Blood & Gold

Smith & Jones Book 2

Beck Todd

Interior maps by Beck Todd

Cover art and design by Alissa Megan

First Printing: May 2026

Print ISBN: 979-8-9862007-8-1

eBook ISBN: 979-8-9862007-9-8

For my family.

Also by Beck Todd

Dionysus Trilogy

Dionysus
Event Horizon
Prospero

Gadyeni Cycle

Ravens in Flight
Ashes of War

Smith & Jones

Smith & Jones
Blood & Gold

Contents

The Malkin Commonwealth
Akena
Shadowlands
Scanlan
Lake Twila
Tallinn Mountains
Lake Aquilo
Lake Bona
Niantic
Crystallus River
Tarrbonn
Amistad Plains
Attakapas River
Kallendon
Saluda Forest
Scaland Caelum Mountains
Lake Fortuna
Malkin
Barra
Malkin City
Greer Island
Ruic Channel
Channel Islands
Fae Islands
Mabinogia
Ruhalleen Empire

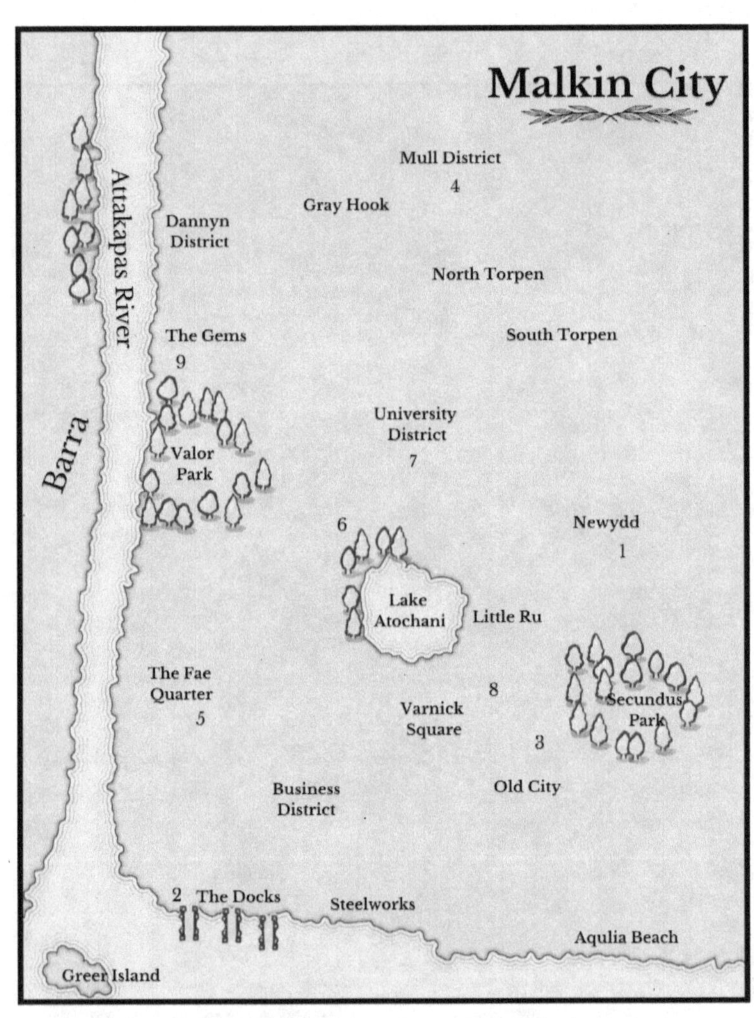

1: Invictus's Boardinghouse
2: Shipping Company
3: Fifth Precinct
4: 21st Street
5: Fae Embassy
6: City Hospital
7: Malkin City University
8: Ciceron Station
9: Grady's House

Chapter 1
The Old City

A waning quarter moon hung in the dark September sky, providing plenty of light for Wulf's Halfling eyes. Gaslamps burned every hundred feet or so. Pockets of yellow-orange light that only served to create more shadows. More places to hide.

Wulf crouched behind an old wooden fence and waited. Everything in this part of Malkin City was old. So old that folks called it "The Old City" and were real proud of its oldness. Some buildings here dated back to the Commonwealth's founding, over five hundred years ago. Or the foundations did, at least.

And the folks who lived in these buildings were rich. Not as rich as folks in the Gems, mind. But no way he'd go back there. Queen Waylinda herself could offer Wulf all the gold in her treasury, and he would still refuse to set foot in that neighborhood.

Not even if his life depended on it.

So when Macsen told him about a smash and grab in the Old City, Wulf jumped at the chance.

Things had been weird since the Grady job. Lots of important folks got shipped off to Greer Island, and lots of others lost their jobs when the shipping company folded. The shop owners who depended on Grady's imports and exports soon found themselves in a bind and scrambled to find new shippers. Within a week, all the importers in the city were overwhelmed, and many shipments arrived late or didn't arrive at all.

Seemed every time Wulf walked into a shop, folks was complaining. Not enough to buy. Not enough to sell. And that made thieving difficult.

How could Wulf steal from folks who were struggling to live the same as him and Ma?

Honestly, it didn't feel right.

But it wasn't like they were strapped for cash. Wulf kept all the hundreds and fifties he had stolen from Grady. Ruthless helped set up a bank account where the money would be safe and earn interest, whatever the hell that meant. Wulf made withdrawals once a week to pay for food and rent. For the first time in years, they weren't behind on rent. Wulf did not have to steal.

Not stealing felt weird. Almost wrong.

If Wulf wasn't stealing, when what was he doing with his life?

Then last week, Macsen got the idea for a job.

Actually, the idea belonged to Macsen's new friend, a timid, skinny Shinnok Halfling named Carlos Vallejo. Carlos worked as a landscaper in a rich neighborhood in the Old City, maintaining their private gardens. He overheard that the owner of 386 Hawthorn Street was going to the Tallinn Mountains for a month-long work vacation. Something to do with birds flying. Wulf honestly didn't care.

A big house crammed full of stuff.

Completely empty.

The perfect job!

Wulf peered over the fence and looked at the clock in a corner store window. A quarter till eleven.

Where the hell are y'all?

Macsen and Carlos were supposed to meet him here at ten-thirty.

Had Carlos gotten cold feet? He wasn't a career thief. Just a guy down on his luck with one missed rent payment away from being on the street. And though Macsen was one of Ruthless's nephews, he wasn't that great a thief. His father was one of the gang leader's many cousins, and his mother was a Shinnok Fae with a nice secretarial job at the Fae Embassy. Good enough to pay the bills, so Macsen didn't need to steal to survive. Instead, he hired himself out as a caser or a shadow.

Did his parents learn about the job and talk him out of it? Or Ruthless?

I can always swing the job myself, Wulf thought as he eyed the house. Completely dark. No sounds. No movement.

Yeah, he could swing it and split the take with Macsen and Carlos. Fifty percent for himself, and twenty-five for each of them. And if they complained, too bad. If they wanted an even share, they should have showed.

Wulf checked his pockets. Lock picks, gloves, handkerchief, and a multi-purpose knife that Bookie gave him as a gift. In addition to a small knife, the Amistadian made gadget also had a corkscrew, nail file, bottle opener, and pliers. A reward for reading his first book.

Not an easy task. The words still got all jumbled up despite it being a kids' book with lots of pictures. But Wulf could recognize about thirty words now, and the story was kinda fun. A brother and sister on a family beach trip.

Would Bookie be disappointed that Wulf used the knife in a smash and grab? Yeah, probably. But Bookie had his new important job at the brickyard, and Wulf... Well, reading a single book did not qualify someone as an educated worker.

Wulf sprinted across the quiet street, sticking to the shadows between gaslamps. This part of Malkin City had yet to see a spark of electricity, making this job much easier.

386 Hawthorn Street was a massive, three-story mansion with tons of windows on each floor and flowering shrubs lining the perimeter. Sneaking shrubs, he and Dav called them. You could sneak around the whole house, and nobody would see nothing. Just shadows.

Two towering oak trees bordered the house. The twisting branches almost reached the rooftop. And best of all, there were no hired guards and no dogs.

Wulf pressed his ear against a window. Silence. Perfect.

He slipped on his gloves and tied the handkerchief over his face as a precaution. Couldn't risk some insomniac walking by and giving his description to the bricks. He then selected the oak tree on the left and climbed up to the second-floor window. He pinned his back against the frame and secured a foot on the opposite side. Nothing short of a gust of wind could knock him out of place.

Wulf opened the knife blade and jimmied the lock. Easy. Very easy. Didn't folks realize how easy they made things for thieves? Sure, they remembered to lock all the doors and windows on the first floor, but that only worked if they lived in a single-story house.

He slid the window up an inch at a time, his ears twitching, picking up dozens of tiny sounds. The shifting of wood on wood. A bat squeaking as it flew overhead, searching for insects. The leaves rustling in the warm breeze.

A cough.

Wulf froze, the window halfway open. Where did that cough come from? Next door? No, it sounded closer. But there was nobody home. Carlos swore up and down that the guy would be gone all month.

But leaving your house empty for a whole month wasn't smart. Did the guy ask a family member or a friend to stay overnight?

Wulf waited sixty heartbeats. The house was silent.

Easing the window up the rest of the way, he slipped inside. He spied a faint light glowing around the corner, flickering. A gaslamp. Who the hell left a gaslamp burning in an empty house? It could cause a leak. Couple years back, a tenement in Gray Hook exploded because of a leak, killing a dozen people.

Wulf slipped the knife into his pocket and crept down the hallway. The plush, dark blue carpet muffled his steps. Oil paintings hung on the dark wood walls, complete with polished, gilt frames. At the corner, a gaslamp burned, lowered for the night.

Either this guy is stupidly forgetful, or someone's here.

Crap.

Okay, not a loss. The house was three stories tall, and it was almost eleven o'clock. Most folks were in bed by now, and bedrooms tended to be on the top floor. Even if someone was sleeping over, he should be okay as long as he stayed on the second floor and didn't venture too far from the window.

Wulf continued down the hallway and carefully tested the doorknobs. Some were locked, but a few were loose. One door opened into a bathroom that smelled like lavender and had fancy white and green tiles. Another a linen closet stuffed with towels and blankets. Those were valuable in their own way. The blankets could be used as they were or cut up to make clothes or socks. Bloody hell, Wulf was fourteen when he first got a pair of socks without holes or patches. Stole them from a tailor shop in South Torpen. Dav had acted as a lookout while...

Voices.

Wulf's heart leapt into his throat. He reached for his gun and cursed under his breath as his hand passed over an empty belt. After the Grady job, Ma made him promise to stop wearing a gun. He had kept that promise for two and a half months.

Besides, he didn't need a gun. He hadn't stolen nothing, and nobody had seen him. If he got to the window in time, there'd be no need for fighting. And he could always try again.

The voices grew louder, rising to shouts. Two men arguing. Part of Wulf wanted to run, but the house was supposed to be empty. Did the guy cancel his trip? Did another gang hear about this place and decide to score?

Wulf crept around another corner. Light spilled into the hallway from an open door. The shouting grew louder, angrier. Wulf's ears twitched, straining to hear, but he could not understand a single word.

That made no bloody sense. The owner was Malkinese. Sure, Bookie spoke two languages, but the words didn't sound like the High Speech. They were sharper, more guttural.

A gunshot fired, echoing.

Wulf's heart leapt into his throat.

An object flew out of the room. It hit the wall between two paintings and fell onto the carpet.

A gun.

Wulf spun on his heels and ran like hell.

Mercy sakes alive, this was supposed to be an easy job! The entire house empty for a whole month. 'Cept it wasn't empty, and someone just got shot!

Did the shooter see him? No, not unless they had a mirror angled into the hall.

And they tossed the gun. Who the—

Wulf skidded to a halt as he turned the corner. A woman stared up at him. She was Malkinese, and in her fifties with touches of gray in her black hair. She wore a traditional maid's uniform...

The woman stood there, frozen.

Wulf rushed past her, racing towards the window. The woman ran in the opposite direction. Towards the gunshot.

The woman screamed. "Oh my God! He murdered him! Oh God! Call the police!" She screamed again, a horrified, blood-freezing scream.

Wulf scrambled onto the windowsill and leapt to the nearest tree branch. He climbed down, hands and feet moving faster than he could think. His foot missed a branch and slipped. He fell the last five or six feet but managed to land in a roll and scrambled to his feet. Half the windows blazed with light. More people shouted. Dogs barked.

Bloody hell!

How could Carlos have gotten this job so wrong? Did he mishear a date? Did the homeowner change his mind?

Or worse. Did Carlos set him and Macsen up?

The idea made his blood turn to ice water. Gang members rarely turned on each other, but it happened. And Carlos wasn't a member of the Marauders. Wulf just met him last week. Macsen vouched for him but...

Wulf shoved the idea away. Carlos was too scared of his own shadow to pull a stunt like that.

And...

And someone was dead.

Killed less than twenty feet away from him.

Wulf ran down the street and headed for the train station. No trains ran this late, but he didn't need a train. Just a direction.

What should he do? Call the bricks? Hell no. They'd never believe a thief, even a thief exonerated by Captain David Reyes himself.

How would he explain it anyway? The second he admitted to breaking into the house, the bricks would have him in cuffs.

No, the bricks weren't an option. He couldn't drag Bookie into his mess neither. Bookie had a good job and a good place to live. Wulf couldn't jeopardize that, and knowing Bookie, he would drop everything to help.

Wulf just needed to lie low for a while, wait for this storm to blow over, and hope the storm surge didn't drown him.

Chapter 2

Case Briefing

Invictus read over the ledger again, checking each number for accuracy. Three sets of numbers for three different paygrades. The same numbers every week.

He sighed. What he envisioned as a wonderful career with the Malkin City Police turned out to be boring and tedious. Instead of investigating fraud, Captain Reyes hired Invictus as the precinct's payroll coordinator. Each week, he would go through the ledger, which rarely changed, and write out the numbers and totals on a spreadsheet which would then be mailed to the City Council, approved, and mailed back. Invictus sat beside the captain's desk and watched silently as Reyes signed every single check.

It could be worse, he guessed. He could be working for a criminal organization, ensuring that all the numbers looked legitimate while they threatened countless people, including himself and everyone he loved.

Invictus shivered.

Yes, it could always be worse.

Someone knocked on the door of his cramped office, barely larger than a storage closet. But it was neat and tidy with every paper and ledger in its proper place and a window with a decent view. The door opened before he could answer. Office Asa Bishop strolled in.

"Reyes wants to see you," he said.

"Okay." Invictus stood and tucked the ledger under his arm. He and Reyes met every Tuesday morning to go over the payroll so the checks arrived on Thursday afternoon, but news reports stated a high probability of bad weather later this week. Reyes probably wanted to complete the payroll early just to be safe. Malkin City had already experienced several bad thunderstorms this summer, flooding the streets and damaging railways in a matter of hours. Another storm would not surprise him.

"Not about that." Asa closed the door and lowered his voice. "Have you seen Wulf Smith lately?"

"No. Why?" He hadn't seen or heard from Wulf all week. Not a surprise. The thief rarely ventured out of Mull District. Invictus tried to visit once a week to check on Wulf and Maria and to give Wulf reading lessons. The Halfling had made amazing progress. Far better than Invictus initially thought. He hoped the new skill would steer Wulf onto a better path, but half the time he visited, Maria explained that Wulf was out. She did not need to elaborate further.

"There was a robbery in the Old City last night."

Invictus's heart sank. "Is Wulf a suspect?"

"Yeah. Reyes wants to talk to you about it."

"But I—"

"He knows you aren't involved. He just wants to talk."

"Very well." Invictus's stomach twisted in knots. *Merciful heavens, Wulf. What have you gotten yourself into this time?*

Invictus followed Asa down the hall. His office was located on the second floor of the Fifth Precinct's new building. The fire caused severe structural damage, and the original building on Highwater Street was condemned. Within the week, the precinct was relocated to a narrow, three-story office building on Varnick Square.

But the architects never intended the building to be used as a police precinct. Renovations were now being made one story at a time. With the first floor complete, the work crews now inhabited the second, painting walls, moving furniture, and knocking down walls and putting up new ones. Some days, it seemed like there were more workers than officers.

They navigated around a trio of carpenters and stopped at the corner office. Asa knocked twice, and Reyes's stern voice told them to enter.

Asa gestured for Invictus to enter first. He did so and froze. A young woman stood next to the captain's desk. She was in her early twenties and wore a dark green police officer's uniform with a long skirt instead of trousers. She had a tan Malkinese complexion, but her hair was tightly curled like an Amistadian's. A halo of thread-of-gold curls. And a constellation of freckles dusted her nose and cheeks.

"Mr. Jones," Captain Reyes said curtly.

Invictus jolted. Was he staring? He didn't mean to stare.

"Are you okay?" the young woman asked.

"Um, yes."

"Take a seat, Jones," Reyes snapped.

Invictus couldn't help but stare.

Asa shoved him.

"Right. I mean, yes, sir." Invictus nearly missed the chair as he sat down, his eyes fixed on the young woman.

"You act like you've never seen a policewoman before," she said, smirking.

"Well, I haven't." There were not, to his knowledge, any women officers in the Malkin City Police.

Reyes rolled his eyes. "Let's get this over with. Jones, meet Office Bishop's new partner Celeste Lawson. Office Lawson, Invictus Jones. Payroll," he added.

"It's nice to meet you, Mr. Jones," Celeste Lawson said, her hazel eyes shining. "I read all about you in the papers."

Invictus's palms began to sweat, and the accursedly humid climate was not to blame. "Oh, that. Um..."

"Don't be so modest," Asa joked. "Not every day a thief and a number cruncher take down a notorious criminal."

"Well, I…"

Reyes cleared his throat. Three pairs of eyes instantly turned his way. "Are we done exchanging pleasantries?"

"Yes, sir," all three of them replied.

Thank God. It wasn't that Invictus did not like talking about the Grady case. It was just… Okay, yes, he hated it. All the attention felt awkward and wrong. Those weeks felt like a nightmare he could never awake from, and Grady had tricked him so easily. How much longer before people stopped talking about Invictus's bravery and started talking about his gullibility? How he was tricked by such an obvious mask?

"Good," Reyes said. "Jones, where were you last night between ten-thirty and eleven?"

Invictus's heart sank. Right, the robbery. "I was at my boardinghouse. The landlady has a very strict nine o'clock curfew." A curfew he had not broken in over two months. Mrs. Ramirez barely huffed whenever she saw Invictus now. He interpreted it as being on her good side.

"Can the other tenants confirm this?"

"Yes, sir." Invictus spent the evening having tea and playing a new card game with two other tenants, Iulianus Bennett and Dr. Samuel Rosario, one that involved dice and a complicated points system. The parlor clock struck ten a couple minutes after they finished.

Reyes nodded. "When was the last time you saw Beowulf Smith?"

"About a week ago. Is Wulf under arrest?" His heart sank further. He genuinely hoped that Wulf would turn a new leaf, and Invictus had grown attached to Wulf, as though he were the little brother Invictus never had.

Reyes opened a file and turned it around so Invictus could read the report. "Beowulf Smith was seen at 386 Hawthorn Street by Mrs. Rosalyn Palacio, one of the maids."

"One of? This household has more than one?"

"Three, to be precise. Do you want to hear the rest?" Reyes asked sarcastically, a sign that his patience was frayed.

Not really. "Yes, sir."

"Mrs. Palacio stated that she heard a gunshot around ten forty-five and went to investigate. She ran into Smith as he fled down the hallway and exited the house through an open window. She went into the study of her employer, Dr. Armand Whateley, and found him dead from a gunshot to the heart."

"No."

"I'm sorry?"

"Wulf would never kill someone."

"The doctor must have surprised him," Asa said.

Invictus shook his head. "If someone caught Wulf stealing, he would run away, not shoot them. Not unless his life depended on it." His mind wandered to Harvey's security firm. Wulf had shot out the light instead of shooting Lewin Manning. A distraction. Invictus's gut told him that Wulf would have reacted the same way, creating a clean getaway. "Did the doctor have a gun?"

"The Whateley family does not believe in owning weapons."

Asa muttered under his breath and crossed his arms.

"Would you care to comment, Office Bishop?"

"No, sir."

"Did the maid see Wulf pull the trigger?" Invictus asked.

"She heard a gunshot, saw Smith running away from the study, and then found the doctor. As well as the gun."

Invictus frowned. "Where was the gun?"

"Smith dropped it as he ran away."

"Then it wasn't him."

Reyes glared at Invictus. He felt like a bug under a magnifying glass, but the invisible string tugged at his mind, assuring him that he was on the right path.

"How do you know?" Office Lawson asked curiously.

"Well..." Invictus collected his thoughts into a logical order. "When we were investigating Emilio Grady and Lewin Manning, Wulf was so angry that he wanted to kill them, but he didn't. Even when he had a clean shot, he controlled himself." The image of Dav's body and seeing the pain in Wulf's eyes appeared in his mind. "Manning killed Wulf's best friend, and Wulf still did not shoot him. In fact, the only times I've seen Wulf shoot someone were in self-defense. And he isn't careless enough to lose his gun."

"The only times you've seen," Reyes said gravely. His dark eyes hardened like amber. "Jones, how long have you known Smith?"

"About three months."

"Would you say three months is long enough to truly know a person? To know their innermost thoughts and secrets?"

"I guess it would depend on the person." A sinking feeling formed in his gut. *No, please don't bring that up.*

"Bishop," Reyes said, confirming Invictus's dread, "how long have you known your cousin Jorge?"

Asa stiffened, his dark eyes turning to stone. "My whole life, sir."

"Did you know everything about Jorge?"

Asa struggled to speak. His eyes watered, but only for a moment. Clearing his throat, he said, "I thought I did, sir."

Reyes shifted his gaze back to Invictus. "A lifetime. You can know someone for an entire life and not really know them."

"But Wulf would not shoot an unarmed person." Invictus struggled to keep his voice level. Bringing up Jorge Bishop, the corrupted officer who worked for Lewin Manning, was cruel and unnecessary. "Are there photos?"

Reyes showed him a few. Three of the house and surrounding gardens, one of the study without the body, and one of Dr. Whateley when he was alive and well. *Perhaps 'well' isn't the right word.* The doctor was pushing eighty and looked frail. No more than a hundred and twenty pounds.

Invictus held up the doctor's photo. "Does this look like the man a skilled thief would need to defend himself against?"

"Looks can be deceiving," Reyes stated.

Embarrassment flooded Invictus as he recalled how easily Emilio Grady had tricked him into believing that he was the kind, grandfatherly type who would never hurt a fly. But Grady's mask never tricked Wulf. And the thief knew when to fight and when to run.

"I don't buy it."

"What type of doctor was Dr. Whateley?" Lawson asked before Reyes could reply.

The captain cleared his throat and turned to another page. "A medical doctor. He immigrated from Scanlan thirty years ago and worked at City Hospital until he retired ten years ago to focus on research."

"What kind of research?" Lawson asked.

"Antibiotics."

"What the hell are those?" Asa asked.

"A type of medicine that reduces the risk of infection after surgery."

"Could Smith have known about this research?" Lawson asked both the captain and Invictus.

"Doubtful," Invictus replied. "Until recently, Wulf was illiterate, and I doubt he's ever been to the hospital."

"Then what could he have been after?" Lawson asked, though it sounded more like a prompt than a query.

"Was Dr. Whateley wealthy?" Invictus asked. *He was wealthy enough to employ three maids, you dolt.*

"You tell me." Reyes held up the photo of the house. A house far larger than most in the Gems.

"Then Wulf saw a big house, assumed it was full of valuables, and tried to rob it."

"But why this house?" Asa asked, pointing at the photo.

Invictus frowned, thinking. The other houses in the neighborhood must be as equally grand. Wulf could have chosen any of them, but he chose the one in which a man was shot and killed. *Why this house?* Was it merely bad luck, or another factor?

Reyes locked eyes with him. "What are you thinking, Jones?"

"I, um..."

"Because if you're thinking of tracking down Smith and questioning him yourself, good idea."

Invictus jolted. "I beg your pardon?"

"Sir?" Asa stared at Reyes as though the captain had slapped him in the face. He looked to Invictus for an explanation, but Invictus did not have one.

"Smith is a career thief," Reyes said. "If he suspects a brick is nearby, he will run. This makes it impossible for an officer to track him down and question. Would Smith talk to you if you find him?"

"Probably." If he could find him. If Wulf had not gone further underground, hidden by Ruthless Wells or another gang leader in Mull District's labyrinth of streets.

"Good. Find Smith and report to Bishop and Lawson. They will be your handlers in this case."

"What?!" Asa yelled at the same time Invictus's heart skipped a beat.

"But I'm not a police officer!"

"Not yet." Reyes studied Invictus. "I saw the exam book on your desk."

Invictus's face and neck grew warm. He got the police exam book the day after he was hired, studying during his free time. He assumed the captain would ask him to take the exam someday, but weeks passed, and he lost hope of Reyes asking.

"Bishop and Lawson," Reyes continued, "will lead the murder investigation. As of now, Wulf Smith is our main suspect. If you manage to find Smith and establish his innocence, we can focus on different avenues."

"What will you do to Wulf? He broke into the house, after all."

"Exactly. According to Mrs. Palacio, Smith was running away from the study. Which means, if Smith is not our killer, then he likely saw the real murderer." Reyes leaned forward. "Dr. Whateley was a very important man. His family wants the murderer found, and they believe that Smith is guilty. So, unless you want your friend to be charged with murder, I suggest you find him first."

CHAPTER 3
Details

INVICTUS LOOSENED HIS SHIRT COLLAR as he walked the now familiar streets of Mull District. The summer had yet to release its stranglehold on the city. Instead of cool September breezes, the people of Malkin City had to contend with warm wind and clinging humidity. By the time he reached the apartment building, he was soaked with sweat.

But the extended summer had one advantage. All varieties of plants and trees thrived, making the slums look halfway habitable, more akin to the nicer parts of Malkin. Vibrant, climbing ivy. Fruit trees. Flowers. Patches of color amid drab, ramshackle buildings.

He spotted a group of children playing in the street, kicking a tattered soccer ball. All wore ragged, ill-fitting clothes that were either too large or too small for their spindly limbs. One boy sat on the front porch steps, cradling his head in his hands.

"Hey, Ozzy," Invictus said as he walked up. "Are you okay?" He could not recall the child ever sitting still. *Is he injured?*

The Halfling boy shrugged.

Invictus jolted as yelling erupted from inside the apartment. The words were too muffled to understand, but he guessed it was two women, judging by the pitches. One cursed and slammed a door. The building's front door burst open, and a furious Malkinese woman strode out, paying no attention to Invictus or Ozzy. The children paused and stared as she stormed down the street. They resumed their game the moment she disappeared around a corner.

"Who was that?" Invictus wondered out loud.

"My mom," Ozzy whispered.

Mrs. Garcia, the landlady, appeared a second later. She hauled Ozzy up by a skinny arm and shepherded him inside. Ozzy did not fight her as she led him into their rooms on the first floor. The door closed softly, the deadbolts sliding into place.

Invictus pressed his ear to the door. Eavesdropping was wrong, but concern overwhelmed him. What had happened?

Mrs. Garcia spoke gently to Ozzy, her voice almost soothing. Muffled crying followed. Invictus frowned. He had never heard that child cry. Even after falling and skinning both knees, the boy was all smiles.

Granted, he had never seen Ozzy's mother either.

Invictus hurried up the stairs, mindful of the wobbly steps. The second floor was weirdly quiet. It was as though the entire building were holding its breath, waiting.

Do they know about the robbery?

Had word reached Twenty-first Street so quickly? Everyone in the building knew about Wulf's ties to Ruthless and the Marauders, and he was the only Shinnok Halfling in the neighborhood.

He knocked on Maria's door. *Please be home. Please be home...*

Maria answered. Dark circles surrounded her bloodshot eyes.

"Are you alright?" he asked.

"Other than working the night shift for a month and my son being a wanted criminal, yes, I'm alright." She gestured for Invictus to enter.

He stood near the kitchen table with his hat in his hands. The dark wood was recently polished. The whole apartment, in fact, was as spotless as ever. Not a dish or an article of clothing out of place.

His eyes settled on the bedroom door. Closed.

"Is Wulf...?" He pointed at the door.

Maria nodded. "Found him in there this morning. Can't get a word out of him." She smirked. "His eyes were glued to a book, and he acted like he didn't hear me."

"How did you learn about the robbery?"

"Read the headlines in the morning paper." She sat down at the table and clasped her hands tightly. "Invictus, my son is a lot of things, but he is not a murderer."

"I know. I want to help him."

Maria nodded. A faint smile tugged at her lips. "Figures." She gestured to the door.

Invictus tried the knob. Locked.

"Wulf?"

No reply.

"Allow me." Maria removed two pins from her hair and swiftly picked the lock.

"How did...?"

Maria silenced him with a look that said 'don't act like you're surprised'.

Two beds separated by a battered dresser crowded the narrow bedroom. An oil lamp and a few brushes and combs rested on the dresser, all made of dark wood. Wulf sat huddled on the floor between his bed and the window. An opened door rested on his knees. He stared at it intently.

"Wulf?" Invictus sat on the edge of the bed and studied his friend. Wulf was pale with bloodshot eyes and disheveled hair. His rumpled, black clothes looked like he had slept in them, but Invictus's gut told him that Wulf had not slept last night.

"Beowulf?"

Wulf's eyes remained fixed on the book. Invictus glanced at the title. *On the Types of Fae.*

Must be one of Ruthless's books. The Blydd Fae owned a small library, neatly stashed away in his apartment. More books than Invictus could hope to read in a lifetime.

"Interesting book?" he asked.

"I ain't done it," Wulf whispered.

"I know."

Wulf glared at him, purple eyes blazing. "How do you know what I'm talking 'bout?"

"Because I work at a police precinct. Listen, you are the main suspect, but Captain Reyes doesn't believe you killed the doctor." Invictus chose his next words carefully. "He wants me to speak with you. As a witness."

"Yeah bloody right! Bet he's just using you to sucker me in."

"No. Listen, Wulf—"

"No, you listen, Bookie. I ain't killed nobody, and I ain't talkin' to no bricks! If they don't get me for murder, they will for robbing."

Invictus waited a moment, both for Wulf to calm down and to give himself time to think. "Did you steal anything?"

"No, but..." Wulf crossed his arms, holding the book close to his chest. "But I broke in. Used the second-floor window just like we planned."

"Who is we?" Invictus leaned forward. Reyes hadn't mentioned anyone else in his report.

"Me, Macsen, and Carlos. 'Cept they didn't show."

Too bad they weren't there. If they were, Wulf would have two people to vouch for his innocence. And two more witnesses who might have seen the real murderer. "Where are they now?"

Wulf shrugged. "Beats me. Oh, hey, Ma." He looked up at his mother. "Sorry 'bout..." His voice faltered. "I'm sorry."

"You don't need to apologize."

Wulf's face turned red, his eyes a shade of violet. "I don't? How many jobs you working now? Two?" Wulf rose to his feet. "You wouldn't have to work so damn much if I just... I mean, I can read now. Kinda. I could get me a grass cutting job, or a... A..." He snarled. "Hell, I don't know!"

Maria walked over and placed a gentle hand on Wulf's face. "Stop beating yourself up, Beowulf. Do you really want to help me?"

"Yes."

"Then work with Invictus. I know you are innocent, but the police will hunt you down and send you to Greer if they can't find a real suspect. Remember what happened to Raul Bain? He was the only one the police were able to place at that fire and..."

"And they shipped his ass to Greer. Ten years." Wulf shivered. "Okay, I'll help. But I won't talk to the bricks. Not yet."

"That's fair," Invictus said. "So, where are Macsen and Carlos?" He met Macsen a few times. Macsen Wells belonged to Ruthless's gang and guarded Invictus's boardinghouse when Lewin Manning was hunting him and Wulf. What had Ruthless called him? A Hybrid. Half Blydd and half Shinnok.

Wulf shrugged. "Don't know. Never worked with Carlos before. Macsen lives on Twenty-second Street. Just down the alley."

"Okay. Let's go." Invictus stood.

"Hold up. What are you going to do?" Wulf eyed him warily.

"Ask why he was absent last night. That's all," he added.

Wulf wavered for a moment and then agreed. He donned his hat and long, black coat, but not a gun. He stopped wearing one after...

A light dawned in Invictus's mind. "You don't carry a gun."

"Yeah. So?"

"Dr. Whateley died from a gunshot wound."

Wulf smiled, revealing sharp teeth. "Hey, that's right! I heard a gunshot and then some guy threw the gun into the hallway. You can tell the bricks it ain't mine. But I never saw no faces. Except the maid." The smile vanished.

"It doesn't matter. We have a point in your favor."

Invictus and Wulf headed out with Wulf promising Maria that he would be careful and run like hell if he saw anyone in dark green. A creeping feeling invaded Invictus. Had Reyes assigned someone to follow him? He thought back to the train ride and the walk here. No one stood out. He hoped to God that if an officer was trailing him, that they were wearing plain clothes. Jeopardizing Wulf's trust was the last thing Invictus needed.

"Don't you want to leave the book here?" Invictus asked as they walked down the stairs.

"Nah. Ruthless said I can keep it." He stuffed the book into a coat pocket, creating a rectangular outline in the fabric. "Did you know there's over twenty different subspecies of Fae?"

"Really? That many?" Invictus assumed there were no more than a dozen.

Wulf nodded, grinning. "Yeah. Some only live on the Islands. A lot of weird ones, too. Ever heard of a Ghillyman?"

Invictus began to reply when the door to Mrs. Garcia's apartment opened. Ozzy, his eyes red and his face tear stained, peered out.

"What happened to you, kid?" Wulf asked.

Ozzy shrugged. "Is my dad upstairs?"

"No. Heard him head out early this morning. Why? Your granny say something to you?"

Ozzy shook his head and quickly closed the door, locking it.

Wulf's eyes flashed. "If that old bat—"

"Wulf," Invictus whispered. "Ozzy's mother was here."

"Oh hell. You sure?"

He nodded.

"Damn. Haven't seen Lola in years. Wonder what brought her back."

Invictus had several questions, but he left them unasked. He needed to focus on the case, and Ozzy's personal life was none of his business. Granted, he felt weird not seeing his parents for a couple months. He could not imagine years. And Ozzy was only ten.

He followed Wulf outside and down a narrow alley filled with moldy garbage, the stench intensified by the humidity. A cloud of flies hovered over a rusty trash bin. Invictus held his breath, trying not to gag.

How can Wulf stand it? Shinnoks had a better sense of smell than humans. Then again, Wulf might just be used to it.

Wulf walked into another apartment building, the mirror image of the one on Twenty-first Street, and went up to the third floor.

Invictus heard a familiar voice followed by the sound of someone retching.

Wulf knocked on the last door three times. Two quick raps followed by a long bang. Loud enough for the sound to echo down the hallway. Another tenant yelled at them to shut the hell up.

The door opened. Ruthless Wells, dressed in a sharp black suit with a dark blue vest and necktie, stood in the doorway. His silver eyes flashed.

"Mr. Jones. Honestly, I'm not surprised. And you." He directed his eerie gaze at Wulf. "What do you have to say for yourself?"

"Where's Macsen?"

Invictus heard retching again. He tried to peer around Ruthless, but the Blydd Fae blocked the entire doorway.

"I asked you a question," Ruthless said to Wulf.

"So did I. Where the hell's Mac?"

Ruthless studied Wulf, his silvery eyes flashing twice. Wulf's own eyes turned violet. Ruthless then moved aside.

The apartment was half the size of Wulf and Maria's, and contained a fold-out couch, a card table with two folding canvas chairs, and a small kitchen. Dirty dishes piled up in the dripping sink.

The retching sounded from the water closet off to the side. The toilet flushed, and a gangly Fae stumbled into the main room. Standing at six and a half feet tall, he was fair-skinned with bright red hair streaked with silver. His bloodshot eyes were purple with silver specks. He collapsed onto the couch, moaning.

"What the hall happened to you?" Wulf demanded. He loomed over the Fae, glaring.

Macsen moaned again, clutching his stomach.

"Is he okay?" Invictus asked.

"As okay as someone with the flu can be. Close the door," Ruthless said politely.

Invictus complied. The apartment felt half as small.

"The flu? You caught the bloody flu the day before a job!" Wulf snarled.

"Didn't catch it on purpose," Macsen said weakly. His eyes fell on Invictus. "Oh, it's that accountant. What's he...?" Macsen scrambled to his feet and made a mad dash to the water closet, retching again.

Invictus tasted bile in the back of his throat.

"Damn. He ain't faking." Wulf grimaced.

"No," Ruthless said. "My cousin-in-law heard rumors that Macsen was planning a job. She came over yesterday to talk him out of it. The flu did the job for her."

Wulf grounded his teeth. "How the hell did your ma find out?" he yelled at Macsen.

"She's a bloody Shinnok." Macsen stumbled forward and leaned his head against the door frame. "Probably heard it from a neighbor. Got thin walls here. Did she tell you or Dad?" he asked Ruthless.

"Your father. Be grateful that I'm here instead of him." His eyes narrowed to slits.

"His father is one of your cousins?" Invictus hazarded a guess. Ruthless had a seemingly endless supply of relatives.

The Blydd nodded. "Very stupid to accept a job without my blessing."

Macsen sneered, revealing a mouthful of sharp teeth. "Don't need your permission for every little thing."

"Breaking into a house is no little thing. Are you aware that the owners were present? Along with all the household staff? I know you inherited Ector's intelligence, but even an amateur thief ought to know better."

"There weren't no people at the house," Macsen said, confused.

"Like hell!" Wulf snapped.

Ruthless silenced Wulf with a glare. He then said to Macsen, "What do you mean?"

"Carlos and I cased the house the other day. Completely empty. The owner won't be back 'til October, and staff only comes by twice a week." He paused, thinking. "Cleaning staff on Tuesdays and landscapers on Fridays. Carlos works for the landscaping company. That's how he found out."

"Well, Carlos was wrong!" Wulf yelled. "The house was crawling with folks!"

Macsen shook his head. "No. Nobody was there."

"Nobody was there when you cased it," Invictus amended. "Could Dr. Whateley have returned early? Or canceled the trip?"

Macsen stared at Invictus as though he had recited poetry in the High Speech. "Who?"

"The homeowner."

"No, it's some guy named Townsend. Works at the University studying birds." Macsen lowered himself onto the couch. His arms and legs shook badly. "Left for four weeks. The University confirmed it."

"Wait, he's a university professor?" Invictus asked.

"Yeah."

"Can you describe him?"

Macsen closed his eyes, thinking. "Malkinese. Forties. Wears glasses. Mostly bald. Why?"

Now it was Invictus's turn to be confused. "It can't be the same person. Dr. Whateley was elderly and had white hair."

"Who?"

"The man who was unfortunately murdered in his home yesterday evening," Ruthless explained.

"Never heard of him."

Invictus and Wulf exchanged glances. The invisible string tugged at his mind. "Macsen," Invictus said, "what is Professor Townsend's address?"

"368 Hawthorn Street."

"386," Wulf said.

Macsen shook his head. "Carlos said 368 Hawthorn."

"He said 386!"

"No, it was 368, you dyslexic—" Macsen dashed inside the water closet again.

"What the hell did you call me?!" Wulf raised both fists and lunged at Macsen.

Invictus grabbed him and pulled him aside. The invisible string tugged harder, giving him a sense of direction. A direction he feared to travel. "Could Carlos have given you and Macsen different addresses on purpose?"

Wulf paled. "Why would he do that?"

"Hear me out. Who cased the house?"

"Macsen and Carlos."

"But not you?"

Wulf shook his head. "Carlos was worried someone would recognize me from the papers, so he told me to stay out of sight 'til we pulled the job."

Invictus nodded. "And someone did recognize you."

"The maid." Wulf's eyes widened, turning a lighter shade of purple.

The tugging grew stronger, impossible for him to ignore. "Wulf, how well do you know Carlos?"

"Only met him last week."

"Is it possible that Carlos knew when Dr. Whateley would be murdered? Did he tell you the wrong address so you would be placed at the scene?"

"You know, I..." He swallowed. "Thought about it. Just for a second." He then shook his head. "But, Bookie, this guy was more scared than you were at Ciceron Station. He could barely put a sentence together."

Invictus racked his brain, searching through every detective novel he had read, looking for an explanation. A piece of logic to connect the numbers. "Maybe he was a go-between. A third party hired him to contact you."

"But why me and Macsen?"

"Good question." He frowned, trying to add up the numbers.

"Your name was in the papers," Ruthless pointed out. "Though contacting Macsen first instead of going to you directly is interesting. What is Carlos's last name?"

"Vallejo."

"His species?"

"Shinnok Halfling. But he's lighter skinned than me and has red hair."

"Like Macsen's hair?"

"No, it's darker. Kinda like rust."

Invictus filed the description away. Malkin City was the most populous city on the continent, but knowing Carlos's subspecies would help narrow the search. How many Shinnok Halflings could there be, anyway?

"I will have my people search for him," Ruthless said. "In the meantime, work with Jones and find the real murderer. Unless you'd like to spend the rest of your life on Greer Island."

Chapter 4
Comparison

Invictus and Wulf decided to split up after leaving Macsen's apartment. Wulf, knowing the police were looking for him, went home to lie low, and Invictus returned to his boardinghouse to think. Ruthless's threat about Wulf spending the rest of his life on Greer Island unnerved him. How could he allow his friend to suffer such a fate?

He spent the afternoon and evening going over everything Captain Reyes, Wulf, and Macsen had said, looking for any converging points. According to Macsen, Wulf misheard Carlos's instructions and robbed the wrong house. But Wulf was a Shinnok Halfling with excellent hearing. He could not have misheard unless Carlos wanted him to. Was it intentional, or did Carlos make a genuine mistake?

A mistake that led to Wulf being a murder suspect.

Invictus tabled the question for now. Once they found Carlos Vallejo, they could hear his side of the story.

So, he turned his investigation to Dr. Armand Whateley. Why would someone want to kill an old man? What did they stand to gain?

Invictus went to the Fifth Precinct shortly after dawn, a good two hours before his shift began. He wanted to go over the case file before the captain arrived. Though Reyes tasked him with questioning Wulf, he was not technically an officer, and he was not sure if he was allowed to view the evidence by himself. But he felt that Wulf's freedom depended on it.

A handful of officers from the night shift milled around. Some greeted Invictus with half-hearted waves and hellos and left him to his work.

He found the file for Dr. Whateley in the top drawer of Asa's desk.

Armand Whateley immigrated to Malkin Province from Scanlan thirty years ago, right before the Scanlan Campaign started. He was survived by his two sons, Alistair and Alfred, his daughter-in-law Gina, and two young grandchildren. The entire family lived in the house on Hawthorn Street and had statements for the night of the murder.

Alfred and Gina, who lived on the third floor, went to bed around ten-thirty. Alfred claimed that he heard a gunshot followed by the maid screaming around eleven o'clock. He went downstairs to investigate and discovered his father's body in the study, as well as the murder weapon in the hallway. He then called the police.

Alistair, also a doctor, was working the evening shift at the City Hospital and did not arrive home until after midnight. All the doctors and nurses working the shift confirmed that he was at the hospital all evening.

But nobody witnessed the murder. The maid stated that she saw Wulf, dressed in a black coat with a wide-brimmed hat and a black handkerchief over his face, running away. Her statement included Wulf's height, approximate weight, and eye color. His clothes and hat hid everything else.

Invictus sat back, thinking. The maid only saw Wulf's eyes. So, how did she know it was him? Shinnoks and Shinnok Halflings were the only Fae subspecies with solid purple eyes, but there must be hundreds in Malkin City.

But only one Shinnok Halfling had his name and photograph in the papers.

Merciful heavens, could the maid have recognized Wulf solely by his eyes? But how? Colored photographs were far too expensive to use in newsprint.

"What are you doing here?"

Invictus jolted and scrambled to his feet.

Celeste Lawson, dressed in her dark green uniform, smiled at him. Her hazel eyes shimmered.

"I, um..." Invictus swallowed a lump in his throat. "I was just..."

"Going over the case file?"

"Yes," he admitted.

Celeste gave him a curious look. "Did you come to work early just to read this?" She pointed at the file.

"Well, I..." His ear decided to ring. Dammit, it had been over two weeks since the last time. He thought it was healed.

"Because we're working on this case together. All you need to do is ask. No sneaking required."

"Oh, right." Idiot. Reyes also assigned him to work with Celeste and Asa, reporting directly to them. Of course he would have access to the files. He just needed to ask. Celeste seemed nice, but Asa was... Well, Asa Bishop was himself. He was nothing but civil towards Invictus, but Invictus sometime caught Asa glaring at him, his dark brown eyes like cold glass. Sure, Invictus worked with the police now, but he had posted Beowulf Smith's bail. He was friends with a thief. "I just thought..."

Celeste sat down at the desk and motioned for Invictus to join her. "What do you think of the case so far?"

"It's tragic." The ringing faded. "But the robber wore a mask and hat. How did Mrs. Palacio know he was Wulf?"

"Good question. When we questioned her yesterday, she didn't have a good answer. She was adamant that it was Beowulf Smith despite only seeing half his face. And there were no other witnesses. Unless you count Dr. Whateley."

"Did anyone discover a motive?"

"The family believes that it was a robbery gone wrong. Dr. Whateley interrupted Smith, and robbery turned into homicide."

"Was anything taken?"

"No."

Invictus read over the file again. Nothing was stolen or disturbed. Nothing dropped or broken. Except the gun.

Wulf claimed he didn't have time to steal anything, and Invictus believed him. Wulf might be an excellent thief, but he was a terrible liar.

And he was not wearing a gun.

"What are you thinking?" Celeste asked.

Invictus glanced around. A handful of tired officers sat at their desks, waiting for the night shift to end. Some of them were Halflings. Invictus lowered his voice, just in case they had keen hearing.

"I found Wulf yesterday. He didn't do it."

"Explain." Celeste rested her elbows on the desk.

Invictus related Wulf's plan to rob a house in the Old City with two other thieves, but the others did not show up, and Wulf confused the addresses.

"See. He wasn't supposed to be there." *Unless Carlos gave him the wrong address on purpose.* The idea tugged at his mind, but he could not complete the equation without hearing Carlos's side first. For all Invictus knew, it truly was a mistake.

"Okay," Celeste said, "then who shot Dr. Whateley?"

"I honestly have no idea. Did he have any enemies? Rival colleagues?"

"Jones, the man was a doctor. He dedicated his life to healing people."

"Could it be because he was Scanlannish?" Though Scanlan was an official province, many questioned its place in the Commonwealth. The Scanlan Campaign lasted for fifteen years, costing thousands of soldiers their lives. A lot of families and veterans harbored ill will towards the Scanlannish. The existence of several rebel groups seeking Scanlan's independence only stoked their hostilities.

"Doubtful," Celeste replied. "Whateley had a good reputation, with both his neighbors and colleagues."

"Then, Wulf is your only lead?"

"At the moment, yes."

Invictus's heart sank. He promised Wulf that he would do everything he could to prove his innocence, but if the police failed to find another suspect...

"Did Smith really help arrest Emilio Grady?" Celeste asked, a curious expression crossing her face.

"Yes, I don't think we could have built a case against Grady without his help."

"We being you and Smith."

Invictus nodded. If he had been by himself, he never would have managed it. Fear would have crippled him, forcing him to work for criminals and making their illegal transactions appear legitimate. And he would have done so for the rest of his life, knowing that if he failed, the Sidhe Family would hurt everyone he loved.

Wulf robbing him, on Lewin Manning's orders, had saved his life.

Weird.

He selected a blank sheet of paper and a pen and jotted down a few notes.

"No witnesses and no suspects."

"No suspects except for Wulf Smith," Celeste amended.

Invictus shook his head. "No. Wulf is not a killer. He would not shoot an unarmed old man. Not when he had a clean getaway."

A light shone in Celeste's eyes. "Right. He's half Shinnok. That kind of Fae have better hearing than humans. He would have heard the doctor long before the doctor saw him. So, how did Smith mix up the addresses?"

"Wulf is barely literate. I think Carlos Vallejo took advantage of that and gave him the wrong information so Wulf would be at the wrong place at the right time." The invisible string returned, tugging at his mind, pulling him further in this direction. "Carlos works as a landscaper. Can you and Bishop find landscaping companies that have contracts in Old City neighborhoods?"

"Shouldn't be too difficult. What does Vallejo look like?"

"I honestly don't know. Wulf said he is a Shinnok Halfling. Average height and thin build. And he has red hair, so he shouldn't be that hard to find." Granted, Invictus had no idea how common Shinnok Halflings were. But red hair. He could count on both hands the number of redheads he had seen this summer.

Celeste raised an eyebrow. "Another Halfling?"

"Small world." His mind wandered to Europa Grady, another Shinnok Halfling, innocent of her grandfather's crimes but a victim, nonetheless. Where was she now? Was she doing okay?

Focus! Invictus scolded himself.

"Perhaps." Celeste crossed her arms. "I have a theory. Want to hear it?"

"Sure."

"You're familiar with the Seelie Court, right?"

Invictus broke out in goosebumps, recalling the banishment Grady had placed on Wulf through the Seelie Court. "Yes."

"The Court prevents Fae from entering places they don't have permission to enter. Such as houses and businesses. However, the Court has less control over Halflings, and the Crown has little love for them. Some noble families have gone as far as disowning Halfling members. That's why more and more are turning to crime. Because they can enter places normal Fae cannot, and cut off from their families, they don't have much of a choice."

"That's very interesting..." Invictus rubbed his chin. Ruthless Wells, a full-blooded Blydd Fae, was a powerful gang leader, but he did not commit crimes himself. He always delegated that kind of work to his gang members, the vast majority of whom were Halflings.

But Macsen is a Hybrid. Wouldn't the Court's laws prevent him from entering certain places, too? How is he a thief?

And Germanicus was an Aziza Fae. Granted, Germanicus did not steal in the same way that Wulf stole. Ruthless placed him in companies, working as a temp and learning the building's layout, employee schedules, and security guard rotations. He stole information, and he had a legitimate reason to enter those buildings, so the Court could not prevent him.

"Very interesting." He jotted down a note. Perhaps the book Ruthless gave to Wulf held an explanation.

A question popped into his mind. "How does the Seelie Court enforce this law?"

"Magic," Celeste replied with a smile.

"I'm serious."

"So am I."

"Magic doesn't exist."

"Doesn't it? How does the Seelie Court function then? There are hundreds of thousands if not millions of Fae in the world. How can the Court, based in the Fae Islands, prevent a full-blooded Fae from breaking into a house in Malkin City? Or in Barra? How do banishments work?"

"I don't know." He recalled the toll Grady's banishment took on Wulf. He looked half dead and might have died if Invictus had not gotten him outside in time. And Wulf was just a Halfling. Ruthless explained that banishments were worse for full-blooded Fae. Often lethal.

Celeste smirked, her hazel eyes shining.

The front door opened, admitting a dozen officers for the day shift, Captain Reyes and Asa among them. But instead of walking to his desk, Asa followed Reyes upstairs.

"Any plans for today?" Celeste asked as she and Invictus stood. He checked his watch. A quarter to nine.

"I have a lot of paperwork to process." Spending the majority of yesterday's shift in Mull meant more work for today. *And I'd rather not see how everyone reacts if payroll isn't processed in time.*

Celeste gathered up the case file. "We'll go through the physical evidence today. And don't worry. We will share it with you."

"It wasn't Wulf," Invictus said adamantly. A few officers glanced his way, including Diego Montgomery, a short tempered Eadryn Halfling. The young officer refused to trust Invictus, believing that a gang planted him inside the precinct in order to steal evidence and alter records. Montgomery scowled at him, his green and brown eyes swirling.

"I want to believe you, Jones," Celeste said. "But I've never met Smith."

Invictus sighed. Yes, Wulf helped the police once, but he was still a thief. Still leery of being near a police officer. If only Celeste were in Invictus's shoes, then she would understand.

"Tell you what," Celeste said. "If we find evidence that proves Smith wasn't the murderer, we will call him in as a witness. But only if the evidence proves it. Deal?"

"Deal."

Chapter 5
Think Like a Thief

Asa Bishop peered down at the Fifth Precinct's desk area from the second-floor railing. Officers hurried about, preparing for a busy day shift as the nightly skeleton crew gathered their belongings and handed over case files. Construction workers also spilled inside, towing an assortment of paints, tools, and wooden planks. Half of those planks would be used for boarding up windows in a few days. News reports stated that a hurricane was due to make landfall around Thursday evening. Yet another thing to occupy everyone's minds.

In all honesty, it was a wonder anybody could think in this mess.

Guess that's why Reyes's office is on the second floor.

In the old precinct, Captain Reyes's office was located down the hall on the first floor, just out of sight of the desk area but close enough if anyone required his assistance. But the new building was narrower. Less space per floor meant redesigning the layout. Asa thought the architects did an alright job, but he constantly found himself walking someplace and remembering it was now on a different floor.

He spotted Celeste Lawson among the chaos. The new officer, a recent graduate from the University's police program, had wasted no time getting to work and seemed to have befriended most of the officers. Even old Stant, who had been on the force longer than Asa had been alive, had warmed up to her. In the same sense that sleet was warmer than ice.

Hard to believe she's only been here a week.

To be honest, Asa had his reservations about a female officer. The Malkin City Police was strictly a male profession. Even the secretaries and clerks were men. But Reyes, like Invictus Jones before him, had a hunch, and this hunch led him to hire Celeste Lawson and pair her with Asa. But Asa was not complaining. Triumvir knew the city needed all the police officers it could get. Most of the Second Precinct officers were shipped off to Greer, along with a couple dozen from the Third and Fourth.

And Jorge.

Asa grounded his teeth. How could his own cousin have fallen so low? Jorge was always so strong and dependable, and a war hero to boot. It wasn't like he needed the bribe money. The military gave him a pension for his service in the Scanlan Campaign, and their family...

A lump caught in Asa's throat.

We would have given you the money if you needed it, Jorge. You didn't have to resort to taking bribes. Why didn't you let me help you?

Perhaps Jorge was too ashamed to ask, and dirty money was, in his mind, the only option.

The hallway clock struck nine times. The official start of the day shift.

Asa shoved all lingering thoughts about his cousin into the recesses of his mind and walked into Reyes's office.

The captain sat behind a massive, dark wood desk with stacks of papers and files on both ends. Each stack was organized in a system that only the captain understood, and he refused to use filing cabinets. Reyes claimed that being surrounded by paperwork helped keep him focused.

The window was cracked open, letting in warm, late summer air.

"Whateley case. Status," Reyes said tersely, not looking up from the letter he was writing.

"Both sons and the daughter-in-law have alibis," Asa said, standing straight with both hands clasped behind his back. "Strong ones. Multiple witnesses. Movements of all the household staff have been accounted for and verified. And all of them are well paid." An early theory postulated that a butler or a cook had killed the doctor for his money, but Dr. Whateley ensured that all his employees received good wages, including free room and board.

And each employee had only positive things to say about the doctor. More than a few were in tears. Asa hoped at least one would hold a grudge, but no dice.

Reyes nodded. He signed a semi-legible signature and placed the letter on top of a stack.

So that one is outgoing mail, Asa noted. He had tried and failed to understand the system over the last five years, but Reyes seemed to change it randomly. If anyone had to suddenly fill the captain's shoes, they were in for a hellacious time.

"What about Mrs. Palacio?" Reyes asked, referring to the maid who saw Beowulf Smith fleeing the crime scene.

"Worked for the family for twenty-three years. Excellent record. She never imagined a thing like this could happen." The poor woman had been scared witless when Asa and Celeste interviewed her, terrified that the Halfling would return and finish off the rest of the family.

"And Smith?"

Asa scowled. They should have shipped that bastard off to Greer months ago! They had him right in their pocket, but no. Invictus Jones and his brilliant hunch decided to post the Halfling's bail, and Smith was back on the streets causing untold amounts of chaos.

Granted, Smith did help Jones take down Lewin Manning and Emilio Grady, as well as a member of the Royal Family. Who would have thought that Prince Hastyr of all people oversaw an extortion ring? Not Asa. Not in a million years.

"Bishop?" Reyes prompted.

"Right. Mrs. Palacio is the only one who saw Smith after the murder. And she only saw his eyes, sir." The scowled deepened.

"Is something bothering you, officer?"

"Yeah," he admitted. Bloody hell, saying that word, that one syllable, was almost as painful as pulling a tooth. "Kind of weird that she was able to make a positive identification just based on his eyes, sir."

"Smith's picture was in the papers," Reyes pointed out. "She likely saw it and then recognized him. Positive identifications have been made with less."

Yeah, in those stupid books Jones always reads. The man had a stack of paperbacks in his office. Each time Asa looked, they seemed to multiply. When would Jones learn that dime novel detective stories had almost nothing in common with real life police work?

"Still." Asa sighed, thinking. He had gone over the maid's statement again and again, hoping to find something more substantial, something more than a pair of purple eyes underneath a black hat. But he couldn't, leading to a conclusion he did not want to explore.

What if the maid was wrong?

What if Smith was innocent?

"Officer Bishop, do you believe in the accuracy of eyewitness reports?" The captain raised an eyebrow.

"Depends on the witness. Remember that pharmacy robbery last year? We asked the clerk if he recognized anyone in the photo ledgers, and he was completely wrong." The real thief was a teenager who had robbed the pharmacy on a dare. They eventually found the kid and gave him a slap on the wrist after making him return the money. But they held the wrong person in custody for four days. The man threatened to sue the police department. Thankfully, Reyes was able to placate the man and his lawyer.

Reyes nodded. "My thoughts exactly." He stood and rounded the desk, standing face to face with Asa. "These are the kind of questions I want my officers to ask. You've met Smith a few times, correct?"

"Yes, sir." *Unfortunately.*

"What do you think of him?"

"I think he's a thief and a liar, and you never should have exonerated him..." Asa tried to stop himself, but the words tumbled out. Clearing his throat, he added, "I mean, in my opinion, sir."

"Your reaction is understandable." Reyes locked eyes with Asa, as though trying to peer into his soul. "What about Jones? What is your impression of him?"

"He's an okay guy. May I ask what you are getting at, sir?"

"Of course. Do you think Jones is the type of person who would associate with a cold-blooded murderer?"

"No, sir." Jones had his flaws, but he was not stupid or malicious.

"Did you see the way Jones defended Smith? No matter what I said, he questioned me. Gave explanations for why I was wrong." The captain smirked, though whether he was proud, amused, or annoyed, Asa could not tell. "What do you conclude?"

"Jones believes that Smith is innocent. Obviously." Asa rolled his eyes.

"You disagree."

"Yes, sir."

Reyes studied him for a very long moment. "What's bothering you?"

"I've been thinking about the case, sir. Going over the evidence and testimonies—"

"No. Something else is bothering you. What is it?"

"I..." Should he really bring it up? The other officers were finally starting to treat him normally again. As though he was not related to Jorge Bishop, disgraced police officer. "I was thinking about my cousin, sir."

Reyes sighed and seemed to age ten years. "God knows I wanted to straggle Jorge. His stupidity put this entire Precinct in jeopardy. It will take years for us to discover how many cases he tampered with. How many crimes he swept under the rug. But," the captain said, standing a little straighter, "it could have been worse. Only Jorge and three more of our own were arrested. Nothing like the Second. Even Captain Mendez was charged." Reyes looked like he wanted to punch a hole in the wall, but he quickly tampered down his anger. "Have you spoken to Jorge lately?"

"No." Bloody hell, why did the captain ask that? Jorge was the last person Asa wanted to think about. Why would he voluntarily talk to him?

The handful of letters Jorge sent went directly into the fireplace.

"Do you know where Jones went yesterday?"

"Probably to Mull District." Asa thanked Triumvir for the conversation change.

"Think he made contact with Smith?"

Asa shrugged. "It's possible."

"More than possible. I assigned Pembroke to track him." Pembroke, a full-blood Shinnok Fae, was one of the few officers from the Second Precinct who was clean. With most of his colleagues in prison, the young Fae asked for a transfer, and Reyes willingly gave him a fresh start.

"Really?" Asa understood the reasoning, but Pembroke was so timid and quiet. He doubted he heard Pembroke say more than twenty words all summer. *How did that kid wind up as a police officer?* Perhaps he had an uncle or a grandfather who was a policeman.

"Of course," Reyes said. "Shinnoks are excellent trackers, and they rarely get caught."

Don't bloody remind me!

"Pembroke confirmed that Jones contacted Smith, and they went to a tenement on Twenty-Second Street."

"Why?"

"Pembroke sensed the presence of more Fae inside and feared he would be spotted. He waited outside until Jones returned half an hour later and followed him back to his residence on Clarke Street."

"You want me to talk to Jones about this, sir?" He saw Lawson speaking with Jones this morning. Maybe she already got the information from him.

"I assigned Lawson that task." Reyes walked over to the window and looked down at the busy street. Pedestrians, carriages, cyclists, and a handful of nosy motorcars circled Varnick Square. An area of vibrant green with a clock tower rising from the center. Every year Malkin City seemed more and more crowded. More people. More crime. More work for people like Asa Bishop.

"Captain," Asa asked hesitantly, "do you think Beowulf Smith is guilty?"

"I think people rarely change. An honest young man will become an honest old man. And a thief will remain a thief. But will that thief become a murderer?" He turned and faced Asa.

"I guess it depends on the thief's circumstances." Greer Island was populated by people under those circumstances. Men and women who started off with petty crimes and then escalated to major ones. People like Beowulf Smith.

"Say you're a thief, Bishop. You see a big house full of money and other valuables. So, you enter through a window when nobody is looking. You walk into a study, planning to steal everything you can get your hands on, but an old man interrupts you. Do you run away immediately, or do you stay and argue with the old man before shooting him dead?"

Asa's mind took a few moments to process the captain's request. Why would a police captain ask his officer to think like a thief? The concept was weird and a little disturbing. "I would run away, sir."

"Why?"

"If the old man sees me," Asa said, trying to visualize the odd scenario, "he will call for help. More people will arrive. Easier to run away from one person than five."

"To clarify, you would *not* stick around for an argument?"

"No, sir."

Reyes selected a file from the nearest stack and opened it. "What was Rosalyn Palacio's witness statement?"

Asa repeated it verbatim.

"Excellent. And Molly Gonzalez's statement?"

Molly Gonzalez was one of the maids. The third, Elena Norris, was in the kitchen chatting with the cook. At the same time Rosalyn Palacio was walking up the stairs to the second floor, Molly was carrying a basket of laundry down the hall to put in the linen closet.

"She claimed to hear arguing," Asa replied, his heart sinking. "At first, she thought Dr. Whateley was on the telephone, but then she heard the second voice. A man's voice, but she couldn't understand him. She then heard the gunshot, followed by Mrs. Palacio screaming."

Reyes locked eyes with him. "Why would Smith stop to argue with the doctor? Why not run away immediately?"

"I don't know, sir." Oh hell. Did this mean that Smith was not guilty? But if it wasn't Smith, then who killed the doctor?

"Tomorrow," Reyes said, mercifully breaking eye contact and sitting down at his desk, "I am giving Jones the day off. He's due for a personal holiday. My gut says he will contact Smith again. You and Lawson will follow him. If you see Smith, approach with caution. I don't want him disappearing on us. Convince Smith to come in for a witness statement."

"So, he isn't under arrest for breaking and entering?" Those charges alone would land Smith on Greer Island for at least a year.

"We will cross that bridge later. For now, I want his side of events. I have a hunch that Smith might be the key to solving this murder."

Asa's vision lurched as though he stood at the edge of a cliff, gazing downward.

"A hunch?"

"Yes." Reyes fixed him with a glare. "Do you have a problem with that, Officer Bishop?"

"No, sir."

Another hunch.

Great.

Chapter 6
Lost in the Woods

Wulf banged on the door. Faint moaning sounded from inside the apartment. Damn, Macsen was still sick, but Wulf couldn't wait for him to recover. He needed answers now.

He knocked again. Loudly.

"Go away," Macsen said weakly.

"Maybe we should go," said Vic. The lanky teen had grown half a foot this summer, making the long brown coat a couple inches too short, exposing his bony wrists. Billy, standing behind his older brother, nodded.

Wulf wasn't sure why he recruited the brothers. He could talk to Macsen on his own, but Wulf saw them milling about on the stairs and the idea took hold. Besides, Macsen was less likely to lie if there were witnesses.

"And leave your cousin to suffer alone?" Wulf questioned. "Is that something families do?"

The two Blydd teens locked eyes and then nodded. At times, the brothers seemed able to communicate without talking. Just a shared look or a nod, and all need for conversation flew out the window. Wulf and Dav could sorta do that, but never as accurately as Vic and Billy.

The brothers knocked on the door repeatedly.

"Shut the hell up!" yelled someone living across the hall.

"You shut up!" Billy yelled back.

The Someone yelled a curse. A real nasty one.

Wulf placed a hand on Billy's shoulder as the boy prepared his own curse. Billy glanced at him, meeting him at eye level. At just fourteen, Billy stood as tall as most adult human men. He'd be as tall as his father in a few years, maybe taller.

For half a second, Wulf wondered if he was taller than his father, whoever he was. Or had been.

He shoved the thought aside and shouted, "Mac, you gonna open this door?"

"No."

"Fine." Wulf selected a lock pick and had the door open in five seconds. He shook his head as the door swung open. You'd think a caser, the nephew of a gang leader no less, would have better locks.

Some people...

Macsen laid face down on the fold-out couch, the blankets tangled around his legs. His normally tan face was chalk white, and sweat matted his red and silver hair.

Wulf strolled up to him. Vic and Billy followed on his heels, closing the door. Faint light streamed in through the moth-eaten curtains, making the small apartment look cramped and dingy. This building was the mirror image of the place Wulf lived in, but the landlord wanted to squeeze every possible cent out of it. So, he had the building gutted and built more walls, making more apartments. Cramped, thin-walled apartments that made Wulf's place look like a proper house.

"Why?" Macsen muttered.

"Just checking the make sure you was still sick."

"Yeah. Still sick. Go away." Macsen buried his face in a pillow.

Wulf grabbed a chair, the only one in the room, and sat down in it backwards, resting his arms across the back.

"You know, this place is filthy," Wulf said, eyeing the pile of dirty dishes in the sink and the layer of dust on the table. And the water closet... Well, the smell alone told Wulf that it was in desperate need of cleaning. "Good thing I brought help."

"What are...?" Macsen glanced over and saw his younger cousins. They greeted him with big, toothy smiles. "Oh, hell."

"Boys, get to work."

"Work? That mean we're gettin' paid?" Vic asked. Billy laughed under his breath.

"Yeah, sure, whatever. Now." Wulf turned his attention back to Macsen as the brothers started tidying. Folks could say all they wanted about Blydd Fae being little more than animals, but they knew how to keep a place clean. In a way, they were better housekeepers than humans. Some of the apartments in Wulf's building certainly needed their expertise.

"Now what?" Macsen glared at Wulf with one eye.

"Where is Carlos Vallejo?"

"Don't know."

"Don't know or don't wanna tell me?"

"First one. Go away."

"Not until you tell me what I want." Wulf leaned closer, studying Macsen. The Hybrid's eyes were completely bloodshot. In fact, he looked the same way Wulf felt the second time he snuck into Grady's house. The banishment had made it hard to move, hard to breathe, as though he had glass shards in his lungs. If Bookie hadn't helped, Wulf would have collapsed halfway to the stairs and been at Lewin Manning's mercy.

I want a fox hunt! Lewin's words echoed in Wulf's mind. He shuddered and shoved all thoughts of the Sidhe away. The golden-eyed bastard was locked up on Greer Island. He'd never lay a hand on Wulf again. Never get his fox hunt.

"Mac, are you really sick?" he asked, tilting his head to the side. "With the flu, I mean."

"Feels like the flu."

"But most folks don't get the flu in the summer. That's more of a winter thing, right?"

"Ain't no doctor." Macsen turned away, covering his face with the pillow.

Wulf leaned back and watched the brothers clean. They'd made good headway. Vic washed and dried the dishes and placed them in the cupboard, and Billy had dusted the table and moved on to the desk, the only other piece of furniture. He leafed through a few papers.

"Hey, Mac, where do you want these?" Billy waved the papers in the air.

Wulf frowned. "Let me see those."

Billy handed them over.

Wulf scanned the papers, looking for familiar words. Familiar names.

"Did Carlos ever write anything down?" he asked Macsen.

"Don't know. Go away."

Wulf found a crudely drawn map of Hawthorn Street. Squares and lines represented houses and roads with numbers written in the squares. Wulf found 386 with ease. Numbers rarely gave him trouble. For starters, there were only ten different kinds and folks always wrote them the same way. Granted, if there were more than five in a line, he had trouble remembering the order. But three numbers? That was easy.

So, how the hell did he mix up 386 and 368?

And their locations were completely different. 368 was in the middle of the street, closer to Elm than Maple, and 386 was only two lots away from Maple with the corner store in plain view. If Wulf had worked as the caser instead of Macsen, he'd never have made this mistake.

"Carlos said 386, right?"

"368!" Macsen sneered, glaring at Wulf. The silver flecks in his eyes flashed.

"Then, how'd I mix them up?"

"Because you can't read!"

"Exactly. Carlos never gave me nothing to read. He *told* me the address." A sickening feeling crept into Wulf's mind as Bookie's question resurfaced. The same question that Wulf wondered as he fled the Whateley house. "Think he told me wrong on purpose?"

"Why would he? That house was the perfect score. If I hadn't gotten sick—"

"If you hadn't gotten sick, you would've been at the met up. You'd have told me the right address."

Wulf stood and started pacing, his arms and legs demanding to move, his mind demanding to think. Bloody hell, this apartment was too small! He could only go five paces before turning around.

"You get sick," Wulf thought out loud. "Carlos doesn't show. I break into the wrong house. The wrong house where some geezer gets bumped off. And now the bricks think I did him in." He ran his fingers through his hair. The sickening feeling worsened, churning his brain and stomach.

Dammit, is this how Bookie felt? Bookie claimed that the Ciceron Station robbery never sat right with him because one detail did not make sense: Birdie instructing Wulf to rob him and only him. Not the women with fancy jewelry or the men with nice suits. The Amistadian guy with nothing to his name 'cept a silver pocket watch.

And now Carlos Vallejo instructed Wulf to rob the wrong house, making him a murder suspect. Carlos, a guy Wulf had met just last week.

"Mac, what did you do the day of the robbery? That morning and afternoon?"

"Didn't do shit. Was too sick to move."

"Okay, what about Saturday?" Wulf kept moving, pacing, fearing that if he stopped, he would lose this line of thought and never find it again. "I met with Carlos early in the morning, right before daybreak, to make sure I had the job right. I laid low until Sunday night. What did you do?"

Carlos was terrified during the meeting, ready to jump out of his own skin at every little sound, afraid that something would go wrong.

"He doesn't own dogs," Carlos had said, his voice trembling. He kept glancing over his shoulder even though he and Wulf were alone in a narrow alleyway between two shops. Neither shop would open for a couple hours. "But he might have hired a guard."

"You ever see guards at the house?"

"No, but..." Carlos shivered, his purple eyes fading to pale lavender. "God, I feel like I'm gonna be sick. You ever feel this way?"

"Not anymore. Now, go over the plan again. Where are we meeting?"

Carlos spoke in a whisper, but Wulf understood every single word. Without a doubt, he said that the guy lived at 386 Hawthorn Street.

"Met with Carlos around noon," Macsen said, his voice muffled by the pillow. "Ate lunch."

"Did you feel sick then?" Wulf paced faster, covering every inch of the narrow apartment and almost running into Vic and Billy. What was wrong with him? Mercy sakes alive, his brain felt like it was on fire! "The flu is weird, you know? Sometimes, you can feel it coming, and other times, it hits you like a gut punch."

"I..." Macsen struggled to sit upright. He failed and laid on the pillow. "I felt okay. Good, actually."

"But not sick."

"No."

"What did you eat for lunch?" Where were these questions coming from? Why did his brain feel like it was spinning?

"Just sandwiches. Turkey and cheese with tomato. Carlos ate the same thing."

Wulf halted. His mind was going somewhere... And now it was lost in the woods. Bloody great. "The same thing? You sure?"

"Yeah, I'm sure. Bastard made me pay for it," Macsen grumbled.

Wulf picked up the papers. A few were blank on one side. "Mind if I borrow these?"

"If I say yes, will you and my cousins leave?"

"Yes."

"Then, yeah. Take them."

Wulf whistled sharply. Vic and Billy froze and locked eyes with him. Wulf smiled, surveying the apartment. The boys did an excellent job, turning Macsen's apartment into a livable space. It even smelled cleaner. Should hold up 'til Macsen was well enough to clean for himself.

"Good work. Let's go."

"Are you gonna by okay, Macsen?" Vic asked, leaning over him.

"Yes. Please, for the love of God, go away!" Macsen pulled the blanket over his head.

"We will, and thanks." Wulf waved the papers in the air. He led the way into the hall and shut the door.

"Boys, is your father home today?" Wulf asked as they walked down the rickety stairway. Far more rickety than the one in his building. A few boards seemed ready to snap under his slight weight.

"Should be. Why?" Billy asked.

"I need some pens and ink and somebody who can read real good."

"I can read," Vic chimed in.

"I said someone who can read good." Wulf glanced at the papers as they walked outside. The sunlight helped, making the paper whiter and the ink blacker. But half the words were meaningless.

Wulf grounded his teeth. He'd been learning all summer, and he still could not read half the words he saw. What was the bloody point?!

"What do those papers say?" Billy asked. He could read okay. Street signs and newspaper headlines. Easy stuff. But when you could count cards and win any game, who needed to read?

"I don't know." But one page had Carlos's name on it. Wulf smiled and silently thanked Bookie for giving him that book. One of the characters was named Carlos. A few lines down was the address for 368 Hawthorn Street.

How the hell did I hear that wrong?

He swore Carlos said 386. He recalled that last meeting and saw Carlos's mouth form the words. Three Eighty-Six.

Wulf might be too stupid to read, but he never, ever misheard someone talking directly to his face.

He grimaced. If Carlos had purposely given him the wrong information...

"Dammit."

"What?" Vic asked as they turned down the street.

"I think..." Bloody hell, was this how Bookie felt? Was this how his brain worked? If so, then Wulf's brain must have gotten infected. "I think I have a hunch."

Chapter 7

Cold Ashes

"I'm sorry?" Invictus asked, stunned by the captain's words. Reyes fixed him with an icy glare. "Sir," he quickly added.

"Do you have a problem with taking a day off work?" the captain asked, sitting behind his cluttered desk with his hands clasped together.

"No, sir. I just..." When Reyes called Invictus into his office this morning, Invictus assumed he wanted an update on Wulf's whereabouts, though he did not have a chance to see Wulf yesterday. Instead, the captain decided to give him a random holiday. It was more than a little strange. "It's the middle of the week." People might request a Monday or a Friday off for a longer weekend, but never a Wednesday.

"Jones, how many days off have you had since you started working here?"

"None, sir." Other than weekends and holidays, Invictus had not missed a single day of work.

"Then you're due for a personal holiday."

"Personal holiday?" Invictus raised an eyebrow. *What in the world is he talking about?*

"It's a new idea I've been toying with. I have a theory." Reyes rounded the desk and stood side by side with Invictus. "Work will become more efficient if people have time to rest. Tell me, Jones. How do you feel after a bad night's sleep?"

"Um, tired?"

"And after working hard all day?"

"More tired?" *Where is he going with this? I thought he wanted me to help with the Whateley case.* Though, if he had the day off, he could visit Wulf and Ruthless and see if either one found a lead on Carlos Vallejo.

"Exactly," the captain replied. "Tired employees cannot work at full capacity. And when one's profession is to enforce the law and prevent crime, the city cannot be properly protected."

"But I'm not an officer, sir."

"No, but you are employed by the Malkin City Police, and I want you to receive the same benefits."

"So, everyone will get a personal holiday?"

"Eventually. I'm thinking once per quarter."

"It sounds like a good idea, sir." But giving employees random holidays still sounded strange. None of the businesses in Amistad followed this practice. *And why wait to tell me about it the day of?* If Reyes had told Invictus about it yesterday, he would not have wasted time commuting to work and could have gone straight to Mull.

Reyes nodded. "Now, get out of here, Jones. I don't want to see your face again until tomorrow morning. We will need everyone to prepare for the hurricane. Understood?" News reports stated that the hurricane was due to make landfall tomorrow evening, but Invictus did not understand why it was such a big deal. Hurricanes sounded like summer thunderstorms, just windier.

"Yes, sir, but what should I do?"

"It's your holiday. Figure it out." Reyes resumed his seat and selected a file from one of the many scattered about the desk. A pickpocket case in Varnick Square reported two days ago. Three people claimed that their purses or wallets were stolen around noon...

"Jones."

"Sir?"

"Leave."

"Yes, sir."

Invictus exited the office and walked downstairs to the desk area. Officers hurried about, talking to witnesses, filing paperwork, and moving furniture and boxes upstairs. He did not see Asa or Celeste.

They must be working the Whateley case.

Should Invictus help them? Reyes said he could use his personal holiday however he liked, but it felt strange to officially work on a case. Nor was his task really official. His sole job was to find and question Wulf and report back to Asa and Celeste. Reyes never told him what he should do afterwards.

He halfway expected Reyes to assign a few officers to trail him. Once he found Wulf, the real officers would question him, and Invictus would sit behind his desk like a good little clerk and hope the police believed a thief's testimony. But nobody had trailed him on Monday.

And Reyes acted like he believed Wulf's innocence.

Was it genuine or some sort of ploy?

A sickening feeling formed in his gut. Was this the real purpose of his 'personal holiday'? Give Invictus a valid excuse to meet with Wulf again, allowing the police another chance to follow?

Were Asa and Celeste already on their way to Mull District?

Well, let them go to Mull. Wulf would see their green uniforms from a mile away and find some tenement or abandoned building to hide in. They would have an easier time sailing to the Shadowlands than finding him.

So, let Reyes play his games. Invictus had more important things to do.

Donning his hat, Invictus walked outside and hailed a cab.

***

"I don't like this," Celeste Lawson said, glancing at Asa Bishop. The other officer rode across from her in the cab. A glossy, black cab owned by the Malkin City Police. A fresh coat of black paint covered the insignia, allowing the cab to blend in with the mid-morning traffic.

Asa shrugged. "It's Reyes's idea. Not mine."

"So?"

Asa shot her a glare. "Do you have a problem with following orders?"

"Maybe," she said a bit indignantly. Celeste was well versed in the methods of the Malkin City Police. Growing up in the Commonwealth's capital, avoiding the latest news and gossip was next to impossible, and the police were a popular subject. Her university professors dispelled a few rumors, but some were accurate. The police often wore plain clothes and other disguises in order to follow suspects, but never had they disguised themselves to follow one of their own.

When Captain Reyes presented them with the idea yesterday afternoon, Celeste balked.

"Sir, Jones is part of this investigation, too."

"Yes, a vital part. Without him, we will never find Smith." The captain then laid out his plan. Asa accepted it with a wordless nod, and he refused to listen to her concerns.

I thought we were supposed to be partners.

Celeste tried to talk Asa out of the plan this morning, but he refused again, stating that the captain gave them explicit orders. And when she tried to warn Jones, Asa interrupted her, saying there was an important call on the telephone.

But there was no call.

A part of her wanted to slap him. The other part, the part that sounded exactly like her mother, told her to be smarter. If Asa Bishop wanted to unquestioningly follow orders, let him. Celeste would do otherwise.

The cab turned south, heading past Varnick Square and trailing Invictus's cab at a healthy distance. Close enough not to lose him in the crowd, but far enough away to go unnoticed. The morning traffic provided plenty of camouflage.

"Don't you think it's odd to follow our colleague?" Celeste asked, attacking Asa's indifference from a new angle.

"Jones isn't a policeman, uh, officer, so he technically isn't our colleague."

"Policeman uh officer or not," she replied, smirking, "he's working with us. Reyes assigned him to this case, too."

"To draw out Smith. Nothing more." Asa stared out the window and frowned.

Celeste closed her eyes, thinking. This case should have been straightforward. A thief breaks into a house. The homeowner surprises the thief. The thief pulls gun and fires. The homeowner dies.

But Invictus Jones had defended Smith's innocence every step of the way.

"Do you agree with Jones?" Celeste asked, opening her eyes.

"Hmm?" Asa continued to stare out the window. The cab turned off the main road and headed into the heart of the Old City. Sprawling mansions and multi-storied shops surrounded by decorative, vine-covered gates and flowering hedges. Most dated back to the founding of the Commonwealth. Five hundred years of history. How much had they seen?

If only buildings could talk. That would make her job a hundred times easier.

"Do you think Smith is innocent?" she asked.

"The evidence points to him."

"What evidence?" Celeste leaned forward, forcing Asa to make eye contact.

"The gun, the maid's statement, and the dead body!" Asa snapped. His dark brown eyes hardened like amber.

"You mean the gun without any fingerprints?"

"Smith was wearing gloves."

"How do you know?" Celeste narrowed her eyes. "Did Mrs. Palacio state that he was wearing gloves?"

"No, but he is a Halfling. He has to wear gloves to handle a steel gun." Steel, an alloy of iron. For most Fae and Halflings, iron caused severe burns, and sometimes the shock alone could kill them. Steel had a lesser effect, but some still found it painful.

"Interesting. What type of gun did Smith use at Ciceron Station?"

Asa looked like Celeste had slapped him. "What?"

"The gun used in the Ciceron Station robbery," she repeated. "What model was it?"

Asa frowned, thinking. "A point 44 Swanson revolver."

"What type of gun did we find at the Whateley house?"

He cursed under his breath. "A point 32 Pax revolver. But this doesn't prove it wasn't Smith." He jabbed a finger in Celeste's face. "He could have gotten a new gun, or stolen it."

"Perhaps. But why a smaller caliber?"

"How the hell should I know?" Asa leaned back and crossed his arms over his chest. He stared out the window, jaw clenched.

The carriage continued down the street, turning onto Maple, and then onto Hawthorn.

That's where you're going. What did Jones hope to find at the Whateley house? All the evidence was in the case file.

"You got any family, Lawson?" Asa asked quietly, almost a whisper.

Celeste blinked. Did she hear him correctly? "Just my dad. Why?"

"I've... I've been thinking." He swallowed a lump. "About my cousin."

Celeste grimaced. The Grady case had dominated the headlines for a solid month. How could it not? The owner of the largest importer in the province was arrested for extortion. Hundreds of businesses were affected, and over a hundred people lost their jobs. Not to mention the dozens who went to prison, including Queen Waylinda's former heir.

The City Council had to scramble to restructure the police force after two-thirds of the Second Precinct were charged with bribery and criminal negligence, along with several officers in other precincts.

Four officers from the Fifth Precinct were also arrested, including Jorge Bishop. A career officer and army veteran with an excellent record.

"I thought... I mean, I looked up to him my whole life, and I never really knew him. So, when Jones vouches for a guy he's only known a couple months..." Asa shook his head.

"Hard to truly know a person in such a short time."

"Exactly." Asa stared out the window and sighed heavily, as though a massive weight was tied around his neck. "Exactly."

***

Invictus spotted the police cab as they turned off Varnick Square. A part of him wanted to give whoever was inside a little chase, but that would be a waste of time and money. So, he allowed them to follow all the way to 386 Hawthorn Street.

He asked the driver to drop him off and watched as the police cab parked in front of the corner store and newspaper vendor. The driver bought a copy of *The Times* and handed it to the person inside. Based on his short stature and pale skin, Invictus guessed the driver was Stant.

Are Asa and Celeste in the cab? But why would they follow him? *I thought we were supposed to work together*, he thought with dismay.

He strolled up the curved driveway, his shoes clicking on the smooth, interlocking stones. Brilliantly colored flowers grew along the driveway's edge, and more flowers adorned window boxes on the first and second floors. Two massive oak trees with twisting branches guarded both sides of the house like silent sentinels.

Invictus imagined Wulf climbing one of those trees, navigating the branches all the way up to the hallway window. All without being seen.

He knocked on the door.

A wiry, fair-skinned man with short, blond hair answered. He looked at Invictus warily.

"Can I help you?"

"Yes, I'm Invictus Jones. I work for the Fifth Precinct." He pulled a business card out of his pocket and handed it to the man. "I wanted to ask a few questions about Dr. Whateley. Is that alright?"

"The police have already been here twice. What more do you people need?" The man studied him with pale blue eyes. Such an odd color. Almost the same shade as the sky.

"We always follow up," he replied, thinking quickly. Going to Hawthorn Street instead of Mull was spur-of-the-moment. A half-formed idea at best. Why was he here? "To make sure we haven't missed anything. Is the Whateley family home?"

"Yeah. I'm Alfred Whateley. Dr. Whateley was my father."

Invictus cursed himself for an idiot. Dr. Whateley and his family were Scanlannish. Why did he assume this man was a member of the staff? He then recalled Hallvard, Mr. Grady's Scanlannish butler. Both men had the same hair and eye colors, but Alfred's eyes held warmth despite the dark circles underneath them.

"I'm very sorry for your loss, Mr. Whateley, and I'm sorry that I don't have anything better to say."

Alfred smiled, but the expression only made him appear more tired. "Thanks on both parts. Honestly, I'm bloody sick of hearing that." He chewed on his lower lip. "Why don't you come inside? I can have one of the maids fix you a cup of tea."

"Thank you."

Invictus followed Alfred inside. The house was both cramped and spacious. The foyer, decorated with several potted plants in brightly painted vases, branched off in three directions with a staircase at the end of the hallway. More rooms lined the hall, and each contained ample furniture. End tables, curio cabinets filled with odds and ends, painted vases both with and without flowers. Not to mention the oil paintings in polished, gilt frames.

Alfred led him into a sitting room, occupied by a variety of couches and armchairs, all in various shades of blue. Even the wallpaper was a faint blue. Invictus sat on one couch while Alfred sat in the nearest chair. A young Malkinese woman dressed in a stark black dress walked in. She eyed Invictus nervously.

"Molly, can you fix us a cup of tea?" Alfred asked.

"Yes, Mr. Whateley." She bobbed her head.

"Which kind do you prefer?" he asked Invictus.

"Do you have black tea?" Invictus said a silent prayer of thanks for the option. He had yet to adjust to iced tea. Yes, it was refreshing on miserably hot days, but the taste was all wrong. Kind of like drinking warm juice.

"Black tea," Alfred relayed to Molly. The young woman bobbed her head again and ducked into the hall.

Invictus retrieved a small notepad and pencil from his jacket pocket and turned to a blank page. He bought the notepad shortly after being hired, figuring he would need it for investigations. All of the pages were blank. "Were you home on the night of the twelfth?" A shiver ran down his spine. The twelfth. The same day Lewin Manning collected the extortion payments. Was it a coincidence or just unfortunate timing?

"Yes." Alfred frowned. "I already gave your colleagues this information."

"We like to be thorough," he replied, hoping it sounded official. He recalled Spes Sherrington saying this line in several books. "Who else was here?"

"My wife and two children. Three maids, the butler, the cook, and the coach driver. My brother was working late." He crossed his arms as though he were cold. "He didn't get home until after."

"No landscapers?"

Alfred shook his head. "We hire a crew that comes by once a week to do maintenance. More cost effective," he added, rolling his eyes.

"You disagree?"

"It was my brother's idea. Alistair thought it would be more modern or something."

"I see. Is Alistair home today?"

"No, he's at work. The City Hospital."

"Oh, he's a doctor, too?"

Alfred fixed him with a leveled look. "Officer Jones, I'm not trying to tell you how to do your job, but why ask the same questions all over again? You already know who killed my father. Why aren't you looking for him?"

Worry crept into Invictus's mind, an invasive weed taking root. Alfred Whateley believed that Wulf killed his father, and he thought Invictus was a police officer. The business card stated that Invictus was employed by the Fifth Precinct, not that he was a policeman.

You already played police officer once. Doing so again won't hurt. Besides, Reyes wants you to work on this case.

Correction. The captain tasked Invictus with finding and questioning Wulf. He doubted the captain envisioned him questioning other witnesses. But unless he found evidence pointing to the real murderer, his friend would be shipped off to prison.

"Because we want to make sure we send the right person to Greer," he replied. Merciful heavens, did he sound nervous? The words sounded so forced and unnatural, Alfred was bound to pick up on it.

Instead, Alfred just nodded. "Yeah, I understand what you're saying, but Mrs. Palacio swears that she saw Beowulf Smith running out of my father's study."

"And the gun?"

"She found it in the hallway, right outside the study. Smith dropped it."

Invictus made a note. "What were you doing at the time?"

"Sleeping. Or trying to. We have a two-month-old baby. My wife and I had just gotten her to sleep about ten minutes before."

No wonder the man looked so tired.

"Is your wife also home?"

Alfred shook his head. "Gina took the kids to the doctor for a check-up. Please do not question her again." He glared at Invictus. "We've been through enough. Hell, we still have to make funeral arrangements and contact family back in Scanlan..." Alfred cursed under his breath. "They don't have a telegraph office. It'll be weeks before..." He buried his face in his hands.

Invictus placed a hand on Alfred's shoulder. "Is there anything I can do to help?"

Alfred looked up at Invictus, startled. Tears glistened in his bloodshot eyes. "What?"

"Maybe I could help clean or sort mail?" *That's the staff's job, moron.* But the staff members had all spoken so highly of Dr. Whateley. Surely they must be grieving, too. And Invictus felt terrible. Here he was, impersonating a police officer and forcing Alfred to talk about his father's death again. He ought to do something useful.

"Every small thing helps," his mother had once said.

Alfred blinked away the tears. "Why would...? I mean, that's very kind of you, Officer Jones, but I can't take you away from your work."

Molly returned with two cups of black tea. She set the platter, made of solid gold, on an end table. She hurried away without a sound.

"Solid gold," Invictus said to himself.

"Yeah. Dad brought it with him from Scanlan. Been in the family for a hundred years. Supposedly." Alfred took a sip of tea.

"Where do you keep this?"

"Pardon?"

"It must be very valuable. Do you keep it on the first floor?"

"Yeah, in the kitchen cabinet. My parents brought a lot of old things when we immigrated."

"Were you born in Malkin City?"

Alfred shook his head. "I was born in Scanlan. We immigrated when I was seven."

"Really? You don't have an accent."

"I, uh..." Alfred's face blushed red. "I learned to drop it. But I can speak like a Scannie if I want to," he said, switching to a thick accent. He smirked. "Anyway, was there anything else you wanted to ask or see?"

"Would you mind showing me your father's study?" Perhaps he could retrace Wulf's steps and see how long it took to run from the study to the window.

Alfred agreed and led Invictus upstairs. Rich blue carpeting covered the floor, and dark wood paneling lined the walls. Landscapes of Malkin's beaches and wetlands decorated the twisting hallway.

"This house is gigantic," Invictus said under his breath. The layout seemed random, almost haphazard. It was a wonder Wulf hadn't gotten lost. Invictus doubted he could navigate his way to the front door.

"Yeah. All of these old houses were built like this. Part of an old Malkinese superstition that's supposed to confuse spirits. Here we are." Alfred paused at the door. He stared at the dark wood for a long moment. He then took a deep, shuddering breath and opened it.

Invictus peered inside. The study was about the size of his room at the boardinghouse. An oak desk stood to the left, facing a stone fireplace. Pictures and awards lined the mantle over the fireplace, and a massive bookshelf occupied the far wall, flanked by two windows. One curtain was open, allowing the morning light to spill in.

Two armchairs faced the fireplace, and another chair sat behind the desk. An incredibly well-organized desk. Not a single pen or paper out of place.

"My father was found there," Alfred said weakly, pointing at one of the armchairs. His hand trembled.

Invictus walked over. A bit of blood stained the fabric, and cold ashes rested in the fireplace. A medical journal sat face down on the end table.

He suddenly felt cold. A man had died here. Had drawn his last breath. Did Dr. Whateley seen his murderer, or was he taken by surprise?

Invictus closed his eyes, recalling the case file. Dr. Whateley was shot in the heart. Yes, he saw his murderer, but what had he seen? A pair of purple eyes underneath a black, wide-brimmed hat, or a different pair?

He turned to ask Alfred a question but stopped. Alfred's eyes were wide, terrified. His breaths came in short stutters, and he trembled as though he were caught in a snowstorm.

"You don't have to see this," Invictus said, quoting another line from a Spes Sherrington novel. One with an eerily similar plot. A man murdered at home in the dead of night with his family left to pick up the pieces.

"Yes, I do." Alfred walked over to the armchair and placed a hand on it. He shivered. "My father, he..." Alfred met Invictus's eyes. "Do you think he will come back?"

"Who?"

Alfred jolted. "Smith. I mean, he didn't have time to grab anything, and you've seen the stuff in this house. That gold platter is worth hundreds. Any thief..." He swallowed. "Do you think he'll come back?"

"No, but I will ask for police protection to be assigned to your house."

Alfred breathed a sigh of relief. "Thank you, officer. Is there anything else you'd like to see?"

"Did your father keep accounting ledgers here?"

"Yes. Do you think they're important?"

"Perhaps."

Alfred walked over to the desk and found a few ledgers. He handed them over. Invictus had no idea if he would find anything useful, but it never hurt to check.

"Anything else?"

"No, I think that covers it."

Alfred nodded, looking relieved, and showed Invictus to the door.

"Thank you for your cooperation, Mr. Whateley. And I truly am sorry about your father. I... If it was my father, I wouldn't be nearly as composed as you."

Alfred smirked. "You should have seen me on Monday. Please call me once you have more information."

"I will."

Invictus walked down the driveway, the ledgers tucked under his arm. He did not expect to find anything pertinent in them, but he hadn't expected to find hundreds of tiny errors in Grady's accounts either. Best to explore every possible avenue.

He strolled down the street to the waiting police cab. Bits of dark green insignia showed through the shoddy paint job. Officer Stant, dressed as a cab driver with gray trousers and coat and a tattered brown hat, scowled. Invictus knocked on the window. Asa Bishop rolled it down.

"Good morning, Asa," Invictus said. "And good morning, Celeste. Have you found any leads yet?" He genuinely hoped so.

"No. We've been too busy following you," Asa replied. He stole a glance at the Whateley house. "Why are you here?"

"I wanted to see the house for myself."

"Find anything?"

Invictus shook his head. "You know Wulf didn't kill the doctor, right?"

"Actually, I don't know that. Nobody knows that. Including you!" Asa snapped.

"What do you have?" Celeste asked, speaking over Asa.

"Accounting ledgers. Celeste, can you ask Reyes to place police protection on the Whateley house? It would give the family more peace of mind."

"No problem," she replied.

Asa scowled and glared at the house.

"Do you disagree?" Invictus asked.

Asa jolted and blinked a few times. "What? No. Good idea. Heading back to the precinct?"

"No, I'm going to Mull District," he called up to Stant. "Do you wish to follow?"

"Hell no." The gray-haired policeman scowled.

Asa leaned out the window. "Then what would you have done if Jones went to Mull in the first place?"

"Turn around. This whole damn case is screwy. Having a clerk do an officer's job. Idiocy!"

"Please don't follow me," Invictus said to Asa and Celeste. "I have a hunch about this case, but if Wulf sees either of you—"

"And he's friends with the lead suspect!" Stant complained. "I swear on Triumvir's holy name, Reyes has lost his damn mind!"

"Thank you for your input, Officer Stant," Celeste said. She turned to Invictus. "We will report back to Reyes and ask for two officers to watch the house. Think the real murderer will return?"

"Doubtful." *Though it would be really nice if he did.*

"Oh, Celeste," Invictus remembered. "Have you looked into the landscaping companies yet?"

"Not yet."

"Landscaping companies?" Asa asked, raising an eyebrow.

Invictus explained that Carlos Vallejo worked for a landscaping company, servicing 368 Hawthorn. "Alfred said that a company comes by once a week. Check if they're the same one."

"Got it," Celeste said.

Asa did not reply, but Invictus was not surprised. He tucked the ledgers under his arm and headed for the nearest train station.

Chapter 8

Nobody Home

The Twenty-first Street apartment was strangely quiet. No people walking about or chatting in doorways. No children playing in the street. And all the neighborhood shops appeared to be closed.

Invictus tucked the ledgers under his arm and checked his watch. A few minutes past eleven.

Where is everybody?

He knocked on the front door. No answer. Well, that was nothing unusual. He tried the knob, and the door swung freely on well-oiled hinges.

"Hello?" he called out. His voice echoed faintly.

His gut twisted in knots. The apartment was never empty. Never silent. Did something bad happen here? Could it be connected to the Whateley case? To the real murderer? The knots twisted further, making him feel sick.

Invictus walked up to the second floor. Relief washed over him when he saw Vic Wells. The lanky teen sat in front of Wulf and Maria's door, playing cat's cradle.

"Ms. Maria is at work," Vic said before Invictus could ask. "And Wulf is upstairs with Dad. But don't go in there. Use the first door on the right."

"Why?"

Vic shrugged. "Dad told me to tell you. He had a feeling you'd come by soon, so he cleared the way."

Invictus froze. "Explain."

"Don't get all jumpy." Vic rolled his silvery eyes. "Dad knows you don't like folks seeing you come by here, so he asked everyone to clear out for the day. Paid them, too. He also said that if any bricks were trailing you, he'd see them from a mile away."

"Makes sense," Invictus muttered under his breath. But it was also unnerving. Yes, Ruthless was a powerful gang leader with countless connections, but how did his influence extend to an entire apartment building?

And the neighboring buildings, too. Invictus had not seen a single person since turning onto Twenty-first Street.

How had Ruthless convinced them? Where did he get the money to pay them?

Invictus filed the questions away for later, thanked Vic, and hurried up the stairs.

The first door on the right was unlocked. Two of Ruthless's cousins, Urien and Allo, sat in the living room, playing poker. The cards looked strangely small in their large hands. Allo, the taller of the two at seven and a half feet, stood and opened a side door.

"What's going on?" Invictus asked.

Allo glared at him, silver eyes flashing. He motioned for Invictus to enter.

Invictus complied. To his surprise, the door led to the adjacent apartment. Fully furnished and completely empty except for Adalhard, another of Ruthless's cousins and Allo's younger brother. Faint music sounded from a record player. So faintly that Invictus could barely hear the tune.

Adalhard jabbed a thumb at another door, which in turn led to Ruthless's apartment.

The massive Blydd Fae, again wearing a sharp, dark blue suit, stood by the door, his arms folded and smirking. "About time you showed up. Had me worried for a second."

"How did you know I would come by today?"

"I have good hearing."

"That doesn't..." Invictus glanced over his shoulder. From this angle, he could see straight into the first apartment. "Do all the rooms on this floor interconnect?"

"Just the ones on this side. My grandmother moved in here when the building was new. Bought this entire side."

So that's how so many people can live here.

Invictus looked around. "Where is Wulf?"

"Bedroom."

Invictus took a few steps and turned. Ruthless remained by the door. "Are you coming, too?"

"No. I'm acting as lookout today."

Invictus walked into the bedroom and saw Wulf seated at the desk with a small stack of papers off to the side. Wulf jolted and reached for a knife. Seeing Invictus, he relaxed.

"Oh, it's you. Find anything yet?"

"No. What are you reading?"

"Some papers I found at Macsen's place. Turns out he really is sick."

"I never doubted it." Invictus pulled over a chair and sat next to Wulf. "Reyes wants me to bring you to the Fifth Precinct for questioning."

Wulf sneered, revealing sharp teeth. "Hell, no!"

"But you're innocent."

"Of killing. But I broke inside. The bricks will charge me with that."

"Maybe Reyes will exonerate you again." The captain had exonerated Wulf for the Ciceron Station robbery without hesitation. But Wulf helped bring down a crime ring and protected officers during the fire. Would Reyes exonerate him again?

Wulf rolled his eyes. "Yeah right. Bookie, tell me the truth. What will the bricks do if they see me?"

Invictus thought it over. He wanted to trust Captain Reyes, but did the captain really believe in Wulf's innocence? Would he have tasked Asa and Celeste with following Invictus if that truly were the case? Did the captain actually want to hear Wulf's testimony, or was it a ploy to trap him? To ensure he could not run away? "Most likely, they will arrest you."

"See! So, you gotta help me."

"Okay." Invictus gathered his thoughts. "Carlos Vallejo took Macsen to the Old City to scout out the house, correct?"

"Yes."

"But not you."

"Nope."

"Why?"

Wulf's face fell. "Been thinking 'bout that, too. I mean, most times, gangs only use one or two casers at a time. One guy looking at a house or a shop is no big deal. But two or three? That's sketchy. People are bound to notice."

"But couldn't Carlos have taken you and Macsen on different days?"

"Not if he wanted me to break into the wrong house."

Invictus had feared this. "Alright. Tell me what you're thinking."

Wulf handed him the papers. "I can't read most of this, but there are numbers and dates on it. The date for the robbery is right, but the address number is wrong. Or right." Wulf ran a hand through his black hair. "Hell, I don't know!"

Invictus set Dr. Whateley's ledgers off to the side and studied the papers. Carlos's handwriting was a weird combination of print and cursive, making it difficult to decipher. But the numbers were clear. 368 Hawthorn Street.

"Was this job all Carlos's idea?"

"As far as I know." Wulf shifted, frowning. "I've been thinking, Bookie. Birdie robbing Ciceron Station was real stupid, but it wasn't her idea. Lewin paid her a stupid amount of money and promised her more if we pulled it off. What if someone paid Carlos?"

Invictus exhaled slowly. "The same thought crossed my mind." He opened the doctor's ledgers, hoping to find a name or a date or an odd transaction, some small clue, but nothing stood out. No errors or discrepancies.

Instead, he discovered that the Whateleys had substantial amounts of money divided into three accounts, one for the doctor and each of his sons. More money than Invictus hoped to earn in a lifetime. The valuables inside the house more than doubled the amount. Did Carlos know how wealthy the family was? *Obviously. Anyone can look at the house's exterior and know that the people who live inside are wealthy.* But why this house?

He closed his eyes, picturing the street. Some houses were twice as large as the houses in the Gems, the richest neighborhood in Malkin City. Carlos could have chosen any house on Hawthorn Street for the job.

But only one house had a murder.

"The owner of 368 is a university professor, right?"

Wulf shrugged. "All I know is that he's gone for a whole month."

Invictus's invisible string returned, forcing him to read over the ledgers again, to look.

Would be nice to know what I'm supposed to look for.

"Hey, you got another number book." Wulf leaned closer. "Who's it from?"

"Dr. Whateley. His son let me borrow it."

"Why? You ain't no brick."

Invictus's blood turned to ice water. What would happen if Alfred discovered that Invictus was not a policeman?

"Oh, hell. Did you fake being a brick again?"

"Yes." He quickly turned the page. So long as Alfred did not call the precinct asking for Officer Jones or speak with Asa and Celeste about him, he ought to be fine. No point in worrying over maybes.

All of the Whateleys' assets were normal. Income from three different people with two main sources: the City Hospital and an art dealership in the Business District. Some of Dr. Whateley's earnings were marked as consultations, and the check numbers were verified by the hospital and the bank.

Medical research, Invictus surmised. The case file stated that Dr. Whateley had worked in research for the last decade.

All of their expenses were normal, too. Gas and water bills, groceries, salaries for the household staff. Very good salaries. The butler earned almost as much as Invictus.

"What does Carlos Vallejo look like?"

"Shinnok Halfling. Dark red hair. Purple eyes. A few inches shorter than me and skinny."

"Then the maid could not have confused you two."

"Not if we were standin' side by side. 'Cept Carlos wasn't there."

The invisible string tugged again. "Are you sure about that?"

Wulf chewed on his lip, thinking. "Yes and no. I heard the old guy arguing with someone before he got shot, but thieves ain't stupid enough to argue with the folks they're robbing. They either run like hell or shoot first before running like hell. And it sounded like they was speaking a different language. Besides, I think Carlos is sick, too."

"Why?"

"He and Macsen ate the same thing for lunch on Saturday. If they got food poisoning instead of the flu, that would explain why neither showed."

Invictus stared at him.

"What?"

"Wulf, that is excellent deductive reasoning."

"It is?"

"Yes."

"Awesome! Wait." His eyes narrowed. "Does that mean I sound like one of those fake bricks?"

"Yes. Which is a good thing," he added before Wulf could argue. "Where does Carlos live? Do you know?"

Wulf nodded. "Yeah, in Dannyn District. Near the river." He gathered up the papers.

"Wait." Invictus selected a page. The handwriting was like nothing Invictus had ever seen, and the words... Well, he wasn't sure if they were words. Straight lines intersected by slash marks covered the page. "Did you see this?"

"Yeah. Makes no damn sense."

"Agreed." Invictus frowned, studying the page. Some lines were shorter than others, and each contained a different number and combination of slashes. Short diagonal ones, long straight ones, long diagonals. Was it a language? He turned the paper sideways, wondering if the words were written vertically. No dice.

"You can't understand it neither?"

"Unfortunately, no. Could it be Faerie?" Faerie had two scripts: a phonetic one and a symbolic one. He knew neither script, but if Carlos, a Halfling, had corresponded with another Halfling or Fae, could they have used the symbolic script as a code?

But what Fae would orchestrate a doctor's death?

A sinking feeling formed in his gut.

"Can Ruthless read Faerie script?"

"No." The Blydd Fae walked into the room. "I suggest giving that letter to the police, Jones. The Fifth Precinct can contact an interpreter from the Embassy to translate."

"How long have you been listening?"

"How long have you been talking?"

That's fair. Blydd had an extraordinary sense of hearing. Invictus made a mental note not to forget.

Shinnok have excellent hearing, too.

"Wulf, you heard arguing, but you couldn't understand it, right?"

"Yeah, at first, I thought it was just because they were yelling. You know how folks yell real loud and you can't understand half the words?"

Invictus nodded, recalling the argument between Mrs. Garcia and her daughter.

"But the words sounded strange. I don't think they were speaking Malkinese."

"But you heard the argument," Ruthless said, looming over them.

"Sure. Surprised the whole neighborhood didn't hear them."

Ruthless nodded. He turned to Invictus. "Jones, I have other business to see to today and cannot follow you. Promise not to get into trouble?"

"I promise," Invictus agreed, a bit worried. How often had Ruthless or one of his gang members followed Invictus without his knowledge?

Is someone following me now? He had not seen Germanicus in weeks, and he had a hunch Reyes assigned an officer to trail him.

Ruthless walked into one of the connecting apartments. He exchanged a few words with Adalhard in Faerie and then disappeared.

Leaving the ledgers and papers in the apartment, Invictus and Wulf headed for the station and caught the train to Dannyn District.

Invictus breathed a relieved sigh at the sight of the crowded train car. Ruthless's weird influence had not spread past his own neighborhood, and Invictus found an odd sense of comfort by being part of a crowd.

Easier to blend in, to go about his business without the fear of being watched.

Dannyn District was directly north of the Gems and bordered the Attakapas River to the west. The buildings, a mixed bag of houses, stores, and manufacturers, were well-to-do with fresh coats of paint. And vibrant green plants flourished in the late summer humidity, giving the impression that the area was one large garden.

One detail immediately caught Invictus's attention. The majority of the people were either Shinnoks or Shinnok Halflings. Each one had purple eyes and angular, foxlike faces, and their hair colors ranged from bright red to brown to black.

Wulf muttered and lowered the brim of his hat.

"Are you okay?" Invictus asked.

"Yeah, sure. I just..." Wulf glanced around. One Shinnok, a woman in her twenties with her coppery hair in a braid, smiled at him. Purple eyes flashed to dark violet. Wulf quickly turned away. "Didn't realize there were so many Shinnoks in Malkin."

The number surprised Invictus, too, but what better place for a Shinnok Halfling to hide?

Every block or two, Invictus looked over his shoulder. No black police cabs in sight. Stant had been adamant about not going to Mull, but what if Asa and Celeste found another driver, or maybe Reyes instructed a second cab to follow him? One with a better paint job?

Now you're being paranoid.

Then why did he have the distinct impression that he was being watched?

Wulf led them deeper into Dannyn, weaving through a maze of streets. Plant life grew in abundance with large patches of green, including several public gardens. A trio of Shinnok women chatted in Faerie as they pruned a small grove of apple trees. The swaying branches shaded the sidewalk, providing blessed relief from the noon sun.

"Here." Wulf stopped and pointed at an apartment complex.

"Are you sure?" Invictus frowned. This neighborhood was nicer than Clarke Street, and fresh, pale blue paint coated the walls. Vibrant flowers grew in window boxes. Two tenants, both full-blooded Shinnoks and both wearing well-tailored suits, stood on the wide porch and talked about the weather.

"Yep." Wulf walked inside and up a flight of stairs. Stairs with recently polished wooden railings and sturdy, carpeted steps.

Why would someone who lives in a nice building plan a robbery?

Wulf paused on the third-floor landing, muttering.

"Is everything okay?"

"Never been here during the day. Only visited once at night." He glanced around. "I think this is the right place."

"Excuse me." Invictus flagged down a passing tenant. He was a Shinnok with reddish brown hair and flecks of blue in his purple irises. A Hybrid or a Halfling, perhaps.

"What are you doing?" Wulf said through his teeth.

"Act normal."

"Yes?" the Shinnok man asked, raising an eyebrow.

"Does Carlos Vallejo live in this building? We're visiting from out of town, and I'm afraid we lost his address."

The man studied Invictus for a moment. His eyes then drifted to Wulf. He smiled and nodded. "Second door on the left." He continued down the stairs.

Wulf exhaled loudly. "Bloody hell, how did you know that would work?"

"Because most people will answer a simple question." *And you being a Halfling helps.* He knocked on the door. "Mr. Vallejo? Are you home?"

No answer.

Invictus knocked again.

"I don't hear anything," Wulf said. He deftly picked the lock.

Carlos's apartment was well furnished with a new couch, and a sturdy, dark wood table with three matching chairs. The kitchen had a polished sink and a new icebox. A dark green rug covered most of the hardwood floor.

"Mr. Vallejo?" Invictus walked into the bedroom. Everything was neat and tidy, and it smelled clean. A few blank papers rested on the writing desk along with a couple of books written in the same odd script. Lines of various lengths interspersed with dashes.

"That explains the letter." But who wrote it?

"Where the hell is he?" Wulf asked, scratching his head.

"Maybe he went to the hospital." If Carlos truly had food poisoning, he might have asked a neighbor to call the hospital or to give him a ride.

"No way."

"How do you know?"

"I just..." Wulf violently shook his head and sneered. "Bloody hell, I don't know! He might have."

An idea formed in Invictus's mind and quickly took root. "Alistair Whateley is a doctor."

"Who?"

"Dr. Armand Whateley's son. We can go to the hospital and ask if Carlos checked in, and we can question Alistair about Sunday night."

Wulf's face turned ashen. "I don't know, Bookie. Won't there be bricks there?"

"Not necessarily. And if there are, I will vouch for you."

"Vouch for me how?"

Excellent question. "I'll think of something." Invictus took one more look around the apartment. New furniture. Clean. Nothing in need of repairs.

Why would a man with a steady job who lived in a nice apartment in a good part of town resort to robbery?

Why would an accountant purposely make mistakes in a ledger?

To draw attention to them. To force someone, anyone, to look. Just look!

Several numbers in this equation were missing, and Invictus was determined to solve it.

Wulf's freedom depended on it.

Chapter 9

Landscaping

Do you run away immediately, or do you stay and argue?

Captain Reyes's question echoed in Asa's mind like a record on an endless loop, haunting him.

"Bishop?"

"What?" He jolted and locked eyes with Celeste. The policewoman stared at him.

"Did you hear me?"

"No." Asa glanced out the window and watched as Jones disappeared around the corner.

We should follow him. Now would be the perfect opportunity to track down Smith. Stant would never drive into Mull District, not even if somebody gave him ten thousand dollars in cash, but Asa's father taught him how to drive a carriage when he was fourteen. He could leave Stant here, and then he and Celeste could finally arrest Smith and...

Do you stay and argue?

Asa grounded his teeth, banishing the question, but it returned a moment later, begging to be answered.

"Are we going to follow Jones's lead?" Celeste asked. The words seemed to come from a mile away. "Check out the landscaping companies?"

Asa stared at the street corner. Ciceron Station stood a couple blocks away. If Jones were going to Mull, he would catch the train there and take a connecting train to Numerius or maybe University Station. Trains ran on a twenty- or thirty-minute schedule. Asa could get out now, catch up to Jones, board the train without him realizing it, and follow...

A very faint but recognizable whistle blew.

"Yeah." Asa sighed, cursing the timing. "Sure."

Celeste instructed Stant to drive back to the Fifth Precinct. The older officer happily complied. Once there, she requested that two officers watch the Whateley house. She then went to the directory room on the third floor.

The directory in the original building had also been on the third floor, and good thing, too. That floor suffered minimal damage, and other than a little smoke damage, all of the records were saved.

Captain Reyes wanted the new directory to be more spacious, allowing for better accessibility, and for it to have an updated organization system.

But thanks to dozens of other renovations, the task had yet to be complete.

As a result, thousands of papers, books, and ledgers crowded a space little bigger than a clerk's office.

Celeste immediately went to work, combing through shelf after shelf until she found the business directories. Massive tomes printed on hundreds of pages of thin, fragile paper.

"How do you want to divide?" she asked.

"What?" Asa blinked a few times and found himself staring at the wall, once again lost in his racing thoughts.

Dammit, he knew the answer to the captain's question. If you are a thief, you don't stop and argue with someone and then shoot them. You run like hell.

It was the obvious, no, the only answer.

So easy and simple.

Asa wanted to scream.

Instead, he prayed.

God, why are You doing this to me? You know what Beowulf Smith has done. He's a menace who belongs in prison. This case can send him away for life, so why are You making this complicated? Where is the justice in this?

"Hey, I'm talking to you." Celeste waved a hand in his face.

"Divide what?"

"We have to call all the landscaping companies to see which ones work in Old City neighborhoods."

"How many companies are there?"

Celeste combed through the directory. "Fourteen."

Asa rolled his eyes. "Fine. I'll take seven, and you take seven."

Celeste handed him a list of names and numbers, and they walked to the telephones on the first floor. That was one major improvement. Instead of two phones, the Precinct now had four, and they were in their own separate room, allowing them to actually hear the person on the other end.

But that did not make talking on one easier. Asa winced each time he dialed a number. Talking on the phone was so strange. Yes, he could hear the other person's voice, but were they smiling or frowning? Were they standing confidently or clenching their hands to keep them from shaking? A hundred little tells. And all he had to go on was their voice.

In the time it took him to call two companies, Celeste had called five and found the right one. Domhan Landscapers.

They collected Stant, who grumbled about having his lunch break interrupted, and rode to the company, this time in a marked cab. Located midway between the Old City and Secundus Park, it was just a couple blocks away from the Precinct.

"You could've walked here," Stant grumbled as Asa and Celeste climbed out.

Domhan Landscapers operated out of a two-story office building with several storage sheds off to the side. A group of men wearing khaki shirts and trousers sat near an open shed, cleaning and repairing equipment.

"Huh," Asa said.

"What is it?" Celeste asked as she studied the building.

"I think I know that guy." Asa took a step forward. One man, about thirty years old with a skin tone a shade darker than average, was inspecting a length of hose for leaks. "Excuse me."

The man and every single one of his colleagues froze. They eyed Asa and Celeste nervously, as though they stumbled on a nest of snakes. A few whispered. Two guys looked ready to make a run for it.

Asa tensed. How many of these guys had records? Bloody hell, the last thing he needed was for them to bolt and take any pertinent information with them.

"Can we help you, officer?" the man asked with a faint accent. He glanced at Celeste and frowned, confused.

The pieces fell into place. This man worked at the Grady Shipping Company. One of the warehouse workers. Barrish. What was his name?

"Yes, you can," Asa replied. "What is your name, sir?"

The man shifted and stole a quick glance at his colleagues. At least three had disappeared. "Can I ask what this is about?"

"Nobody is in trouble," Celeste addressed the group. "We just wanted to ask your employer a few questions. He is a witness in a pickpocket case. Is he available?"

"Uh, sure. But which employer?" the Barrish man asked.

Teo Julio Arias!

Information flooded Asa's brain. Arias was thirty-one. Immigrated from Barra two years ago. Worked for the Grady Shipping Company until it folded. Clean record. Also acquainted with Jones. Did he also know...?

"Wait, what?" Asa asked, processing Teo Julio's question.

Teo Julio shrugged. "It's kinda weird." He motioned for them to follow him inside. The other employees resumed their work, whispering and wondering when the City Police started hiring women. "See, we just got a new boss. The old one quit a couple days ago."

"How come?" Celeste asked. They walked up a flight of stairs.

"His great-uncle or something died and left him a hundred thousand dollars. Can you believe that? One day, out of the blue, you get a telegram, and suddenly, you're rich! Anyway, he quit, and this new guy took over the company."

"When was this exactly?" Celeste asked.

Asa's mind raced. Was this coincidental, or was this connected to the case? If this Vallejo guy really did play a role in the murder, and if he really worked for this company, could the original owner have been in on it? Did he skip town once the murder was committed, creating a fake story? But why? What did either stand to gain from killing an old man?

And what about Smith?

Smith is guilty. You know he is!

Would you run...?

Shut up, shut up, shut up!

"Monday afternoon," Teo Julio replied. "New boss started yesterday morning." He knocked on the door.

"Who is it?" asked a deep, muffled voice.

"Two police officers wanna speak with you, Mr. Fisher. Something about a witness statement?"

Mr. Fisher told them to enter.

Teo Julio opened the office door, and Asa's heart leapt into his throat.

Behind the desk sat a massive Blydd Fae. Easily seven feet tall, the Blydd had pale skin, silvery gray hair combed back and cut short on the sides in a new style popular with younger businessmen, and silver eyes. Eyes far keener than any human's.

Those eyes fell on Asa and narrowed. His blood turned to ice water.

"Hello, officers," the Blydd said, his voice deep, almost a growl. He stood and proved to be taller than Asa's estimation. His head brushed against the ceiling!

But the Blydd wore a pressed, dark blue suit with a matching tie and waistcoat. The clothes of a respectable businessman and not a wild animal. Asa forced himself to relax. All those stories about Blydd Fae hunting down travelers in the woods and stalking remote villages were just that. Stories. Stories created to frighten humans. They were as safe and civil as every other Fae subspecies.

And they were not alone. A pretty Malkinese woman sat at a small desk off to the side, typing notes. Nothing to fear here.

The Blydd sniffed.

Asa's heart skipped a beat. His father always said that Blydd could smell fear.

"They're wolves in human form," his father had claimed. And seeing this Blydd, Asa was inclined to believe it.

"Good afternoon, sir," said Celeste, not in the least bit fazed. "I'm Officer Lawson, and this is my partner Officer Bishop. We have a few questions, if you don't mind."

"I see. Thank you, Mr. Arias. You may go."

Teo Julio nodded and closed the door. Perhaps it was Asa's imagination, but the Barrish man looked relieved. Though relieved to be away from the Blydd or from the police, Asa could not say.

"Questions about what? Oh, thank you, Maria," The Malkinese woman handed Mr. Fisher a document and quietly returned to her desk. Mr. Fisher removed a pair of glasses from his coat pocket and began reading. "Apologies. I'm new to the company, and I'm still familiarizing myself with all of our clients."

"No problem, sir," Celeste replied.

"You said it was a pickpocket case?"

How the hell did he hear that? Celeste had invented that detail while they were outside!

“Not exactly.” Celeste clasped her hands behind her back, like a student about to give a recitation. “Mr. Fisher, does your company service 386 Hawthorn Street?”

“Let me see.” He ran a finger down the page. The secretary selected a paper out of a folder and handed it to him. “Thank you again, Maria. She’s an absolute godsend,” he said to Asa and Celeste. “I’d be lost without her. Oh, yes. We service them once a week. Fridays. Why...?” Mr. Fisher shook his head, his expression grave. “Of course. I read about Dr. Whateley’s death in the papers. Please forgive me.”

“No worries, sir,” Celeste said. “We think one of your employees might have witnessed some suspicious activity. Perhaps someone casing the house in the days leading up to the murder. We think he is a Shinnok Halfling named Carlos Vallejo.”

Mr. Fisher turned to his secretary.

Maria went to a filing cabinet labeled ‘Employee Records’ and selected a file. She eyed Asa and Celeste warily as she resumed her seat.

Asa frowned. Everyone here was so jumpy. Why? People were supposed to respect the police, not fear them.

“Hmm...” Mr. Fisher frowned and then shook his head. “No, I don’t see anyone by that name.”

“What about Carlos?” Celeste asked.

“There are two, but neither are Halflings. Are you sure that is the right name?”

“As far as we know.” Celeste glanced at Asa.

“It’s very important that we speak with him,” Asa said, taking the hint. “We think he is involved with the case.”

Correction, Jones thought this Vallejo guy was involved. But who was he really? Jones was not one to make things up on the spot. Did Smith give him the name? A false lead to keep the police busy while Smith planned a getaway? Hell, if Smith had half a brain, he would be in Barra or Amistad by now. Then what would become of this case? Another dead end in the police's records. Another one of Asa's failures.

Mr. Fisher grimaced, revealing sharp teeth. "Do you think this person joined the company under an assumed name in order to plan this crime? I've heard rumors about gang leaders placing people in certain roles, but I never believed they were intelligent enough to pull it off."

"We're not sure," Celeste replied.

Though it made sense. A lot more sense than a thief arguing instead of running away. *What were they arguing about?*

Asa frowned. Too bad Molly Gonzalez had not heard them clearly. *How long were they arguing? A minute? Two? But why?*

"Well, I certainly hope you find this man, whatever his real name is," Mr. Fisher said. "Is there anything I can do to help? I never met Dr. Whateley, but to be killed in your own home..." He shuddered.

"Please, give us a call if you find anything. Perhaps he is a former employee," Celeste suggested. She handed Mr. Fisher a business card. The card looked impossibly small in his large hand.

"I will look into it, Officer Lawson." He smiled. "Lawson. What an appropriate name for an officer of the law."

Celeste smiled back.

"Would you run?" Asa muttered under his breath, the question invading his mind again. He knew the answer, knew it as soon as Captain Reyes asked. The answer was no. No, he would not stay and argue when he had a clean getaway. No, he would not shoot an unarmed, old man. And his gut told him that Smith would respond the same way.

But if Smith didn't kill the doctor, who did? Nobody else was in the house. Everyone has an alibi. Was it this Vallejo person? How does he factor in?

Dammit, this was supposed to be an easy case!

"Pardon?" Mr. Fisher asked.

Asa jolted. "Just a random question. Don't worry about it."

"Are you asking if I run for exercise?" Mr. Fisher leaned against the desk, his arms crossed.

Asa was not sure how to respond. For some bizarre reason, people in Barra decided that it was a good idea to run around for fun. They called it some weird word, and the trend had made its way to Malkin.

"Jogging?" Celeste asked. She raised an eyebrow, no doubt wondering if Asa had lost his mind.

Maybe I have.

"Yes, do you like jogging, sir?" Asa asked.

"No, not particularly. But my youngest son loves to run." He smiled, silver eyes gleaming. "Somedays, I can't get him to stand still."

"Good. Great." Asa glanced out the window. The office had a decent view of Secundus Park. The steeple of Our God of Mercy Cathedral rose above the trees. Bright, afternoon sunlight reflected off its brass surface.

Okay, Triumvir, what's going on here? Smith might not be guilty of murder, but he broke into the house. He wanted to steal from the Whateleys, an action that demands judgment for him and justice for the family.

And only You know how many crimes Smith has committed. So, would it still be considered justice if he was charged with this crime?

But what about the real murderer? Is it this Carlos Vallejo person, or someone else?

Can You give me a sign?

Growing up, Asa had heard miraculous stories about people receiving signs and visions from God. Was it too much to ask for a sign for himself?

"Well, I certainly hope you find Dr. Whateley's killer," Mr. Fisher said. "I know I will sleep better once this monster is off the streets."

"Thank you, sir." Celeste shook his hand, and so did Asa. The Blydd's hand completely enveloped his, reminding Asa of meeting various uncles and grandfathers as a small child.

Celeste and Asa exited the office and headed downstairs.

"So, jogging?" she asked with a smirk.

Asa rolled his eyes. "Sorry. I was thinking about something Reyes asked me. Lawson, if you were a thief, would you stick around to argue with the homeowner, or would you run away?"

"I'd run away," she replied without hesitating.

"Yeah." Asa sighed heavily. "I was afraid you'd say that."

Chapter 10

Undercover

Maria Smith waited until the two police officers closed the door before shooting a glare at Rufus.

Rufus returned the glare with an infuriating smirk. "What?"

"Do you have any idea how close that was?"

He shrugged. "I've come closer to getting arrested. I'd rate this encounter as mildly alarming."

Is that supposed to make me feel better? If her son's life was not in danger, Maria would not have gotten involved. When she created her deal with Rufus, she made it clear that she would not take unnecessary risks. But to risk inaction, to watch from a distance and wait for events to play out, was far too great. The police only had one suspect in this case, and they would not pass up the opportunity to put a career thief behind bars.

Or swing him from a rope.

Maria's heart ached.

"But I suppose," Rufus said, studying the policewoman's business card and putting it in his pocket, "this is a good sign. The police are actively looking for Carlos Vallejo. Same as us."

When she returned home for a two-hour break between jobs yesterday afternoon, Maria found Rufus Wells waiting in her apartment. Nothing out of the ordinary. Maria had made a deal with Rufus to help her and her child, and he never broke it. Nor had he abused it.

"What now?" Maria had asked a bit harshly. Fatigue and stress made her head hurt.

"I just need a small favor."

"Define small."

Rufus smiled, his silver eyes flashing even in the dim light. "Have you ever worked as a secretary?"

"A few times."

"Would you care to work as one again?"

When Maria demanded to know why, Rufus explained.

Macsen had told him everything he knew about Carlos Vallejo on Monday, and Rufus wasted no time getting to work. He put in call's to all of his contacts, searching through census records, bank accounts, apartment leases. Nothing turned up. It was as though Carlos Vallejo did not exist.

Instead of giving up or getting frustrated, Rufus found a new avenue. He asked his contacts to find the landscaping company that serviced the Whateley house, and they did not disappoint. Maria did not know who they were or how Ruthless enlisted them. The less she knew, the less risk involved.

Rufus then wrote an official-looking letter to the business owner, explaining that his great-uncle, who lived in a small town a hundred miles up the coast, had passed away and left him a sizable inheritance.

An inheritance that did not exist.

Rufus wanted to conduct this search himself. Therefore, he needed a legitimate reason to enter the building and search the company's records. Once the company went up for sale, Rufus made a successful bid and gained ownership. A clever way to avoid the Seelie Court's laws. Laws that prohibited Fae from entering a building without permission or ownership.

Maria thought the ruse was unnecessary. As a full-blooded human, she could have acted as the original owner's secretary and looked through the files herself. But no. Rufus was adamant about doing this job himself.

His nephew is involved, too, Maria reminded herself. Rufus's reason for being here was the same as her own.

Which led her to a disturbing conclusion.

"Are the Families involved?"

"Possibly."

The very idea made her skin crawl. Lewin Manning had orchestrated a robbery in order to trap her son and all of his gang members. A clever way to get rid of unwanted trouble. Now, all the members of the Twenty-first Street gang were dead. All except for her son.

All because Invictus Jones had paid Wulf's bail.

Did Invictus realize that he was saving her son's life?

No, of course not. He was just a confused man who had read a few too many detective novels and wanted answers.

But his decision also led to Lewin Manning's and Prince Hastyr's arrests. The Five Families and the Royals had suffered because of a simple hunch. The Old Man lost his Right Hand, his last surviving son, as well as his royal liaison. Was this murder some sort of ploy to destroy Invictus and Wulf?

In the light of this possibility, Maria felt compelled to help. She spent twenty-three years keeping her son safe. She refused to fail him now.

Rufus crossed his arms and shook his head. "Should have known Vallejo was using a pseudonym. Are you sure Beowulf didn't say anything else about the job?"

"He never talks to me about them." Wulf started running with the Mull Marauders when he was ten years old, learning how to case buildings and pick locks. But he did not confess the truth to Maria until he was fourteen. He was too ashamed to admit that he stole food and clothing, that the money in his pocket was his cut from a recent job.

Maria had known the entire time. Rufus told her, wanting her to understand that, in a strange way, he was still protecting her son. Life in Mull District was cruel. Those who did not steal starved. A young boy in Wulf's position, and with his Fae heritage, was destined to wind up in a gang. So, why not join a gang with a leader who actually gave a damn about him? Who would actively work to ensure he avoided the law? To make sure certain people continued to believe that he was just a no-good, bastard Halfling?

In a twisted way, the argument made logical sense. But Wulf had grown too stubborn to accept protection. Too independent. And this was the consequence.

"If only Macsen hadn't gotten sick." Rufus glanced at her, silvery eyes flashing, a sign that he was thinking. "A bit early for the flu, don't you think?"

"Maybe. Do you think it's something else?" *Out with it, Rufus. Tell me what you're thinking.* But Rufus had an odd way of giving out information. He forced people to guess, think, provide their own input before giving his own.

"His father was the same way," Lady Constance had once told her. One of a mere handful of times she had mentioned her late son.

"I think it's very inconvenient," Rufus replied. "And Wulf's dyslexia does not affect his hearing."

Maria frowned. According to Macsen, Wulf had confused the addresses. She didn't buy it for a second. "Could you find Vallejo based on his description? Lear can draw. Could Wulf describe him, and Lear draw a portrait?"

Rufus smiled. "Maria, you're a genius. But," he looked at the wall clock. Ten minutes to two. "We must maintain appearances. What time do businesses like this close?"

"Five o'clock." Maria had arrived at nine, two hours after the other employees reported for work. Rufus did not arrived until noon. He provided no explanation other than taking care of work in Mull.

"So, three more hours of playing pretend. Unless you'd like to come down with the flu, too?"

"I'll pass. I'm getting paid, correct?" She sent word to the laundry that she felt too ill to work this afternoon. The job paid by the hour and had no accommodations for sick workers.

"Correct."

Maria never asked where Rufus got the money. A portion came from his grandmother and his father's inheritance. But inheritances only lasted for so long, and Lady Constance, in all likelihood, received only a token stipend from the Blydd noble houses.

Is Rufus's name on the books? She doubted it. His father made several enemies on the Islands, including members of the Royal Family, and Rufus was wanted in Malkin and Barra Provinces. The Royals, despite controlling the Five Families like a quintet of puppets, publicly disapproved of criminal activity. Once a noble broke the law, and got caught, they were disowned, stripped of all their lands and titles, and in Razanur Wells's case, exiled.

Prince Hastyr was the most recent example of Queen Waylinda's wrath.

And good riddance.

Maria recalled the last time she saw Hastyr. She was working as a maid for Emilio Grady. Party guests packed the house. Wealthy business owners, City Council members, Fae nobility, all mingling together in a cacophony. Only Maria had noticed Clayton Tyler sneaking upstairs.

Curiosity got the better of her. She followed Tyler into Grady's study and witnessed him hand a stack of cash to Lewin Manning, his gold eyes like twin suns. Hastyr supervised the exchange. With his keen sense of hearing, the Shinnok Fae heard Maria and pulled a gun.

"Do you want to live?" he asked, purple eyes burning.

Maria nodded, too terrified to speak. Terrified that Hastyr would pull the trigger anyway and make her son an orphan.

"Get out. You breathe a word of this, and I will hunt you down myself."

Behind him, Lewin Manning laughed, a thin, reedy cackle that made her skin crawl. Tyler stared at his shoes, biting his lip so hard it bled.

Two days later, Maria lost her job and was blacklisted from the Gems. But she was alive, and she never had to fear running into the prince again.

"Does this job bother you, Maria?" Rufus asked.

"Yes. Why wouldn't it?" she snapped. She then sighed. "Sorry. I know you're trying to help. I just..."

Rufus placed a gentle hand on her shoulder. Far more gently than she had first thought possible. "He would protect Beowulf if he could. I know I'm a poor substitute, but don't you think he would do the same?"

Tears stung Maria's eyes. She had lost her love so long ago. She hadn't realized that she was pregnant when... She bit down on her tongue. Thinking about Wulf's father, of everything they almost had and then lost, of her own terror as she watched her love being ripped away, the overwhelming sense of hopelessness... She shoved the fear away. She was no longer a helpless, terrified girl. And she was no longer alone.

Rufus was right. Wulf was so much like his father. The same smirk. The same beautiful, mischievous eyes. And the same mind. Beowulf was so much like his father that sometimes it scared her.

"He would not stop until he discovered Carlos Vallejo's real identity and shook the information out of him." Maria smirked, picturing his smiling face. The image faded, replaced by a face covered in blood. "Rufus, if the Families are behind this, we can't go to the police. I know the Fifth Precinct is mostly clean, but look what happened last time. It's a miracle more people weren't hurt."

"Then what do you advise?" Rufus folded his hands behind his back, looking oddly like a teacher.

"Have Wulf or Macsen give Vallejo's description to Lear, and then send your people searching. I doubt Vallejo pulled the trigger, but he is the strongest link we have. We need to find him."

"And if finding Vallejo leads to a Family member?"

Maria chewed on her lip, thinking.

"The police will need to get involved eventually," Rufus said. "Someone must be arrested for Whateley's murder."

"Maybe..." She grimaced. The idea was terrible, but drowning people did not look for options. They clung to the nearest piece of driftwood and hung on until help arrived. "Maybe use Invictus Jones as a go-between. His connections in the Fifth Precinct are good, and I think Captain Reyes trusts him."

Rufus nodded. "I will send Germanicus to Jones, see if we can work something out. In the meantime," he sat at the spacious desk, "might as well figure out how a landscaping company works. Could be useful."

Maria rolled her eyes. "Yeah. Sure." She had a sneaking suspicion that Rufus would retain ownership after the real owner returned, creating a dozen more eyes and ears for his organization. How far did it extend? Did she really want to know?

She glanced out the window and saw a church steeple rising above the trees. She said a silent prayer, hoping that the police found the real murderer before they found her son.

Chapter II
Motives

The ride to the hospital was thankfully uneventful, and the train car was only half full. People carried grocery bags and other supplies. Invictus and Wulf sat near the back. Wulf, dressed in his long, black coat and wide-brimmed hat, seemed more shadow than person. Anybody who walked by would be unable to identify him.

Should I dress similarly? Invictus wondered. He quickly banished the idea. No, he was employed by the Malkin City Police and was assigned to this case by Captain David Reyes himself, despite not technically being an officer. He had no reason to hide or conceal his identity.

In a sense, he had much in common with Aurelia Jayne and Spes Sherrington and half a dozen other fictional detectives. Not police officers by trade but trusted enough to work side by side with them. Investigating crimes. Finding clues.

Except, those detectives never had to worry about their friends going to prison if they failed.

The train came to a screeching halt. Invictus and Wulf disembarked and walked the short distance to the hospital. A massive stone and glass structure painted white and surrounded by curated trees and flowering shrubs.

Invictus's stomach twisted in knots at the same time his ear rang. The last time he visited the hospital, he questioned Tomas Navarro and learned about the Five Families, the true rulers of this city.

What if they are here? Invictus shook his head. *Don't be ridiculous! If the Families wanted to hurt you, they would have done so months ago. Stop being paranoid!* But how could he not feel a little paranoid? He spent weeks running from these people, and then he spent all summer looking over his shoulder, terrified that the Mannings would come for him in the dead of night or ambush him on the train. Or worse, hurt his family.

But nothing happened. No muggings. No break-ins. No knives in the night.

Invictus had testified against Lewin and Grady along with a dozen others. Both men were on Greer Island for life. And not a single witness had been harmed or threatened.

Perhaps working for the police granted Invictus an extra layer of protection.

And the case was so high profiled that the Mannings could not retaliate without the public putting the pieces together. After all, Invictus's name and photo were in all the major newspapers.

Maybe they're waiting until everyone forgets.

"Bookie, you good, man?" Wulf asked.

Invictus blinked. He stood a few feet from the hospital's entrance, frozen like a deer in the crosshairs. How long had he stood here, plagued by his racing thoughts?

"Yeah. My ear was ringing." The ringing, fortunately, subsided.

Wulf frowned. "It still does that?"

"From time to time. But not nearly as bad as before," Invictus assured him.

Wulf nodded grimly. The Halfling had felt terrible when Invictus told him about the ringing ear. The result of Wulf firing a gun right next to his head.

Invictus steadied himself with a deep breath and walked inside. Wulf trailed at his heels. He glanced nervously at everyone who walked by and kept reaching for a gun he no longer wore.

"Breathe."

"What?" Wulf jolted. His eyes faded to pale purple.

"Wulf, take deep breaths."

"What the hell for?"

"Because," Invictus lowered his voice to a whisper, "you're acting like a frightened deer. You need to calm down." *Has he ever been to the hospital?* Invictus doubted it.

Wulf took a few rapid breaths. "Ain't workin'. Bookie, what if someone recognizes me?" His photo was in the papers, too. Probably how Carlos Vallejo discovered him. But it begged the question. Why contact Wulf through Macsen instead of going directly to Wulf?

"They won't," Invictus assured him.

"Like hell," Wulf muttered. He walked right behind Invictus, stepping on his heels.

Invictus went to the information desk. The nurse on duty was organizing patient files. Dark circles lined her tired eyes.

"Excuse me, do you know which room Carlos Vallejo is in?"

The nurse checked the records. "I don't see anyone by that name. What did he come in for?"

"Food poisoning. He was sick over the weekend, so he might have checked out already."

The nurse looked through several more files. She shook her head. "I'm sorry. No one named Vallejo was admitted within the last week."

Invictus got a sinking feeling in his gut. If Carlos wasn't at his apartment or the hospital, where was he? Did he skip town? If they couldn't find him...

"Different name?" Wulf whispered, hiding behind Invictus.

"Did he ever tell you a different name?"

"No." Wulf cursed under his breath.

"Is everything okay?" the nurse asked. She stood and tried to look at Wulf. Wulf pulled his hat over his face.

"Yes, ma'am." Invictus positioned himself between the nurse and Wulf. Merciful heavens, the nurse recognizing Wulf as a murder suspect was the last thing they needed. "My friend gets very nervous around doctors. Thank you." Lightning flashed in his mind. Mercy sakes alive, he almost forgot the second reason they came here. "One more question, if you don't mind. Do you know if Dr. Alistair Whateley is working today?"

The nurse frowned. "Why do you ask?"

"We're friends of the family. I went to the University with his brother Alfred." A bit of a stretch. Alfred was about five years older than Invictus. He hoped the nurse wouldn't notice.

The nurse nodded solemnly, which made her look even more tired. "Then, you know..."

Invictus sighed. "Yeah, it's... Well, when Alfred told me..."

"Of course. I can't imagine finding your own..." She shivered and lowered her voice. "You know, the hospital board told Dr. Whateley that he could take time off, but he refused. Said it was better for him to keep his mind busy. Help people. You know?"

"Yes, I understand."

"Dr. Whateley is working today. Post-op ward. Do you think you could talk to him? Convince him to take a day or two off? Honestly, he looks terrible, and we..." Another nurse walked past the desk, escorting a patient with a plaster case over his wrist. The desk nurse put on a smile and waited until they were out of earshot. "We're worried about him."

"I'll do my best."

Invictus thanked her and found a hospital map. The post-op ward was on the second floor. Alistair Whateley, however, was not there.

"Maybe the guy decided to go home early," Wulf suggested as he nervously stared at the doctors and patients. Most of the patients were asleep, and all of them had blood or saline drips attached to their arms. Wulf stared at the transfusions in mute horror.

"Possibly. Or... Excuse me." Invictus flagged down a doctor, a young man with slightly pointed ears and brown eyes with blue specks. "Do you know where Dr. Whateley is?"

"Who?"

"Dr. Alistair Whateley. We can't find him anywhere, and we need to speak with him."

The young doctor shrugged. "I've no idea. Sorry."

"You work here, don't ya?" Wulf snapped, his eyes flashing.

The doctor scowled. "Yes, but I'm new, and I don't know everyone by name."

"Could he be in an office or private room?" Invictus asked, placing himself between Wulf and the doctor. *I thought you were worried about being recognized.*

"I guess. Why do you need to know?"

"We're friends of the family." Invictus lowered his voice. "His brother sent us to find him. Please, it's very important."

"Look, I..." The doctor's face turned ashen. "Whateley. Hey, is he related to that man who was killed?"

"Yes. His father."

The doctor peered down the empty hallway. "Doctors sometimes have private officers on the third floor. Visitors aren't allowed in that wing, but..." He chewed on his lip. "I guess they'll make an exception. Given the circumstances."

"Thank you."

A bell rang. The doctor hurried into a patient's room.

"Bookie, how did you learn to talk like that?" Wulf asked as they walked up a flight of stairs.

"I just think of what people will most likely respond to."

"Huh?" Wulf titled his head to the side, looking foxlike.

"Remember when we met in the interrogation room? I asked different questions, seeing which ones you responded best to."

"Really?"

Invictus nodded. "Most people are willing to help another person."

"So when you mentioned being sent by Alistair's brother, the doctor wanted to help."

"Exactly."

Wulf halted. "Hold up." His eyes narrowed. "Books. You got all of this stuff from books, didn't ya?"

"Yes," Invictus said a little too harshly. Wulf had stopped making fun of him for liking detective novels once he started learning to read, but Invictus could not help feeling a little defensive.

"Don't get me wrong, Bookie. I understand why you like reading now, but don't you think it's kinda dumb? I mean, folks write the books, right?"

"Correct."

"And they write them certain ways. The good guys always win, and the bad guys always go to prison."

"For the most part." Invictus recalled a handful of books where that was not the case. Those tended to be less popular.

"Meaning they control the way folks answer questions. Them fake bricks learn everything they need to learn because the writer wants them to learn it."

"That's the way it works." They exited the stairwell and turned a corner. Rows of office doors with names displayed on frosted glass windows lined the hallway.

Alans, Civilis, Connors...

"Yeah, except you ain't Spes Sherrington, fake brick. You're Invictus Jones, numberer. What makes you think the guys will give you the right answers? Help you learn what you need to learn?"

Invictus sighed. Wulf had a point. "I just have to follow my string."

"Your what?"

Great, now Invictus felt silly. "My invisible string. It's like a force that tugs on my mind, leading me where I need to go."

"And you followed this string the first time?"

"Yes. It led me to question you, in fact."

Wulf locked eyes with him. "Bookie, please tell me you realize how stupid that sounds."

Invictus rolled his eyes. He started to argue but stopped. A familiar voice echoed down the hall. He motioned for Wulf to be quiet.

He peered around the corner and saw Dr. Samuel Rosario, one of the tenants in his boardinghouse, speaking with a tall, blond man. The man was in his early forties and wore a white doctor's coat. Dr. Rosario wore a similar coat, except the breast pocket had the crest of the Malkin City University stitched on it. An open book in front of a rising yellow sun.

"I can't thank you enough, sir," Dr. Rosario said, his dark brown eyes shining. "For a while, I thought I wouldn't get it, and with your father's passing... Well..."

"You can thank the board as much as myself," said Alistair Whateley in a faint Scanlannish accent. "They're the ones who made the final decision."

"Wait, they're Scannies?" Wulf whispered.

Invictus signaled for him to hush.

"But you helped. You and your father, Triumvir rest his soul." Dr. Rosario jolted as though he had touched static electricity. "Oh, are you Triumvirans? I never..."

Alistair Whateley smiled, faint crows' feet forming around his eyes. "My mother worshipped the old gods, but my father was never particularly devout about anything except his work. My brother and I are Triumvirans, though. We try to attend holiday services."

"You never said they were Scannies," Wulf whispered in Invictus's ear.

"Shut up!"

Dr. Rosario relaxed. "I see. Well, I hope Armand is at peace. And thank you." He and Alistair shook hands, and Dr. Rosario left.

"The hell was that about?" Wulf whispered.

"Good question." Dr. Rosario worked as a chemist for the University, teaching the occasional undergraduate class. Perhaps it was related to his research.

Alistair wrote a few notes on a notepad, muttering and frowning. He then let out a heavy sigh.

"Excuse me?" Invictus asked as he walked up to Alistair. *Is this a good idea?* He wanted to speak with Alistair, but Alistair was not home during the murder. What insight could he provide? *Only one way to find out.*

Alistair gave him a confused look. "Can I help you, sir?"

"You're Dr. Alistair Whateley, correct?"

"Yeah."

"My name is Jones. I'm with the Fifth Precinct—"

"I already spoke to you people," Alistair snapped. "Twice!"

"I am aware, sir, but—"

"Did you find Smith?"

Invictus paused. Did he hear Alistair correctly? "Pardon?"

"The thief who murdered my father. Did you find him?"

Invictus stole a quick glance over his shoulder. Wulf, thank God, was nowhere in sight. "Actually, we no longer believe that Beowulf Smith is the murderer. New evidence has come to light and..."

Alistair glared at him, his eyes like blue fire. "What?! Mrs. Palacio saw Smith running out of my father's study immediately after the gunshot. How could he not be the murderer?"

Invictus struggled to speak, to find the right words. "Because he was working with at least two other men. One of them cannot be found. We think—"

"What other men?"

Invictus searched for a believable explanation. "A neighbor said that he saw three men running away from your house on Sunday night. He positively identified two of them, but we haven't been able to identify the third. We believe he is the one who orchestrated the robbery."

"Really?" Alistair crossed his arms and stepped closer to Invictus, looming over him. "And how do you know this?"

"We have one of the thieves in custody. He told us everything," he stammered.

"But not Smith."

"No, sir."

Alistair studied Invictus for a long, silent minute. "Okay, so you have a guy, but not the bastard who killed my father. Is that right? You came all the way here just to say that?" His voice rose to a shout.

"Yes, sir." Invictus's palms began to sweat. *Bloody hell, Invictus, what were you thinking? That Alistair would be as amenable as his brother? That he would be happy to hear that we have no new information? No evidence pointing to the real murderer? You stupid idiot!* "I'm sorry, but cases of this nature take time, and—"

"Yeah, the other policeman already gave us that excuse." Alistair's eyes narrowed. "Your name is Jones?"

"Yes." Knots twisted his gut.

"Invictus Jones?"

The knots turned into ice, freezing him in place.

Alistair smirked. "I thought you looked familiar. The accountant turned policeman. One hell of a career change."

"Yes, it's..." He swallowed. "It's been an adjustment."

"I'll say. You took down a crime ring. You and Beowulf Smith."

Invictus felt dizzy, lightheaded. Merciful heavens, this conversation had gone from bad to worse in a heartbeat.

Alistair leaned closer until their faces were almost touching and asked, "Do you really have another thief in custody, or are you just protecting your friend?"

Invictus forced his fear into the back of his mind. "Yes to both."

"All because a neighbor saw three men running away from my house on Sunday night?"

"Yes, sir."

"Which neighbor?"

"They wish to remain anonymous."

"Bullshit!" Alistair grabbed Invictus's jacket collar. "I know all about you, Jones. You ain't a brick. You're just a number cruncher who got lucky. And I swear by Triumvir and all the gods of this land, if I see your face again, I will sue the Malkin City Police and tear Mull District apart until I find that Halfling. Do you understand?"

"Yes," Invictus trembled. He forced himself to speak. "Yes, Dr. Whateley. I understand."

Alistair released him and stormed away. "Stay the hell away from my family!" He walked into an office and slammed the door shut. Invictus's ear rang.

He leaned against the wall, his heart pounding and blood rushing painfully in his ears.

What the hell were you thinking? Your names were in the papers! Did you really think that Alistair wouldn't recognize your name? That he would forget that you and Wulf know each other? How could you be so foolish?

A hand grabbed Invictus's shoulder, and he screamed. He saw Wulf and suppressed the urge to yell at him.

"You good?"

"No."

"Want me to rough him up?"

"Absolutely not." Alistair stood a head taller than Wulf and outweighed him by about fifty pounds. The skinny Halfling wouldn't stand a chance. "He's mad enough to kill you."

Wulf titled his head to the side, looking more foxlike. "Mad enough to kill, huh? Bookie..." A pair of doctors rounded the corner, discussing a patient's history. Wulf motioned for Invictus to follow him into the stairwell. Once inside, Wulf continued, "Bookie, do you think one of Dr. Whateley's sons could've done him in?"

"Doubtful. The police already checked that theory, but neither son has a motive, and they both have solid alibis."

"Oh." They reached the ground floor. "I was just thinking. This Alistair guy's got a temper, and I heard arguing before the gunshot."

Invictus shook his head. "It's a good theory, Wulf, but Alistair was working the evening shift on Sunday. Hospital records confirm it along with twenty other doctors and nurses," he added before Wulf could rebuttal.

"Fine. So, now what?"

"I want to talk with Dr. Rosario." They exited the hospital, and a cool breeze greeted them. A much-needed relief from the humidity. And the sky was a perfect, cloudless blue.

"Who?"

"The man Alistair was speaking to. We live in the same boardinghouse. Are you okay with visiting the University?"

"Sure. Better than sitting 'round all day. And maybe Rosario will back me up." Wulf smiled, revealing pointy teeth.

"Alistair Whateley was not home Sunday night," he said adamantly.

"But his brother was. Bet they was in on it together."

"Okay. What was their motive?"

"Money. The old guy was loaded, right?"

"Yes, but so are Alistair and Alfred." As a doctor, Alistair earned enough money to buy a house in the Gems if he wished, and Alfred earned both a yearly salary and commission at the art dealership.

"Then they wanted more money."

Invictus rolled his eyes. He then stopped in his tracks. "Wulf, you didn't know their ethnicity."

"Their what?"

"You didn't know the Whateleys were Scanlannish," he amended.

"Course not. Thought I was breaking into a different guy's house."

"Oh, right." Another reason why they needed to find Carlos Vallejo. The odds of Wulf breaking into a house at the same time a murder occurred were too small, almost impossible. Unless someone wanted him to be there in order to take the fall for Armand Whateley's murder.

But why Wulf? Why chose him out of the hundreds of thieves in Malkin City?

And why would anyone want to kill a doctor?

He hoped Dr. Rosario could lead them to an answer.

Chapter 12
Metals

"Still, you have to admit it's possible," Wulf said as he and Invictus walked through the University's campus. Plant life enveloped the area, turning it into a massive garden with the brick and wood structures barely visible underneath. Towering oaks with twisting branches covered in bright green ferns and gray moss guarded walkways. A pair of willows shaded the entrance to a dorm. Bits of grass and flowering weeds grew in the cracks of the brick pathway they walked on.

And there were hundreds of students. The bells had rung a few minutes ago, giving the students ten minutes to arrive at their next class. Invictus and Wulf quickly moved to the side as a group of students hurried by. Some talked excitedly with friends while others read books or notes.

"They seem to be enjoying themselves," Invictus commented. He then saw a notice on a bulletin board stating that classes were canceled on Thursday and Friday due to the oncoming hurricane.

Right. The hurricane. Every person in Malkin City, it seemed, was talking about the storm. All of the tenants in his boardinghouse appeared worried and discussed buying extra food and water and boarding up the windows on the first floor. Even Mrs. Ramirez, the landlady, looked concerned and asked everyone to be home early on Thursday evening. Not told, asked.

Invictus could not help but raise an eyebrow. Honestly, it just sounded like a large thunderstorm. What were they getting so worked up over?

There was one thunderstorm back in August that caused major flooding along the docks, but nobody paid it much heed.

"And it's kinda weird," Wulf continued as they turned onto a broad walkway paved with gray river stones. The Math and Sciences Center stood at the end, facing a fountain surrounded by poplars. "Most Scannies is as poor as me and Ma. How'd they get so rich?"

"Because doctors earn a lot of money. And stop calling them Scannies," Invictus said, dropping his voice to a whisper as a trio of fair-skinned students passed them. They could have been Scanlannish, but the dark hair and eyes indicated that they were more likely Kallendonic or Saludan. Still, best not to say a word that would start a fistfight.

"Why?" Wulf asked.

Invictus almost yelled at him, but then realized that Wulf was serious. The man honestly did not know. "Wulf, let me put it this way. How do you feel when Germanicus calls you Fox-face?"

"I wanna break every damn bone in this stupid face." He sneered, purple eyes flashing.

"Well, that's how Scanlannish people feel when others call them Scannies."

Wulf's eyes widened, shocked. "Wait, really?"

Invictus nodded.

"Oh hell. I've been calling them Scannies my whole life. I mean, everyone up in Mull does. I just..." He locked eyes with Invictus. "You mean, I've been insulting them this whole time?"

"Yes."

"Damn. I've got a lot of folks to apologize to."

"Save it for later. Are you sure you're up to talking with Dr. Rosario? He's a very nice man, but he is bound to recognize you."

Wulf thought it over. "Yeah, I guess. 'Sides, I'll be with you, and you'll vouch for me."

They walked into the building, and it proved to be far larger than Invictus imagined. Easily twice as long as it was wide, the Math and Sciences Center contained four stories, each one with scores of classrooms, student labs, and offices. The first floor alone boasted twenty classrooms and labs, according to the directory.

"Okay. Where is Rosario?" Wulf asked, looking around. Bright, electric lights hung overhead, arranged in the shape of molecules. He squeezed his eyes shut. "Bloody lights. Why's it so bright in here?"

"Because people need to see." *It's no brighter in here than at the Fifth Precinct.* Were Fae more sensitive to artificial lights? Invictus supposed it made sense. Shinnoks had keener eyesight than humans. He scanned the list of names on the directory. Dr. Rosario was not listed.

"Maybe he's in a different building," Wulf said.

"No, he ought to be here." Dr. Rosario's chemistry lab was funded by the University, so it made sense if it was on campus. But Dr. Rosario never said *where* on campus.

Invictus flagged down a student, a young Malkinese woman with her hair in a long braid. "Do you know if Dr. Samuel Rosario works here?"

"No." She hurried along.

Wulf smirked. "Okay. My turn."

"What are you...?"

Wulf hurried over to a small study area. Several benches, chairs, and desks filled the space as well as typewriters that students could rent by the hour. He grabbed a chor battery powered lamp and walked back to Invictus, looking around. "They got folks in charge here?"

"There's an information desk," Invictus said, pointing. "I don't know what you mean. Why do you have...?"

The Halfling smirked and walked over to the desk with the word 'Information' painted in gold letters overhead. A man in his early twenties sat there, reading a paperback book.

"Hey, I got this delivery for Dr. Rosario. You know where he is?"

The desk clerk, who looked terribly confused, asked, "What delivery?"

"This thing." He held up the lamp, hiding his face.

"Shouldn't it be in a box?"

"Hell if I know. Look, man, I just deliver the stuff, not package it. So, is Rosario here or not?"

"He works here. In a lab in the basement. You can leave the lamp here, and I will..."

"Thanks." Wulf, still hiding his face with the lamp, hurried towards the stairs. Invictus followed, just as confused as the poor clerk.

"What on earth was that?" he asked once they were inside the stairwell. The lamp glowed a warm yellow-orange color, providing additional light.

Derived from ichora flowers, chor nectar was used to power any number of mechanical devices. Some, like the lamp bulb, provided light, and others powered anything from radios to iceboxes to motorcars. The nectar was terribly expensive, so most people still relied on oil or gas for lighting where electricity was not available. Invictus had no idea how chor nectar worked, only that it did.

"I was just doin' what you did. Pretending to be someone else to get answers. Worked real good, huh?"

"I guess." Well, Wulf's plan confirmed where Dr. Rosario worked, but what if the chemist was not here? What if he did not have the answers Invictus needed?

The invisible string tugged at his mind, leading him downward.

The basement contained a long hallway that branched off at multiple points, creating a maze of laboratories. Invictus peered into the first one. Four scientists in stark white coats studied a group of white mice. Two took the mice's measurements and weights while the third wrote everything down. The fourth then injected them with... Something. Invictus shivered. He could still feel the cold metal from the handful of times he received inoculations.

He walked to the next lab. One scientist poured liquid into a breaker, causing the contents to change color while another scientist took notes.

Did Dr. Rosario have a lab partner? Invictus tried to recall everything the chemist said about his work, but Rosario got easily sidetracked. One moment, he was discussing the corrosive effects of acids, and then someone would mention a random word or he would glance at the newspaper. The subject would veer sharply, and Rosario would speak at length about track and field statistics or how the weather impacted train schedules. And all attempts to get Rosario's mind back on track were next to impossible.

He finally found Rosario in the lab at the end of the hallway. A dozen breaks lined the bench. Dr. Rosario jotted down notes as he moved from one to another. Invictus knocked.

Dr. Rosario glanced up, confused, and then locked eyes with Invictus. He smiled brightly and opened the door.

"Invictus, what a surprise! What brings you here? Did Mrs. Ramirez send you on an errand?"

It took Invictus a moment to realize that Rosario was referring to hurricane preparations. Mrs. Ramirez had singled out everyone as they left this morning, giving them a list of supplies to buy. Rosario managed to slip out while she gave Invictus his list for extra lamp oil and various spices. She adamantly instructed him to only buy oil from the store on Ellison Avenue, stating that everywhere else sold inferior products. The note was still in his jacket pocket.

"No, my friend and I," Invictus grabbed Wulf by the arm and dragged him into the lab, "are working on a case, and we thought you might be able to help."

Dr. Rosario's eyes brightened. "Yes, of course!" He jotted down a few notes, placed the notebook on the counter, and lowered the temperature on the beakers. "How can I help?"

"Where do you want this?" Wulf held up the lamp.

Dr. Rosario arched an eyebrow. "Um, I didn't order a lamp."

"Yeah, I know. Should I just put it here?" Wulf pointed to a corner with his foot.

"Sure." The chemist shrugged.

Wulf tossed the lamp into the corner. The bulb shattered, and the porcelain base cracked in three places. Bright yellow chor liquid oozed onto the floor. "Oops."

Wulf, I am going to maim you.

Invictus took a deep breath, regained his composure, and said, "Sorry to intrude, and sorry about him."

"It's not trouble. Is he a policeman?" Dr. Rosario whispered.

"He's more of a consultant." It was the nicest word Invictus could think of.

"Good." Relief washed over his face. "Now," he said, returning to a normal volume, "how can I help you?"

"How well did you know Dr. Whateley?"

"Which one?"

"Well, both I guess. Have you known Alistair Whateley for long?"

"Yes, I've known him for years. The City Hospital finances half of my research while the University finances the other half. Alistair has always championed medical research, and he helped me and my colleagues secure funding."

"What y'all researching now?" Wulf asked, studying the beakers.

Dr. Rosario smiled like a child at Festival. "Base metals."

"Huh?"

"Gold, silver, copper, lead, tin, iron, and mercury." Dr. Rosario walked over to the beakers. Bits of sediment rested at the bottoms. "We are studying the properties of each, seeing if they have any medical applications. Mercury, for example." He selected a small glass vial with numbers written on the side and filled with a reddish liquid. "Mercury can be used to measure one's temperature."

"But thermometers have been around for years," Invictus said.

"True, but how accurate are they? Alistair Whateley noted that he used five different thermometers in the course of a week, and all five were different! The numbers were written too close or too far apart, or the mercury was no longer viable. When he learned about this project, he asked for a better thermometer."

"That sounds... Very useful." Invictus pictured Alistair Whateley. The man had been furious and threatened both Invictus and Wulf, but he was mourning his father. He had every right to be upset. And despite his grief, he was at work caring for his patients. Perhaps working to prevent someone else's grief.

"What about gold?" Wulf asked. A devious smile crossed his face.

"Gold is an excellent electrical conductor."

"Okay." Wulf's face fell a bit. "What does that have to do with medicine?"

"I don't know," Dr. Rosario replied cheerfully. "But electricity is becoming more commonplace, and gold and copper are excellent electrical conductors," he reached for a vial, "as well as silver!"

"No!" Wulf leapt up and hid behind Invictus, shivering.

"Did I... Oh my God! You're a Halfling." Dr. Rosario placed the small sample of silver on the bench. "Please, I meant no harm. Truly!"

"No worries, Dr. Rosario," Invictus assured him. "Your research sounds fascinating. Perhaps you can explain it more this evening."

"Yes, I'd be glad to." But Invictus got the impression that the subject would slip Rosario's mind, or another topic would sidetrack him mid-conversation.

"I take it that Alistair Whateley has a good reputation?" Invictus asked, steering them back to the original question.

"Oh, yes. He's a wonderful doctor. Quite talented, and he takes good care of his patients."

"What area of medicine does he specialize in?"

"Surgery and post operation care."

"I see. And his father?"

Dr. Rosario paled.

"What was Armand Whateley like? Wulf, get off me." Invictus shrugged Wulf off his shoulders. The Halfling let go but kept a healthy distance from the silver.

He knows I still have a silver pocket watch, right?

"Armand Whateley." Dr. Rosario shivered. "I, um, only met him a few times. Tragic what happened. That's what you're investigating, right? His death?"

Invictus nodded.

"Yes, tragic." Dr. Rosario returned to his beakers, adjusting the temperatures. He jotted down some notes. A long list of numbers with times and temperatures. Invictus tried to find a pattern, but Dr. Rosario's notes were halfway illegible. Dr. Rosario muttered under his breath and adjusted the temperatures again, bringing some beakers to a boil.

"Was Armand Whateley also involved in research?" Invictus asked. According to the case file, Dr. Whateley devoted the last decade of his life to medical research. Did the research play a role in his death? If so, why?

The chemist selected a vial with a few flakes of iron and placed it on a balance.

Invictus sighed. Dr. Rosario's mind had wandered again.

"Hey, we're talking to you!" Wulf snapped.

Dr. Rosario jolted. "Right. Of course, yes. Sorry. My work is time sensitive."

"We understand," Invictus said, shooting a glare at Wulf. "Did you ever work with Armand Whateley?"

"No, not really. He was a brilliant doctor. Excelled at research and diagnosing illnesses. Terrible bedside manner," he added quickly.

"So, he was a jerk?" Wulf asked.

Dr. Rosario laughed bitterly. "That's certainly a way to describe him. But I'd say he was more aloof. Often kept to himself and only had a few friends. Most of his relatives were still in Scanlan, but they didn't talk. Disagreements over the war. Very sad." Dr. Rosario shook his head. "Do the police have any leads?"

"Not yet." Invictus stepped closer to the bench and studied the beakers. He could not make heads or tails of the chemist's work. He glanced at the notes, but Rosario's handwriting was a mess.

Is this how Wulf feels when I try to explain accounting to him? No wonder the Halfling looked lost half the time.

Dr. Rosario turned back to his work.

Invictus locked eyes with Wulf and gestured towards the door. As he placed his hand on the knob, Dr. Rosario spoke.

"They say it was a thief." He continued to take measurements. "But I doubt it."

"Why?" Invictus's palms began to sweat. He had one hunch, one terrible hunch, but he hoped it was not true.

"Well, Armand, he..." Rosario opened and closed his mouth, trying to speak. "Never mind."

"Dr. Rosario, please. Every bit of information counts in a case like this. Please..." *Please save my friend,* he almost said.

"I understand, Invictus." He met Invictus's eyes, pleading. "And please understand that my research is very important, despite the University Board's views. If the hospital pulls their funding..." His eyes shimmered, on the verge of tears. "Please, Invictus."

"Dr. Rosario, is someone threatening you?" The invisible string tugged on his mind again.

The chemist glanced over at Wulf who was inspecting the broken lamp, trying to put the pieces back together. "Do you trust him?"

"With my life." Did Rosario recognize Wulf? He almost asked, but a small voice in the back of his mind told him to be quiet, listen.

"Good. It's important to trust people. I wish... I wish Armand had been more trusting. Trusted better people. Do you have the time?"

Invictus checked his watch. "Just past three."

"I have a meeting at three thirty. I need to finish this experiment before then." Dr. Rosario locked eyes with him, pleading.

"Dr. Rosario, I can help you."

"No." He shook his head vehemently. "No, I'm just tired. My research and the board... It's a headache. No, I fear the only way you can help me is with a check for five hundred dollars, but," he tried to smile, "I won't bother you with my problems. Just know that Alistair is a good man, and his father was a trouble man. But not a bad one."

"I understand. Thank you."

Dr. Rosario returned to his experiment. As he adjusted temperatures and wrote down notes, the tension seemed to ebb away. The air around him felt calmer, more focused.

Invictus grabbed Wulf by the elbow, hauled him to his feet, and exited the laboratory.

"Where are we going now?" Wulf asked.

"To the library. Dr. Rosario wanted to tell me something about Dr. Whateley, but he's too afraid. I have a hunch that some powerful people are involved."

Wulf paled. "The Families?" he whispered.

Invictus nodded as his stomach twisted in knots.

"Damn. I thought we were done with those bastards."

"So did I."

Chapter 13
Informant

Wulf did his best to help. He really did. When Bookie asked the librarian for newspaper articles about Dr. Armand Whateley and for any research papers he wrote, Wulf stood quietly by his side, not saying a word. But the librarian, a stuffy Malkinese woman with her gray hair in a tight bun, acted like Wulf would jump her and steal her wallet if she took her eyes off him for a second. And he was just standing there!

Could have been worse, he guessed. She could have told him to get lost or threatened to call the bricks.

Once he had the papers, Bookie found an empty table on the third floor and started reading. Wulf sat across from him, sitting backwards in the chair with his arms crossed over the top, and looked around. A lot of students were nearby. Reading, writing, studying, and other studenty things. Things Wulf never considered until recently.

What would it have been like to learn how to read as a kid? What if he had stayed in school? He guessed he could have worked for Ruthless on nights and weekends. Kids only had to stay in school a couple hours a day. But how long would he have stayed? Long enough to learn reading and writing, or long enough to graduate high school? Long enough to consider going to University? But what would he have studied? He doubted professors taught classes on how to be a better thief.

Three students, two girls and one boy, sat at a nearby table. They smiled relieved smiles as they finished up a project. Some big paper with photos glued on it and words written underneath. One girl, a pretty

Bannock Halfling with blue-green eyes, suggested going to a nearby restaurant for fizzies to celebrate. The boy and the other girl happily agreed. They gathered up the project and left, chatting and smiling.

Could Dav and I have done that? he wondered, watching the students leave. Dav had been real good at school. Well, not when it came to reading, but he was great at math and numbers and remembering names and dates. He probably would have stayed if he didn't need to steal food in order to eat. And Wulf...

No, these kinds of things, going to classes and studying in quiet libraries, were not for him.

Wulf pulled the small book out of his pocket. *On the Types of Fae.* Ruthless owned several copies, and when he found out that Wulf was learning to read, he gave one copy to Wulf.

"Might as well learn about yourself in the process," he had said.

Wulf skipped ahead to the chapter on Shinnoks, but he only understood a few small words. He glanced at one of the newspapers. Some words were jumbled up messes, but he recognized a few.

"Can I help?"

Bookie looked up.

"With reading, I mean. Can I help?"

"Um, sure." Bookie selected a newspaper article and handed it to Wulf.

See, even Bookie doesn't think you can help.

Shut up! Wulf snarled at himself.

He started with the headline. Big, bold words. Easy to read. Except, half the words were complete nonsense. All he could figure out was: Dr. Word Word and word words new word words.

Wulf grounded his teeth. Dammit! Why the hell was he so stupid?

"Are you okay?" Bookie asked.

"No! What does..." He snarled. "What does it say?"

"Dr. Armand Whateley and colleagues announce new surgical techniques."

How the hell...? Wulf shook his head. "What does it mean, though?"

"The article states that Dr. Whateley worked more with research than with patients. This was written twelve years ago, so the technique is widespread now."

"So, not the reason he was murdered?"

"Not unless the murderer has a problem with reducing the risk of bacterial infections." Bookie sighed and rubbed the bridge of his nose.

"Anything connecting him to the Families?" Wulf whispered. All the students seemed focused on their work, but Ruthless had eyes and ears everywhere. No doubt the Families did likewise.

"Nothing obvious. Every article has only good things to say about the doctor, but they also said good things about Emilio Grady. They're only part of the equation."

"Grady's still on Greer, right?" A shiver ran down his spine. For half a second, he was back in the old man's house, the banishment creeping into him like vines climbing up a tree, making it difficult to think and breathe.

"Yes."

"And his granddaughter?"

Bookie's face fell. "She... Europa is innocent. She didn't know anything about Grady's scheme. Last I heard, she moved to a small town farther upriver." He sighed again.

"Good." The last thing they needed was for those folks to start interfering again. And Wulf wasn't too keen about Europa being innocent. Ma knew Wulf was stealing long before he admitted it. Europa likely knew the truth but got away free thanks to her great-grandmother, Queen Waylinda.

"Yes, good." Bookie selected one of the research articles and started reading.

Wulf opened his book to the chapter on Shinnoks and got an idea. He and Carlos were both Shinnok Halflings. Could the book tell him more details about his kind? Maybe give him an idea about Shinnoks' way of thinking and where Carlos might be hiding out?

He paced his fingers on the page, isolating each word, and forced himself to look at each letter and think about the sounds. Putting the sounds together, he slowly began to read.

On the Shinnok, the chapter title read. *Most something to foxes, the Shinnok tend to be tall and thin with something, something words. The something have red hair and purple eyes, making them something. Large word and another large word that the word humans who first something Shinnoks...*

Wulf's head hurt. He tossed the book onto the table and rubbed his eyes.

"Do you want a break?" Bookie asked.

Wulf sneered. "No, I don't want a bloody break. Can't take a break if I ain't done nothing. Bookie, maybe we're making this harder than it really is. So the doctor researched a bunch of crap, and he creeped out your friend. Don't mean he was working for the Families. If you ask me, the guy's sons bumped him off for the money."

Bookie shook his head. "Alistair and Alfred both have reliable sources of income."

"So did Grady. Didn't stop him from stealing. Why would it stop them?"

"Excellent question." Bookie frowned. He looked off to the side, thinking.

The hairs on the back of Wulf's neck stood on end, making the iron burn scar itch. He glanced over his shoulder and saw a woman wearing a dark green shirt and skirt standing next to him, staring.

Wulf leapt to his feet, knocking the chair over. The woman smiled, hazel eyes shining. She looked Amistadian, except her skin was lighter and her curly hair was midway between brown and blonde. She kept staring at Wulf, studying him.

"Celeste? What are you doing here?" Bookie asked. He rounded the table and stood next to Wulf.

"Checking on your progress. I see you've found Beowulf Smith. Captain Reyes will be pleased."

Wulf's blood turned to ice water. Those dark green clothes, so dark it was almost black. They were the same shade of green as brick uniforms. And Captain Reyes... He was in charge of the Fifth Precinct! Wulf looked at Bookie. He... He didn't look surprised to see her.

Not surprised to see a brick.

Wulf took a step back, his heart pounding and blood racing. She said... The brick said that Reyes will be pleased that Bookie found Wulf. Why would...?

"No." Wulf shook his head. "Bookie, please, tell me you didn't..." It couldn't be true. Bookie was his friend. Sure, he worked with the bricks, but... No, Bookie would not betray him.

Would he?

"It isn't like that, Wulf," Bookie said quickly. Too quickly? "Captain Reyes believes you are innocent. He wants to talk to you about the case, but he knows you feel uncomfortable at the Precinct."

"What'd you tell him?" Wulf's eyes darted. The main exit was just behind and to his left. To his right were bookshelves. He could fake left and head right, running around the shelves until he created some distance between himself and the brick, and then head left.

But how many bricks were waiting downstairs?

"Only what you told me," Bookie said. He placed a hand on Wulf's shoulder. Wulf flinched. "Reyes knows that you are innocent," he repeated. "And the police are looking for Carlos Vallejo."

"But we can't find Vallejo without more information," Celeste said. "Please, sit, Mr. Smith. I want to ask you a few questions, and then I will be on my way."

Wulf stared at Celeste. Was she telling the truth? Nothing about her showed that she was lying, and she didn't have a gun or handcuffs. But she was a brick! Everyone in Mull knew to run the second they saw dark green. And Bookie... Bookie was his friend. He wouldn't lie to him. Right?

"It's okay, Wulf," Bookie said. He and Celeste sat at the table. Celeste took the seat between them and glanced at the papers.

Wulf wanted to sit, wanted to believe Bookie, but he was one step removed from being a brick himself. Thieves and bricks were not friends.

"What kind of questions?" Wulf asked. He took a step closer but did not sit down. Easier to run away when you were standing and the other person was sitting.

Invictus is your friend. You can trust him.

The voice sounded kinda like Ma's.

"Questions about the Whateley case," Celeste said. "We already know you broke into the house, so don't lie. And, if you cooperate, Reyes will drop the charges."

"Cooperate? You mean, work with the bricks?"

Celeste nodded.

Wulf had known a few brick informants. People who gave the bricks information in exchange for money or other favors. Every single one had ended up dead in an alleyway or shipped off to Greer.

"I ain't no snitch."

"I didn't call you one." Celeste placed a satchel on the table and removed a large piece of paper and some ink. She placed the paper on the floor. "Let me see your boot."

"What for?"

"Evidence in your favor. Boot, please."

Wulf removed a boot and handed it to her. Celeste coated the bottom with ink and pressed it against the paper, leaving an impression. "Are these the same boots you wore on the twelfth?"

"Only got one pair."

"Do you recall any rain that day?"

"Yeah, in the afternoon." This time of year, it seemed to rain three or four times a week, leaving everything all muddy and...

Wulf cursed. Was the ground around the Whateley house muddy? The lawn was mostly grass, but there was dirt around the oak tree. Had the rain turned it to mud? Had he been careless enough to leave muddy footprints?

Ruthless will tan my hide.

Celeste returned the boot and retrieved another paper. One with a partial boot print. She compared the two.

"Identical."

"What does this mean?" Bookie asked.

"This print was found near the Whateleys' second floor hallway window. All of the prints were partials, and they faded quickly, which is to be expected. We then discovered traces of mud in the hallway carpet, but there was no mud inside the study."

Bookie's eyes widened. "Then you have proof that Wulf didn't kill Dr. Whateley."

"Exactly."

"Hold up." Wulf's head spun. "You believe me?"

"Of course."

Wulf honestly did not know how to feel about that. His ma and Ruthless believing him was one thing. They were family. Celeste was a stranger and a brick.

"You, Beowulf Smith," she declared, "are innocent of one crime. However, a jury will not take your testimony at face value. After all, you still broke into the house. We must establish your innocence further."

"Okay. How?"

"Excuse me," said a student, a skinny boy with black hair down to his shoulders. "We're trying to study. Do you mind—"

Celeste showed the student her gold brick badge.

The boy's eyes widened. "A police officer?"

"Yes."

"But you're a girl."

"Excellent deduction. Now, shoo." Celeste waved him away.

The boy returned to his table and whispered to the other students sitting there. They stared at Celeste, Wulf, and Bookie.

"Can we establish my innocence somewhere else?" Wulf asked, pulling his hat over his eyes. Did the student see that they were purple? Did he recognize Wulf's face or name?

"Why?"

Wulf glanced at the students. His sharp ears picked up their whispers.

"What are they investigating?" another boy asked.

"A murder, I think."

"Are the other two officers?"

"Maybe."

"I think I've seen that Amistadian guy before."

Wulf's skin crawled.

"Now," Celeste continued, "Dr. Whateley was found sitting in his armchair. Beowulf, stand in front of me." Wulf did so. "Excellent. Now, pretend you have a gun and aim it at me." Wulf did so again, and Celeste frowned. "You're left-handed."

"Yeah. So?"

Bookie stood and walked over to Wulf and Celeste. "At what angle was the doctor shot?"

"Straight on. Are you right-handed or left-handed?"

"Right."

"Okay, pretend to aim a gun."

Invictus did so, and Celeste smiled. "Very good. The real killer, a right-handed person, shoots Dr. Whateley in the heart at close range." She slumped over. "And Dr. Whateley dies immediately."

An invisible fist clenched Wulf's heart. Seeing Celeste pretend to die in a chair, a chair almost identical to the ones in that dockside bar... The bar where Lewin took Dav, tied him up, and tortured...

"Wulf, are you...? Wulf!" Bookie grabbed Wulf's arm at the same time his knees buckled. A second later, Wulf was sitting and Bookie stood over him. His lips moved, but the sounds were far away, echoing down a long tunnel.

Wulf blinked and he was there again. Dav's bruised and bloodied body tied to a chair. Tortured to death for information he did not have. How did Dav get out of jail? Did someone pay his bail? Did he escape? Ruthless promised to find out, but he never did.

Dav shouldn't have been here.

He shouldn't be dead.

"Should I call a doctor?" Celeste asked, her voice sounding far away.

Wulf blinked again and he was back at the library. He felt cold and shaky, as though he was coming down with the flu. He glanced around. Bright lights overhead, too bright for comfort. The students kept whispering. Staring.

Wulf looked at Bookie and focused on him. He was there when they found Dav. He could have bolted right then and there, but he didn't. He stayed by Wulf's side. Even now he stayed by Wulf's side, refusing to abandon him. The shakiness began to fade.

"Wulf, what happened?" Bookie asked.

"I don't know. Just... The doctor died in a chair. Dav died..." Tears stung his eyes. He bit his tongue and buried his face in his hands. No! He already cried for Dav. He wasn't gonna start crying again. Not in front of a brick.

"Who's Dav?" Celeste whispered.

Invictus explained, leaving out the gory details.

"Oh my God. Beowulf, I'm so sorry."

Wulf wiped away a few stray tears and met Celeste's eyes. Sincere eyes. "Why do you care?"

"Because no one should have to die like that. Did the police find the ones responsible?"

"Yeah. The bastard's on Greer now."

"Good."

Wulf searched Celeste's eyes for the lie, but there was none. Celeste, a brick, actually cared about a thief. Why?

"I think I have enough evidence for today," she said to Bookie. "I'll report to Bishop and Reyes. Do you think you'll be available to speak with us later this week?" she asked Wulf. "Say, after the hurricane?"

"Speak where?" No way he'd walk inside the Fifth Precinct. Not for a thousand dollars.

"Wherever you like."

Wulf thought it over. "Maybe." Sincere or not, Celeste was still a brick. "But I think looking for Carlos Vallejo is a dead end. I think the sons did it."

"Wulf..." Bookie began, but Wulf cut him off.

"Alistair Whateley has a temper. He threatened Bookie when we talked to him today."

Celeste frowned. "What do you mean you talked to him?"

"Bookie and I went to the hospital, and Bookie asked Alistair about the robbery, saying he was a brick."

Celeste gave Bookie a stern look.

"Reyes asked me to help," Bookie stammered.

"He asked you to find and question Smith. Questioning the family is my job."

"Still," Wulf said. "I think the sons killed him."

"Then how do you and Carlos Vallejo factor in?" she asked.

Wulf shrugged. "Guess they wanted us to take the fall."

"Interesting." Celeste collected her papers and ink and slung the satchel over her shoulder. "What do you think, Jones?"

"I think something connected to the doctor's research got him killed. Check his personal finances for any unusual payments. I'll bring the ledgers tomorrow, and we can analyze them then."

"Noted. Oh, Reyes wants everyone to come in an hour early tomorrow to help with storm preparations."

Bookie did his best not to frown. "Yes, of course."

Celeste told them both goodbye and left.

Wulf wrapped his arms around himself, shaking. A brick. He spoke face to face with a brick, and he wasn't arrested. Instead, she believed him and listened to his ideas.

Why?

Did this make him an informant now?

He hoped to God it didn't.

Chapter 14
Underground

Invictus and Wulf waited in a small park adjacent to the hospital and watched as the setting sun dyed the sky shades of orange and red. Invictus had not been too keen on returning to the hospital. Instead, he wanted to go home and analyze the Whateleys' accounts again. He did not find anything unusual the first time, but if the doctor was involved with the Five Families, even indirectly, it ought to be reflected there. A single discrepancy or a strange notation could lead them onto the right path.

But Wulf had other ideas.

"Come on, Bookie. You know one of the doctor's sons did him in."

"There is no evidence and no motive," he said. Again.

"What's your deal, man?" Wulf sneered. His eyes flashed a deeper shade of purple. "If you get a hunch, we follow it. But if I get a hunch, we ignore it? How the hell is that fair?"

Invictus sighed. "You have a valid point."

"And your brick friend thought it was a good idea, too."

Celeste never stated that, but a wave of guilt struck Invictus. Wulf had followed him every step of the way so far. It was only fair that he gave the Halfling the same credit.

They left the University campus and headed north to the hospital, waiting for Alistair's shift to end.

In all, the waiting wasn't too bad. It gave Invictus time to think and order events in his mind, analyzing every detail. He was grateful that

Celeste found them at the library. She provided more evidence in Wulf's favor and confirmed that Reyes had an officer trailing him. Not a surprise. Cases of this nature always had multiple officers assigned in various tasks. But who could have followed him and Wulf without being seen or heard? He shelved the question for later and focused on the evidence.

The boot print and muddy tracks proved Wulf did not commit the murder though it firmly placed him at the scene, making him a witness. He asked Wulf to list everything he remembered.

"The house was real quiet," Wulf said, glancing every time someone walked within twenty feet of them. The small park had ample space for people to walk about without accidentally overhearing them, and the shady trees gave them addition coverage, both from watching eyes and the afternoon heat. "I couldn't see any lights from outside. A gaslamp was burning in the hallway. Then I heard voices. People shouting."

"But you couldn't understand them, right?"

"Right. It definitely wasn't Malkinese, and I don't think it was High Speech either."

"Would you be able to recognize the language if you heard someone speak it?"

Wulf shrugged. "I don't know. Maybe."

"Could it have been Faerie?" If Dr. Whateley had ties to the Sidhe Family, he might have spoken some Faerie. Invictus's mind snapped back to Harvey's Security Firm, overhearing Lewin threatening Harvey. Had another Family member threatened Dr. Whateley? Was the doctor dead because he refused to cooperate?

"No," Wulf said. "Hey, maybe they were speaking Scannie. I mean, Scanlannish."

"Possibly. Did you see anyone?"

"Just the maid. Whoever did the doctor in threw the gun into the hallway. Never saw his face. Guess he did that to make it look like I dropped it."

"Interesting." Invictus made a mental note. Dropping the gun in the hallway meant that the murderer planned for Wulf to be present. They wanted him to take the blame.

They must have coordinated this with Carlos.

Unless Carlos was the murderer. But why? What motive could he have?

The park's clock tower chimed seven times.

How long are medical shifts? Invictus wondered as he confirmed the time on his watch. For most businesses, the day shift ended at five.

A quarter hour later, several doctors and nurses exited the hospital. Some walked towards the train station while others hailed cabs. Alistair Whateley, with a satchel slung over his shoulder, accompanied the group heading towards the station.

Invictus and Wulf followed at a distance.

Alistair arrived in time to catch the train to the Old City, but he did not board. Instead, he sat down on a bench and waited.

"What's he doin'?" Wulf whispered. He and Invictus stood across the street, hiding behind a newsstand. People crowded the stand, buying evening additions of the *Malkin City Times.* This evening's main headline stated that the hurricane would make landfall sometime Thursday evening. Smaller headlines stated a sharp rise in petty crimes throughout the city.

"Good question." If Alistair was not going home, then where?

Maybe he just doesn't want to be home right now. Invictus recalled how his grandfather had acted after his grandmother passed away. Grandpa Gratian created every reason under the sun to not go home. Visiting friends. Working late at the tailor shop.

"Every time I'm there," he eventually admitted, "I expect to see her, and I have to remember that she's gone."

It had taken months for Grandpa to regain a sense of peace. To adjust to her absence.

The next train arrived, and Alistair boarded. Invictus and Wulf raced across the street and boarded the adjacent car. They watched Alistair through the connecting door's window.

"Where does this train go?" Invictus whispered even though only a handful of other passengers occupied the car.

Wulf shrugged.

The train whistle blew, and the massive vehicle lumbered to life, heading north.

Invictus's stomach twisted in knots as the train passed the Gems and Dannyn District and turned northeast. Only two possibilities awaited them: Gray Hook and Mull.

Why would Alistair go to the worst parts of Malkin City? Was he meeting with someone? A connection to the Families?

He shivered, picturing Lewin Manning's eerie gold eyes.

The train stopped at Numerius Station, right on the edge of Gray Hook.

Alistair disembarked. Invictus and Wulf followed, sticking to the shadows. The sun had sunk below the horizon, creating a myriad of shadows. Wulf, wearing all black, blended in perfectly. Invictus hoped his gray and brown clothes were suitable camouflage.

"Do you know where he might be going?" Invictus whispered as they turned a corner, getting lost in the maze of streets.

"No idea. I don't venture into Gray Hook often. Some parts are worse than Mull."

Bloody great.

As night fell, the streets grew livelier and more dangerous. Invictus spied at least three gangs stalking alleyways and eyeing everyone who passed their way. One group acted like they were going to mug Alistair, surrounding him on all sides and brandishing knives. Invictus almost called out, but one look from the doctor sent them running.

Invictus sighed in relief. "That was close," he whispered.

Wulf said nothing. His eyes shifted constantly, focusing on every little movement.

Alistair finally stopped at a nondescript building with a faded sign on the side advertising laundry services. The paint had chipped away, making the company's name unreadable.

The doctor knocked three times. The door creaked open, spilling light into the darkened street. He slipped inside. The light vanished.

"Wait." Invictus grabbed Wulf's arm as the Halfling continued forward. "What is this place?"

"The place Alistair Whateley walked into. Are we still following him?"

"Yes, but... It's just..." A knot of pure ice twisted Invictus's gut. "What if it's a meeting?"

Wulf shrugged out of Invictus's grip. "Then it's a meeting. Big deal." He knocked on the door before Invictus could stop him.

A large man, nearly as tall as Ruthless, answered. He wore a tattered jacket over an equally tattered button-down shirt, and his eyes gleamed a strange, silvery green. A Blydd Halfling or Hybrid, Invictus guessed.

"We want in," Wulf said.

The man nodded and opened the door wide enough for them to slip inside. He then closed the door and slid three deadbolts into place.

Invictus balled his trembling hands into fists. *What is this place?* Why did it require a door guard? And why did the guard allow Wulf and Invictus to enter without some sort of payment or password?

"Hey, Bookie, check this place out!"

Invictus turned. Wulf stood along a railing that circled the ground floor. The section within the railing was open, revealing a massive basement. The ceiling was also missing, allowing people on the second and third floors to gaze downwards.

The basement itself was divided into three rings circled by wooden stands. The two rings in the corners were half the size of the central ring. People crowded the central ring, some sitting and others standing. Most wore ragged clothing, but a few were nicely dressed, the clothing new and clean. Invictus looked around the railing and noted more men in finely tailored suits. Even a few women in silks.

"What is this place?" Invictus wondered out loud.

"It's a fighting ring!" Wulf smiled from ear to ear like a child at the Festival of Lights.

A bell sounded.

A man wearing a bright blue coat and vest sauntered into the central ring. He waved his hands over his head, and the crowd silenced. "For our first fight," he announced, his voice echoing, "we have Gray Hook's own Grant Valdez." The crowd cheered. "And the terror of the Attakapas, Tomas Aron de Alzed!"

The cheering erupted into a roar. The ringing in Invictus's ear returned with a painful vengeance. Grimacing, he joined Wulf at the railing and watched as two men entered the ring. One wore a blue belt while the other wore a white one. The man in the blue clothes instructed them to shake hands. Other men, also wearing blue, walked through the crowd and collected bets. One man walked up to Invictus.

"Valdez or de Alzed?" he asked.

"Pardon?"

"Your bet, sir."

"What are the odds?" Wulf asked.

"Three to one in Valdez's favor."

"I like those odds. Bookie, place a quarter on Valdez."

"No."

"But—"

"We didn't come here to place bets," he said firmly.

The man in blue shrugged and went to the next person, a woman wearing a matching purple dress and hat. She handed him a dollar, and he wrote her name in a ledger.

Wulf sneered.

"I'm serious, Wulf. Merciful heavens, five minutes ago, we didn't know what this place was."

"True, but three to one? You can spare a quarter on that!"

Invictus rolled his eyes and then scanned the crowd. "Do you see Alistair?"

"Nope."

Another bell rang. The two men started boxing. After a few punches, the man in the blue belt slammed his elbow into his opponent's head. The man in the white belt responded by jabbing his knee into Blue Belt's ribs. The crowd cheered.

"Um, isn't that against the rules?" Invictus grimaced as Blue Belt received another knee jab to the ribs.

"Ain't no rules in a place like this, Bookie."

Invictus turned away from the fight and surveyed the crowd. He spotted a single blond head standing next to the ring. Grabbing Wulf's wrist, Invictus hurried down the stairs and made his way through the crowd.

"Dr. Whateley?" Invictus needed to shout to be heard over the cheering. "Dr. Whateley!"

"Yeah?" Alistair turned and scowled. "What the hell are you doing here? Did you follow me?" His eyes fell on Wulf. "You son of a bitch!" He grabbed Wulf by the shirt collar and shook him like a ragdoll. "You killed my father!"

"Like hell I did!" Wulf kicked Alistair in the kneecap. The doctor screamed and lost his grip. Wulf backed away and snarled, revealing pointy teeth. Alistair lunged at him, but Invictus stepped between them, holding up his hands.

"Wulf is innocent," he shouted over the crowd. "The police proved that he wasn't in your father's study. He is not the murderer."

"But he was there." Alistair glared, his bloodshot eyes burning.

"Yes." Invictus locked eyes with the doctor. Mercy sakes alive, what if Alistair did not believe him? Would he contact the police or take matters into his own hands?

Alistair, thankfully, relaxed. Straightening his jacket, he said, "Alright. You didn't murder my father. Did you see who did? And don't give me any crap about anonymous neighbors," he said to Invictus.

"I saw nobody except the maid," Wulf replied.

Alistair stared at Wulf for a moment and then glanced at the fight. Blue Belt managed to wrap his leg behind White Belt's ankle and twisted, sending them both to the ground. The crowd shouted. A few people jumped up and down in the stands.

"Was anyone with you?" Alistair asked Wulf, looking him in the eyes.

"No, just me. The other two didn't show. Got food poisoning."

"Good. They deserve it."

"Dr. Whateley," Invictus said, "what are you doing here?" Was Alistair a gambler? Nemo Bonaventura got into debt with the Malkinese Family because of his gambling habit. Had Alistair or his father fallen into a similar trap?

"I'm a medic. I stitch up the fighters and reset broken bones after each round."

"You get paid for that?" Wulf asked, his head titled to the side.

Alistair shot him a glare, balling his hands into fists.

"Are you here on a volunteer basis?" Invictus asked, stepping between Wulf and Alistair.

"In a sense." Alistair redirected his glare to Invictus. "These fighters can't go to regular hospitals. Doctors ask questions, and then the police get involved. So, I help out."

"How did you get involved?" If one of the Families was involved...

"Jones, has anyone ever told you to mind your own business?"

"I'm just curious, sir. Could someone here have learned where you live? They might have broken in and—"

"No way." Alistair's glare turned red hot. "Without people like me, these fighting rings would not exist. They know better than to mess with the doctor."

A sickening snap echoed through the basement, followed by a bloodcurdling scream. The crowd erupted into madness.

Invictus looked at the ring. White Belt's leg was bent at an unnatural angle, as though he had a second knee joint. Bile rose in the back of Invictus's throat. He quickly turned away, taking deep breaths.

"If you will excuse me, I have work to do." Alistair climbed into the ring and examined the injured fighter. The man in blue held up Blue Belt's hand. Blue Belt, his face and torso severely bruised and blood pouring out of his nose, looked like he also needed Alistair's attention. But he was able to stand while his opponent was on the ground. In the crowd's eyes, that was all that mattered. Half a dozen men in blue hurried through the crowd and along the railings, distributing winnings.

"See, I told you to bet on Valdez," Wulf said.

Invictus swallowed, forcing the bile to stay down.

"We asking anymore questions?"

Invictus wanted to, but who would he ask? Alistair would not tolerate further questioning, and what if this ring was controlled by a Family? The owner might report to his superiors if Invictus started interrogated his employees.

Perhaps his hunch was wrong.

"No, let's go."

Walking up to the ground floor, Invictus spied a familiar face standing next to the railing. Germanicus Hillman, dressed in a fine gray suit with a rose in the lapel, tipped his hat and motioned for them to follow. He then headed up the stairs.

"Oh hell, what's Germanicus doing here?" Wulf muttered.

"You're gang members. Shouldn't you know where he is?"

"Yeah," Wulf said as they reached the second floor. "Don't mean I have to like him. 'Specially since he's been calling me the Shinnok version of Scannie this whole time."

Blue and green checkered carpeting lined the second-floor hallway, and the dark wood paneling lined the walls. Gaslamps in gilded scones lighted the way. Germanicus waited under one lamp, midway down the hall. He leaned against a doorframe and waved them over.

"Interesting seeing you here, Jones," Germanicus said. "Never pictured you as a fights man."

"Wulf had a hunch. What are you doing here?"

"Ruthless assigned me trail you and Fox-face. Followed you here and sent word for Ruthless to join. Shouldn't be too long now." He gestured at the doorway. The door itself was long gone. Even the hinges were missing. But the wood was smoothed over and polished, leaving no signs of damage.

The room was more luxurious than the hallway. Plush couches lined two walls, and a table made of solid oak rested in the center, complete with matching armchairs. A bar took up the back wall and included top shelf liquors and an attendant wearing a blue uniform, the same as the men collecting bets. The gaslamps burned low.

"Sit," Germanicus said.

Invictus and Wulf sat at the table. Germanicus remained by the door with his arms crossed over his chest. The attendant, a short, wiry man with orange and green eyes set in a pale, angular face, asked if they would like anything to drink. They both declined.

"What the hell sort of fighting ring is this?" Wulf asked.

"One that serves a wide variety of clientele," the attendant replied in a strangely accented voice.

"So the poor folks watch in the pit, and the rich folks watch from up here?" Wulf asked.

The attendant nodded. "Would you care to listen to the fight? We have wireless radios available."

"No, thank you," Invictus said before Wulf could reply.

Wireless radios? Thanks to new innovations, wireless radios had become more commonplace over the last decade. Mrs. Ramirez had one installed in the sitting room, and even Maria and Wulf had a portable one that they shared with Ruthless. But the replacement batteries cost more than a month's rent. Supplying each room with its own private wireless would cost a small fortune. How did they afford it?

Perhaps his hunch was correct. One of the Families owned the ring and furnished it with luxury items to attract wealthy betters. Though boxing was a legal sport, it had very strict rules, and breaking a single one could end a fighter's career faster than a broken leg.

And the City Council placed strict limits on betting. Several members wanted to make it illegal, viewing it as another vice plaguing the city.

"Got a question, man," Wulf said, turning around in his chair. "Y'all got gator wrestling?"

"Only on Mondays, sir," the attendant replied as calmly as though Wulf had asked about the weather.

Wulf grinned maniacally. "Bookie, this place is awesome!"

"Well, that's certainly a word." He checked his watch, and his heart skipped a beat. Eight forty-seven! Bloody hell, Mrs. Ramirez would roast him alive for breaking curfew again.

The attendant hissed.

Invictus glanced up. The attendant gripped the bar's edge so tightly that his knuckles turned white. He glared at Invictus, his pupils narrowing to slits. Just like a cat's eyes.

Or a snake's.

Fae are allergic to silver, idiot.

He quickly pocketed the watch. The attendant resumed working, keeping his narrowed eyes on Invictus.

"Which subspecies is he?" Invictus whispered to Wulf.

"Probably at Neydir. They got weird eyes."

You all have weird eyes.

"Good evening, Jones." Ruthless Wells sauntered into the room and sat at the table next to Invictus. Germanicus and Lear, a short Eadryn Fae with red and brown eyes, joined them. The attendant asked if anyone cared for a drink. Ruthless ordered a shot of whiskey. Germanicus and Lear declined. The attendant poured the drink and placed it on the table. He kept his eyes fixed on Invictus, ready to run or lash out at a moment's notice.

"What's got him spooked?" Lear asked. His eyes were stripped like wheel spokes, and he wore a brown bowler hat with a bright red band to match. A brown satchel with red trim was strapped over his shoulder.

"He saw Bookie's silver watch," Wulf explained.

Lear raised an eyebrow. "You still have that thing?"

"Well, yes."

He let out a low whistle. "Man, you are just asking for trouble."

"What Jones wishes to carry on his person is his own business," Ruthless said. He drank the whiskey and nodded, impressed. "What do you think of the good doctor's nightly activities?"

"You knew about this?" Invictus frowned.

"Not until recently. I ran a check on this ring. The owner is connected to the Malkinese Family, but only slightly. The Family receives a ten percent cut, nothing more. Everyone else is clean. Including Alistair Whateley."

Well, that's a relief. "What about Armand Whateley? Did he have any connections?"

"Yes and no." Ruthless leaned forward, locking eyes with Invictus. The silver irises appeared almost golden in the low light. "Armand Whateley's research, from what I've found, was funded by three groups: the City Hospital, the Malkin City University, and the Barrish Family. Don't worry. The Barrish have always been interested in scientific research for research's sake. Nothing criminal. And Whateley was not connected to anything criminal either, nor anything that could have contributed to his death."

"How did you find this out?"

"I have my resources."

And that tells me absolutely nothing.

Invictus recalled the business card Nemo Bonaventura gave him. The one stating that Ruthless worked as a detective for the Commonwealth. He still had the card, tucked safely away in his favorite Aurelia Jayne novel. He tried and failed to find more information about the agency, and even the police officers he asked offer no explanation.

How much was a fabrication, and how much was true? Living undercover in a slum would be difficult, but if Ruthless had outside resources, it could be manageable.

A part of him wanted to ask, but he held his tongue.

"Beowulf, your mother wants you to be careful," Ruthless said, turning his eerie gaze to him.

Wulf rolled his eyes. "She always says that."

"Still. You ought to listen to her. The person or persons who killed Armand Whateley want you to take the blame."

"But Macsen and Carlos would have been there too if they didn't get sick."

Ruthless shared a grave look with Germanicus.

"Yeah," the Aziza Fae said. "If they didn't get sick."

"You think they were poisoned intentionally?" Invictus's ear rang.

Ruthless nodded. "We think another party is involved. They used Carlos as the go-between, and then got him and Macsen out of the way, leaving Wulf alone with no one to verify his claims. Beowulf, can you describe Carlos Vallejo?"

"Sure."

Lear placed the satchel on the table and removed a drawing pad, pencils, and a few pieces of colored chalk. "Okay. Describe away."

"Shinnok Halfling."

"What human ethnicity?"

"Huh?"

Lear rolled his eyes. "The human half. What is he? Malkinese? Barrish?"

"Malkinese, I think."

"Age?" Lear turned to a blank page. Invictus caught glimpses of other sketches. People, flowers, buildings. All expertly drawn.

"Around twenty. He never said."

"Build?"

"A little thinner than me." Wulf paused, thinking. "Angular face. Pointy ears. Purple eyes. Dark red hair."

Lear quickly sketched an image, adding color for the hair and eyes. "What about skin tone?"

"Tan, but not as tan as me."

"Lighter skin?" Lear raised an eyebrow.

"Yeah."

"Interesting." Lear added to the drawing. "What about nose and mouth shapes?"

"Thin lips, like mine. Thin nose that looks like it got broken and reset once or twice."

"Eye shape?"

"Same as mine." Wulf's eyes were slightly oval, the same as Maria's eyes.

Lear finished the drawing and presented it to the group. Invictus stared at the drawing, shocked. The portrait appeared so lifelike, as though it would start moving and speaking, giving the answers they desperately needed. It was miles beyond what the police sketch artists could create.

How had Lear fallen in with a gang of thieves? Why hadn't he become an artist?

Did Ruthless recruit him because of his talent?

Invictus tabled the questions away for later and studied the drawing. The man looked similar to Wulf, but they were the same subspecies and around the same age, so no surprise there. His red hair would certainly stand out in a crowd.

"Did he ever cover his hair?" Invictus asked Wulf.

"Wore a hat."

"Makes sense," Germanicus said, studying the drawing. He acted like he was about to speak but shook his head. "No. Don't recognize him."

"Neither do I," Ruthless muttered as he polished off his drink. "This is good stuff. Mr. Hillman, leave a generous tip."

"On it." Germanicus placed two crisp dollars on the table.

Two dollars? That was more than the shot of whiskey cost.

"Are you going to search for Carlos?" Invictus asked.

"Of course. Lear, create three more drawings. We will distribute them to lookouts and see if it rings any bells."

"Yes, sir." Lear placed the sketchpad and supplies in his satchel.

"Jones, do you have any plans for tomorrow?" Ruthless asked.

"I have to help with hurricane preparations at work." He did not understand why everyone was making such a fuss. Hurricanes were just large thunderstorms. But nobody bought extra groceries or boarded up windows for thunderstorms. Nobody acted concerned.

Should he be concerned?

"Excellent," Ruthless replied. "We have storm preparations to do ourselves. Wulf, your mother wants you to lie low tomorrow and help her."

"No problem."

Ruthless stood, signaling everyone else to do so. He shook hands with Invictus. "Good luck, Jones, and stay safe during the hurricane. I hear it's going to be a nasty one."

"If you say so, sir."

Ruthless glared at him, silver eyes flashing. "I do say so. You've never experienced a hurricane, have you?"

"No." Goosebumps broke out on his arms. But why? He wasn't afraid. It was just a large storm and... Should he be afraid?

The Blydd smiled wolfishly. "Figures. Be safe, Jones, and stick close to your newfound brick friends."

"What is that supposed to mean?" Was he referring to Asa and Celeste or the entire Fifth Precinct? What did he know about them?

Ruthless studied him for a silent moment. Voices echoed upwards from the basement, cheering as the next fight was announced. "Does the phrase have more than one meaning?"

"Normally, no."

"Then, in the normal sense, be safe, Jones." Ruthless, with Germanicus and Lear in tow, sauntered out of the room.

Chapter 15

An Offer

Invictus sequestered himself in his small office, analyzing Dr. Whateley's ledgers. Everyone at the Precinct was busy with hurricane preparations. Hurrying this way and that, carrying supplies, or taking furniture and important items upstairs. Boarding up windows. Invictus tried to help, but just like at his boardinghouse, every time he tried, he felt like he was getting in the way. He slipped away half an hour ago, and nobody had questioned his absence.

The ledgers, as far as he could tell, were perfect. All of the numbers added up, and everything was accounted for. No discrepancies or mistakes. No mysterious sources of income or unexplained expenses. Nothing out of the ordinary.

But what about money not listed in a private ledger? Invictus wondered. *Did the doctor receive any unrecorded cash payments, or payments disguised as research funds?*

Dr. Rosario was reluctant to talk about Armand Whateley. Was he fearful of the man himself or someone connected to him? Invictus tried to bring up the subject last night, but Rosario claimed he had a terrible headache and retired early. Invictus suspected that Mrs. Ramirez's wrath played a significant factor. The landlady had yelled at him for breaking curfew, starting the moment he walked through the door. Apparently, she had been waiting in the parlor since nine o'clock sharp.

"She's just worried," Cuchallain explained once Mrs. Ramirez stormed into her room, slamming the door. Iulianus nodded in agreement. "Hurricanes make her nervous. There was a really bad one about twenty years ago. Ruined a large portion of the city and flooded out her old house. Now, whenever she hears about one, she goes all to pieces."

"Don't let her hear you say that, Cuchallain," Iulianus whispered. He glanced down the hallway, as though worried she would materialize out of thin air.

"She took a sleeping draught. She'll be out in five minutes."

"How do you know that?"

Cuchallain smirked and pointed at his ears. His orange eyes flashed.

Invictus attempted to speak with Dr. Rosario this morning, but the chemist stayed close to Mrs. Ramirez's side, performing every little task for her. Each time Invictus got within ten feet of them, Mrs. Ramirez glared at him, her dark brown eyes as hard as bullets. He hurried out of the house, knowing he would not get a single word out of Rosario about Dr. Whateley.

Ruthless claimed that the Barrish Family's involvement in research was purely scientific, but what about the other Families? Did they have a stake in Whateley's work? If so, did Rosario discover this and now fear for his safety?

But how would Invictus prove their involvement? He could request a report on the hospital's research funds. The hospital was bound to comply, but Invictus was not a police officer. Perhaps he could ask Asa or Celeste. Asa would roll his eyes, but Celeste might be open to the idea.

Granted, any funding from the Families would likely be disguised to make the transaction appear legitimate.

Why would crime families care about medical research? Invictus thought, dismayed. Ruthless never explained why the Barrish funded scientific research or what they received in return. The Sidhe Family worked with Emilio Grady because they earned a substantial amount of income each month. But what would the Families hope to gain by donating money to doctors?

A sharp knock sounded at the door.

"Yes?"

Officer Hector Riggs, the ever-present scowl marring his face, peered inside. At first, Invictus assumed that Riggs disliked him because he was friends with Wulf, but the policeman greeted everyone with that scowl. "Captain Reyes wants to see you."

Invictus nodded and gathered up the ledgers. He saw Asa and Celeste walk into the captain's office earlier. The captain, no doubt, wanted an update on the case.

If only I had an update.

Other than Celeste comparing Wulf's boot prints and a sketch of Carlos Vallejo, he had nothing.

Officers hurried up and down the stairs, carrying buckets of sand or planks with nails and hammers. Invictus glanced over the railing. Most of the windows on the first floor were boarded up. One officer accidentally bumped into him. Invictus almost lost his grip on the ledgers. He clutched them closer to his chest. Reyes would skin him alive if he lost or damaged a single piece of evidence.

Riggs barged into the office without knocking. Captain Reyes stood off to the side, reading a letter while two officers boarded up the windows.

"Wait!" Reyes said. "Light the lantern."

One officer, a Shinnok Fae named Pembroke, nearly jumped out of his skin hearing the order. He complied and lit the oil lamp on the captain's desk, his fingers shaking and sweat beading on his forehead. He then returned to his task. Within moments, the soft, yellow glow was the room's only source of light.

"You wanted to see me, sir?" Invictus asked.

"Sit down."

Invictus did so, placing the ledgers on Reyes's desk. Riggs stood off to the side, his arms crossed. Reyes waited until Pembroke and the other officer, Invictus was ninety percent sure his name was Nunez, left.

"Where did these come from?" Reyes pointed at the ledgers.

"They're Dr. Whateley's personal ledgers, sir."

"Okay. Why do you have them?"

"Alfred Whateley gave them to me, sir." His palms began to sweat.

The captain scowled. "When was this?"

"The other day, sir. I, uh, spoke to him about the case. He, Alfred I mean, um..." Bloody hell, how would Reyes react to him impersonating a police officer? "You wanted me to work on the case, sir, and I..."

Reyes pinched the bridge of his nose. "Of course. I should have known you would pull some stupid stunt. Smart, but stupid," he added. He handed the letter to Invictus. "This arrived for you."

Invictus's name and the Fifth Precinct's new address were written on the envelope. He did not recognize the handwriting, and there was no sender name or return address. Strange.

He unfolded the letter and read:

Hello Mr. Jones,

I hope your time with the police has been enlightening. Working with detectives instead of reading about them must be quite the experience. I read about a very unnerving case in the papers on Monday. A man killed by a thief in his own house. It's the stuff of nightmares. I only had the privilege of meeting Dr. Armand Whateley a handful of times, but I am familiar with his work. He was a fascinating individual, to say the least, and I am sorry to hear about his untimely passing.

I want to shed what little light I can on the case, but on two conditions. One, visit me on September sixteenth in the afternoon, not a day before or later. Two, do not bring your thief friend. Break either condition, and I will withdraw my offer.

Sincerely,

Emilio Grady.

Goosebumps broke out on Invictus's skin. He struggled to find words as memories of the trial overwhelmed him. He was sitting in the courtroom, waiting for the judge to call his name, to testify against his former employer. Grady had glared icy daggers at Invictus the entire time, as though this was all his fault. And in a way, it was. Invictus refused to ignore the discrepancies, refused to ignore the oddity of Wulf robbing him and only him. And more importantly, he refused to work for a criminal.

Yes, Grady's arrest and twenty-year sentence to Greer Island were all Invictus's fault, and he did not regret it for a second.

"When did this arrive?" he asked, finding his voice.

"About ten minutes ago. Hired courier." Reyes stepped closer, looming. But he was not glaring or frowning. Instead, he looked worried. "I hope you don't mind me reading it first."

"I don't." Invictus bit his tongue, grounding himself in the here and now. "Why did he send this to me? I'm not a police officer. Just a clerk."

"A clerk who I assigned to this case."

"But how does Mr. Grady know that?" Grady could only know about Invictus's involvement if he had a spy inside the Fifth Precinct. He told Reyes.

The captain nodded gravely. "I thought we caught all of those bastards. One must have slipped through my grasp." Reyes clenched his hands into fists, as though he wanted to personally strangle the spy.

"What are you going to do, sir?"

"Me? I'm going to finish hurricane preparations. You and Riggs are going to Greer Island to speak with Emilio Grady."

"What?" Invictus stood, his knees threatening to buckle, and met the captain at eye level. "Why me?"

"Because Grady addressed that letter to you, and I want to know any information he's hiding. It might bring us one step closer to finding the murderer. Unless you want Beowulf Smith to hang for a murder he didn't commit."

"Hang?" Invictus's stomach twisted in knots. "But he... The evidence..."

Reyes locked eyes with him. "Trust me, Jones. Smith will hang. The Whateley family is putting pressure on us to find the murderer, and half the news articles name Smith as the killer. The public wants justice just as much as the Whateleys. Someone must pay the price."

A bottomless pit formed in Invictus's gut at the same time the invisible string tugged at his mind. If Emilio Grady held a missing part of this equation, could he really risk not speaking to him? Even if it meant sailing to Greer Island?

"Jones," the captain said, "do you believe that Smith is innocent?"

"Yes. Officer Lawson proved it by taking his boot print. Nobody found any mud in the doctor's study."

"Boots can be removed, Jones," Reyes said gravely. "How do you know Smith didn't remove them in order to literally cover his tracks?"

"Because Wulf would never kill an unarmed man!" Merciful heavens, how many times did he have to explain this!

"And how do you know? Didn't Smith rob you at gunpoint?"

"He tried to—"

"Didn't his actions result in a permanent injury?"

Invictus's ear rang, emphasizing the captain's point. "That was an accident! And his gang was hired to scare me, not kill anyone."

"How do you know he wasn't hired again?" the captain all but yelled. "Smith claims there was a third thief. Except, no one can find him. Did he hire Smith to kill Dr. Whateley?"

"No!" Invictus forced himself to calm down, to breathe. Screaming at the captain solved nothing. "Why are you asking me this? I thought you believed Wulf was innocent."

"I think there is a strong possibility of his innocence." The captain's expression softened. He almost looked sad. "But can you prove it in a court of law?"

A heavy weight settled on Invictus's shoulders. For all the evidence in the world, Wulf was still a thief. A judge and jury, already prejudiced against him, would view Wulf as a thief first and a witness second.

They would never believe him.

"These are the type of questions," Reyes said, "that a lawyer will ask at the trial. And yes, there will be a trial. The only way to keep Smith alive is to find the third thief and find enough evidence to convict him.

"I don't know what information Grady has," he continued, "but I want it. I have arranged for a cab to take you and Riggs to the docks. Police boat number fourteen will take you to Greer Island. Captain Tartan will meet you there. Of course, you can say no. I won't force you to go."

Invictus stared at the letter, thinking. Yes, the traces of mud ended several paces short of the study, but only so much mud could stick to a boot. The traces would run out eventually. And Invictus never imagined Wulf taking off his boots. It was simple. Remove the boots. Walk into the study. Shoot the doctor. Then, run back into the hallway and drop the gun while putting the boots back on...

No, Wulf would never do that!

Taking his boots off and putting them back on again would slow him down. Wulf's single goal was to steal. Get in, grab, and get out. All in as little time as possible.

But will a jury believe a thief? They might view the theory as Wulf being a clever Shinnok Halfling who almost got away with murder.

He pictured Wulf with a rope around his neck, swinging lifelessly.

"Okay. I'll go."

Chapter 16

Lectures

Wulf nailed the last plank into the window frame. The sky was still bright and blue, but the wind blow stronger and faster, picking up speed, and fast-moving clouds darkened the horizon. The guy on the radio said the hurricane would make landfall around nightfall, but one look at the horizon and folks knew it would arrive hours sooner. This hurricane was bound to be a powerful one. Wulf felt it in his bones.

"Okay, that's all of them," Wulf said, turning to his mother. They had split up hurricane duties. Wulf collected wood from the stack Mrs. Garcia bought and boarded up the windows while Ma collected water and made sure all the lamps had plenty of oil.

Ma sat at the table. Three ceramic jugs of water rested on the floor by the sink, and both lamps were on the table, but Ma hadn't put oil in them yet. Instead, she stared at the old wall clock, watching it tick, tick, tick. The clock had been there for as long as Wulf could remember. *Bloody miracle the thing still works.*

"The windows are done, Ma."

Maria startled as though someone had grabbed her from behind. She took a breath and said, "Yes, good." She then lit one of the lamps. The flickering flame glowed a soft yellow.

The sight took Wulf back to his first hurricane. He was five years old. The winds buffeted the building, and rain leaked through the boarded windows. An early gust had thrown a tree limb at the window, shattering the glass. He and Ma sat huddled together on the couch, waiting for the storm to pass.

They ran out of lamp oil two hours after sunset.

That night felt like it would never end.

"Shouldn't we wait 'til evening?" Wulf asked. Early or right on time, the hurricane wouldn't reach Malkin City for hours yet. Wulf shivered, thinking of enduring another storm through the long night. Night was a dangerous time for a storm. During the day, you had a bit of light to see by, but at night? The wind, rain, and flying debris would make it impossible for the Blydd with the keenest eyesight to see.

And rising waters made the danger ten times greater. Not for the first time, Wulf was grateful to live on the second floor. If things got real nasty, they could go upstairs and stay with Ruthless.

"Ma?" He walked over to the table. In the low light, her eyes looked so tired and hollow.

What was the last time she slept?

Granted, sleep was hard to find when you worked the day shift five times a week and the night shift four times. And Wulf being wanted by the bricks only made matters worse.

"Yes?" she finally answered.

"Shouldn't we wait 'til evening to light these?" He pointed at the lamp.

Maria smirked, erasing a bit of her tiredness. "You might be able to see without it, but I can't."

"Oh, Right." Sometimes, he forgot how much better his senses were than Ma's. Recognizing faces from half a block away. Overhearing a whispered conversation. Things only a Halfling could do.

"Is everything okay? I know me being wanted by the bricks ain't good, but..."

Maria sighed heavily. "It's more than that. I..." She paused for a long moment, staring at the flame. "Beowulf, please sit down."

Wulf complied, his blood turning cold. Ma only used that tone when she wanted to give him a lecture. Bloody hell. He was an adult. He was too old for lectures. But she was still his mother.

"Do you want me to stop thieving?" he asked. The lectures usually pointed to this. The earliest lectures explained the importance of trusting the right people and running from the wrong kind. The kind wearing dark green. The next set were about him going back to school so he could have a future. Every person, even those in Mull, needed an education. The rest involved him choosing a better path. He would not have to be a thief if he got a real job.

Why didn't you teach me to read then? he thought bitterly. He shoved it away. Ma did try teaching him after he quit school, but he was too damn stubborn.

Maria smiled, but it didn't reach her eyes. "Yes, but there is something else I want to talk about. I haven't been fair to you, Beowulf. I've kept secrets. I..." Tears gleamed in her dark eyes.

"Ma, are you okay?"

"I met your father when I was sixteen," Maria began, staring into the flickering flame. Wulf sat absolutely still. His father. Ma never talked about his father. Never even said his name.

"I was working as a maid in a townhouse near the Fae Embassy," she continued. "The owner rented out rooms to Fae visiting the city. Because of the Seelie Court's laws, Fae can't stay in hotels. They must be invited into the house and invited again to spend the night.

"A Shinnok family was visiting from the Islands and intended to stay with relatives, but the youngest son had a rebellious streak and wanted space away from the family." She smirked. "Seventeen-year-olds are the same no matter what their species. He, um..." She cleared her throat. "He asked the owner if he could rent a room for a few months. The owner agreed. He preferred long-term renters. As silly as it sounds, it was love at first sight. From the first moment we met each other's eyes, I knew that I loved him, and he loved me."

Maria paused, watching the flame. Wulf did not dare to move a muscle or make a sound. This was more than he had ever heard about his father. What if she stopped? What if he never learned more?

What is his name? Please, just tell me his name.

"At first," she finally continued, "we just talked. Stealing a few moments here and there to ask about one another's lives. Likes and dislikes. Plans for the future. We had to be careful. The owner would have been furious if he caught me speaking casually to a guest. And your father's family was very traditional. Very strict. If they learned that he was in love with a human, they would have dragged him back to the Islands."

"Is he alive?" Wulf's voice faltered. He feared that Ma would not answer, that she would stop talking, leaving him forever in the dark.

"His older brother found out and told the rest of the family," Maria said. A tear ran down her face. "They threatened to disown him, but he didn't care. He wrote a letter stating that he wanted to break away from the family, forfeiting his name."

Wind swept through the street and rattled the apartment. The lamp flame flickered. Wulf waited for his mother to continue. When she did not, he asked, "Where is he?"

"We planned to run away together," Maria went on as though Wulf had not spoken. "Start fresh in a new town. His family discovered the plan. They sent his brother and a group of humans to stop him. The men broke into the house and demanded that he come with them. He refused. They started beating him. I... I was so afraid. I hid in a closet. I couldn't breathe or move." She closed her eyes. More tears fell. "He stopped moving. God, there was so much blood. The men dragged him away. I wanted to contact the police, but the owner refused. He said it was none of our business, and we should forget that he ever stayed here.

"I kept waiting for your father to send a letter or return, but he disappeared. The family sailed back to the Islands. And when I discovered that I was going to have you, I feared that the men who hurt your father would hurt you. So, I packed my few belongings and went to Mull. Not the best place to hide, but it was the last place anybody would look."

"Who were they?"

Maria stared at him, her dark eyes glistening.

"The men. Who were they?"

"They were family men."

A chill ran down Wulf's spine. "The Five Families? My father was involved with those guys?"

"He was a distant relation, but not distant enough. He wanted to break away, but he knew too much. Had told me too much."

The room spun. Wulf tasted bile in the back of his throat. "What was his name?"

"Camden," his mother lied. He knew it was a lie, but the lie gave him a strange sense of comfort. The rest was the truth. "Camden Pritchard o'r Shinnok." She met Wulf's eyes. "I see so much of him in you, Beowulf. You have his eyes and his smile, and the way you throw yourself headlong into things without thinking." She shook her head, smiling. Truly smiling. "You're so much like him."

Wulf heard the words, but he didn't know what to do with them. He guessed he should feel happy. Lots of folks commented on how a kid looked or acted like their mom or dad. Dav had his mother's eyes, and Suzette, a girl who lived on the third floor before getting married, had her father's temper. But whose eyes did Wulf have? Where did his Shinnok half come from?

Well, he had some answers now.

"Thanks, Ma, but why tell me this stuff now?" *Why did you wait?* Where were these answers when he was six years old?

"Because you've gotten yourself involved with strange people."

"C'mon, Ma. Bookie ain't that weird."

"I meant Lewin Manning."

"Oh." The apartment grew silent save for the clock ticking and other tenants moving around, the movements and voices muffled by the walls.

"I feared," Maria continued, "a member of the Sidhe or Halfling family would see your photo in the papers and recognize you as Camden's son. Have you noticed anyone strange following you? Faces in a crowd that look familiar?"

"Not really." But the thought got his mind racing. Had someone followed him? Watched from a distance? Ruthless had eyes and ears everywhere. One of them would have noticed.

But if the person were a Shinnok...

"What about this Carlos Vallejo person?" Maria asked. "How did you meet him?"

"Mac introduced us."

"Who introduced him to Macsen?"

"I don't know." Wulf felt cold, numb. Macsen never said how he and Carlos met. It hadn't seemed important. "Do you think the Sidhe Family sent Carlos to get me and Macsen involved in this Whateley business? Is that why he up and vanished?"

"Ruthless and I searched every available public record. No one named Carlos Vallejo lives in Malkin City."

Wulf cursed under his breath. Mercy sakes alive, how could he be so stupid twice? When Birdie explained the Ciceron Station job, he knew it sounded too good to be true. Hadn't he thought the same about this job? A guy gone for a whole month, leaving his big fancy house empty? A thief's dream job.

Too good to be true.

"Carlos gave me and Macsen different addresses on purpose. He wanted me to be alone when I broke into Whateley's house. That way,

I'd get the blame." Wulf locked eyes with his mother. "How much do me and Camden look like?"

"Other than your hair color and eye shape, you're his spitting image."

"Bloody hell. Then someone in the Sidhe family recognized me, right?"

Was this the reason Ruthless told him to lie low? Did he know about Wulf's father? But why? Why would Maria tell him and say nothing to her own son?

"It's possible." She placed a hand on Wulf's shoulder. "I can't force you to stay inside and hide. As much as I want to. You're an adult. Please be careful, son."

"I promise, Ma."

Maria gently brushed a lock of hair away from his eyes and went to the cabinets. She removed two more pitchers and began filling them with water. "Would you mind carrying these up to Mrs. Avita? I'm worried she won't have enough."

"Sure, Ma."

Wulf watched his mother, wondering if he should ask her again. Maria never said if his father was still alive. Wulf's gut told him that Camden, or whatever his real name was, was dead. But what if he was alive? Could Wulf talk to him, or would it be too dangerous? He might still be involved with the Five Families. But if he was alive and involved, why would he allow this to happen? It made no bloody sense.

Taking the pitchers upstairs, Wulf decided not to ask.

In a way, it was better if his father was dead.

It meant that he hadn't abandoned them.

Chapter 17
Dead Ends

"What is the normal procedure with cases like this?" Celeste asked as she and Asa walked down a commercial street in the Business District. Gray clouds raced across the sky, heading westward. The handful of shoppers rushed down the street, hoping to get home before the hurricane made landfall this evening. One person bumped into Asa and shouted a quick apology as he hurried away.

"What do you mean?" he asked.

"We know that Wulf Smith is innocent. We've established that fairly well. So, what do we do? We can't condemn an innocent man."

Asa rolled his eyes. "Smith is hardly innocent. He broke into the Whateley house on the twelfth. He even admits it!" *Why the hell does everything happen on the twelfth?* Emilio Grady, acting under Lewin Manning's orders, collected extortion payments on the twelfth, and his son, Julian Grady, was killed by a mugger on the twelfth. Was there a connection or just a coincidence? From what Asa had seen, Manning had a cruel streak. He must have chosen the twelfth as a way to rub salt in Grady's wound.

Granted, Manning didn't seem like he was forcing Grady. At the trial, Grady had stared directly at Manning while he testified, explaining every detail of their scheme. The old man kinda seemed happy about it, in a twisted kind of way.

"Innocent of murder," Celeste emphasized. She pulled a small notebook out of her skirt pocket. "None of the neighbors saw anyone suspicious that night, nor did Dr. Whateley have any enemies."

"No obvious clues either." Asa sighed. They had no real evidence or leads, which was why they were going to question Alfred Whateley again. This time at his place of business.

Asa thought it was a weird choice. They spoke with Alfred the morning after the murder, and Jones talked to him a few days later. Both testimonies were identical. No deviations or added or missing details. But Reyes insisted that they keep searching and keep asking question until they found the real killer.

He never thought Smith was guilty, Asa realized, a light dawning in his mind. From the very beginning, when the maid swore that Beowulf Smith was the one, Reyes did not buy it. Why?

"What?"

"Nothing." Reyes's question echoed in his mind. *Would you stay and argue, or would you run like hell?*

"Run like hell," Asa muttered.

"What's that?" A gust of wind blew by. Celeste ducked, avoiding a piece of newspaper.

"Just thinking. Perhaps Alfred remembered something new." *Please, God, show me what to do. Tell me which questions to ask.*

Would you stay...

Asa squeezed his eyes shut, banishing the question.

"Are you feeling okay?" Celeste asked. "We can question Alfred later."

"Later might be too late."

They walked another block and arrived at Venegas Collections, an art dealership specializing in paintings and antiques from across the Commonwealth. The vases and trinkets in the display window were each worth a small fortune. Asa didn't get it. Sure, some of the landscape paintings were nice to look at, but spending three months' salary on one single thing?

Then again, the people who bought these paintings and vases made more money in a week than Asa earned all year. They had to spend the extra coin on something, he guessed.

A bell chimed as they walked inside. More paintings, vases, and odds and ends crowded the space. A young woman with long, dark brown hair tied in a ponytail navigated the space and greeted them with a warm smile.

Asa's heart skipped a beat. It was Esmeralda Banning, the Brownie Fae who worked as Emilio Grady's secretary for two years. Clean record. And she testified against Grady, speaking vehemently about how horrible she felt working for a man who had no qualms about hurting others, and hoping that he got every bad thing he deserved.

Her testimony might have sounded over the top, but she was a Brownie. The subspecies was predisposed to helping others. In their minds, no job was too big or too small so long as they could be helpful. Many gravitated towards secretarial or social work.

Then how the hell did she wind up working at an art dealership?

And what were the odds of Asa running into two of Jones's former coworkers?

Esmeralda's large brown eyes widened. "I know you! You're one of the nice police officers who helped Invictus!"

Asa managed to turn his grimace into a smile. Jones had helped the police, not the other way around, but dammit if the newspapers didn't get it backwards. An average man taking down a crime ring was far more interesting, and far more likely to sell papers, than the police doing the same thing. In other words, doing their bloody job!

"Your name is Bishop, right?" Esmeralda asked.

"Yes, and this is my partner, Officer Lawson."

"Nice to meet you. Are you here to buy a painting?" she asked sweetly.

"No. We want to see Alfred Whateley. Is he available?"

"I don't know. He and Mrs. Venegas, she is the owner, were in a meeting. I'll see if they are done. Oh." Her face fell. "Are you here about Alfred's father?"

"Yes, ma'am."

"I see." Esmeralda dry washed her hands. "Did you find the one who... The person who did it?"

"Not yet, but we have a few suspects." *A few suspects. I bloody wish!*

Esmeralda nodded gravely and walked into a back room.

Asa glanced at the wall clock, the wooden casing carved to mimic a rising sun at the top and oak trees on the sides. A quarter till noon. The hurricane would make landfall this evening, right around sunset. He had plenty of time to go home after this and check on supplies. His parents were always nervous about storms and rushed to the store the moment they heard that one was approaching, buying extra lamp oil, food, water, and even blankets. If the corner store near his apartment was already closed, he could ask...

He bit down on his tongue. No, as much as he wanted to ask, wanted to see them...

Celeste wandered over to the paintings. Each one was set in a gold gilt frame, polished to a mirror shine. "This one is from Kallendon," she said, pointing at a painting of mountains. The peaks seemed to stretch all the way to the sky, hidden in the clouds. The small plaque read: "View of the Scalaad Caelum Mountains" by Hector Owens, F.C. 472.

"You ever been?" Asa asked, grateful for the distraction. He glanced around. Another employee was helping a customer, fidgeting nervously as she took her sweet time choosing between two nearly identical vases. The other employees carefully carried paintings and antiques into the back room for safekeeping.

His mind wandered back to Esmeralda Banning. What were the odds of him running into her on another case? The Business District alone boasted hundreds of shops, ranging from antiques to mechanical supplies to stationery. She could have worked in any of them, but instead, she worked for the same business as Alfred Whateley.

Granted, the odds of Wulf Smith also being involved were just as slim. And yet, here he was, trying to prove the innocence of a career thief.

Asa wanted to scream.

Celeste nodded, light brown curls bouncing. "Once as a kid. My father grew up there. Told me all kinds of stories. What about your folks? Where are they from?"

Asa's skin crawled. Why did Celeste need to know? His family was none of her business. Why did she even think she could ask...

It's just a question. She doesn't mean anything buy it.

"My mother and father are both Malkinese. Born and raised right here in the city. I hope you don't mind me asking, but does everyone in Kallendon look like you?" Not the politest way to ask that question, but as long as it got them away from the subject of his parents, so be it.

Celeste smirked. "No. Most Kallendonic are as pale as the Scanlannish. My mother was Amistadian."

"Really? How did they meet?" Those provinces were on opposite sides of the Commonwealth.

"Dad was a wanderer. He met my mother while walking down the Attakapas River. Passed through her town and found a reason to stop wandering."

"You mean sailing?"

"No, walking. He wanted to walk the entire length."

"That's... ambitious." It was the nicest word he could find. The Attakapas River was almost a thousand miles long, starting in Scanlan and ending at the Ruic Channel. "How did he wind up in Malkin City?"

Celeste hesitated. Focusing on the painting, she said, "Mom passed away when I was ten. Dad thought a fresh start would be best." She paused. "He said he couldn't walk down a single street, see a single building or tree, without thinking about her and knowing that she was gone. Said that was no way for a person to live."

"Sorry," he said quietly.

"Anyway, it was for the best. I had access to the best schools and universities in the Commonwealth, and Dad always had work."

Esmeralda walked up to them, a bounce in her step. "Alfred is ready to see you. He's waiting at the counter." She smiled.

Asa glanced over and locked eyes with Alfred. The man's eyes were blue ice.

Wonderful.

Asa and Celeste walked over to the counter, Celeste one step ahead. Alfred was more receptive towards her during the first interview.

"Good morning, Mr. Whateley," Celeste said politely.

"Get to the point," Alfred snapped.

"Okay, fine. What happened on the night of the twelfth? Do you remember anything new?"

"No, I already told you. My wife and I were on the third floor, trying to get the baby to sleep. We didn't hear or see anything unusual until the gunshot. I heard Mrs. Palacio scream, rushed downstairs, and found my father's body. I called the police immediately."

"You didn't hear anyone arguing?" Asa asked.

"No."

Another man, Malkinese and in his late sixties judging by his white and gray hair, walked over to Alfred. "We need to move the inventory upstairs."

"I know!" Alfred snapped. He grimaced and said, "Sorry, Jose. Just give me a moment. Please."

Jose looked like he was going to retort but held his tongue. He picked up the nearest vase and carried it into the back room.

A little boy, about six or seven years old with the same blond hair and blue eyes as Alfred, peered through the doorway. He stared at Asa and Celeste curiously.

"Arlan, go sit in Mrs. Venegas's office," Alfred said. "I'll be done in a few minutes."

"Is he your son?" Asa asked. He met Alfred's wife and brother, but he never saw the children.

"No, officer, I just met him today." Alfred glared at him.

"Are you a policeman?" Arlan asked. He took a hesitant step closer. Asa noted a plaster cast on the boy's right arm.

"Yes, he's a policeman, and I'm a policewoman. Your dad is help us solve a case." Celeste smiled at the boy. Arlan shyly smiled back.

"What case? Do you have a badge?"

"A very important case." Celeste removed the golden badge from her belt and handed it to Arlan. "Do you know what these words say?"

"Malkin City Police," he sounded out.

"Wow, you're a great reader!" Celeste smiled brightly, her hazel eyes shining. "What grade are you in?"

"Second. Mrs. Townsend's class at Secundus Park Elementary. But we have a new teacher 'cause Mrs. Townsend and her husband are on a vacation."

"That sounds fun. Do you like school, Arlan?"

"Yes."

Asa's skin crawled, as though hundreds of invisible insects were scurrying over his arms and back. What did the boy say? Asa tried to recall each word, but he was only halfway listening. Bloody hell, what was it? Secundus Park? The park and surrounding neighborhood were due east of the Old City. Made sense Arlan attended school there. No, not the school. Another word, another detail. Asa grounded his teeth. It was so close, but it was like reaching for a plate on the top shelf. So close, his fingers just barely able to touch...

"What happened to your arm, Arlan?" Celeste asked.

Alfred placed a protective hand on the child's shoulder. "Playground mishap. Arlan fell backwards out of a swing."

"Oh dear!"

"I have to wear a cast for a whole month," Arlan replied.

"That's no fun. Are you out of school today?"

"Yeah." The boy's eyes lit up. "Because of the hurricane. I've never seen one before." Arlan glanced down at the badge and then met Celeste's eyes again. "Are you going to find the person who hurt my granddad?"

Asa's heart sank. Of course the kid knew. Kinda hard to hide the fact that a loved one was gone forever.

Celeste looked at Arlan for a silent moment. She then said, "Yes, I promise we will find them."

Arlan looked up at Alfred, as though for confirmation. A few yellowish bruises mottled the skin under his collar, along the collarbone and the back of the neck. Asa recalled getting similar bruises after falling out of a tree.

"Go sit in the office, Arlan," said Alfred. "And give Officer Lawson her badge back."

The boy complied and disappeared through the doorway.

"Thanks," Alfred said quietly. "We're trying to protect him from the worst of it, but he's a smart kid. He knows his grandfather isn't coming home again. We..." He swallowed a lump in his throat. "Look, I know y'all are just doing your job. I shouldn't be an ass about it. I just..."

"It's hard to lose a parent," Celeste said. "And to lose one so suddenly." She shrugged.

"Yeah." Alfred glanced around. The handful of customers were gone, and employees carefully moved the inventory. Two boarded up the display window. "Listen, if I had more to tell you, I would. But there is nothing else. Just the gunshot, and Mrs. Palacio swears she saw Beowulf Smith." He frowned. "You know, I read about him in the papers. I thought he was going clean."

"We thought so, too," Asa lied. Smith was a bloody thief. The papers could praise him all they wanted, but that did not change the facts. "Well, Mr. Whateley, if you need us, don't hesitate to call." Asa shook his hand.

They walked outside, and a blast of wind nearly knocked them down. People quickened their paces, clutching bags of food and supplies in their arms. One man lost his hat, but he hurried along, not seeming to care.

"What do you think?" Celeste asked, frowning.

"That this is a dead-end case." The words left a bitter taste in his mouth. The Malkin City Police recorded a few dead cases every year. Cases left unsolved due to lack of evidence or witnesses. The idea of having a dead case on his record galled him.

Celeste's frown deepened, and she looked away.

"What?"

"I just... I never fell out of a swing set."

"Neither have I, but trees." Asa smirked. "Damn near broke half the bones in my body falling out of trees."

Celeste nodded and said nothing.

Okay, what's bothering her?

Asa glanced up at the sky. The gray clouds inched closer, turning darker.

"Come on," he said, walking faster. "Reyes will wonder what's keeping us."

Chapter 18

Greer Island

Invictus gripped the boat's railing so tightly that his knuckles hurt. Each time the boat pitched in the choppy water, he feared being thrown overboard. His stomach twisted in knots just thinking of being submerged, unable to surface, unable to breathe.

He tore his eyes away from the water and glanced at the sky. Dark clouds gathered near the horizon. The gusty wind propelled them closer and closer.

It hadn't looked so bad at the docks, he thought as lightning flashed.

Granted, Captain Tartan, the officer in charge of the boats ferrying to Greer Island, had looked at him and Riggs as though they had two heads when they explained their task. Tartan, despite reading the orders from Captain Reyes three times, hesitated and asked if this was really necessary.

"Can't y'all wait a few days?"

"What do you bloody think?" Riggs asked, jabbing the order form with his finger. He glared at Tartan, and the captain relented.

"God, grant these idiots Your mercy," Tartan muttered under his breath as he went to ready the boat. "Myself included."

"This is bloody stupid," Riggs complained as the boat pitched again. The officer complained the entire way, starting the second they left Captain Reyes's office. But he carried out the captain's instructions, nonetheless. "Out on the water right before a hurricane makes landfall. Bloody stupid!" A wave crashed onto the deck, soaking his and Invictus's shoes. Riggs shouted a curse that Invictus had never heard before and did not care to hear a second time.

Invictus spied a green and gray mass near the horizon. Greer Island, the largest and most secure prison in the Commonwealth, and the current residence of Emilio Grady.

He felt like he was going to be sick.

Could he really face this man again? The man who had smiled and earned Invictus's trust while wearing a mask the whole time? What if Grady wore another mask today? A mask that Invictus would foolishly trust?

No, you saw through the mask once. You can see through it again.

The boat sailed into a small harbor. A single pier with only one boat, tied securely to the dock and with the mast taken down. Two guards in dark green stood guard, and both were armed with swords in dark green scabbards.

"Why do they have swords?" Invictus wondered out loud.

"No guns allowed on the Island," Riggs said. "Less chance of the prisoners getting hold of them and escaping."

Invictus nodded, appreciating the simple logic. *Well, that's one less thing to worry about.*

A massive wave crashed into the pier, soaking the two guards. Both stood their ground, but the sight sent panic rushing through Invictus's veins. Could he have withstood that wave? Or would it have sent him plunging into the water?

Does Mr. Grady know I can't swim? Thanks to the spies sent to Niantic, Grady knew a disturbing amount of information about him. Did Grady choose today because of the rough weather? Did he want Invictus to be on edge? To be frightened?

A third guard walked down the pier, asked if the other two were alright, and then addressed Riggs. "Do you have any weapons?"

"No, sir."

"Good." He signaled for Tartan to toss him the towrope. He deftly tied it to the dock and motioned for Invictus and Riggs to follow him.

Invictus stepped onto the pier, his legs shaking. The water made the wood slick. *Dear God, please, let me keep my balance.*

"What the hell are you doing here?" asked one of the guards. He was as tall as a Blydd Fae, but his hair and eyes were both dark. He gripped the hilt of his sword, ready to draw.

"We received—" Invictus began, but Riggs cut him off.

"Official police business. We need to speak with one of your prisoners."

"Which one?"

"Emilio Grady."

The guard gave Riggs a dubious look. "Couldn't this have waited until after the hurricane?"

"No." Riggs glared, his hands clenched into fists.

The guard shook his head. "Fine. But if you stay too long, you will be stuck here until the storm passes."

A knot formed in Invictus's gut. Being stranded on the prison island never crossed his mind, but it made logical sense. Boats could not sail in rough weather.

How long does it take for a hurricane to pass? Thunderstorms rarely lasted more than an hour, but some storms lingered the entire day. Was this another part of Grady's plan? Give Invictus timely information and then ensure he cannot leave, delaying the case? Allowing the real murderer to escape?

Did Grady know the murderer's identity? But how?

Save the questions for later. You'll have the answers soon.

He hoped.

They followed the guards down the pier and up a short hill to one of the gray stone buildings. Massive stone walls topped with barbwire surrounded the prison complex. Guard towers, rising five stories into the air, lined the walls, and each one employed a trio of archers with archaic crossbows.

The rest of the island was a healthy, vivid green. Lush green grass rippled in the wind, and knee-high reeds grew along the water's edge. But there were no trees or shrubs.

Nowhere for prisoners to hide, Invictus guessed.

They entered the nearest tower. The guard stationed there quickly locked the door. Three deadbolts secured by combination locks. One of the guards from the docks relayed Riggs's message to the tower guard. The tower guard, who looked like a Bannock Fae with shimmering green eyes and pointed ears, nodded.

"May I see these orders?"

Riggs handed him the letter with Reyes's signature and the Fifth Precinct's seal.

The tower guard returned the letter and led them down a long, narrow hallway. Invictus could have stood in the center and touched both sides with ease, it was so narrow.

"Stop," the tower guard ordered when they reached a small room. Two more guards were stationed in front of another locked door. They searched Invictus and Riggs. Riggs sneered and muttered curses under his breath but complied. Invictus felt uncomfortable as the guard searched his pockets. The guard removed a fountain pen and placed it on a nearby table.

"Why are—"

"Could be used as an improvised weapon," the Bannock guard explained. "Trust me, you don't want a pen in your eye."

Invictus tasted bile in the back of his throat. "Is that a possibility?"

"A remote one. We keep the prisoners well-guarded, but best to be cautious."

"What should we do with this, sir?" The guard held up Invictus's pocket watch. The silver gleamed in the low light.

The Bannock guard eyed it warily. "What is it made of?"

"Silver," Invictus answered. "But I always keep it in my pocket," he quickly added, seeing the unease on the Bannock guard's face.

"Which prisoner do you want to see?"

"Emilio Grady."

"Grady is a full-blooded human. Let him keep it," the Bannock told his colleague.

With the search complete, the Bannock guard led them down a narrow, windowless corridor. Gas lamps, protected by metal casings, illuminated the hall every twenty feet, creating pockets of darkness in between.

The guard rounded a corner, and the corridor turned into a maze. Invictus tried to keep track of all the twists and turns, but it felt like the guard was leading them in circles, disorientating them on purpose. The guard then unlocked a random door and led them into a room that was divided in half by a mesh gate.

Desks and chairs were set up on both sides of the mesh, but the furniture on the opposite side was nailed to the floor. Neither side had windows.

They really don't want to take any chances with prisoners escaping.

"Wait here." The Bannock guard hurried out, closing and locking the door behind him.

Invictus took a seat and checked the time. Five minutes past noon.

"Damn stupid," Riggs muttered as he paced around the narrow room. "Should have waited until tomorrow."

"Will it really be that bad?" Invictus asked.

Riggs glared at him.

"The storm, I mean."

The policeman sneered. "Ain't no storm. It's a bloody hurricane! If we don't get off this bleeding island soon, we'll be stranded until it passes. Damn thing could last all night!"

Invictus feared that any response, even agreeing with Riggs, would anger the police officer further, so he held his tongue.

The gaslamp guttered and almost went out as wind buffeted the building. Invictus silently prayed that the lights would not go out, stranding them in darkness.

The door on the opposite side of the mesh opened. Emilio Grady, escorted by a massive Blydd Fae guard, sat down across from Invictus. The older man, though a bit pale, appeared healthy. His white hair was recently trimmed, and his face was cleanly shaven. His dark red prison issued shirt and trousers were also clean and in good repair.

Mr. Grady eyed Invictus curiously.

Invictus's palms began to sweat. He had not been face to face with Mr. Grady since the trial. The entire time, he was terrified that the Mannings would retaliate, or that Mr. Grady would twist facts around and try to implicate Invictus alongside himself.

Neither happened, but Invictus was a nervous wreck and suffered nightmares for weeks afterward.

"So, you did receive my letter," Mr. Grady said. "I feared they weren't being delivered."

"There was more than one?" Invictus stammered. He dug his fingernails into his palms. He was in control, not his fear. And what did he have to fear? Mr. Grady was on the other side of a gate and under a prison guard's watchful eye. What did Invictus have to fear?

"Not to you." Mr. Grady shot a glare at Riggs. "What is he doing here?"

"I'm escorting—"

"I asked for Mr. Jones, not his babysitter. You are dismissed."

Riggs's face turned dark red. "Listen here, you old—"

"I want him dismissed," Mr. Grady said to the Blydd guard as though he were speaking to his butler.

The guard glared darkly at Riggs. "Leave."

"But—"

"Leave." His silver eyes flashed, reminding Invictus of Ruthless.

Riggs opened his mouth to protest. He then sneered and stalked towards the door. Finding it locked, he grounded his teeth and pounded on it.

"What's wrong?" the Bannock guard asked. Riggs shoved him aside and slammed the door shut. The echo reverberated through the room, making Invictus's ear ring.

"Why did—"

"How have you been, Mr. Jones?" Mr. Grady asked cordially.

Invictus blinked, unsure how to respond. He stole a glance at the guard. The guard, also armed with a sword, stood beside Grady as still as a statue. The same posture Hallvard the butler had assumed during the dinner party. And he obeyed Mr. Grady just as swiftly. Why?

"Fine, I guess."

"Do you like your new job?"

"It's not what I expected." Invictus swallowed a lump in his throat. *No, be brave. You have to be brave.* He tried to summon Spes Sherrington's bravery and confidence, recalling all the times the detective interviewed criminals. The criminals were never able to harm Spes, and Mr. Grady, sitting on the other side of a mesh gate, could not harm him. "But it's better than working for a crime family."

Mr. Grady smirked. "I see. Have you seen Europa lately? I sent her several letters, but she hasn't replied yet."

"Are you surprised?" he asked harshly and then winced. Europa Grady left Malkin City the day after the trial concluded.

"No, not really." Mr. Grady sighed heavily. "I'm glad you received my letter, Mr. Jones. I read about Dr. Whateley's unfortunate death in the papers. Terrible. Just terrible." He shook his head solemnly.

"They allow prisoners to have newspapers?"

"An incentive for good behavior."

Invictus chose his next words carefully. If he was not careful, Mr. Grady would take control of the conversation, leading it to where he wanted it to go, and tricking Invictus into believing that he had important information.

"Did you know Dr. Armand Whateley?"

"Only in passing. He was Taran Manning's personal physician for many years."

Invictus's heart skipped a beat. Taran Manning. Lewin Manning's father and the head of the Sidhe Family. "Really? I would not have thought a Sidhe Fae would have a human doctor."

Mr. Grady smiled. "One would think. Regardless, Armand Whateley had a healthy connection to the Sidhe Family, as well as the Malkinese and Halfling Families."

"And people with healthy connections to the Families aren't killed in their homes," he hazarded.

"Precisely."

Okay, so that crossed three names off Invictus's list. "What about the Barrish and Amistadian Families?"

"Well, someone has done his research." Mr. Grady smiled, slipping on another mask. Three months ago, Invictus would have believed that mask, thinking that Grady was truly impressed. "But no, Mr. Jones. Your assumption is wrong. The Families work together. Never against. Peace is the Commonwealth's best interest."

Well, so much for that hunch.

But Dr. Whateley was connected to the Families.

"Was he killed by someone working against the Families?"

"I doubt anyone would be so stupid."

"Then who?"

"Mr. Jones, I have been locked up on this godforsaken rock for months. How could I possibly know the killer's identity?"

"But if you don't know, why did you send for me?" Frustration built in his voice. He bit his tongue. *Stay calm. You have to stay calm.* If he did not, Grady would gain the upper hand.

"To give what little information I have. How good is your memory?"

"Fairly good."

Mr. Grady shook his head. "Don't sell yourself short. Now, listen closely." He told Invictus a string of numbers. "Repeat it."

Invictus did so.

"Excellent. Tell me, what do you think it means?"

"It's too long to be a telephone number. Bank account?"

Mr. Grady nodded. "Excellent work, Mr. Jones."

"What am I supposed to do with it?" Did the account belong to Dr. Whateley? Invictus reviewed his ledgers, but if the account was secret, it would not be reflected in official reports. Did it contain the money he earned from treating Taran Manning? But how was it relevant to the case?

"You are the one working with detectives, Mr. Jones. Detect." Mr. Grady addressed the Blydd guard. "This meeting is over. Goodbye, Invictus. I hope you weather the storm well."

"Wait, that's it?"

Mr. Grady eyed him curiously. "Did you expect more?"

"I... I don't know." He shrugged.

"Perhaps I will have more next time." The guard escorted Grady out of the room.

If he just wanted to give me a bank account number, why not include it in the letter? Why have Invictus sail all the way to Greer Island?

Did Mr. Grady merely want to see if Invictus would obey his instructions, no questions asked?

If so, Invictus had played right into Grady's game.

Feeling a bit foolish, he knocked on the door. The series of locks clicked, and he joined Riggs in the corridor.

"What did he want?"

"He gave me a bank account number." But which bank? Malkin City Trust was the largest in the city, but there was also First City Bank, Commonwealth Central, and half a dozen smaller ones.

"What? That's it?" Riggs's expression darkened.

"Yes."

"A bloody bank account number! That bloody—" Riggs disintegrated into a series of curses that made Invictus's entire face burn red.

The Bannock guard, hearing the tirade, sprinted down the corridor. He had his sword partially drawn. "What is it? What happened?"

"Officer Riggs is just upset," Invictus said. "The meeting didn't go as well as we hoped."

"I see. Officer Riggs, I will reprimand you for foul language if you don't—"

"Fine! Bloody fine. Sir," he added, seething from head to toe.

"Be grateful it was a short meeting," the Bannock guard told them. "The hurricane is stirring up the Channel. The harbormaster is closing all ports in half an hour. Let's get you off this rock."

***

They reached the mainland just in time. The wind had picked up considerably, and waves crashed onto the dock, threatening to seize anyone unfortunate enough to be walking by and drag them under.

Invictus peered around the docks. Other than a handful of workers securing boats, the area was deserted. The dockside shops, usually brimming with activity this time of day, were closed with their doors and windows boarded up.

Perhaps a hurricane is worse than a thunderstorm.

Invictus, Riggs, and Captain Tartan hurried down the dock.

"Mercy sakes alive, I'm never sailing in a storm again," Tartan breathed. "What was your captain thinking, sending you to Greer?"

"Good bloody question," Riggs said through his teeth. The officer had raved during the entire voyage. Invictus barely paid attention as he gripped the railing, praying they would return to the docks safely.

"Well, we're back. Thank God." Tartan disappeared inside the harbormaster's office, a stout, square building adjacent to the marina.

"Come on," Riggs snapped. "No need to keep Reyes waiting."

"Wait." Invictus grabbed Riggs's arm. The officer whirled around and glared at him. Invictus let go and shrank back. "We should find the bank account's location."

"It can wait."

"Just one bank," Invictus pleaded. "If the account isn't there, we'll go to the Precinct. Please."

Riggs relented. "Which one?"

The invisible string tugged at Invictus's mind. "Malkin City Trust."

The bank was located in the heart of the Business District, a mile north of the harbor. A few people hurried down the nearly empty streets. Every building had their windows boarded up, and the bank was no exception.

"How bad are hurricanes?" Invictus asked as they walked up the front steps.

"Depends," Riggs replied. The walk seemed to calm him down. "Some are no more than glorified thunderstorms, but others are deadly. When I was a kid, one hurricane flooded out the docks. Some boats were found half a mile inland. Took months for everything to get fixed. Most of the shops on the docks were destroyed, too."

"Did that include importers?" Did Mr. Grady's business suffer damage? Did the Sidhe Family help pay for repairs, ensnaring him further?

"Probably. Don't really remember."

Invictus walked up to the teller, a wizened, Malkinese man with very thick eyeglasses. "Excuse me, sir. I need to verify a bank account number."

The old man, his dark brown eyes magnified by the glasses, studied him. "Right now? We're about to close."

"Official police business." Riggs showed the teller his badge.

The teller squinted, reading the words on the badge, and then nodded. "Very well. Which account?"

Invictus repeated the number.

His hunch proved correct. The account was at Malkin City Trust. A safety deposit box under the name Julian R. Grady.

"Would you like to view the contents?" the teller asked.

"Yes, sir. Please." Invictus checked his watch. Ten minutes to two.

The teller shuffled into the bank vault, disappeared for several long minutes, and then returned with the box. He led Invictus and Riggs into a private room.

"I assume you want privacy, the teller said.

"Yes, sir. Thank you."

The teller shuffled away.

"What could Grady have hidden in here?" Riggs muttered as he unlocked the box.

A single piece of folded paper laid inside.

"What? That's it?" Riggs sneered.

Invictus unfolded the paper, revealing a charcoal drawing of a man with blood red eyes. The skin surrounding the eyes was pitch black with streaks running down the face, as though he was crying tar. The man's face was gaunt with prominent cheek and eye socket bones.

The blood red eyes glared at Invictus. He shuddered and handed the drawing to Riggs.

"What the hell?"

"Fae don't have red eyes," Invictus said, thinking out loud. He recalled everything Ruthless and Wulf had taught him about the Fae. Over a dozen subspecies and hybrids. Not a single one had solid red eyes.

Riggs stared at the drawing, his hands shaking.

"Do you recognize him?"

"Maybe. I..." He carefully folded the drawing and placed it in his pocket. "We need to show Captain Reyes."

Chapter 19
Folklore

The first raindrops started to fall as Invictus and Riggs returned to the Fifth Precinct, the cryptic drawing safely tucked in Riggs's pocket. The wind had grown dangerously strong, at times threatening to knock Invictus down, and the sky had taken on a strange, green tint. Massive black clouds dominated the horizon, advancing on the city with each gust of wind. Invictus shuddered.

"Is this normal?" he asked, pointing at the sky.

"Sometimes. Must be one hell of a storm," Riggs replied, barely sparing a glance upwards.

Invictus's gut twisted in knots. All this time, he thought hurricanes were little more than thunderstorms, but thunderstorms did not turn the sky green. The winds did not threaten to knock him over, and people did not board up windows or collect supplies or fill bathtubs with drinking water. This morning, when he overheard Pedro and Lucia, the young couple who lived across the hall, going over their list and making sure they filled the bathtub with clean water, he thought they were overreacting. But what if they weren't? What if this storm was strong each to destroy buildings and throw boats half a mile inland?

What if, during the chaos of the storm, the real murderer got away? He could sneak out of the city while everyone's minds were focused elsewhere. Merciful heavens, the murderer could have left Malkin City days ago.

The Fifth Precinct's windows were boarded, and two officers stood outside, setting long planks beside the door.

"Status?" Riggs asked them.

"Reyes wants the precinct vacated within the hour. Once everyone is gone, we'll board up the front door."

Riggs nodded and hurried inside. Invictus followed on his heels.

The emptiness struck Invictus like a punch to the chest. A mere handful of officers remained, milling about the desk area and finishing last minute storm preparations. Chairs and wastebaskets were stacked on desks, and small, personal items were gone, tucked into pockets or satchels. The officers spared them an anxious glance and quickly resumed their work.

Riggs led Invictus up the stairs and continued upwards.

"Why are you going to the third floor?" Invictus asked.

Riggs shot glare over his shoulder, not slowing for an instant.

"Don't you want to speak with Captain Reyes?"

"Later. I wanna check something first."

Riggs continued up the stairs and walked down the hall to the records room where the Precinct stored all the photos and case documents. The cramped room was barely larger than Invictus's office. Shelves lined every wall, each one filled with boxes and files. Riggs selected a photo album and placed it on the table. He unfolded the drawing, studied it, and flipped through the pages, muttering under his breath.

"Do you recognize him?" Invictus asked. He looked at the photos. Mugshots of men and women. Most appeared to be Halflings, but it was difficult to tell in black and white.

"No, I..." Riggs chewed on his lower lip. Invictus felt cold. *Is Riggs worried?* Was that possible? "I think this guy might be a type of Fae."

"But Fae don't have solid red eyes."

"Not officially." Riggs fixed Invictus with a glare. His expression then softened into a frown. "Can I tell you something?"

"Um, sure."

"I saw a Grayman once."

Invictus stared at him, puzzled. Graymen were a Fae subspecies that warned people of impending doom. They were also fictional. Every province in the Commonwealth had their own version of a Grayman, ranging from a physical creature to a spirit to a messenger from God Himself. Invictus always viewed Graymen as folklore, a popular subject for summer campfire stories, more shadow than substance.

"I'm serious," Riggs snapped.

"Okay, but I don't see—"

"Shut up and listen." He dropped his voice to a whisper. "Remember the hurricane I told you about? The one that destroyed the docks?"

Invictus nodded.

"I was nine years old. My parents were out buying supplies. We lived near the beach, so my little brothers and I decided to go shell collecting. Dad told us to stay away from the beach because of the storm, but we were kids. We didn't care. Didn't understand the danger.

"I rounded a dune and saw a man in tattered gray clothes standing near the water. I thought he was a tramp, but then I noticed his clothes."

"Clothes?" Invictus raised an eyebrow.

"Yeah. They were old. Like the clothes people wore hundreds of years ago, when the Commonwealth was founded. Long shirt with a belt, cloak, laced sandals. Those type of clothes. And they were all gray. Same as his hair and eyes and skin." Riggs shivered. "Those eyes seemed to look into my soul. The Grayman pointed at me and told me to run, to get as far inland as possible 'cause the storm would kill us if we stayed.

"He freaked me out, so I hauled ass, grabbed my brothers, and dragged them back to the house. When our parents got home, they asked why I was so scared. I was afraid they wouldn't believe me, but they got the truth out of me. Then it was Mom's turn to freak. She's real superstitious and begged my father to take us to her cousin's house in North Torpen, just on the other side of the tracks from Mull. Dad usually was a stubborn bastard, but he listened. We spent the night in a cramp townhouse, listening to the wind and rain."

"Then what?" Gusty wind buffeted the precinct. Invictus's arms broke out in goosebumps.

"Next day, Dad goes to check on the house. Except, it was gone. Only the foundation and part of the chimney were left." Riggs swallowed. "Half the neighborhood was gone. They said it was a rogue wave. If we had stayed, we would have all drowned."

Chills ran down Invictus's spine. "So, the Grayman saved you."

Riggs nodded. "Yeah. And if anyone tells you that the Graymen ain't real, remember that." He pointed at the strange drawing. "I think this guy is a rare Fae. One most people think is a myth. Grady is connected with strange Fae, right?"

"The Sidhe." The Sidhe, however, were the most well-known subspecies. Queen Waylinda herself and most of the Royal Family were Sidhe, after all. But all of them had gold eyes, not red.

Could they have hidden certain types? Kept them on the Islands? Invictus admitted that it sounded like a stretch, but according to Ruthless, the Five Families had secretly controlled Malkin City for over five hundred years. All with the Royal Family's blessing. If the Royals could keep that a secret, hidden in plain sight, what could they be hiding behind the palace's walls?

"Yeah, I've heard some weird stories about the Sidhe. Hypnotize people by locking eyes with them, right?"

"I've heard about that, too." Invictus refused to admit that Lewin Manning came within a hair's breadth of hypnotizing him. "What other mythical types of Fae are there?" He studied the drawing. How much was exaggeration and how much was factual? Anyone with a face so thin must have suffered a long illness, and red eyes surrounded by inky blackness... This past summer, Invictus had seen Fae and Halflings with every eye color and color combination imaginable. All except solid red. The exception never occurred to him until he saw this drawing.

"There are," Riggs counted off on his fingers, "Aosi, Fomori, Ghillymen, Changers, Banshee, Coylle—"

"Wait, stop!" Invictus grabbed a nearby fountain pen and wrote on the back of the drawing.

"You know that's evidence, right?"

"Yes," he said weakly. Probably should have used a different piece of paper, but too late now. "How many are there?" He had not seen any of these names listed in official books about the Fae. How did Riggs know them?

"Hell if I know. There are those and about a dozen more my grandmother told us about."

"And there are no official records?"

"None that the Royals have published. What about up in the Plains? Don't y'all have stories?"

"Yeah, I recognize Ghillymen." Would Riggs believe that Invictus saw a Ghillyman lurking in Valor Park? He might, but Invictus did not have time to explain now. "We also have will-o-wisps."

"What are those?"

"They're kind of like sprites, except they lead people away from their homes, getting them lost. Some stories claim they lead people to a different land. One that is parallel with our world." One of many stories Grandpa Gratian told him, along with tales of leviathans and hippocamps. Strange and wonderful creatures inhabiting the deep seas. Invictus always viewed them to be as fictional as Spes Sherrington, but what if they held a grain of truth?

"Huh, interesting. I'll have to ask Mom if Gran had any stories like that."

"Did any of those stories include red-eyed Fae?"

"None of them had that detail." Riggs paused, thinking. "Maybe Changers. Those can alter their faces and mimic humans."

"Alter their faces?"

"Yep. Gran said the Changers could perfectly copy a person's face, but sometimes it's just the voice. One story was about a man who got lured into the woods by a Changer mimicking his late wife's voice. He was never seen or heard from again. Course, it's just a story. I think," he added, frowning.

A shiver ran down Invictus's spine as he imagined a Fae copying his face, mimicking his voice. "How can they mimic people?"

"Beats me."

The Precinct's intercom system crackled to life. Captain Reyes's voice said, "Attention everyone. The Precinct will shut its doors in half an hour. Get what you need to take with you. We will unlock the doors at seven tomorrow morning. If you need help with storm preparation, see me in my office." The intercom crackled off.

Invictus folded up the drawing and put it in his jacket pocket.

"That's evidence, Jones."

"True, but Reyes said for us to take everything we need, and..."

Riggs's dark brown eyes narrowed. "What if you lose it?"

The thought had not crossed his mind. He unfolded the drawing and placed it on the table. The charcoal was smudged in one corner. He feared it would not survive much more folding and unfolding. "Do we have a camera?"

"Sure, but—"

"Take a photo. We can leave the original here and take a copy."

"I don't bloody know how to develop a photo! Listen, Jones, I'm only helping you because Reyes ordered me. I have my own cases to work on. I don't need—"

"Please." Invictus held up his hands. "I promise I won't lose it. I have a friend who's a graduate student at the University," he quickly formulated a lie. "He's studying anthropology and folklore. Maybe he will recognize the subspecies or whatever the drawing is referencing."

"A friend, huh?" Riggs crossed his arms. "What's his name?"

"Victor Wells." Invictus said a silent prayer that Riggs would not ask to accompany him or look up enrollment rosters. The officer, no doubt, would launch into another tirade if he discovered the lie.

Riggs scowled, staring at Invictus. He then relented. "Fine. I'll tell Reyes what we found. When are you meeting this friend?"

"Right now."

"Are you insane? Wait until tomorrow." Raindrops fell onto the roof, growing stronger and another gust buffeted the building.

"But I..." The invisible string tugged at Invictus's mind, assuring him that he was heading down the right path, and he needed to hurry. "I have a hunch."

Riggs rolled his eyes. "Like the hunch you had about Smith?"

Invictus did not know how to respond.

"The hunch that led to us arresting Grady and Manning?"

"Yes."

Riggs relented. "Okay, Jones, show your friend the drawing. But if you lose evidence, I'm throwing you under a moving carriage. Got it?"

Invictus nodded, not bothering to ask if the threat was metaphorical or actual.

Pocketing the drawing, he hurried out of the Precinct and down the street, catching the last train to Mull District.

Chapter 20
Theories

Officers Zorita and Nunez stood outside the Fifth Precinct as Celeste and Asa arrived in the carriage. The first band of the hurricane arrived, bringing with it spitting rain and strong winds. Stant needed to stop twice in order to calm down the horses. They climbed out, and Stant flicked the reins, leading the horses to the Precinct's stables. Nunez signaled for him to stop.

"All horses are being held at the First Precinct's stables."

"That's two miles away!" Stant protested. The grizzled police officer gripped the reins so tightly his knuckles turned white.

"Yeah, two miles inland," Nunez clarified. "Reyes doesn't want to take any chances. Oh, and if there is anything inside that you need, get it now. We're boarding up the doors in fifteen minutes."

Stant rolled his eyes. "Let me guess. Captain Reyes."

"Who else?" Zorita snapped. He then turned to Celeste and Asa. "That goes for y'all, too."

"Understood." Asa headed inside. Stant, fuming and muttering curses under his breath, flicked the reins and rounded Varnick Square, heading northwest. Celeste watched as he disappeared down a side street. The square, usually filled with pedestrians and vendors this time of day, was eerily silent. The clocktower chimed three times, echoing.

A gust of wind threatened to knock her down. She leaned against the stair railing, struggling to keep her balance.

"You should go," Nunez said to her. He was young, around twenty-five, and had a handsome face with kind, dark brown eyes. He glanced up at the green-tinted storm clouds, his expression a mixture of awe and fear.

"In a minute. Do you know if Invictus Jones is here?"

Nunez shook his head. "He left about five minutes ago. Ran all the way to the train station. Smartest thing I've seen him do," he added under his breath.

Celeste cursed her bad timing. She really needed his input on the case. Arlan's injuries and the way Alfred Whateley brushed them off unnerved her. Sure, plenty of kids got broken bones on the playground, and Triumvir knew she was one of them, but the way he reacted to her and Asa being police officers...

Arlan wanted to tell us something.

Something he did not want Alfred to overhear? Or something Alfred had instructed him not to talk about?

"Thanks." She walked inside.

Her footsteps echoed in the strangely quiet space. Less than a dozen officers remained, hurriedly collecting their belongings and checking to make sure they did not leave anything important. She spotted Asa near the back of the desk area speaking with Hector Riggs. Riggs, wearing his customary scowl, had his arms crossed over his chest. He nodded as Asa spoke.

"Hey, do you know where Jones went?" Celeste asked Riggs as she joined them.

"Yeah. Going to meet a friend. Except he didn't say where, and he took the only piece of evidence we found." Riggs looked like he wanted to punch a hole in the wall.

Celeste jolted. "Evidence?"

Riggs related Jones receiving a letter from Emilio Grady, meeting with him on Greer Island, and discovering a strange drawing stored in a safety deposit box.

"We think it's a rare Fae subspecies," Riggs concluded. "Jones's friend is some sort of expert." He rolled his eyes.

"Why didn't you go with him?" Asa asked, arching an eyebrow.

"In this weather? The first band is already here. I'll be lucky to get home without getting soaked to the bone."

Asa muttered under his breath. He then walked over to his desk, grabbed his small statue of Triumvir, and tucked it into his jacket pocket. The three-faced statuette stared at Celeste with small, dark wood eyes.

"Why does God have three faces?" she recalled asking her father when she was seven years old. They were traveling across the Commonwealth from their small town in the Plains to her father's home province of Kallendon to visit family. A chance to put faces to names, her father explained. Along the way, they stopped at a cathedral in Barra so her mother could pray for safe travels.

Gus Lawson crouched down beside her, his wild, light brown hair sticking out in all directions. He looked up at the decorative, stained-glass window. Triumvir, surrounded by His angels, winged creatures composed of interlocking rings and covered in a multitude of colorful eyes, stood in the center. All three faces, including the Face of Judgment, smiled, and His eyes were kind.

"So He can watch all three types of life at once," Gus had answered. "Humans, Fae, and animals. Each one is precious to Him, and He did not want to neglect the other two while watching one, so He created two more faces for Himself. This way, He cares for everyone and everything all at once."

Since then, Celeste felt comforted by this interpretation of God, though many believed that the three faces were symbolic. But if God was all powerful, why wouldn't He be able to alter His form?

The lights flickered as a massive gust shook the Precinct, followed by rolling thunder.

Riggs cursed and headed upstairs to find Captain Reyes.

"Asa, what do you think about this case?" Celeste asked.

He let out a heavy sigh. "It's strange. I thought Smith was our killer, but now..." He glanced down at the statuette. "What do you think?"

"When I talked to Smith, he assumed one of Dr. Whateley's sons killed him for the inheritance money, but both have good sources of income, so the theory doesn't hold merit." And Smith was not what she expected. Yes, he was a career thief who was nervous about being near a police officer and immediately searched for an exit. But he seemed nice and was surprisingly cooperative. Invictus's presence certainly helped, too.

And the way Smith reacted to seeing Celeste pretend to die in a chair, the same way his friend had died...

"Right," Asa said. "We ruled that out pretty quickly."

"But what if they had a different motive for killing him?" Celeste's theory stood on shifting sand. She had no evidence to back it up. None except Arlan Whateley's reaction to seeing two police officers. "Was there any history of abuse?"

"Not that I'm aware." Asa frowned, thinking. "You think the old man was hurting his sons? Lawson, the man was a hundred pounds soaking wet."

"True, but did you see Arlan's injuries? Sure, you can break an arm by falling out of a swing set, but what about the bruises on the back of his neck?"

"What bruises?"

Celeste described them.

"They sound like the bruises someone gets in a fall. And Dr. Whateley was a feeble old man. I doubt he had the strength to twist open a jam jar let alone break someone's bones."

Celeste had considered this flaw in her theory. Armand Whateley was in his late seventies and was as thin as a twig. His sons, however, were both healthy, and Alistair stood a head taller and outweighed his father by about seventy or eighty pounds. If Armand tried to hurt them or his grandson, either could have easily overpowered him.

But the location of Arlan's bruises and his reaction to her and Asa being police officers and wanting to ask them questions nagged at her. She wished Jones was still here so she could run the theory by him. Jones was not an officer, but he had a unique way of looking at things. Honestly, who else would befriend the thief who tried to mug them because one little detail did not add up?

Perhaps he could fill in a missing piece.

"Lawson." Asa tapped her on the shoulder. She looked up and saw Reyes walking down the staircase. The dozen or so remaining officers gathered around him.

"Is everybody ready?" Reyes asked the group. Everyone nodded. "Good. Now—"

"I need medical records for every person in the Whateley family," Celeste said.

Every eye turned her way.

Reyes fixed her with an icy glare. "What?"

"I would like to get them today, sir."

The captain's expression hardened like amber. "Not happening. Ask again tomorrow."

"But, sir—"

"Lawson." His voice sounded like thunder.

She relented. "Yes, sir. Tomorrow."

"Bishop, Riggs, see that Officer Lawson gets home safely. We will arrange for you to view their records after the storm."

"Yes, sir," Asa replied. Riggs sneered.

Celeste wanted to protest, but she held her tongue. If other members of the Whateley family had a history of broken bones and mystery bruises, it could validate her theory. Dr. Whateley, after all, was not born old and feeble. Could she somehow access the records today? It would only take an hour or two.

There is a giant, life threatening hurricane about to make landfall, Celeste. You can't investigate a case if you get injured yourself.

And Reyes agreed to get her the records. She just needed to be patient.

Reyes shepherded everyone out of the building and waited until Zorita and Nunez nailed the planks into place. The small crowd quickly dispersed. Most walked, but a few were able to hail cabs, the few remaining vehicles on the street. The horses stamped their hooves and rolled their eyes, frightened by the gusty wind and rain.

"Where do you live?" Asa asked. Riggs had wandered off.

"You really don't have to escort me home." Did Reyes honestly think she would go to the hospital and ask for the records? Not that it was a bad idea...

"I'd rather not piss off the captain," Asa whispered.

Celeste stole a glance at Reyes. The captain glared daggers at the sky, as though daring the hurricane to damage his precinct.

"Newydd Hill, a couple blocks away from South Torpen."

Asa nodded and walked down the street with her. Everywhere they looked, houses and shops had their windows boarded. Storefronts were dark. Celeste could count on one hand the number of people they passed.

"You know, the hurricane will last most of the night," she said. "You might be stuck with us. Dad won't mind having an extra person to talk to, but wouldn't you prefer to stay with your family?"

"I..." Asa's face fell. "We ain't on speaking terms."

"Oh. Sorry."

They walked another block, and then Asa said, "You aren't going to ask?"

"Your business is your business." *And I read about your cousin in the papers,* she almost added but thankfully did not.

Asa stared straight ahead. The wind rushed past them, whipping at their clothes and hair. Celeste wished the train station was not closed. The sign on the station door read that all public transportation would resume tomorrow morning. A way to ensure more people stayed inside, she guessed.

"So, what does your father do? Workwise, I mean?" Asa asked.

"He did a lot of odd jobs, picked up several trades and hobbies, but nothing lasted more than a few years."

"A jack of all trades then?"

"Pretty much. Until ten years ago. Dad worked as a chor engineer, studying the nectar's properties and applications. It was steady work, paid well, but Dad got bored. He decided to enroll in law school." Celeste watched Asa, bracing for his reaction.

Asa's pace slowed as his mind processed the words. "A lawyer? Your father is a bloody lawyer?"

"Yes." She smirked. Exactly as she expected!

"What's his name?"

"Augustus Lawson."

Asa racked his brain, muttering under his breath. "I... I think I met him. Yeah! A year ago, during the Clara Tesana case. Remember her?"

"Of course." Clara Tesana was a pickpocket. She worked independently of the gangs and targeted people as they exited banks on payday, hoping to steal as much cash as possible. She was arrested by two officers from the Fifth Precinct, but she put up a fight. One officer hit her in the face with his gun, knocking out a few teeth.

"Augustus Lawson is the reason we had to let her go!" Asa all but shouted.

"Because the officers used excessive force."

Asa paused for a moment, his mouth partially open. "That's... Yeah, Reyes created a bunch of new rules afterwards. And Carter was given a month's leave without pay."

"Exactly."

"Did your father have something to do with that, too?"

"Of course. Just because someone steals a couple hundred dollars does not mean they deserve to lose their teeth."

"But what about the people she stole from? Don't they deserve justice?"

"Obviously. The courts worked with the banks and were able to reimburse the stolen funds. Granted, that didn't stop some people from exaggerating the amounts." Celeste rolled her eyes. One man claimed that Tesana had stolen over a hundred dollars from him. Gus Lawson did not buy it for a second and checked the bank's records. The man had only withdrawn ten dollars.

"Right. What ever happened to her?"

"Move to a small town up the coast. Works in a papermill. She seems happy."

"Hold up." Asa narrowed his eyes. "How do you know that?"

"She and Dad exchange letters. He likes to stay in touch with his clients. Make sure they're doing okay. And obeying the law," she added.

"Huh. Weird. But it makes sense." Asa sighed and rolled his eyes. "Still, waiting out a hurricane with a bloody lawyer..."

"Would you rather be alone?" Celeste intended the comment to be sarcastic, but seeing the hurt look in Asa's eyes, she realized that he was alone. "Sorry."

"It's fine. Hey, do you mind going over your theory again?"

"Sure."

Lightning skittered across the sky, illuminating the horizon. Roaring thunder followed, and the light rain turned into a deluge.

The driving rain soaked her and Asa within seconds.

"When we get home," Celeste yelled over the wind and rain.

"Agreed."

Chapter 21
Eyes of Red

The rainfall started halfway between the train station and Twenty-first Street. What began as a trickle quickly turned into a downpour. Invictus sprinted the last two blocks. His sides burned, and his jacket and hat were soaked by the time he hurried inside. He checked on the drawing. One corner was wet, smudging the charcoal, but the rest of the drawing was otherwise intact.

I hope Captain Reyes won't mind.

Granted, the captain had yet to see the drawing. Invictus could claim that it already had water damage.

"What are you doing here?" a stern voice asked.

Invictus jolted and spun around. Mrs. Garcia glared at him, but her eyes were rimmed with red and bloodshot. Had she been crying?

"I wanted to check on Ms. Smith and Wulf. See if they're okay."

Mrs. Garcia waved him away with a huff and retreated into her apartment. He heard at least three locks click.

Invictus had a hunch that something was bothering her, but he did not have time to investigate. Plus, she struck him as the type of person who would bite his head off if he asked a personal question.

He walked up to the second floor, but the invisible string tugged him upwards to the third floor. Of course. He followed the string and knocked on the third door on the right. Allo, one of Ruthless's cousins, answered.

"Is Ruthless here?" Of all the people in Malkin City, Ruthless ought to know about strange types of Fae.

Allo did not reply. He merely opened the door long enough for Invictus to slip inside.

The apartment looked like a storage locker. Crates and supply boxes of varying sizes were stacked against the walls, and every member of the Wells family appeared to be present. All five cousins, their spouses, multiple children ranging in age from elementary school age to mid-twenties, and several others who Invictus had yet to meet. Each one turned their weird, silvery eyes towards Invictus, studied him for a brief moment, and resumed their various conversations and activities.

Ozzy sat on the couch between Ector, the largest of the cousins at eight feet tall, and Lady Constance who hummed quietly as she knitted a scarf. Ozzy read a book, and his silver eyes were also rimmed red.

Ruthless, dressed in a simple button-down shirt and trousers instead of a suit, strode out of his bedroom and greeted Invictus.

"Are you planning to wait out the storm here, too?"

"No, sir." The pieces quickly fell into place. Everyone was here to wait out the hurricane, and each member of the Wells family bought extra supplies, same as everyone else in Malkin City. "I have a question. Do you recognize this subspecies of Fae?" He showed him the picture.

Ruthless's face was an unreadable mask. He spared a glance at the window. Rain streaked down the glass, turning the city into a blur.

"I also have a question for you, Jones. Would you rather I lie as a means of keeping you here longer, forcing you to wait out the storm in safety, or would you rather I tell the truth, prompting you to run headlong into a hurricane and putting yourself in danger?"

Invictus's blood turned cold. "Then, you know—"

"Where did you get this drawing?"

Invictus explained his meeting with Mr. Grady.

Ruthless cursed under his breath. "You sailed to Greer..." He shook his head. "No, only you would be foolish enough to sail to Greer Island and back at the advent of a storm. Let me guess. You had a hunch."

"Yes, sir." A part of him felt like the Commonwealth's greatest fool, but what choice did he have? He could not risk any evidence slipping through his fingers. Couldn't risk Wulf being imprisoned or executed.

Ruthless sat down in an empty chair opposite the couch. An interior door opened, admitting Vic, Billy, and a Blydd woman who was tall and thin with silver hair in a braid halfway down her back. She stood half a foot taller than Invictus and was easily one of the most beautiful women he had ever seen.

More beautiful than Celeste?

Invictus's face grew warm.

Where did that question come from?

"Oh, Invictus," Ruthless said, "meet my ex-wife, Verona. Verona, this is Invictus Jones."

Verona smirked, revealing an elongated canine tooth. "Wulf's human friend?"

"Yes, ma'am." Why was Ruthless's ex-wife here? Based on their expressions and postures, he judged they were on good terms, but wouldn't she prefer to wait out the storm in her own home?

"Interesting. I thought you'd be taller." Verona sat at the kitchen table along with two of the cousins, Cuthbert and Wyn, and their wives, and an assortment of children. Each one had silver eyes and grayish-white hair, except Wyn's wife who had ink black hair and brown eyes speckled with silver. A Halfling, Invictus guessed. Vic and Billy joined a group of teens near the window, watching the rain and lightning.

Taller? Did Ruthless tell her about me? That seemed odd, and a bit creepy. How many other members of the Wells family knew about him? *Everyone in this room, I guess.*

"Waiting out the storm with us?" Verona asked.

"No, ma'am. I just had a question." He showed her the drawing. Verona cursed in Faerie, a sharp, guttural sound. The other family members had similar reactions. Cuthbert and Wyn whispered nervously, their eyes flashing. And Cuthbert's wife, Invictus thought her name was Elyna, forced a little girl to look away.

"A Changeling?" Verona spat, her eyes flashing like lightning. "Where the hell did you get a picture of one of those creeps?"

"Thank you, love. You just cost me at least fifteen minutes of stalling," Ruthless said, narrowing his eyes.

"Oh, damn. Well, no point in stalling now." Verona leaned forward and locked eyes with Invictus. "So, Tu'atha'dyn, where did you get that drawing?"

"What did you call me?" Was it an insult? Her tone made it sound like an insult.

"Tu'atha'dyn is the Faerie word for humans," Ruthless explained. "The more accurate translation is 'field worker', since the majority of humans during the Contact lived in small, agrarian societies, along the coast and river—"

"Are you really trying to stall me?" Invictus interrupted. Twenty pairs of silver eyes turned his way. "Sorry."

"Don't apologize." Ruthless stood, took the drawing, and studied it. "I am trying to stall, and please don't take offense. A man who faced a silver-mad Sidhe, in my opinion, would not hesitate to track down a Changeling. Even at the risk of his own life. Or am I wrong?"

"That depends." Invictus's palms began to sweat. At the risk of his own life? How dangerous were Changelings? Riggs mentioned a type of Fae called Changers. Were they one and the same? He recalled the man being lured away, thinking he heard a loved one's voice, never to be seen again. "Could a Changeling be involved in the Whateley case?"

"Perhaps. Perhaps not. Remember, Emilio Grady was loyal to the Sidhe Family for decades. He could be steering you in the wrong direction, or maybe he wants revenge. Loyalty, after all, only goes so far."

"Are Changelings connected to the Sidhe Family?" Was that how Grady acquired the drawing? Or did he draw it himself, creating it as a form of leverage?

"According to rumor. But do detectives follow rumors, or do they follow facts?" Ruthless handed back the drawing.

"Facts, obviously, but..." Invictus studied the drawing and its eerie, red eyes. "But why would Grady send me down this path if there wasn't a connection? And the Sidhe Family can't be involved. Dr. Whateley was Taran Manning's personal doctor."

Ruthless's eyes widened. "Grady told you that?"

"Yes, sir."

"What else?"

Wind gusts rattled the apartment as driving rain pelted the windows. Ozzy huddled closer to Constance who lovingly stroked his hair while humming softly. Vic, Billy, and a few other teens excitedly watched the storm and shouted as lightning flashed, followed by rolling thunder.

Why isn't the window boarded up?

Before Invictus could ask, the interior door opened again. A Blydd man entered, carrying a little girl. Though he stood as tall as Ruthless, he had a narrow, almost willowy frame, and his silver hair hung past his shoulders. He walked over to Verona and handed the little girl to her. The girl wrapped her arms around Verona's neck and stared fearfully at the storm.

"Thunder woke her up," the Blydd man explained. His voice had a gravelly quality, but it was not as deep as Ruthless's voice.

"Jones," Ruthless said, "let me introduce Verona's current husband, Mathyn Howell, and their daughter Tierney."

"You're... Wait, what?" Invictus tried to solve the equation, but the numbers refused to add up.

"Rufus told us—" Mathyn began, but Verona interrupted him.

"Rufus insisted that we all stay with him during the storm," she said, eyeing her husband.

"Yes, you see, Blydd prefer to gather together during storms. It makes us feel safer," Mathyn explained, but Invictus did not quite believe him. He looked at the other relatives for confirmation. They refused to make eye contact.

A question for another day.

He checked his watch. A quarter after four.

"Hey, can I look at that?" Vic asked, pointing at the watch.

"It's pure silver," he reminded the teen.

"Silver?!" Mathyn placed himself between Invictus and his wife and daughter. His silver eyes flashed, turning almost white. Cuthbert and Wyn both bared their teeth, and the smaller children shied away.

"Calm down, Stepdad." Vic donned a pair of leather gloves. "See?"

Invictus recalled Quintus using that same tone when he asked their parents if he could spend a weekend at the lake with friends.

"Victor Servius," Verona said in a warning tone.

Vic bristled at being called by his full name. A weirdly Amistadian name, meaning Preserving Conqueror in the High Speech. The teen then looked at his father.

"Let the boy learn," Ruthless said. "The gloves ought to afford some protection. But if your skin starts burning, give the watch back."

"Understood." Vic held out his hands.

"Are you okay with this?" Invictus asked, raising an eyebrow.

Ruthless nodded.

He gave the watch to Vic, being extra careful not to touch the teen's skin. Wulf's horrible shriek echoed in Invictus's memory. He never wanted to cause that kind of pain again. Vic, smiling from ear to ear, hurried over to the window, watching as the lightning reflected off the silver.

"You're a dumbass," said one teenaged girl who had streaks of red in her silver hair. Mascen's sister, Invictus guessed. *Is Mascen here, too?* He could be in another room. Invictus hoped he had recovered from food poisoning.

Vic stuck out his tongue and held the watch by the silver chain.

"I suggest," Ruthless said to Invictus, "treading very lightly. Changelings are dangerous. Here." He went into the bedroom and returned with a small, leather-bound book. Gold leaf in the shape of vines decorated the spine and front cover. The title, also in gold leaf, read: *My Travels in the Fae Islands by Varius Sanders.* "It discusses Changelings and other rare subspecies. I have an extra copy, so don't worry about getting it wet."

"Thank you." Invictus scanned the table of contents. Most chapters discussed common subspecies, but he also recognized a few that Riggs had named. Coylle, Banshee, Fomori... "Wait, why would I get it wet?"

Ruthless gestured to the window. "Are you really going to wait out the storm, or are you going to prove Beowulf's innocence?"

A part of Invictus, the cautious, logical part, told him to wait. No point in running about during a potentially dangerous storm. But the other part, the part being tugged by that bloody invisible string, told him to go. Find the connection between the drawing and Dr. Whateley's murder. Find the evidence that would prove his friend's innocence.

"Could a Changeling have killed Dr. Whateley?"

"Sure. They can handle a gun just as well as a human."

"But what can Changelings do? I know Blydd and Shinnok have better senses than humans. What about Changelings?"

"They can alter their appearances," Verona said, clinging to Tierney as tightly as the little girl clung to her. "The rumors vary. Some say they can only change enough to hide their true faces. Others say they can mimic another person perfectly."

Invictus shivered. "Another person? Does that mean a human or a Fae?"

Verona shrugged. "One is just as easy to mimic as another."

"I suggest you read this first," Ruthless said, tapping the book. "Don't go into this blind."

Perfectly mimic another person. Could that be the connection? Was Carlos Vallejo, the Shinnok Halfling who talked Wulf and Macsen into this job, really a Changeling? Could he have killed Dr. Whateley while disguised as someone else? Disguised as Wulf?

"Where is Wulf?" Invictus asked. Anxiety built up inside him, threatening to escape and take over.

"With his mother. Are you thinking of bringing him along?"

Invictus nodded.

"Smart." The deluge slowed to a trickle. "The first band will be over soon. I suggest leaving within the next few minutes. Unless I can talk you into staying?"

Invictus considered it for a moment. But only for a moment. Wulf's life depended on him discovering the truth. This storm could provide the perfect opportunity for the real murderer to get away. Away from the city or the province or the Commonwealth itself.

He could not allow anything, not even a hurricane, to get in the way.

Invictus's eyes wandered to the crates. Why did they have so many? Some were large enough to hold a week's worth of supplies.

The entire family is here. Perhaps each person brought something. But it still did not account for the quantity.

Think about it later, he told himself.

"No, thank you. I need to solve this case. Wulf will be tried for murder if I don't."

Ruthless nodded. "Then go. And please, don't do anything stupid."

Chapter 22

Changeling

"A Changeling?" Wulf asked as he and Invictus walked the deserted streets of the Old City. The train stations closed over an hour ago and were not scheduled to resume operation until tomorrow morning, pending possible delays. Each station sat dark and strangely empty.

The sight unnerved Invictus. The trains never stopped running. Dockside Station occasionally closed for a few hours due to flooding, but only for a few hours. Never half a day, and never every station.

He glanced up at the dark, cloudy sky. The rain had let up. The first band, Ruthless had called it. What did he mean by that? Invictus read in the newspapers that hurricanes had a unique shape, but for the life of him, he could not picture it. Did it mean hurricanes proceeded in waves? A short period of wind and rain followed by another and another? How many in total?

The weather reports stated that it might last all night.

Panic shot through him. *Is this why Ruthless's entire family was at the apartment? Is this why they had dozens of supply crates?*

Their preparations seemed more suitable for a long trip than a single storm. But if hurricanes were not one, single storm...

"I've heard of them," Wulf continued, drawing Invictus out of his thoughts. "But nobody has ever seen a Changeling. Most folks don't think they're real. Just weird stories told to scare little kids."

"But if Changelings can alter their appearance, it would be next to impossible for someone to identify them."

"True. You think a Changeling did the doctor in?"

Invictus nodded. "I think Carlos Vallejo is a Changeling."

Wulf turned pale. "You... I mean, he looked just like a Shinnok Halfling. Even smelled like one. Be real hard to fake that."

"Not necessarily. There are hundreds of Shinnoks and Shinnok Halflings in Dannyn District alone. If he rented the apartment for the sole purpose of studying Shinnoks in order to mimic one, it could be plausible."

Wulf muttered under his breath, eyes narrowed. He quickened his pace as they turned onto Hawthorn Street. Massive oak trees swayed in the gusty wind. Myriad leaves littered the ground, and one branch had snapped off, landing in the neighboring yard. Thunder roared, and light raindrops fell on Invictus's face.

Invictus paused in front of the Whateley house. The Townsend house stood across the street, several plots away. The windows were dark with the curtains drawn. Nobody had bothered to board up the windows. He doubted the professor knew anything about the hurricane.

Wulf stared at the Whateley house, frozen.

"You can wait here." Invictus cursed himself for a fool. The Whateleys believed that Wulf killed the doctor. They were able to convince Alistair of Wulf's innocence, but what about the rest of the family? Did Alistair convince them as well, or did they 'talk sense' into him? Of course a thief and his friend would persuade you that he was innocent. What were you thinking?

Alistair, after all, had made no attempts to speak with the police on Wulf's behalf.

Perhaps Invictus ought to speak with the family privately.

About what? That you think a mythological Fae conspired to murder their father?

And what was the Changeling's motive? He could not be working for the Families. Dr. Whateley was Taran Manning's personal physician, and the Families always worked together, never against. Drawing the ire of one Family meant drawing the ire of all five. No one would be foolish enough to invoke that kind of wrath.

"Bookie, can I tell you something?" Wulf shifted his feet like a sprinter preparing to run.

"Of course."

"I thought..." Wulf hesitated, staring at the Whateley house. "When I first met Carlos, I thought he kinda looked like me. You think it was on purpose? That this Changeling made himself look like me?"

"It sounds plausible."

"But do you think he did?" Wulf's eyes faded to the palest purple. He trembled from head to toe.

"I think it's possible." But why would the Changeling go to the trouble of recruiting Wulf and Macsen? Why not break into the house himself while disguised as Wulf and kill the doctor? The maid would have still seen Beowulf Smith. He still would be framed for murder.

Maybe Changelings have to be close to a person before they can mimic them. Listen to their voice, study the way they walk.

"Wulf, when you heard the argument, did any of the voices sound familiar?"

"No." He stared nervously at the house.

"Do you want to stay out here?"

Wulf glanced up and down the street. All was silent save for the wind and the patter of rain hitting the road. A potted tree on the neighboring porch toppled over, and the ceramic pot shattered. Wulf whirled around, facing the sound, and reached for a gun. His hand brushed empty air. He grimaced.

"These people don't own guns, right?"

"Right."

Wulf stared at the house for a moment and said, "Okay. I'll go with you."

Invictus walked up to the front door and knocked. Nobody answered. He knocked again and received the same result.

"Maybe they left town because of the storm?" Invictus had overheard a few police officers making travel arrangements earlier this week.

"No, I hear voices inside." Wulf got out his lock picks and went to work. The door swung open. Invictus could not help being a little impressed.

The interior was completely dark. No lights. No opened curtains. It felt like he was peering into a mausoleum.

Faint voices drifted down the hallway, whispering, worried. One voice sounded like Alistair Whateley.

"Hel—"

Wulf clamped a hand over Invictus's mouth.

"Something's wrong here, Bookie," he whispered. He stared into the dark hallway, shivering.

"Did you feel it when you broke in?" Invictus also felt worried, but the invisible string tugged, urging him forward.

Wulf shook his head. "No. Different wrongness. We should go."

"But—"

Wulf shot him a pained look, pleading.

The invisible string tugged again, begging Invictus to walk inside, to ask the questions he wanted to ask. No, the questions he needed to ask. Otherwise, his only lead would vanish, leaving him with no suspects.

And leaving Wulf in a prison cell.

Or swinging from a rope.

Invictus shivered and forced himself to step inside. Wulf, whimpering like a kicked dog, followed.

Invictus almost tripped over a vase in the dark hallway. Wulf leapt forward and steadied the vase before it fell. Invictus waited a moment, allowing his eyes to adjust. Faint outlines formed. The shape of a doorway. A lampstand a little farther down the hall. And voices. The whispering voices led him into the sitting room where he had questioned Alfred Whateley.

Alfred, Alistair, and a woman who Invictus assumed was Gina Whateley sat huddled on the couch nearest the empty fireplace. A lantern rested on the central coffee table, providing some light. Two maids sat off to the side. Their faces were pained, worried. The youngest of the pair, the one who had served Invictus tea, looked like she was on the verge of tears.

Wulf tugged on Invictus's sleeve. The Halfling cocked his head towards the front door. Invictus shook his head. Wulf mouthed the word 'please'. Invictus's heart sank. He had never seen his friend look so scared, as though he were walking into a nightmare.

"What do we do now?" Alfred whispered, his voice shaking.

"Why are you asking me?" Alistair snapped. His voice sounded strange. More scratchy, as though he had a sore throat.

"Maybe we—" Gina Whateley began, but the older maid noticed Invictus and inhaled sharply, covering her mouth.

The Whateleys turned.

Invictus's blood became ice water. All three had blood red eyes. Their skin, now a deathly pale, was drawn, as though they suffered a long illness followed by starvation. Their red eyes, surrounded by pitch black circles, seemed to glow. The dark pigmentation seeped down their faces, like ink thrown against a wall.

"What the hell are you doing here?" Alistair demanded, sneering. His voice altered, becoming deeper and scratchier. He looked like Grady's charcoal drawing come to life.

Was it a drawing of Armand Whateley?

A newfound horror crept into Invictus's mind. Of course Taran Manning, a Sidhe Fae, did not have a human doctor.

He had a Fae one.

Alistair's blood red eyes fell on Wulf. He blinked a few times, startled. Black liquid oozed out of his tear ducks, creating new tracks.

"Al, what...?"Alfred turned and saw Wulf. Red eyes widened. He cursed under his breath.

"What are you?" Invictus asked, but he already knew the answer. Changelings. The Whateleys were Changelings!

A viselike grip seized Invictus's wrist and dragged him down the hallway and towards the front door.

"Wulf, what are...?"

Footsteps thundered behind them. Invictus glanced over his shoulder. Alistair and Alfred, red eyes flashing like evil sprites, chased after them. Invictus forced his legs to move faster.

They rushed out the front door and all but flew down the steps. His leather shoes pounded against the pavement. The sound sent him back to that sunny June afternoon when he and Wulf went to see Tacitus Harvey. Instead, they found Lewin Manning. Wulf had grabbed Invictus's wrist and forced him to run. Run for his life. A part of him, the part that worried late at night that the Mannings would come knocking, felt like he had never stopped running.

Fingertips brushed his shoulder.

Invictus screamed and ran faster, forcing his burning legs to keep pace with Wulf.

The wind buffeted him, threatening to knock him down, to leave him at the Whateleys' mercy.

Lightning scattered across dark clouds, followed by deafening thunder. Invictus's ear rang, loud and painful, obliterating all other sounds.

The sky opened the moment they reached the street. Driving rain fell in sheets. Invictus, his soaked clothes and shoes weighing him down, could not see more than a few feet in front of him. A black shadow moved just ahead. Wulf. He kept running, his eyes fixed on Wulf, trusting the Halfling's heightened senses to lead them to safety.

"Leave them!" Alistair called out, his voice barely audible over the storm.

"But they know!" Alfred screamed, sounding like a scratchy record. "They'll ruin us!"

Alistair shouted back, but the wind and rain drowned out the words.

Invictus and Wulf ran down the street, completely disorientated. He thought they turned east, heading towards Secundus Park, but did they turn again? Or twice? He was so preoccupied trying to follow Wulf, trying to outrun the Whateleys, that he failed to pay attention. But if they could find a landmark or a street sign, they could reorientate themselves. The Fifth Precinct was a few blocks north of Secundus Park. If they could make it there...

A massive gust of wind slammed into Invictus, knocking him down. He crashed onto the pavement, his hands and knees smarting. Was he bleeding? There was too much rain to tell. Wulf helped him to his feet.

"Over there!" He pointed.

"What?"

"A light! Look!"

Invictus blinked rainwater out of his eyes. A faint light shone down the street. "What is it?"

"A lantern. Go, go, go!" Wulf took off running, heading for the light. Invictus followed, his legs and knees burning and his waterlogged coat weighing him down.

The faint light grew brighter with each step. The outline of a man formed. He stood on a doorstep and waved to him and Wulf.

"Hurry," the man called out. "The storm is worsening. Hurry!" The man wore a gray raincoat and a gray hat.

Is he a Grayman? Invictus wondered. Had Riggs's Grayman appeared to save them?

Invictus and Wulf raced up the steps and into the house. The man shut the door and slid two deadbolts into place. Wind and rain battered the house, demanding to be let inside. The man faced them, but instead of being completely gray, the man had fair skin and pale blue eyes the color of a summer sky. He removed his hat, revealing thin, white hair.

Not a Grayman. Just a neighbor.

Is he a Changeling, too? Outwardly, the man appeared human, but so did Alistair and Alfred.

Invictus shivered. His wet clothes clung to him, and the knees of his trousers were both torn. One knee bled a little, but the other was just skinned up a bit. Same with his hands. And the wind had blown away his hat.

He glanced around the hallway, lit by a single lantern. The house was smaller than the Whateleys', but furniture packed every available space, barely leaving any room to walk. Couches, chairs, end tables, potted plants. The walls were equally covered with paintings, ranging from landscapes in oil to children's crayon drawings.

But the house was warm and dry. Outside, the storm raged.

"Thank you," Invictus said, his teeth chattering.

The man nodded. "It's no trouble. I saw you a few days ago. You're a policeman, correct?" he asked in a thick, Scanlannish accent.

"Yes, I work with the police." Not a complete lie, just... Yes, a lie. Invictus was bloody sick of lying.

The old man smirked. "Spend a lot of time with the Fae, I see. And you." He swung his lantern so the light shone on Wulf. Somehow, he had managed to keep his hat. "I remember you. Caused quite the commotion."

"Wait, you saw Wulf break into the Whateley house?" But there were no official eyewitnesses outside the household.

"Yes. All dressed in black. Strange for a Fae to dress that way." He gestured to Wulf's long coat. Water dripped off it, pooling on the hardwood floor. "And even stranger for one to enter a house uninvited."

"I'm a Halfling." Wulf shivered so badly that his teeth chattered.

The old man nodded. "I see. I am Norri. You are welcome to stay in my home. Please, have a seat. My son is about your size," he said to Invictus. "I have some of his old clothes upstairs. They ought to fit. Though they'll likely hang off of you like a scarecrow," he said to Wulf.

"Thank you, sir. My name is Invictus J—"

"No." Norri held up his hand. "First names only, if you don't mind. Names are powerful things. Don't give them out freely."

"Very well. I'm Invictus, and this is Wulf."

"A pleasure to meet you both. Please, make yourselves comfortable. I'll just be a moment." Norri headed upstairs, taking the lantern with him.

Invictus and Wulf went into the sitting room. Another lantern shone on the coffee table, glowing a soft yellow. Neither wanted to get the furniture wet, so they sat on the floor with their backs to the couch. Invictus's ear rang.

"He saw me," Wulf muttered. "How the hell...?" He shivered violently and wrapped his soaking wet coat around himself. He shivered again, his teeth chattering. Invictus hoped he was not getting sick. His mother always warned him and Quintus that they would catch pneumonia if they ran about in the rain.

"That is odd. Why not talk to the police?" No eyewitnesses had come forward, and Asa and Celeste questioned all the neighbors. Invictus closed his eyes and pictured the case file. A dozen names written in Asa's precise handwriting, but Norri's was not among them.

Perhaps he was not home at the time. Or he pretended not to be home. *But his neighbor was murdered, and he saw Wulf fleeing the scene. Why wouldn't he tell the police?*

"Changelings," Wulf muttered. "A bunch of bloody Changelings."

Invictus reached into his pockets. Ruthless's book had water damage on the back cover, and the last few pages were ruined. But the rest of the book, including a short chapter on Changelings, was intact.

The drawing, however, was ruined. The paper crumpled and tore as Invictus tried to unfold it. He sighed heavily and shoved the wadded mess back into his pocket. Reyes would skin him alive for ruining evidence.

"Grady knew." Invictus shook his head and cursed himself for a fool. Mr. Grady was in Taran Manning's pocket for years. How could he not know?

"Huh?"

"Grady knew that—"

A gust of wind shook the house so hard that Invictus feared it would be ripped off its foundation.

"Are hurricanes always this bad?" Invictus asked Wulf.

"Depends on the size and the speed," Norri answered. The old man carried an armload of clothes and blankets. He set them on the couch. "According to the weather scientists, this one is going to be quite bad. Looks like we're in for a long night."

Chapter 23
Hurricane

Wulf wrapped a second blanket around his shoulders, huddled in dry clothes that were a size too large, and none of them were black. He sat close to Bookie and watched Norri's every move.

This old guy saw him break into the Whateley house and didn't tell the bricks nothing. Why? What was his game?

Norri adjusted the lantern so the flame glowed a comfortable yellow and sat down in a padded rocking chair. Wulf and Bookie sat on a couch. One of three in the cramped living room.

Why the hell do Scannies always have so much furniture?

No, not Scannies, he reminded himself. Calling a Scanlannish person a Scannie was just as bad as Germanicus calling him Fox-face.

But why all the furniture, he couldn't help wondering. *So much stuff for one old man. What gives?*

The wind howled. Driving rain pounded the roof and windows, demanding to be let inside.

He hoped Ma was alright. They had planned to wait out the storm with Ruthless and his family, then Bookie showed up and explained his plan to Wulf. Running around during a hurricane sounded crazy, but so did spending the entire night with twenty some odd Blydd. Ruthless insisted that the whole family do so, including extended family. Wulf had spied Esmeralda and her mother walking down the street as he and Bookie left, protected by colorful umbrellas.

Was there something to this storm that only Ruthless knew? Sure, the weather scientists and the newspapers all said it was gonna be a bad one, but Esmeralda lived in South Torpen, and Verona and her husband lived in a neighborhood a block north of the Business District. Neither area flooded much. What had gotten Ruthless so spooked?

"How long will the storm last?" Bookie asked.

Norri looked up at the ceiling and listened. "It's early evening now. I guess it will end around midnight or so."

"Midnight?!" Bookie jolted. "But it's a storm. It—"

"It's a hurricane, Bookie," Wulf muttered, pulling the blankets tighter. Bloody hell, couldn't the old man light the fireplace? "Most last all day, or all night."

Wind shook the house again. Outside, glass shattered. A broken tree branch must have smashed a window.

Bookie looked around the room. He then reached into his coat pocket and remembered he was wearing someone else's coat. He asked Norri, "Did you see a pocket watch in my waistcoat?"

"I don't recall." Norri stood and hobbled into the kitchen where their clothes were drying on the table. While the old guy did find Wulf's lock picks and multi-purpose knife, he did not find Bookie's watch.

"Damn. Must have dropped it outside." Bookie gazed at the shuttered window.

"You ain't goin' out there," Wulf said. Most folks didn't need the reminder, but Bookie was, unfortunately, himself. The poor fool didn't even know how bad hurricanes were. Thought they were just thunderstorms with a fancy name.

Bookie sighed and huddled in his blanket, upset over a stupid watch. A stupid *silver* watch. Wulf was glad the damn thing was gone. He felt a sight better without it.

Norri sat in his chair, rocking gently.

"Do you live by yourself, Mr. Norri?" Bookie asked.

The old man nodded. "My son and his family live in one of those newer neighborhoods. I visit from time to time."

"Why not wait out the storm with them?"

"And listen to six screaming kids all night?" The old man laughed. "I love my grandkids, but my childrearing days are over."

"You really saw me?" Wulf blurted out, locking eyes with the old man. Norri flinched, but he held Wulf's gaze.

"I did," he admitted. "Like a shadow. You see, I don't sleep well and often go outside for fresh air. That night, I saw a shadow climb into Armand Whateley's second-floor window. And not five minutes later, that same shadow ran like the wind. Half an hour later, the police arrived. Figured it was a robbery, but they took Armand out on a stretcher with his face covered." Norri glanced at the window, towards the Whateley house.

"You didn't tell the bricks what you saw?"

"No."

"But you witnessed a potential murderer flee the scene of a crime," Bookie said, sounding like one of those idiot storybook detectives. Seriously, the man spent the whole summer working with the bricks. When would he snap out of it?

Norri pointed a gnarled finger at Bookie. "You said a word there, Invictus. Potential. Meaning this one," he pointed at Wulf, "did not pull the trigger."

Bookie blinked. "I... Yes, sir. Wulf was set up."

"Like that Sherrington novel. What was the title?" He snapped his fingers a few times. "*Dead of Winter*?"

"Yes, sir." Bookie smiled, his eyes brightening like he had found an envelope full of cash.

Wulf rolled his eyes. *Great, another book-brained idiot.*

"That one was set in the mountains, remember? Torold's Pass, midway between Amistad and Scanlan. The young man in that story was set up, too."

"By his uncle. The uncle," Bookie said to Wulf, as though he actually cared, "wanted to inherit his brother's fortune, but his nephew stood to inherit the majority. So, he killed his brother, making it look like the nephew committed the murder."

"Good for him. How does this help me?"

Bookie's face fell a little. "Well, the uncle slipped up, and..." He sighed. "You're right. This doesn't help."

"No, lad, I see where you're going," said Norri. "Someone killed Old Whateley and didn't want to go to Greer for it, so they set up your friend. Interesting choice to use a Halfling to kill a Changeling."

The hairs on the back of Wulf's neck stood on end, causing the iron burn scar to itch. "You know what those bastards are?"

Norri paused for a moment, thinking. "I knew the family in Scanlan, long before they moved south. Everyone in the village knew what they were. Each village, it seemed, had their Fae family. We happened to have Changelings."

"Were they dangerous?" Bookie sat on the edge of the couch.

"No, just strange."

"Can they alter their appearance to look like other people?"

Norri shook his head. "Changelings don't work that way. See, their true form is the one the Whateley boys showed you. Blood red eyes, pale skin, dark liquid seeping out of their eyes, dying the skin. Terrifying to look at, but mostly harmless."

"Define mostly," said Bookie.

Norri leaned in his chair, rocking back and forth.

The hurricane raged around them. Wulf was thankful they made it inside. The windows were not boarded, but Norri closed and latched the shutters. The latches looked pretty sturdy. Ought to hold up if the glass broke. But the house was so bloody cold! He glanced at Bookie. The human seemed fine. A bit scuffed up, but he weren't shivering or nothing.

"You work with the police, Invictus. You tell me. What makes a person dangerous?"

"It depends," Bookie said after a moment. "They could have a knife or a gun or a violent disposition."

"Would you say that the Fae are the same?"

"Yes, sir."

Norri smirked. "That's where you are wrong. Have you heard of the Seelie Court?"

"Yeah, what of it?" Wulf snapped. The howling wind sent chills up and down his body. He huddled inside the blankets and looked around. Was there another one? Maybe Bookie could share his.

"The Seelie Court creates laws for the Fae. Laws that live in their blood. Your blood is mixed with human blood," he said to Wulf, "allowing you to break into houses, enter without permission. A full-blooded Fae cannot do that."

"That's a load of crap." Wulf had seen Ruthless enter houses and businesses without permission tons of times, and he was a full-blooded Blydd.

"Are you sure?" the old man asked in an insufferable tone, like he thought Wulf was a stupid idiot.

"Yeah, I'm damn sure," Wulf snapped. He bared his teeth. Sharp and pointy. But not strong like a Blydd or a Bannock's.

"Wulf," Bookie admonished, sounding just like Ma. How the hell did he do that?

"You should read the laws more closely next time, my friend."

"Ain't your friend," Wulf muttered. He tucked his feet underneath the blanket and huddled into a ball. Why was it so bloody cold in here?

Neither human seemed bothered by it, and Bookie was always complaining about the temperature.

"I certainly hope you are my friend." Norri leaned forward. "Otherwise, you are in for a very chilly night."

Wulf tilted his head to the side, locking eyes with the old man. "You're making it cold?"

"What are you talking about?" Bookie asked.

"The Seelie Court protects humans just as much as Fae. More so, at times. In accordance with the law, I have set a ward against unfriendly Fae and Halflings. My friends are warm and comfortable, but those who are not my friends freeze as though they were in Scanlan in the middle of winter."

"And if I say I'm your friend," Wulf said through chattering teeth, "I won't be cold no more?"

Norri shrugged. "Depends on how much you mean it."

Wulf listened to the storm. The wind grew louder, stronger, and the air around him grew colder. No way he could spend the entire night like this.

"Okay, Norri. I mean it. I'll be your friend." The temperature continued to drop. Wulf's fingers and toes felt numb. Bloody hell, why didn't it work? "I mean it, I swear!"

Norri smiled. "I accept your friendship, Wulf."

Warmth flooded him, banishing the cold. Mercy sakes alive, the house felt like the beach in the middle of July. It was wonderful! He unwounded the blankets and tossed them onto the floor.

Why didn't Ruthless never teach me about this stuff?

Maybe it was in the book Ruthless gave him. *On the Types of Fae.* Too bad he left it at the apartment. He couldn't read half of it anyway.

Bookie stared at Norri, his mouth hanging open. "How... Please, tell me how this works."

"Magic."

"No, seriously."

"Do you think I would lie to my guests?" Norri raised an eyebrow.

"No, sir. I..." Bookie frowned. "Well, it's just that magic does not exist."

"Perhaps not the magic of folk stories, but the magic of names and of blood, that is very real. The Seelie Court could not function without it."

"Can I use it?" Bookie asked.

"Of course."

"How?"

"You speak it into existence. If you want to protect your house the same way I have protected mine, simply say that all unwelcomed Fae will burn or freeze if they enter, but all your friends shall be safe."

"Simple as that?"

"Yes." The old man smiled.

Bookie looked kinda skeptical, but Wulf believed Norri. Grady's banishment had worked the same way. Words spoken in accordance with the Seelie Court.

"So, that's why nobody in your village was afraid of the Changelings," Bookie said. "The Seelie Court protected them."

"Precisely. And so long as we did not harm them, they did not have a reason to harm us."

"When did the Whateleys leave?"

"A few years before I did. Old Whateley had earned a medical degree, disguising himself as a human and traveling to Malkin for several months out of the year. The family left so he could practice medicine in a land where Changelings were considered myths."

"They just wanted a new life?" Bookie asked. "They weren't running from the law or anything?"

"Yes and no." Norri hesitated, looking in the lantern flame. "Things in Scanlan had changed. The Commonwealth tried for decades to annex the land as a province. Whateley supported the decision, thinking it would benefit the people. But most people just wanted to be left alone. Our ancestors had gotten along fine without the Commonwealth's interference, and so could we."

"And you?"

Norri's face fell. "I wanted my homeland to be free, but I didn't want it destroyed by war either." Tears welled in his eyes. "I saw the sons and daughters of my neighbors, children who I watched grow up, come home with missing limbs or in coffins..." He blinked the tears away. "I didn't want my son to share their fate. We left before the war began in earnest."

"Did the Whateleys have any enemies because of his views? Or maybe someone here in Malkin City who knew they were Changelings?"

Norri thought it over. "A few of us from Scanlan know, but in a city full of Fae, who cared? Changelings, to us, are no different than Sidhe or Shinnoks." He smiled at Wulf.

"Then no one had a reason to kill him." Bookie's shoulders slumped.

"I never said that, lad."

Bookie frowned at him.

"Carlos Vallejo?" Wulf asked.

"Never heard of him." Norri leaned forward and clasped his hands together. "Armand always kept to himself. The whole family did, but there was nothing odd or wrong about that. Folks up in Scanlan tend to be private. It was shortly after Armand started traveling south for medical school that we began to notice the changes. He became short tempered, started yelling at his wife and sons, even in public. I never heard him raise his voice until then. And he became secretive, almost skittish. Always made excuses not to talk and went out of his way to avoid certain people. People who liked to talk."

"Was it part of being a Changeling?" Bookie asked.

The old man shook his head. "We assumed so, but he was like that every time. For weeks afterward, he'd act like a spooked horse. Sometimes, he didn't leave his house. And just when he was back to his normal self, he would have to return to Malkin City, and the pattern repeated."

"What kind of work did Armand Whateley do before he attended medical school?" Bookie asked.

"He was a trapper. Made some money selling furs and skins to traders in Scanlan and to foreign visitors."

"But not enough to afford tuition," Bookie guessed.

A faint smile crossed Norri's face. "Last I heard, the cost of attending medical school is twice the cost of attending the University. Are you college educated, Invictus?"

He nodded.

"How much did a single year cost?"

"Amistad Central College costs one hundred dollars a year, and tuition does not include the cost of textbooks. Many of those cost between five and ten dollars."

"You paid ten dollars for a bloody book?" Wulf stared at him. Just stared at him. What in the hell was wrong with these people?

"Yes, and I lived at home, so I didn't have to pay for room and board. Depending on the college or university, that could be upwards of twenty dollars a semester."

"The average trapper in Scanlan stood to earn a hundred Malkinese dollars a year. If it was a good year," Norri added.

Bookie sat back, staring into space as his mind worked. Wulf's mind worked, too. Letters were dicey, but he understood numbers. Twice one hundred was two hundred. Adding another twenty dollars made two hundred and twenty. And then, there were the stupidly expensive books. And food and clothes and train fare. All of which cost way more than one hundred.

"How'd this guy afford to go to medical school?" Wulf asked.

"Not to mention the travel costs and supporting his family back home." Bookie asked Norri, "What kind of work did Armand's wife do?"

"She sewed and fixed little things for the folks in the village. They might have given her some coins now and then, but most paid in food."

"Why did Armand want to study medicine?" Bookie asked. "Did he ever tell you?"

"No, but he was the curious type. Always wanting to learn new things. And I think he wanted to help people." The old man stared at his hands. "Granted, it's hard to help folks if they are afraid of you."

"Then he needed to relocate to a new town where people didn't believe in Changelings, and doctors dedicate their lives to helping others. Those two add up. But where did he get the funds for his tuition? Did he apply for scholarships?"

"Not that I'm aware of, but scholarships rarely pay full tuition, correct?"

"It depends," Bookie said. "And most scholarships are awarded to high school students with good grades and military veterans. Did Armand Whateley graduate high school?"

"Scanlan didn't have a formal education system at the time. Most people only learned how to read and write and do simple math. From what I know, Armand traveled to Malkin City, took a test, passed, and enrolled in medical school a month later."

"Hmm." Bookie looked around the room, thinking.

"Maybe he got help," Wulf said.

Bookie's eyes widened. "Did he have connections in the city?"

Norri nodded.

"Dammit, just tell us!" Wulf snapped.

"You aren't being very friendly," Norri warned.

Wulf shivered as the cold threatened to invade him again. "Sorry. But we need to know. I don't wanna go to Greer just 'cause you don't tell things straight."

"I guess that is fair. While he was studying, Armand also had to work. His wife mentioned that he got a job at the hospital, running errands for doctors and nurses, cleaning after hours. The job paid some of his tuition, and he occasionally sent money home. While there, he met a few recurring patients. People who live with chronic illnesses."

"Taran Manning," Bookie whispered. His face turned ashen as though he had heard a banshee scream.

Norri nodded. "You're a smart one. Taran Manning was not the head of his House back then—"

"Wait, you know about this stuff?" Wulf interrupted. *Is he connected to the Families, too?*

Norri shushed him and continued, "Taran was not the head of his House, but he was set to inherit. So rumors say," he added with a smirk. "Taran befriended Armand and promised to help pay for his tuition if he promised to become his personal physician after graduation."

"But he still worked at the hospital," Bookie said.

"Correct. He also aided Taran whenever he called. I lost count of the times I saw him leaving in the middle of the night."

"Did anything else happen during this time?" Bookie asked. "What caused his paranoia? Was he worried Manning would cut off his funds, or did he overhear something while visiting the Manning house?"

"Unfortunately, I cannot say. Armand dutifully worked as Manning's personal physician for thirty years, and he never had to repay a dime."

"But he was in the Manning family's pocket. The Sidhe Family," Bookie emphasized.

"I don't keep up with rumors." Norri waved his hand dismissively.

Yeah, and I'm the Emperor of Ruhalleen, Wulf thought.

"Most rumors are completely wrong, anyway. But I think Armand learned a lot of things while visiting the Manning house. Things that terrified him."

"Is that why they had him killed?" Wulf asked.

Bookie shook his head. "No, Mr. Grady said Whateley was valuable to the Mannings. Taran would not have ordered him to be killed."

"Then who did, and why drag me into it?"

"Armand is a well-known man," Norri said. "You cannot kill a well-known man and expect no one to react. I think they needed a fall guy."

"And they picked me. Great." An idea popped into Wulf's head. "Hey, Bookie, you think it was one of his sons?" Bookie tried to interrupt, but Wulf kept talking. "Maybe they learned that their father was working with the Sidhe Family, tried to talk him out of it, but he refused. Was in too deep, or something. So, they killed the old guy and framed me as a way to protect the rest of the family."

"Well..." Bookie paused, thinking. "I assume it's possible. But they don't own guns, and Alistair was ready to kill you the other day."

"True. Dammit." Alistair genuinely believed that Wulf had murdered his father. He could still feel the bastard's hands wrapped around his throat, see the hatred in his eyes.

"And if the sons wanted no connection to the Sidhe Family, they could have moved away," Bookie continued. "They each have good finances. They could have easily relocated."

Norri muttered under his breath in Scanlannish and went into the kitchen. "Would either of you like a cup of tea or something to eat? I have plenty."

"A sandwich, if that's okay," Bookie said.

"Ham?"

"Yes, please."

"And you, Wulf?"

"I ain't hungry. But thanks," he added. Truthfully, he was starving. Hadn't eaten since breakfast, but his stomach was all in knots. Likely couldn't eat even if he tried.

Norri disappeared around a corner.

The wind died down, and the rain slowed, turning into a light drizzle. A moment later, it stopped. The world grew eerily quiet.

"Oh, thank God! The hurricane is over!" Bookie smiled.

"No, man. We're in the eye," Wulf corrected him.

"The what?"

"Hurricanes have eyes. Inside, there ain't no rain or wind or nothing. Only been in the eye one other time."

"And it was like this?"

"Yeah." Wulf was five years old, terrified by his first hurricane. He and Ma huddled together on the couch in Mrs. Avita's apartment. A tree limb had crashed through their window, sending glass shards in every direction and knocking the oil lamp off the table. Wulf screamed as the apartment plunged into darkness.

"Don't worry," Ma said. "I'm here." Together, they walked up the stairs. Mrs. Avita and her husband, whose health was starting to fail, invited them to stay the night.

Wulf held onto Ma tightly and listened to the howling wind and pounding rain. So much rain. And then, nothing. Wulf believed the storm was over, too.

"The other half was terrible," he told Bookie. "Made the first half seem like a spring shower."

"Oh."

"We probably got half an hour." Wulf pulled the blankets over himself again. Not that he was cold. The room was downright comfortable. But the memories from that first storm overwhelmed him. He wished he was home. He wished he was with Ma. Was she doing okay, or was she worried sick about him again?

Gotta stop doing that. He wrapped the blankets tighter.

"At least we're safe here," Bookie said.

"Yeah." Wulf glanced at the shuttered window. If those Changelings were mad enough, they could run over here, break inside, and...

What if Norri don't consider them friends?

Or the old man might have a stronger law against them. A banishment. If Armand Whateley was connected to the Families, a banishment would make more sense.

Wulf felt warmer, safer. Exhaustion seized him. He tried to keep his eyes open, but they were so heavy. And he'd been running nonstop for days. When was the last time he slept?

He leaned his head against a pillow and fell asleep.

Chapter 24

Mercy and Justice

Asa was grateful Celeste only lived a half mile from the Precinct. The torrential rain made the trip feel twice as long, and they were thoroughly soaked by the time they reached the old townhouse in Newydd Hill; three stories tall and very narrow, resembling the trunk of a palm tree. Her apartment occupied the entire third floor and the attic.

"Dad insisted on attic space," she explained as they walked up the winding staircase, leaving small puddles in their wake. Asa hoped the landlord would not mind. The man who owned his building would have a fit if Asa trudged in this much water, hurricane or no hurricane.

"Why?"

"Reminds him of home, living up in the mountains."

"He's Kallendonic, right?" Asa recalled the mountain painting at the art dealership.

"Yeah. Grew up in the foothills of the Scalaad Caelum Mountains." She unlocked the door. The rooms were sparsely furnished with a couch and two chairs facing a small fireplace. A kitchen stood off to the side. And in the corner stood a bookcase overflowing with books. More books were stacked on the floor and the kitchen table. Hell, there were also books on the chairs.

Asa counted three interior doors and assumed they were bedrooms. He saw no sign of Celeste's father.

"Is he home?"

"Should be." Celeste knocked on the door between the kitchen and the sitting room. A muffled voice echoed down. "Yes, it's me!" Celeste called up.

Asa heard footsteps walking downward. The door opened, and a pale skinned man in his fifties with graying, light brown hair that looked like it had not been combed in over a week, stepped through. His pale gray eyes fell on Asa. He raised an eyebrow.

"Who is this?"

"Officer Asa Bishop. My new partner," Celeste replied.

The eyebrows narrowed. "I see. Waiting out the storm?"

"Yes, sir." Asa introduced himself and shook his hand, a rough, calloused hand. Not the hand he expected from a lawyer.

Augustus Lawson smirked. "No need to be overly polite, son. You can relax."

Asa had not realized he was standing at attention. He relaxed his posture.

Bright, white lightning scored the sky. Deafening thunder followed a second later, bringing with it a torrent of wind and rain. It made what they had just walked through seem like a spring shower. The weather scientists predicted it would be a bad storm. Looked like they were right for a change.

"Are you going to stand all day, or would you prefer to sit?" Augustus asked. He walked over to the kitchen.

"Uh, sit." Asa almost asked about his wet clothes, but neither Celeste nor her father seemed to mind.

He sat on the couch while Celeste sat in one of the armchairs. She lit a lamp, filling the room with a soft, yellow glow that reflected off the windows.

"The windows aren't boarded!" Asa jolted.

"Of course not," Augustus said. He retrieved a box filled with odds and ends from the kitchen counter and sat in the other chair. "Can't watch the storm that way."

"Watch the storm?" Was this man insane? Hurricanes were notorious for snapping tree limbs and throwing debris miles away. People needed to replace broken windows after every storm. It had gotten so bad that the city started giving away free boards a couple years ago.

Augustus arched an eyebrow.

"No offense, Mr. Lawson, but most people board up their windows."

"Don't see why I should be offended by a question. And call me Gus."

"Okay, sir. Gus." Asa fidgeted. His wet clothes clung to him, making him chilly.

"I never saw a hurricane before immigrating to Malkin Province," Gus said as he placed the box on a footstool. He selected a few screws and wires. "Got caught completely off guard. Thought it was just a glorified thunderstorm. Merciful heavens, was I wrong!" He laughed. "But it was amazing. The way the wind gusted, bending the rain to its will. It was like watching the hand of God at work."

Asa glanced down at the statuette of Triumvir in his pocket. He always prayed for protection during storms. The hand of God was something that protected, not brought about destruction.

"I see you're a religious man, Bishop, and with a religious name, too."

"Pardon?"

Gus pointed at the statuette. "That's Triumvir, isn't it?"

"Yes, sir." He cradled the small statue in his hands. "But Asa isn't a religious name."

"But Bishop is. At least, it is out in Kallendon."

"It is?" He did not know where the name came from. It wasn't Malkinese nor from the High Speech. His parents didn't know either.

Gus twisted the ends of two wires together and connected them to a small, metal plate with screws in the corners. "Course, out here the church is structured differently. You have priests, senior priests, and acolytes. Out west, we also have bishops and deacons. People who oversee the laws and courts."

"Don't you have lawyers?" Asa raised an eyebrow.

"Nope. Everything you attribute to the government and the courts here, we attribute to the church."

"So, you're a priest, too? Celeste mentioned that you're a lawyer."

"I have a law degree, and I practice law in court, but I am not a priest. Not out here." He finished connecting the wires to the plate and then attached a third wire, securing the other end to a cylindrical battery. Pale yellow chor nectar sloshed inside. Gus selected another wire from the box and used it to connect the battery to the other lamp. The lightbulb began to glow, radiating a yellow-white light. Gus smiled. "See, told you it would work."

Celeste smirked and gave him a half-mocking clap.

"Wait, you're an engineer, too?" *Right, Celeste said he worked as a chor engineer before studying law.*

"Not anymore. Now, I'm just curious." Gus placed the battery contraption beside the lamp. "Would you like anything to drink or eat, Asa?"

"No, sir." Asa leaned forward, getting a better look. The chor battery was similar to the ones that powered radios and the precinct's intercom system. But how the batteries worked was a mystery. The liquid was derived from the nectar of ichora flowers, but the flowers were rare and only grew on the Fae Islands. All attempts to grow them on the Continent failed.

"Well, I do. What about you?" he asked Celeste.

"Sure." They walked into the kitchen.

Thunder roared, and the wind rattled the windows, threatening to shatter the glass. But the glass held steady.

Asa looked at the little statue of God.

Are You really causing this storm? Is this Your hand at work?

Well, why not? God created all things. The world, the moon, the stars. Humans and Fae and animals. Of course He also created storms. It just... It seemed too destructive.

How could God create something that destroyed?

"Are you alright, son?" Gus asked as he resumed his seat. Both he and Celeste had a mug of iced tea.

I'm not your son! Asa almost snapped, but he stopped himself in time. Barely. "No. I mean, yes, sir."

Gus shared a look with Celeste. "I see. So, how is work?" he asked his daughter.

"Not great." She summed up the Whateley case and explained the two main theories.

Gus nodded. "Both hold merit. But the thief one is too obvious, if you ask me. Too clean cut. The battered child one, though..." He whistled low. "I'd put my money on it."

"Put money on it?!" Heat rose in Asa's face. "You're betting on a murder case?"

"Why not? People bet on everything else."

Asa balled his hands into fists, so hard that his knuckles hurt. "But you can't! A man is dead. A thief broke into his house and killed him!"

The room fell silent save for the rain. Asa's gaze shifted back and forth between Celeste and Gus. They both just stared at him. "What?"

"We already established that Wulf Smith was not in the study when Dr. Whateley was killed," Celeste said. "There is no evidence—"

"But he was there!"

"Yes, we established that," Celeste said calmly but firmly. How the hell did she do that? "Being present at a crime scene does not make one guilty."

"Guilty?!" Bloody hell, why did Reyes have to assign someone so damn stubborn as his new partner? "Lawson, the guy broke into the house. He wanted to rob them!"

"But not murder them." Celeste sighed. "Do you remember the bruises on Arlan's neck and back?"

"Yeah, the kid fell out of a swing set. Onto his back," he emphasized.

"I thought he fell onto his arm."

"Well, maybe both." Asa pinched the bridge of his nose. His head hurt. And his hand hurt. Asa glanced down and saw his fist wrapped around the statue. He relaxed his grip. The Face of Mercy, the right-side face, stared up at him. Searching. "Look, I lost count of the number of bones I broke as a kid. And my parents never beat me! Hell, they loved me! They never did anything to—"

Asa realized he was shouting. His face burning, he settled back into the chair, holding the statuette in both hands. "I'm sorry. I didn't..." Tears stung his eyes. He bowed his head, fighting them. Bloody hell, he did not want to cry. He hadn't cried once since... Since...

"Bishop, is everything alright?" Celeste asked.

He looked at the statue, praying for the right words, praying for a way out of this conversation. But the statue, as always, was silent.

"I don't feel like talking."

"Too bad," Gus said.

"Excuse me?" Asa glared at him.

"No, you are not excused. Is this case bothering you?"

Asa did not want to answer, but he was stuck here for the next several hours. He could not spend them in silence. He'd had his fill of silence. "Yes."

"Why?"

"Because..." Asa looked out the window. The hurricane raged on. Oak trees swayed as easily as beach grass in a gentle breeze. "Because we had him. Beowulf Smith, I mean. We had him at the scene, a reliable witness, and a case that would have put him away for life. I don't care if he helped Jones during the Grady case. He's still a thief. This case proves that Smith will never change. Better to get him off the streets for good."

"But he is not your murderer," said Gus.

Asa let out a sigh and felt the weight of everything, the lack of viable evidence, the grief of the Whateley family, and Captain Reyes's question, threaten to crush him. "No. Smith is innocent. He even agreed to help Jones and Celeste with the case." When Celeste explained Smith's cooperation, he struggled to believe it. And he was pissed off that he missed a chance to arrest the bastard. Did Celeste assume that he was mad at her? He hoped not.

"But he didn't agree to help *you*," Gus inferred.

"I haven't spoken to him." How could he? Asa wanted nothing more than to see Smith shipped off to Greer. "What the hell was Reyes thinking? Having a thief help with a case. It's bad enough that Jones is involved. The man's just a glorified number cruncher. Doesn't belong on the force. Hell, he..." *Oh hell, I'm speaking out loud.* How much did he say? He met Gus and Celeste's eyes and felt strangely ashamed.

"You don't think Jones should help?" Celeste asked gently. Always gently. At first, he did not understand why Reyes allowed a woman to join the Fifth Precinct. Was this the reason? If Riggs or Stant or any of the other guys had used that tone, Asa would have assumed it was a joke. But hearing that gentle tone from Celeste, how could he not answer her?

"Don't get me wrong. Jones is a good guy. Helped bring down some terrible people, but he almost got himself killed in the process. He doesn't have the training to be a police officer."

"And if he did?"

Asa shrugged. "Sure. Maybe."

Celeste thought for a moment. "Is this why you won't listen to my theories? You want Smith to be the murderer."

"Yes," he admitted. From the moment he learned about Smith's involvement, he wanted him to be the murderer, to be guilty.

But then Reyes had asked that infernal question.

If you were a thief...

Storm winds buffeted the house. The oil lamp flickered, but the one powered by the chor battery glowed steadily.

Merciful God, will it ever end?

"I take it you have something personal against this Smith guy," Gus said.

"No, I..." But it was personal. Smith had humiliated Asa and his colleagues and enjoyed every second, smiling like a smug cat. They had finally captured the Twenty-first Street Gang. The petty criminals were off the street for good. Reyes was so proud and even talked about promotions.

But then Jones paid Smith's bail, allowing the Halfling to escape justice. When Smith failed to appear in court, Reyes was furious. Not the kind of furious that Asa expected, but the quiet kind of furious. The silence that spoke volumes.

By allowing Jones to pay Smith's bail, Asa Bishop allowed a criminal to go free.

He had failed.

"I hate him," Asa whispered, remembering the press conference. Reyes had paraded Smith onto the stage, exonerating him and pinning a small medal onto his black coat. The same black coat he wore during the Ciceron Station robbery, turning him into a living shadow. "Seeing him on the stage. Watching people take his picture with Reyes. Calling him a hero..." Asa grounded his teeth. "I hate him."

A gentle hand rested on Asa's shoulder. Celeste sat next to him. Her hazel eyes, midway between brown and green, were soft and kind. He looked away. He did not deserve her kindness.

"Have you talked to Reyes about this?" she asked.

"Tried to, but..." He wanted to speak with Reyes about it, but then Reyes asked his question. Would Asa stay and argue, or would he run away? "What's the point? I'll just fail again."

"How?"

Asa sighed. How could he begin to explain?

"What about your folks?" Gus asked after a silent minute. "Have you talked to them about this case?"

"We aren't allowed to discuss cases with civilians." Another one of Reyes's new rules. Not that it stopped people from talking.

"Well, guess I'm in trouble," Celeste said with a smirk. "Dad and I talk about cases all the time."

Asa honestly was not surprised. He had just listened to Celeste summarizing the case, and Jorge used to tell him stories all the time. Chasing down criminals and the like. Those stories were half the reason why Asa became a police officer.

"You'd be surprised by the kind of insight an outsider can bring," Gus said. "You should talk to them after the storm. See what they think about Smith."

"I can't. They hate me."

"What do you mean?" Gus frowned, his light brows bunching together.

"You read about the Grady case, right?" Gus Lawson nodded. "You know about my cousin?" Asa looked them in the eyes and knew it was true. "My family, they..." More tears stung his eyes. He didn't bother fighting them. "Nobody knew what Jorge was doing. They didn't know he was dirty. And when the truth came out, they wondered if I could be dirty, too."

"But you aren't dirty. You helped collect evidence against Grady," Celeste said.

"An excellent cover." The anger and fear in his father's eyes emerged, haunting him. Instead of seeing his own son, he looked like he was facing a monster.

"Did you know?" his father asked. News about the Grady case broke the day before. Every paper in the city had article after article, each offering their own theories and speculations. Jorge's arrest received less attention. In the same sense that nine was less than ten.

"No, Jorge never told me." Asa grimaced as his shoulder throbbed. A bullet graze. The doctor told him that he was lucky.

His father glared at him. "Stop lying, Asa."

The accusation felt like a punch to the ribs. Lying? He never lied to his parents.

"You knew. You and Jorge are like brothers, and you're telling me that you didn't know?" His father stepped closer, seething. "Did you make a deal with that captain of yours? Jorge goes to prison, but you go free by telling him everything?"

"There's nothing to tell!" Panic seized him. His throat and chest felt unbearably tight. He spun around and faced his mother. She refused to look at him. "You know I'd never do that. Why don't you believe me?"

"I used to believe that Jorge was a good man." In his father's eyes, if his own nephew, the boy he had loved like a second son, could hide such terrible secrets, what secrets was his own son hiding?

His parents told him to get out.

They had not spoken to him since.

The world grew quiet. Asa glanced at the window. The wind stopped, and the rain slowed to the trickle. Was the hurricane over?

"We're in the eye." Gus walked over to the window and looked at the city. The sun had just set below the skyline. The first stars appeared, glowing faintly. He turned and faced Asa. "I'm sorry your folks reacted that way. They had no right. No evidence," he said pointedly.

Asa grimaced and squeezed his eyes shut. "I swear, if you compare me to that bloody thief—"

"Why not?" Gus walked over and rested his arms on the back of the couch. "Both of you are being unjustly accused of crimes you did not commit, and you have people who view you as guilty with minimal evidence. Including evidence in your favor."

Asa looked down at the statuette of Triumvir. The faces of Mercy and Justice peered up at him, waiting for his response.

"How do I prove it?"

"You're the police officer. You tell me."

"But I don't know!"

"Well," Gus said, resuming his seat, "you have all night to think about it. And if it helps at all, I believe you, Bishop. You are innocent, and to hell with anyone who thinks otherwise."

Asa smirked. "Thanks." He studied the statue and wondered. Mercy and Justice. Was God trying to tell him something?

Wish You could be a little more direct.

As a police officer, it was his job to bring people justice. But what about mercy? How did that factor in?

"Celeste, go over your theory again. Tell me every detail."

Chapter 25
Exchanges

The storm ended an hour or two after midnight. Invictus had long since stopped paying attention to the soft chimes of the grand clock in the hallway. The chimes were nothing compared to the incessant wind and rain and thunder. As midnight approached, he wondered if he would see the sunrise in the morning, or if the world had been transformed into one massive, unending storm.

He must have fallen asleep because when he cracked his eyes opened, he saw thin rays of sunlight peering through the window shutters.

Invictus got up from the couch, his back stiff and his skinned knees aching, and opened the shutters. He could not see much. Several large tree limbs and hundreds of twigs and leaves littered the street, but the houses directly in front of him were still there. Still intact.

"We made it," he whispered.

Judging by the brightness, he guessed it was early morning, less than an hour after dawn. He reached for his watch, and his heart sank. The watch was gone, lost somewhere between here and the Whateley house. The wind and rain, no doubt, had washed it away.

He sighed and glanced over at Wulf. The Halfling had no trouble sleeping through the storm. Curled up on his side of the couch with a blanket halfway on the floor and wearing those borrowed clothes, Wulf looked like a high school kid wearing hand-me-downs.

He is a kid, Invictus thought. Wulf was only twenty-two. Almost a decade younger than Invictus. At his age, Invictus was in his final year of college, excited about graduation and planning for a bright future.

He walked over to Wulf and shook his shoulder. One purple eye opened and glanced around.

"What happened?" Wulf asked, yawning.

"You fell asleep."

"Yeah? Then what?"

"The hurricane is over." Invictus looked around the crowded sitting room. The lantern, the flame long since extinguished, rested on the coffee table, but Norri's rocking chair was empty.

"Mr. Norri!" he called out.

A muffled voice sounded from upstairs. Invictus peered into the hallway. Norri walked down the staircase. The old man's hair was combed, and he wore a red house robe over his shirt and trousers.

"Ah, good morning, Invictus and Wulf. Get any sleep?" Norri asked with a smirk.

"Yeah," Wulf said. He joined them in the hall. "Real good sleep. That have something to do with your Seelie Court business?"

Norri smiled. "Perhaps. And you, Invictus?"

"Not really. What time is it?" Captain Reyes stated that the Fifth Precinct would open at seven o'clock. Dr. Whateley's ledgers were still in Invictus's office. Now that he had a better idea of what to look for, he wanted to analyze them again. He also wanted to request a funding report for the doctor's research. He had a hunch that Taran Manning disguised his payments as research funds.

But it still did not address the question. Who killed the doctor? The Five Families would not kill someone so valuable to the Sidhes. There must be another factor. A rival faction within the Families? Was it possible?

Or maybe he became a liability, just like Clayton Tyler.

Could Dr. Whateley have been planning to go public with his knowledge of the Families? If so, why put himself and his family at risk? Why wait all these years?

Was Dr. Whateley sick? Invictus recalled the photograph. Dr. Whateley was terribly thin, almost skeletal. Was it due to old age, or was he ill? Terminally ill? Invictus made a mental note to check the doctor's medical history.

Panic jolted through him as though he touched static electricity. He rushed to the front door and peered outside. The Whateley house, standing half a block away, was quiet. In fact, the entire street was quiet. Downed tree limbs and other debris littered the pavement, and a handful of leaves stirred in the breeze. But there were no people.

"Where is everyone?" Did the Whateleys do something to them?

Don't be ridiculous. What could they have possibly done?

But they were Changelings. If they could alter their faces, what else were they capable of?

"To answer your first question," Norri said, joining him at the door. "It's a couple minutes past six o'clock. As for the second question, everyone is likely asleep. Hard to get a good night's sleep during a hurricane."

"Oh, right." Invictus closed and locked the door, just to be safe.

"Would you care for breakfast?" Norri asked as he walked towards the kitchen.

"You got any bacon?" Wulf asked.

"Yes, plenty."

Wulf grinned. "Bookie, he got real bacon!"

"Good for him." Invictus again reached for his watch and again remembered that it was gone. Mercy sakes alive, how could he have been so careless? His grandfather bought the watch over fifty years ago, and now it, and all the memories it carried, was gone.

"What's wrong?" Wulf asked. "We got through the storm okay."

"I lost my watch."

"Good. Damn thing was no good anyway." Wulf showed off the circular scar on his wrist. The scar was now pale white.

Invictus started to argue, but guilt seized him. That burn scar was his fault, and if he were a Halfling, he would not want to be around a silver watch either.

He joined Norri in the kitchen. Their clothes were strewn over the table. He gathered up his clothes. Dry but wrinkled, and the tears in the trousers were hastily mended. Oh well. He doubted anyone would care.

"Do you mind if I change first?"

"No problem." Norri got a package of bacon out of the ice box.

Invictus and Wulf took turns changing in the upstairs washroom. Looking at his reflection, Invictus saw a pair of bloodshot, brown eyes, and black stubble covering his face. He thought about using Norri's shaving kit, but he decided to wait. Knowing the captain, Reyes would unlock the Precinct's door at seven o'clock sharp. Best not to waste any time.

He joined Norri and Wulf in the kitchen. The Halfling, now dressed in black clothes, black coat, and black hat, happily ate strips of bacon and downed a glass of milk in one gulp.

"Acts like he hasn't eaten in days," Norri said with a smile. He placed two more strips on Wulf's plate and set out a plate for Invictus. Three sweet smelling bacon strips with a side of scrambled eggs and fruit.

He probably hasn't. Invictus recalled seeing Wulf without a shirt. Underneath a score of bruises, he could see every one of the Halfling's ribs and his collarbone. If Wulf ate regular meals, then Invictus was a member of Parliament.

"So, what now?" Wulf asked after stuffing both bacon strips into his mouth. "We arresting the Whateleys?"

"On what charges?"

Norri finished cooking and sat at the table.

"They killed their old man," Wulf said, purple eyes flashing. "And they set me up."

"Correction. Carlos Vallejo set you up."

"Yeah, but maybe the Whateleys hired him. You know, same as Lewin hiring us for the Ciceron job."

Invictus relented. "Okay, I admit it's plausible. But what is their motive?"

"They, um..." Wulf frowned. He muttered under his breath.

"Those boys are very loyal to their family," Norri said. "They would not kill their father for no small reason."

"Okay, then they did it for a big reason," Wulf said.

"What about Dr. Whateley's connection to the Mannings?" Invictus asked Norri. "How much do you know?"

"Well, I can't be certain. Armand never said anything directly, but I saw expensive carriages and sometimes a motorcar pick Armand up at all hours. Day and night. And it was always the same two or three drivers."

Invictus paused, thinking, trying to add up the numbers. "Taran Manning hired Armand Whateley as a personal doctor. Why? Why not see a doctor at the hospital? Is his illness a secret?"

"In a sense." Norri lowered his voice. "I keep my ears close to the ground. Easy to do when you're a Scannie. People don't pay you much attention."

"Don't call yourself that," Wulf said.

"Pardon?"

"Scannie. It's an insult, ain't it?"

"Depends on who is saying it." Norri smiled. "And words are only insults if you allow them to be."

"Huh. Weird." Wulf downed another glass of milk. He then stared longingly at Invictus's uneaten bacon. Invictus rolled his eyes and slid the plate over to him. The Halfling snatched the bacon, eating one strip and stuffing two in his pocket.

"Anyway, a lot of wealthy families hire personal doctors," Norri continued. "Nothing out of the ordinary there. Taran can spend his money however he wishes."

"And he would not harm his own doctor." Invictus ran a hand over his hair, thinking, trying to make the equation work. "The other Families wouldn't dare harm him either. Are there others who would want to cause the Families and their allies harm?"

"Yes. Idiots," Norri said simply. "I don't know how often you listen to rumors, but most state that the Families have connections in Parliament, the City Council, the Fae Embassy, and the Royal Family. The only ones who would want to harm the Families are those who take issue with the Commonwealth itself."

"So, Scanlannish people?" Wulf asked.

"A good guess." Norri smirked. "But there are also the Akenali and a few factions in the Ruhalleen Empire." The Akena Island Chain was north of the Commonwealth. For decades, their government fought against Commonwealth annexation and were finally able to prevent it by creating extensive trade agreements. And the Ruhalleen Empire had grown to rely on the Commonwealth more and more, causing many to view it as an unofficial province. The Ruhalleen Emperor did not take kindly to that view.

"But why kill a Changeling doctor?" Invictus asked. "If someone wanted to hurt the Families, why not go after a Family member?"

"Why not tie a sack of rocks to one's feet and jump in the river?" Norri asked, raising an eyebrow.

"Okay. My head hurts," Wulf said. "Got any more milk?"

A light dawned in Invictus's mind. He reached into his jacket pocket and retrieved the small book Ruthless had given him. The back cover and last few papers were warped by water damage, but the chapter on Changelings was intact.

"Changelings can alter their appearance so they look like normal humans," Invictus said as he skimmed the text.

"We know that," Wulf interrupted.

"Hush. Changelings can exist among any people, altering their appearance to match the local ethnicity. They are bound by the laws of the Seelie Court." Several paragraphs of legal verbiage followed. Invictus skipped over it. "In the past, the Court has noted instances of Changelings exchanging their children with human children... What in the world?"

"You didn't know about exchanges?" Norri asked.

"No. Why would they do this?" The very idea made his skin crawl.

"Helps with the mimicry. And Changeling brains are different. They learn faster. Why, I recall little Alfred Whateley being able to talk when he was just six months old. And in complete sentences." Norri grinned wryly. "That was an eerie sight."

"Would've been real nice to know this earlier," Wulf muttered.

"And it explains how a trapper with no formal education was able to graduate from medical school," Invictus said, thinking out loud. "Are all Changelings like this?"

"Yes. Incredibly smart. And the Court put an end to exchanges decades ago. Now, they must ask permission."

"Still creepy," Wulf said. "Hey, you think Whateley did that with one of his kids? Giving them to another family and then the sons found out, got pissed, and killed him?"

"Wulf, for the last time..." The invisible string tugged at his mind. "Norri, did the exchanges only occur with human children, or with other Fae?"

"I've only heard of it done with humans."

"I'm wondering, could Carlos Vallejo be a Changeling who was raised by Shinnoks?"

Wulf's eyes widened. "You think he's Whateley's kid, and he killed the doctor for revenge for sending him away?"

"Possibly." It was a potential lead. One that only held an ounce of logic, but it also contained a true motive for the doctor's murder. "We will have to check birth records. The Fifth Precinct should be able to get copies from the hospital. But they were exchanges, correct? The Changeling family took a child in exchange for their biological one?"

Norri lowered his voice. "As far as I know, Turi Whateley only gave birth to two children. But Armand was in the city for months at a time. A man can get pretty lonely. Who's to say he didn't have a third child?"

"It could be Carlos," Wulf said, his eyes turning a darker shade of purple. "Is that why we can't find him? The Mannings are hiding him?"

"Or the Whateleys." How loyal would Alistair and Alfred be to an illegitimate sibling? Would they hide him even after he killed their father?

Could they really be in on the murder?

The grand clock chimed seven times.

"We have to go," Invictus said. He stood and shook Norri's hand. "Thank you for helping us. I wish we had a way to repay you." If they were in the Plains, Invictus and Wulf each would have given Norri a gift. A blanket or perhaps a pound of salt.

"Your friendship is payment enough, and you are welcome to visit anytime. That includes you, Wulf."

"Thanks." He also shook Norri's hand and then slipped on his black gloves. "And thanks for not telling the bricks about me."

"Why didn't you speak with the police, Mr. Norri? If you don't mind me asking," Invictus added.

"Well," he hesitated. "I know too many people who had bad experiences with the police. I didn't want to have an experience of my own."

"I hear ya," Wulf said.

Invictus thanked Norri again. He then checked his pockets, making sure he was not forgetting anything, and walked into the bright sunlight.

Broken tree limbs, leaves, and odd pieces of debris littered Hawthorn Street, and rainwater pooled along sidewalks. But all the houses were still standing. No major damage.

He glanced down the street at the Whateley house. All the windows were dark with the curtains drawn. He heard no sounds. Saw no movement. *But can they see us?* Invictus's skin crawled, imagining the Whateleys peering through the curtains, watching him with blood red eyes.

"You really think the bricks can find this information?" Wulf asked as they turned the corner and headed for Varnick Square. A mere handful of people cleaned up debris, piling branches and twigs at the edge of sidewalks.

"I hope so." He hoped Asa and Celeste were at the Precinct. Perhaps they could shed new light on this theory. Or better yet, they might have evidence pointing to the real murderer.

"Think they can also find death records?" Wulf asked quietly.

"Death records?"

"Yeah." Wulf bit down on his lip. "My uh... Ma said my dad's name was Camden Pritchard o'r Shinnok. Didn't say much else. Only that he died before I was born. So, about twenty-three years ago. Think they can find more information?"

"They can certainly try." And if they refused, Invictus would find the records himself. Wulf never spoke about his father. Never had a reason to.

Wulf pulled his hat down, hiding his eyes. "Thanks, Bookie, and thanks for believing me."

"Of course I believe you. You're my friend."

Wulf smiled. "So, uh, do I have to walk into the Precinct, or can I just wait outside?"

"That's up to you." They turned onto Varnick Square, and the Fifth Precinct came into view. Invictus's heart sank. "Merciful heavens."

Chapter 26

Facts

The Fifth Precinct was ruined. The trees lining the perimeter were uprooted and laid scattered about like discarded toys. One tree pierced the boarded windows, the roots sticking out of jagged glass like malignant vines. From across the street, Invictus saw that one section of the roof had caved in, creating untold damage.

Varnick Square was not spared either. Half of the trees were missing, and the remaining half had lost most of their branches. Debris littered the once peaceful square, and several benches and part of the stone fountain were shattered. Water no longer poured out of the fountain's miniature waterfall.

And the old clock tower, the clock that Invictus had set his watch by for the last two months, was missing both hands. One hand speared the soft earth between the clock and the fountain, and the other jutted from the roof of a neighboring building.

A lone figure in dark green stood in front of the Precinct's steps, gazing upwards.

"Captain Reyes?" Invictus asked as he and Wulf walked up to him. At first, he thought Reyes did not hear him, but then the captain slowly shook his head.

"First fire, and now water." He faced Invictus. Was it just the light, or did his hair have more gray than black? "There are a few officers inside, assessing the damage. Firefighters came by half an hour ago and turned off the electricity, so there's no risk of fire. But the third floor is off limits.

The damn roof caved in…" He sighed heavily. "Do you need to be here today, Jones?"

"I hoped to go over the Whateley case with Bishop and Lawson. Are they here?"

"No. Sent them home with the others yesterday evening. Lawson was dead set on getting the Whateleys' hospital records. Surprised she isn't here yet."

Invictus's heart skipped a beat. Was Celeste on the same trail as himself? Did she and Bishop find a clue pointing to an illegitimate child? The invisible string tugged again.

Reyes's eyes fell on Wulf. "Mr. Smith. Interesting seeing you here."

Wulf stared at the captain like a deer cornered by a pack of wolves. His hand brushed against his belt, reaching for a nonexistent gun.

"Jones and Lawson got partial statements from you," the captain continued. "Would you care to give me an official one?"

Wulf locked eyes with Invictus. The Halfling was pale and shaky, acting like he would run away and disappear.

Talk to him. Please, you need to talk to him. Don't run.

"Where?" Wulf asked, looking at the captain.

Reyes gestured towards the Precinct. "Or if the lack of structural integrity concerns you, there." He pointed at Varnick Square. A sole bench near the fountain had survived.

"You gonna arrest me?" Wulf asked, his voice little more than a whisper.

"Have you committed a crime recently?"

"No. Not recently. 'Cept breakin' into the Whateley house," he admitted.

"We will cross that bridge later. For now, the doctor's murder is far more pressing. And Jones, I believe your colleagues are here."

Invictus turned and saw Celeste and Asa walking down the street. They stopped in their tracks, staring at the damage. Celeste's eyes grew wide, concerned, and Asa muttered a curse under his breath.

"Are you okay?" Invictus asked them. Neither appeared injured, and their clothes were neatly ironed, unlike Invictus's rumpled shirt and trousers.

"As okay as we can be," Celeste replied with a smile. "I see you made it through the storm in one piece."

"Yeah. Wish I could say the same for the Precinct."

"Dammit." Asa surveyed every inch of the damage. "We were less than a mile away. How did we miss this?"

"Hurricanes are weird." Celeste noticed the captain and saluted. Asa did likewise.

Should I have saluted, too? Reyes either did not notice or did not mind.

"If you don't need to be here, I suggest heading home," Reyes told them.

"Alright." Wulf made it three steps before Invictus grabbed him by the elbow and steered him around to face the captain. Wulf snarled at him, showing off his teeth.

"You need to speak with Reyes, and you'll be out in the open, so don't worry. You can run away later," Invictus added, whispering.

Wulf stared at the captain, eyeing him up and down. "You got a gun and cuffs?"

"Yes," Reyes replied.

"Throw them away."

Reyes studied Wulf for a long, silent minute. He then unbuckled his holster and placed it on the sidewalk. He tossed the handcuffs into the bushes. Those had survived. "Satisfied?"

Wulf pointed at Varnick Square, not taking his eyes off the captain for a second. "You see that bench by the fountain?"

"It's the only one left."

"We'll sit there. Okay?"

"Okay."

"Bookie, will you be close by?"

"I promise. We will be inside for a few minutes. We need to write up paperwork in order to obtain documents." Assuming the hospital had not sustained damage. And assuming the doctors and nurses were not overwhelmed with patients. *How many people were injured during the storm?*

"Well, good luck with that." Wulf addressed the captain, "How long will this take?"

"No longer than ten minutes."

Wulf nodded. He and Reyes walked across the littered street to the Square.

"Hey, Smith," Asa called out.

"Yeah?"

"I..." Asa chewed on his lip, grimacing. "I believe you."

Wulf titled his head to the side. "Really? Cool, man."

Reyes sat on the bench. Wulf looked around, acted like he would run away, and then, mercifully, joined him.

"He looks just like a fox," Celeste noted.

"Yeah, a fox with black fur." Asa rolled his eyes.

"Did you mean that?" Invictus asked him. "About believing Wulf?"

"Well..." Asa shared a look with Celeste. "Kinda. I've been so focused on arresting Smith that I haven't looked at the evidence like I should. Not very professional of me."

"And now that we've established the obvious." Celeste smirked.

"Hey!"

"What paperwork do you have in mind?" she asked Invictus.

"I want to look at hospital records for all members of the Whateley family and anyone they are closely associated with."

Celeste beamed a smile, her hazel eyes shining. "Excellent!"

They walked inside. A handful of senior officers and a pair of firefighters inspected the structural beams, ceiling, and staircase. A small oak tree had crashed through a window and landed in the center of the desk area, reducing several desks to kindling. Natural light poured in through the shattered window.

"Bloody hell," Asa muttered as he walked towards his desk. Bits of glass and wood crunched underneath his boots. One of the branches had crushed his chair, and twigs and leaves were strewn around the desk. But the desk itself was spared. Asa opened the top drawer. The case file for Armand Whateley was pristine. "Thank God."

"Okay, where do you want to go over the evidence?" Celeste asked.

Invictus studied the staircase. A few stairs and part of the railing were missing, but otherwise, it looked sound. He stopped Officer Campos, a Barrish man with a streak of white in his black hair. "How badly damaged is the second floor?"

"Half the windows are gone, and there is water damage on the ceiling. Gets worse the farther you go down the hall. The captain's office..." He grimaced.

"What about my office?" Invictus asked. A jolt of panic coursed through him. If Dr. Whateley's ledgers were ruined...

Campos shrugged. "We haven't checked."

"May I?"

"Sure." Campos went with a firefighter to inspect the interrogation rooms.

Invictus, Celeste, and Asa carefully navigated the stairs. In addition to missing three steps, two were badly cracked, and the rest were warped by water damage, causing them to shift precariously. Part of the railing lay in a crumpled heap on the floor. But the hallway floor was sound.

Invictus's office, mercifully, suffered minimal damage. One of the windowpanes was cracked, and one corner of the ceiling had water damage, but all of his files had survived. He whispered a prayer of thanks as he inspected Dr. Whateley's ledgers. Not a single drop of water.

"Will this do?" he asked Asa and Celeste.

Both officers nodded.

"Okay, Invictus, tell me why you want hospital records," Celeste said as she sat on one corner of the desk. Asa took a seat in a spare chair, sitting backwards with his arms crossed over the top.

Invictus sat in his own chair, grateful to still have a chair, and said, "The Whateleys are Changelings. A type of Fae that can alter their appearances and..." He explained Dr. Whateley's history with the Manning family, notably Taran Manning, the rumored Old Man of the Sidhe Family. He then explained the doctor's change in behavior, the odd hours he kept, and the old practice of Changelings exchanging their own children with human ones.

"That's... disturbing," Asa said. He shivered.

"Do you think Dr. Whateley continued the practice?" Celeste asked.

"We aren't completely sure. Both of his sons are Changelings, too." Invictus explained that he and Wulf went to question them right before the hurricane made landfall.

"Jones." Asa massaged the bridge of his nose. "This is why you question people with an officer present. What if they had injured you? Locked you in a closet or something?"

"I..." Invictus's gut twisted in knots, imagining himself and Wulf tied up, helpless. His mind wandered to Dav Martinez, tied to a chair before Lewin tortured him to death. Would Alistair and Alfred have done the same? "Well, I didn't know they were Changelings at the time."

"Save the lecture for later," Celeste told Asa. She motioned for Invictus to continue.

"I think Dr. Whateley had an affair while in medical school, and Taran Manning helped set the child up for adoption. In exchange for his silence, Manning asked Whateley to be his personal doctor. And Whateley probably learned a lot of secrets while working for him."

"Secrets that got him killed?" Asa asked.

"No, Whateley was valuable to Manning. I think the child is Carlos Vallejo, the thief who talked Wulf into robbing the Whateley house. I think he wanted Dr. Whateley to officially recognize him as his son. But Whateley refused, so Carlos killed him in anger. Remember, Wulf said he heard arguing before the gunshot."

"Alright, then why drag Wulf into this?" Asa asked.

"Maybe Carlos always knew it would end with murder," Celeste said, her face turning pale. "Invictus, did you meet Alfred's son, Arlan?"

"No."

Celeste explained meeting with Alfred at the art dealership and seeing Arlan. The child had his arm in a cast and bruises along his neck and collarbone.

"I know those bruises could have resulted from a fall, but I got the impression that Arlan was trying to tell us something and didn't want his father to overhear. I think he knows more about our murder, and," she swallowed, "I think Dr. Whateley was abusive towards his family."

Invictus let the information sink in, the numbers adding up. "Could both be true?"

Asa jumped up and started pacing. "Hold up, if both are true, then the Whateley family and this Carlos Vallejo person conspired with each other?"

"Possibly." The invisible string tugged again, telling Invictus that it was more than possible.

"Which is why we need medical records," Celeste said. "You said that Whateley changed while attending medical school, right? Becoming more volatile?"

"Yeah."

"Maybe that's when the abuse started. When the family immigrated to Malkin City, they were isolated, surrounded by strangers. They had nobody to confide in, and the Scanlan Campaign had just started. People here had little love for the Scanlannish. And Dr. Whateley was connected to powerful people."

"Yeah, powerful in the wrong way," Asa muttered.

"Those same people could have held a secret child as leverage," Invictus added.

"Again," Asa said, continuing to pace, "we need evidence. I came within an inch of convicting Smith with minimal evidence. No way I'm letting you two fall into the same trap."

"Okay." Celeste grabbed a piece of paper and a pen. "We need hospital records for Alistair and Alfred Whateley as well as extended family members. And records for any children born while Dr. Whateley was attending medical school."

"Medical school takes four years to complete," Asa countered. "Do you know how many kids are born in Malkin City every year?"

"Then we narrow the search to children without fathers listed on their birth certificates," Invictus said.

"When was Dr. Whateley in medical school?" Celeste asked.

Invictus racked his brain. "Alfred is thirty-seven. He said the family immigrated when he was seven years old, so thirty years ago. A child born thirty to thirty-three years ago."

But Carlos is around Wulf's age.

Invictus recalled meeting Prince Hastyr and Prince Talos. Both men were in their forties, but they could easily pass for thirty or thirty-five. If Carlos was around thirty years old and had a young-looking face, he could pass for someone in his early twenties.

If and could. There were too many 'ifs' and 'coulds' in this case for Invictus's taste.

"Got it." Celeste jotted down a note. "We also need medical records for Arlan. He might have suffered previous injuries."

"But how does Wulf Smith factor in?" Asa asked. "If the Whateleys and Vallejo conspired to kill the old man, why not have Vallejo act as the thief and run away. Hell, nobody would have needed to see him. Just stage a robbery."

"Unless they wanted to guarantee an arrest," Invictus said, his heart sinking. "Carlos recruited Wulf and Macsen, and then he poisoned Macsen so Wulf wouldn't have an alibi. He would be arrested. The Whateleys would have justice for their father's death, and Taran Manning would have justice for his doctor."

It must be the missing key. The Whateleys and Carlos could not simply commit the murder themselves. Even if the Whateleys allowed the case to grow cold, the Mannings would not stop until they found the real murderer. The Whateleys needed someone to take the fall.

"But it was still a risk," Asa replied. "What if Wulf decided not to break into the house by himself? What if he decided the risk was too great?"

"Wulf thought he was breaking into a different house. Carlos told him that Professor Townsend was out of town for the month. No thief would pass up such an opportunity."

Asa froze as if Invictus had smacked him in the face. "Who?"

"Professor Townsend. He lives at—"

"368 Hawthorn Street. Gone for a whole month." Asa cursed under his breath. "Jones, I think you're on to something. Lawson, you're right. The kid was trying to tell us something. Townsend."

Celeste gasped. "His teacher! Arlan said he had a new teacher because Mrs. Townsend and her husband were on vacation. Alfred must have learned that from the school. He..." Her eyes widened. "We need those records."

"What if the Whateleys run?" Invictus's gut twisted in knots. He knew the Whateleys' secret. It was only a matter of time before the police came knocking, demanding answers. Unless they already escaped.

All of the curtains were drawn. He pictured the Whateley house after the storm. Quiet. So, eerily quiet. Did they already leave? The storm ended sometime between midnight and sunrise. They could have left in the dark. Nobody would have noticed.

"Jones, head to the desk area and ask the first officer you see to place a watch on the Whateley house," Asa said. "Then asked for a carriage. Don't let them give you any flack. Lawson, you and I will write up the paperwork. Once we get those records, we'll question the bastards again."

Invictus complied and hurried down the stairs as quickly as the broken steps allowed. Most of the officers were sweeping up leaves and broken glass. Two others studied the tree, debating the best way to chop it up. Pembroke, the young Shinnok Fae, glanced around, looking like a lost child in a busy marketplace.

"Pembroke, I need you to watch the Whateley house and make sure nobody leaves."

"What?" The boy stared at him in a daze. He then shivered and blinked a few times. "I mean, yes, sir. Um, where is it?"

Invictus gave him the address.

"Okay." Pembroke shifted his feet and nervously touched the buttons on his jacket. "But what if they want to leave?"

"You're a police officer. Order them to stay."

Pembroke paled. "I don't think I—"

"Pembroke," Invictus firmly placed both hands on the boy's shoulders. "Tell them that the order comes from Captain Reyes."

"But I heard it from you." His purple eyes filled with fear.

Right, he's a full-blooded Fae. He has to obey the Seelie Court's laws. One law forbad certain subspecies from telling direct lies. Oddly, it did not apply to all. Invictus made a mental note to ask Ruthless about it and then said,

"Well, Reyes told me, and now I'm telling you."

"Alright." Pembroke took two hesitant steps, paused, and looked like he wanted to tell Invictus something. Instead, he hurried out of the Precinct.

Invictus looked around. Several officers were nearby, but they were busy assessing the damage and cleaning up the debris. Would one of them be willing to drive a carriage to the Old City?

Granted, he could get the carriage himself. The idea, however, filled him with dread. He had only driven a handful of times, and horses were intelligent creatures. Most refused to let strangers handle them, and some had a tendency to bite.

You can do this. You just have to drive a few blocks. But before that, he needed to attach the harness to the horse without getting bitten, then attach the horse to the carriage without getting kicked...

He shoved the fear away. Police horses were trained animals. They were used to reins and harnesses and drivers. And maybe Invictus didn't need to drive. Asa and Celeste might know...

"Reyes ordered all the horses to be housed at the First Precinct," he remembered with dismay. The First Precinct was two miles away. Too far to walk in a timely manner.

Maybe there's a cab.

It was a longshot, but what other choice did he have?

Invictus walked outside and peered up and down the street. A few more pedestrians had ventured outside, but there were no carriages. No cabs or motorcars.

"Invictus Jones?" asked someone behind him.

"Yes?"

A pair of hands seized him and pinned his arms behind his back. He tried to call for help, but another pair tied a gag around his mouth and placed a burlap sack over his head. Invictus tried to kick them, but they lifted him off his feet and carried him away. Invictus screamed, but the gag muffled all sounds.

The hands threw him, and he landed on a padded surface, the air knocked out of his lungs. A door slammed shut. A motor started, and the vaguely floral scent of chor filled the air.

A motorcar. I'm in a motorcar.

The car lurched into motion, heading away from the Precinct.

Chapter 27

The Captain

The bench was a good spot. From here, Wulf could see the street corner, the Precinct, what was left of it, and most of Varnick Square. Only a handful of people milled about, and tree branches and other debris littered the square. Debris he could easily jump over while running away. The captain would never catch him. And the captain had sat down first. Dumb mistake. Easier to run away from someone when they was sittin' and you were standin'.

The captain studied him with dark eyes, waiting.

Wulf, against his better judgment, sat down on the edge of the bench. He glanced around. None of the people seemed to be watching. And why would they? They were just two people sitting on a bench. Out in the open.

I hope Germanicus ain't close by.

The Aziza would report this meeting to Ruthless in a heartbeat. In most gangs, speaking to a brick meant a beating or exile, sometimes death. But Ruthless had a brain in his skull. He knew Wulf was no snitch, and he knew all about the Whateley case. Probably more than Wulf did. He'd put two and two together.

But what if Germanicus tells Macsen?

Bloody hell, Ruthless would understand, but what about the rest of the Marauders? Would they still trust him or wonder if he'd turned informant?

"Are you alright, Mr. Smith?" Captain Reyes asked, studying him like he was some weird looking bug. Thank God the man had no gun or cuffs. It made running away all the more easier.

But I gotta talk to him. Bookie promised up and down that Reyes believed Wulf was innocent, that the captain just wanted to hear his side of events. Was it true? Bookie, despite all his book learning, was not too keen when it came to folks lying.

"Sure. Fine." Wulf glanced across the street. Bookie walked inside the Precinct with the two bricks. Celeste Lawson seemed nice, but Asa Bishop was the brick who arrested Wulf at Ciceron Station. The brick on duty when Wulf got out on bail. Each time, he looked like he wanted to punch a hole in the wall.

Bishop said he believed me. What was that about? Some sort of brick trick to make him feel more at ease? The captain must have put him up to it.

"You've had quite a week, Mr. Smith," Reyes said calmly, as though he wasn't talking to a wanted thief.

"My name's Wulf." His skin crawled. Why was the captain calling him 'Mr. Smith'? Sure, it was his name. Part of it. But Mr. Smith sounded like a City Council member or a strict teacher who liked to smack kids' knuckles with a ruler.

"Very well. Care to talk about Sunday night, Wulf?"

"I ain't no snitch!" he blurted out.

"Good." Reyes's eyes narrowed, a perfect mirror of Ruthless. "I don't want snitches. I want information from a reliable source."

"That's what a snitch is, dumbass."

Reyes smirked. "Not quite. A snitch, from my experience, is a person who is willing to sell information about the people who trust them. Such a person, in turn, is not worthy of my trust. Understand?"

"Yeah, man. Crystal." *Huh, never thought about it that way.* But it made sense.

"Excellent. Now, tell me about Sunday, the twelfth. Everything you saw, heard, and smelled."

Wulf sat perfectly still as he glanced around. He saw no familiar faces, but who knew if anyone was listening? A bright yellow sprite bobbed around a flower bush, one of a handful with their roots in the ground. Was it a free agent, or was it a trained bug? Ruthless told him to swat any sprite that acted too smart.

"The Fae like to use them as spies."

"Ain't we Fae?" Wulf, then twelve years old, had asked.

Ruthless smiled wryly. "In a sense."

"Wulf?" Reyes studied him with those dark, human eyes.

Swallowing, Wulf said, "Okay." Against his better judgment, he told the captain everything. The big house with its tall trees. Picking the window lock. The gaslamp burning in the supposedly empty house. Two voices, both male, arguing.

A gunshot.

The maid seeing him. The terrified look in her eyes followed by a scream.

Wulf squeezed his eyes shut. Bloody hell, he could still hear her scream.

"Anything else?" Reyes asked. A faint breeze brushed through the square. The yellow sprite glided away on the current.

Bloody hell, was it listening?

"No," Wulf answered.

"Tell me about the two men who were supposed to meet you."

"I ain't no snitch!" Wulf's face burned. No way he'd sell Macsen out. No bleeding way!

"Good. Now, tell me why they failed to show." The captain watched him, both hands clasped together. The way he watched was so similar to Ruthless it was kinda creepy.

"Got real bad food poisoning. Could barely get out of bed."

"Both of them? You saw both men when they were severely ill?"

"No. Just Mac. I never found Carlos." The leather gloves creaked as Wulf balled his hands into fists. He forced himself to relax. Reyes wanted to help, and he was asking the same questions as Bookie. Important questions. And unlike Bookie, Reyes had the resources to actually help.

You sure about that? Ruthless and his people searched the whole city. Carlos Vallejo is nowhere. Probably ain't his real name.

And now Bookie thought Carlos was a Changeling, able to alter his appearance. How were they supposed to find someone who could blend in with every crowd?

"I checked the city records," Reyes said. "According to the latest census, there are no Shinnok Halflings by that name."

"He could've just gotten to the city. You won't find Bookie's name in the census either. He's only been here a couple of months." The City Council conducted a census every five years in January. Bookie's name wouldn't officially be on the books for another year and a half.

Reyes studied him for so long that Wulf began to sweat. "Are you educated, Wulf?"

"No, I..." He lowered his head, unable to meet the captain's eyes. "I can barely read."

"And yet, you found the flaw in my search immediately. Neither are you afraid to voice that flaw." Reyes sighed and shook his head. "If only half of my officers were able to do the same." He paused, thinking. "Why do you refer to Mr. Jones as 'Bookie'?"

"Cause he works with numbers."

"But he is not a bookmaker."

Wulf shrugged. At first, he didn't see the difference between a bookmaker and an accountant. Both wrote numbers in ledgers, and both handled money. He understood the difference now, but Bookie... Well, he looked more like a Bookie than an Invictus.

"Do you think Mac's food poisoning was accidental?"

"Hell no."

"Someone was responsible?" The captain raised an eyebrow.

"Yeah. We think Carlos poisoned him so I would be alone and break into the wrong house."

"The wrong house." The captain looked down the street, towards the Old City. "Explain."

Wulf did so. A week ago, he would have run like hell. No thief in their right mind spoke to a brick. And here he was, speaking to the head brick himself. But what choice did he have exactly? Ruthless failed to find Carlos, and Bookie was doing his best, but even his best had failed. Same with the other bricks. Lots of ideas and theories, but nothing solid. No real evidence. No real motive. It was either talk to the captain or risk hanging from a rope.

I still might hang. Hangings were rare nowadays, reserved only for the worst criminals. When he was thirteen and cocksure of his thieving skills, Ruthless took him to a hanging. One of the city's last public hangings.

"What did he do?" Wulf asked, struggling to keep down his lunch. The man's neck broke instantly, the sickening snap echoing in his ears. Some people cheered while others watched solemnly, nodding their heads once the deed was done.

"He robbed a carriage belonging to a member of Parliament," Ruthless replied, his silvery eyes fixed on the swinging body. "Normally, he'd get five to ten on Greer, but the Parliament member has friends in the court."

"So, he ordered this?" Wulf felt numb.

Ruthless said nothing, just watched.

Wulf wondered if the Whateleys had similar pull.

To hell with the Whateleys. The doctor worked for Taran Manning.

And Manning held sway with all kinds of powerful folks.

"Professor Townsend." Reyes studied the sky. A perfect blue with no clouds. If Wulf didn't know any better, he would never have guessed that it stormed half the night. "Resides at 368 Hawthorn Street, diagonal from the Whateley house at 386 Hawthorn. Very interesting that the numbers are the same, but in a different order. Easy to confuse."

"I didn't confuse nothing! Carlos told me the address several times. He..." Wulf snarled. "He set me up, and I don't even know why. What did I do to him?"

"Perhaps nothing. Your name and photo were in the papers. Finding your connections in the underworld likely wasn't difficult. It was all a matter of timing."

"But why kill the doctor?"

"What do you think, Wulf?" The captain narrowed his eyes, again looking eerily similar to Ruthless.

"Bookie thinks that Carlos is the doctor's bastard kid, and he wanted revenge for getting thrown away."

"And you? Do you feel the same way towards your own father?"

Wulf's heart skipped a beat. "What?"

"We have a copy of your birth certificate. Beowulf C. Smith. Born on April twelfth, 496 F.C. to Maria B. Smith. No father listed."

"My father's dead," Wulf managed. His heart twisted at the same time his mind reeled. Reyes had a copy of his birth certificate? What the hell for? "Died before I was born."

"I'm sorry to hear that."

Wulf studied the captain's face, searching for the lie. Bricks didn't care about thieves. This was just an act to gain Wulf's trust, to get the information he wanted before shipping Wulf's sorry ass to Greer. But the captain's face was blank, unreadable.

"But," Reyes continued, "you did not tell me what you think."

"I just—"

"You told me what Jones thinks."

Wulf blinked. Huh. Weird.

"So, what do you, and only you, think, Wulf?"

"I think this whole job's screwy." He shook his head furiously. "Bloody hell, I knew it was too good to be true. No thief ever got that lucky. Sure, the house is empty, but there are dogs or guards or a brick making the rounds. And if ya manage to avoid all those, you gotta keep quiet, or others will hear and want a cut of the score.

"Carlos never stole before. The guy was terrified of his own shadow." The little Halfling shook so bad during their last meeting that Wulf feared he was coming down with something. "I think that if he wanted to kill the doctor for revenge, he'd have just done it. No need to drag me and Macsen into this mess."

A light dawned in his mind. "You know, I bet Carlos was hired by the real killer. Maybe the doctor does have a bastard kid, and they hired Carlos. They told him to get me involved so I'd take the fall. Bloody hell, that would explain a lot." Carlos was real jumpy, too. Far too jumpy to make a good thief. And Wulf caught Carlos staring at him a couple times. Studying him. Watching him. Did he want to tell Wulf the truth?

"You okay, man?" Wulf had asked early Saturday morning. The alleyway between shops was cramp and narrow and the nearby trashcan smelled something awful, but it was private. Too far from either street for people to see or overhear them, and too early in the morning for anyone to care.

"I, um..." Carlos shivered, his purple eyes reflecting the growing sunlight. "I've never broken into a house. I mean, I went inside a few times to collect pay, but..." He pulled his jacket tighter, shivering.

"Hey, don't sweat it." Wulf placed a hand on Carlos's shoulder. "Like you said, easy in and easy out."

"But, Wulf, I..." Carlos locked eyes with him. His mouth opened and closed a few times, trying to form words. He shook his head.

"You wanna scrap the job?"

"No!" Carlos shivered again. "No, we can't. I..." He took a deep breath. "I will meet you at the drop. Me and Macsen. Okay?"

Wulf had half a mind to scrap the job himself. He and Mac could swing it, but Carlos had no real skills. Just thinking about the job scared him witless. What if he got cold feet? Or what if someone else got wise to the job and pressured Carlos to share part of the take?

Both were possible, but now he wondered if Carlos had set him up in more ways than one. What if he was an informant?

"Is Carlos Vallejo one of your people?" he asked Captain Reyes.

"If he was, I wouldn't be talking to you."

"Another precinct?"

Reyes shook his head. "We have a list of informants. And it isn't written down," he added.

Wulf cursed in his head. Sure would be nice to steal that list.

"You know the Whateleys are Changelings, right?" Wulf asked.

"We do now."

"What if you can't find the real killer?" Wulf's hands began to sweat. "What will happen to me?" And what would happen to Ma? He knew Ruthless and half a dozen neighbors would look in on her, but would she be okay?

"That is for the courts to decide, but I will vouch for you."

That was a small comfort.

Wulf caught familiar movement out of the corner of his eye. He saw Bookie walk out of the Precinct and looked up and down the street.

"Over here, Bookie!" Wulf stood and waved his hands over his head.

Bookie was looking in the wrong direction.

Wulf rolled his eyes. Yes, human hearing was worse than Fae hearing, but Wulf was right bloody in front of him.

Two men rounded the Precinct and grabbed Bookie. One pinned his arms behind his back, and the other placed a sack over his head. Before Wulf could think, they dragged Bookie away.

"Bookie!"

Wulf's heart leapt into his throat. He found himself on the docks, the moon hiding behind the clouds. Men surrounded him on all sides. Two held Dav, barely conscious and badly beaten. Wulf's mind raced, thinking of his next move, but there was no escape.

He ran across the street, forcing his legs to move. But the other men were faster. They shoved Bookie into a motorcar and sped away.

Cursing, Wulf ran his hands through his hair. Dammit, if he had only been faster... If he had a gun...

Captain Reyes ran up to him.

"Stop them!" Wulf yelled at the captain. But the man just stood there, watching the motorcar speed away.

Wulf spied the holster on the sidewalk and picked it up. A 38 Bricker. Six shots. Excellent condition. Who in their right mind...

He grimaced. The captain's gun. Wulf told him to toss the weapon, thinking he would have a better chance of running away. But if the captain had this gun with him, he could have fired off a warning, gotten the men to freeze. Even if it was just a second or two, Wulf could have saved Dav.

Bookie.

He grimaced as tears stung his eyes.

"What do you plan to do with that gun?" the captain asked.

"Save my friend." Wulf tied the holster around his waist. The weight felt good, natural.

He made it two steps before Reyes grabbed his arm.

"What the hell—"

"You'll never catch a motorcar on foot. Come with me."

Chapter 28
Eyes of Gold

Blood rushed in Invictus's ringing ears. He tried screaming for help, but each time the gag cut into the sides of his mouth. The motorcar lurched as the thugs turned a corner, speeding away. He tried to scream again. One of the thugs yelled at him to shut up. Not that it made much of a difference. He doubted anyone could hear him over the motorcar's engine.

Invictus cursed under his breath. Did anyone see the thugs grab him? Were the police on the way?

His heart sank. All of the Fifth Precinct's horses were over a mile away, and even if a horse and carriage were available, they would never catch up to a motorcar.

Invictus forced himself to breathe evenly. Inhale, exhale. Through the nose. Panic threatened to overwhelm him, to take control. No, he needed to stay calm, think. He did not see either man's face. Were they connected to the Whateley case?

Of course they're connected! Why else would they grab you?

He tried to move his hands, but his wrists were bound too tightly. Damn.

Okay, Invictus, think. Someone connected to Dr. Whateley. Is it Alistair and Alfred? Doubtful. Neither would risk kidnapping Invictus in front of a police precinct. The action would only invite more questioning. And Wulf knew their secret, too. Kidnapping Invictus solved nothing.

Then it must be someone else. Someone who did not fear repercussions from the police.

The Five Families?

The Manning family had close ties to Dr. Whateley, and Invictus was responsible for Lewin Manning's arrest. Did they want revenge? Get rid of him before he could bring more of their crimes to light?

Think, Invictus. The Mannings are Sidhe Fae. They have to obey the Seelie Court.

He recalled the protection Norri placed over his home. Could Invictus do the same for himself? Norri made the process sound so simple. Speak a few words in the name of the Seelie Court and it was done. But was it really that simple? Invictus wished he had asked more.

Too late now.

Moving his jaw and tongue, he managed to push the gag out of his mouth.

"I, Invictus Jones," he whispered, his mouth unbearably dry, "hereby, in the name of the Seelie Court, prevent all Fae from harming me. And um..." Norri worded his protection so all unfriendly Fae would feel extreme cold. Could Invictus do something similar? Something more abrupt? "And any Fae who try to harm me will have terrible headaches. So bad that they cannot see or move. And I... um, I create this protection on myself in the name of the Seelie Court."

Invictus waited. Did it work? He did not feel different, nor did the protection sound legally binding. But if the Mannings did not kill him, he would count it a blessing.

The motorcar turned this way and that through the streets of Malkin City. Were they merely avoiding storm damage, or did they want to disorientate him?

I barely know half the streets, and I have a bloody sack over my head!

The motorcar made a final turn, slowed to a stop, and the engine cut off.

Invictus's heart pounded in his chest and throat, and his ear rang painfully. Where were they? The river? Merciful heavens, what if they weren't Fae? What if they were humans? Would they just toss him into the water and wait for him to drown?

His chest tightened as his mind wandered back to that bright, summer day at Lake Bona. His parents were busy talking with the other adults. Boring conversations about work and chores and whether the Provincial Council would raise taxes this year.

Invictus watched Quintus wander off with a group of older kids. They swam in the lake, splashing and diving and playing blind man's bluff.

He knew he should ask before joining them, but his parents were too absorbed in their conversations. And besides, Invictus was eight years old. He was grown up enough to make his own decisions.

He walked down the pier, the rough wood warm on his bare feet. The cool, blue water reflected the lazy clouds. He waved at Quintus, but his older brother did not see him. Quintus's eyes were fixed on the pretty girl swimming beside him.

Invictus gazed down at the water. His reflection stared back at him. He did not know how to swim, but Quintus and the other kids made it look so easy. Just moving their arms and legs.

Taking a deep breath, Invictus jumped in. Cool water enveloped him. He moved his arms and legs, but nothing happened. He sank deeper. His lungs began to hurt. Panic seized him as he frantically stroked and kicked, slicing through water but sinking deeper and deeper. He screamed for help. Water choked him.

His vision blurred. A shadow appeared at the same time the water turned black.

A moment later, he was on the pier, coughing up water as Quintus knelt over him.

"Are you okay?" Quintus asked, his voice shaking. His older brother looked so scared. But that wasn't right. Nothing scared Quintus.

Nothing except the possibility of me drowning, Invictus thought as the motorcar door opened. Two pairs of hands grabbed him and dragged him to his feet.

His knees almost buckled as he imagined cold water enveloping him, pulling him under. If they did throw him into the river, no one would be there to save him.

Would anybody even know what happened?

"Remove the hood," said a woman's voice.

"But we aren't—" one thug protested.

"Remove the hood," she said more forcefully.

The thugs obeyed.

Invictus blinked in the bright sunlight and glanced around. Instead of the river's edge, they stood on a gravel driveway. Massive stone walls covered with crawling ivy hedged them in, blocking the view of the road and neighboring houses. A large fountain sculpted in the shape of a woman with flowing hair emptying a pitcher rested in the center of the green lawn. Rose bushes surrounded the fountain, and more roses lined the driveway, leading to a mansion.

The mansion was far more opulent than anything in the Gems or the Old City. Reaching four stories into the sky, the mansion was easily three times as wide as Invictus's boardinghouse. Flowering vines reached as high as the third-story windows. The exterior was a pristine white with the window shutters and front door painted a soft blue, almost the same color as an autumn sky. Columns decorated with ivy and gaslamps in stained glass housings lined the front porch.

"Where are we?" Invictus wondered out loud.

"Shut up!" one of the thugs ordered. He stood a head taller than Invictus and had a tan, Malkinese complexion with short, black hair. Shimmering turquoise eyes gave him away as Fae. A Bannock Halfling, Invictus guessed.

The other thug had paler skin. His eyes were purple flecked with gold. A Shinnok-Sidhe Hybrid, most likely. Despite his wiry build, he held Invictus's arm in a vise-like grip.

And the woman, who stood eye to eye with Invictus and wore an ankle length blue dress, had deep, bronze skin with black hair and gold eyes set in an angular face. A Sidhe. Invictus's stomach twisted in knots.

The Sidhe Family.

"Take him into the parlor," the Sidhe woman said. "And untie his hands. He isn't going anywhere."

The two thugs complied and followed the woman into the mansion.

The interior was equally beautiful with white walls adorned with oil paintings, and plush green carpeting lined the hallway. Invictus would have been impressed if he was not terrified.

Every ten feet, gaslamps burned low in ornate glass and marble scones vined with gold.

No iron, Invictus noted. He saw no trace of metal in the house. No silver, either.

The parlor contained a writing desk, several plush chairs arranged in a semi-circle around an empty fireplace, and dozens of potted plants. Ferns and flowers and one cactus, no doubt imported from Ruhalleen. The window curtains were open, flooding the room with bright, morning light.

The Bannock thug shoved Invictus into one of the chairs.

"What do you want?" he asked the Sidhe woman. His voice sounded hoarse, and his ear still rang.

"My brother will be here shortly. Vester," she addressed the Fae with purple and gold eyes.

"Yes, ma'am?" He stood at attention.

"Make sure Mr. Jones doesn't wander off. Sean, come with me." She turned on her heels and strode out of the parlor.

"Yes, Ms. Manning," both thugs replied. Sean the Bannock Halfling followed her. Vester stood in the corner near the windows. He kept glancing outside but never took his eyes off Invictus for more than a few seconds.

Invictus clasped his hands tightly, struggling to control his fear. Ms. Manning. The thugs had addressed the woman as Ms. Manning. Did that mean this was the house of Taran Manning, the Old Man of the Sidhe Family? She was too young to be Taran's sister. Maybe she was Lewin's sister or his cousin. Invictus felt lightheaded.

A clock on the mantle chimed nine times.

Invictus wished he still had his pocket watch. He could threaten the Sidhe with silver and escape.

No, that was a terrible idea. The two thugs had overpowered him in a matter of seconds. Even if he had the watch and created a solid plan, they would subdue him and take away the watch in no time. And then what would happen to him? Nothing good.

The invisible string tugged at his mind. Invictus glanced up at the same time a man walked into the parlor. He was the same height as Invictus but looked like he weighed thirty pounds less. His expensive black suit hung off him as though he were a child trying on his father's clothes. His black hair was trimmed short and recently combed. And his eyes were a deep, burning gold.

Invictus's vision lurched. For half a second, he was face to face with Lewin Manning again, but no silver burn marred this Sidhe's face. A smile crossed his thin lips.

"Invictus Jones?" the Sidhe asked.

"Yes?"

The Sidhe held out his hand. "Jacob Manning."

Invictus studied the hand, his heart in his throat. Was it a trick? Did Jacob Manning want to lure him into a false sense of security? He stole a glance at Vester. The Hybrid stared at him, his head titled to the side, oddly foxlike.

"Hello," Invictus said, shaking Jacob's hand.

Jacob Manning smiled brightly, showing off white teeth, and sat in the chair next to Invictus. "It's nice to finally meet you, Mr. Jones. I've read all about you in the papers."

Invictus stared at him, trying and failing to find words. Officially, Jacob Manning was a member of the Malkin City Council with aspirations of being elected to Parliament. An upstanding citizen who had the misfortune of being cousins with an extortionist. Jacob claimed that the family had a falling out with Lewin over a decade ago, and feigned shock after his arrest.

But Ruthless explained that, with Lewin out of the way, Jacob was now the Old Man's heir. The new Right Hand.

Jacob frowned, concerned. "Did Sean or Vester hurt you? I gave them explicit orders to bring you here unharmed." He shot a glare at Vester.

The Hybrid jolted. "Sir, we didn't—"

Jacob raised a hand. Vester bowed his head and retreated farther into the corner.

"They didn't hurt me," Invictus said quickly. "Just frightened me."

"I see." Jacob's smile returned, but Vester huddled against the wall, refusing to make eye contact.

This isn't the first time the Mannings have threatened to hurt him, Invictus guessed. Based on the reaction, they must have made good on those threats.

"I apologize for bringing you here on such short notice," Jacob continued. "But I didn't want Reyes's people snooping around. The police do an adequate job of protecting and serving, but they can be a terrible nuisance. Don't you agree?"

Invictus did not know how to respond.

"Of course," Jacob said, "working with the police, you must have a different perspective. Have they found any credible leads on Dr. Whateley's murder?"

Invictus relaxed a little. The Mannings did not want revenge. Just answers. Answers he did not have. "Not yet. But they're getting close."

"No names?"

"A few." Invictus's palms began to sweat. Did they suspect Wulf? But Wulf was across the street in Varnick Square. Why not grab him instead?

Unless they already did.

His heart lurched.

Jacob smirked, his gold eyes flashing. "Do you play cards, Invictus?"

"No, sir."

"Too bad. You have the instinct for it." Jacob shook his head. "What am I doing? Here you are a guest in my house, and I haven't offered you anything to eat or drink. Would you care for anything?"

"No, thank you," he said even though his throat was terribly dry. But a cup of tea was an excellent way to conceal drugs or poison. He'd read countless detective stories about people being drugged by an innocent looking beverage.

"Are you sure? Our maid makes excellent blueberry tea."

"I'm sure."

Jacob studied him for a silent moment, his eyes like twin suns. "We really ought to teach you to play cards. With your talent for numbers, I'm certain you'll take to the game like a fish to water."

"Or a bird to air," Invictus replied, forcing all thoughts of water out of his mind.

"Exactly."

Invictus shifted in his seat, stealing a glance into the hallway. He did not see anyone. A grand clock stood opposite the parlor's doorway, ticking away. Gold inlays shaped like vines decorated its wooden face.

"I, um, guess you made it through the hurricane alright," Invictus said.

"Yes, it wasn't nearly as bad as the weather scientists feared."

Wasn't nearly as bad? The wind was so bloody strong, Invictus feared the roof of Norri's house would rip off. And the Fifth Precinct suffered terrible damage.

What about my neighborhood? Had the boardinghouse survived? Were the other tenants alright?

"Now that pleasantries are over." Jacob sat on the edge of his chair, his bony fingers laced together. "I want to talk with you about Dr. Whateley. Your associate was the main suspect for a while, correct?"

"Yes, but he's innocent. The police found evidence that—"

"Calm down, Invictus." Jacob locked eyes with him.

Invictus's heart skipped a beat. The Sidhe could manipulate people by locking eyes with them, making them do or think whatever they wished. But Invictus did not feel calm. The opposite, in fact. Was it the Seelie Court's protection?

Merciful heavens, I think it's working.

Invictus forced himself to relax anyway. Let Jacob think his influence was working.

"Very good," Jacob said. "How much do the police know about Dr. Whateley's professional life?"

"He was a doctor who later specialized in research." Invictus hesitated. "And he was Taran Manning's personal physician."

Jacob nodded. "My uncle distrusts hospitals. He has employed personal physicians for most of his life. Armand Whateley was one of a few he trusted."

"And Whateley was the only Changeling."

Jacob's eyes flashed dark gold. "How did you come by this information?"

Invictus almost told him about Mr. Grady's letter, but his gut told him to keep quiet. "I accidentally saw Alistair and Alfred's real faces," he admitted.

"Idiots!" Jacob sneered and slammed his fist against the armrest. Vester flinched.

I should help him, Invictus thought. But how?

Jacob composed himself. "No matter. The police were bound to discover the truth eventually. So, I've nothing to hide."

Except your family's criminal activity. Invictus bit his tongue.

"My uncle," Jacob continued, "is very particular about who he chooses to trust, and who he allows into his house. I'm sure he will have a fit once he discovers your visit."

"A fit?" Sweat beaded on Invictus's brow.

"Don't fear. He is resting. The storm kept him awake half the night." Jacob shook his head. "Dr. Armand Whateley was the only doctor my uncle truly trusted, and with his untimely death, the family is in a bind. My uncle needs a new doctor. Without medical treatment..."

"What illness does he have?" Invictus asked hesitantly.

"Tuberculosis. Dr. Whateley's treatments have slowed the disease's progression, but without a cure..." Jacob shrugged.

"I'm sorry."

"You..." Jacob blinked a few times. "You actually mean that. Why?"

"I, um... Well, tuberculosis is a terrible disease, and he just lost his doctor. He..." A thought quickly formed. "How many people know about your uncle's illness?"

"Just a select few outside of our immediate family. Many suspect that he is ill, but Uncle does a decent job of covering up the severity."

"Then why share this information with me?" Newfound fear took root, making it difficult to appear calm. He dug his fingernails into his palms.

"Because you are harmless, and you know the one person who was in Whateley's house the night he was murdered."

"But Wulf didn't see anyone."

"But did he hear or smell anything?" Jacob leaned forward. "People tend to discredit Halflings, but with Shinnoks, you have to be at least three generations removed before the Fae instincts cannot be felt. Tell me what Beowulf Smith heard and smelled."

Invictus felt a faint compulsion to speak, his mouth and vocal cords wishing to move. He fought it down and said, "He heard an argument. Two men yelling. He thought they were speaking a different language. Maybe Scanlannish or Faerie."

"Armand was fluent in both languages. Any smells?"

Invictus shook his head. He never thought to ask about smells.

Jacob nodded, thinking.

"Could it have been another Family?" Invictus asked.

"What do you mean?"

"I mean, um..." Grady was adamant about the Five Families working together, but he only had strong ties with the Sidhes. Only knew the inner workings of one Family. "The Amistadians or Barrish or Malkinese."

"No. Absolutely not." Jacob waved the idea away. "Believe what rumors you will, Invictus, but my uncle is well-respected both within and without his circles of influence."

"But if he lost his doctor and then died as a result, what would happen?" Was that the real motive? Was Whateley's death part of a wider plot to kill Taran Manning?

But how does Carlos Vallejo factor in?

"I would take his place, and my sister would take mine," Jacob replied matter-of-factly.

"Has it always been this way?"

Jacob's face fell, his eyes fading to pale yellow. "Jack should have been the Right Hand, but Lewin..." He grimaced.

"Jack was Lewin's older brother, right?"

"Yes, and he was a good man. A bit of an idiot, like you, but a good man."

"Then, someone outside the Families must have killed Dr. Whateley. Did he have any enemies?"

"Not anymore."

Invictus suddenly felt cold.

Laughter pierced the air. Innocent, carefree laughter. A boy and a girl, both around seven years old, raced into the parlor. The little girl shared Jacob's bronze skin and bright gold eyes. Her long, black hair was tied back in a ponytail with blue ribbons. But the boy's skin was deathly pale, and his black hair was lanky, unkept. His clothes, though new and clean, hung off his skeletal frame, making him look like a scarecrow.

And his eyes were blood red.

"Julia, Alexander, what are you doing?" Jacob snapped. He rose to his feet and crossed his arms. The children stopped running and gazed up at him, smiling and giggling.

"We're playing tag," the little girl replied.

"In the house?" Jacob asked incredulously, but he was smiling.

"It was Alexander's idea."

"But it was Julia's idea to run inside," the boy chimed in. His voice sounded like two rocks scraping together.

Invictus's skin crawled. The strange tone sounded identical to Alistair and Alfred's true voices. Harsh, unnatural.

"Is he—"

"Don't you see we have a guest?" Jacob asked the children, cutting Invictus off. "Where are your manners?"

The children faced Invictus, their eyes curious.

"It's nice to meet you, sir," Julia said with a small curtesy.

"Hello, sir." Alexander bobbed his head. He blinked and black fluid leaked out of his eyes. The fluid seeped into his skin, creating dark patches under his eyes. The child looked like a corpse.

A corpse with blood red eyes.

"It's nice to meet you both," Invictus managed, his voice shaking. And his hands, and his legs.

"Where is Mrs. Kay?" Jacob asked.

"I'm here, sir." A woman dressed in a gray dress with a white apron hurried into the parlor. Her eyes, a deep shade of orange, were wide and shimmering as though she were on the verge of tears. "I'm so sorry, Mr. Manning. I was watching them, truly, but they slipped away."

"Don't fret." Jacob glanced at the grand clock. "I believe it's time for their studies. Take them to Mr. Smith."

"Smith?" Invictus's heart skipped a beat.

Jacob smirked. "Yes, their tutor. Mr. Juan Smith. He specializes in literature and history. No relation to your associate, Mr. Jones," he added coldly.

"Do we have to?" Julia asked. She gave Jacob sad, puppy dog eyes.

"Of course! Every young lady must have an education. Same for young men," he said to Alexander.

"Very well," Julia replied. "May we have taffy afterwards?"

"Only if you mind your lessons." His gold eyes shimmered.

Mrs. Kay gathered the children and shepherded them upstairs.

Jacob resumed his seat. "I apologize for the interruption. Where were we?"

"A Changeling," Invictus blurted out. "That boy is a Changeling!"

"Yes, he is."

"But why do—"

"Allow me to explain. My wife and I wanted a large family, but she almost died giving birth to Julia. We couldn't jeopardize her health, so we adopted Alexander. Dr. Whateley helped us arrange it."

"But why a Changeling?" The invisible string tugged, tugged, tugged at his mind. But which direction? He felt like he was navigating a dark cave with just his hands to guide him.

"The subspecies is quite rare. Almost extinct. When Dr. Whateley learned about an orphaned Changeling, he asked if we would be interested." Jacob smiled again, his eyes shining like stars. "And Alexander is a wonderful child. So full of light."

"So, you and your uncle both owe a lot to Dr. Whateley."

"Yes. Do you understand why we want his murderer found?"

"I do, but why talk to me instead of the police?"

Jacob rolled his eyes. "The police ask the wrong questions. Besides, you work alongside them. You understand their methods without being hindered by their rules."

"What is it you want me to do?" Invictus's mind raced. A Changeling child. Adopting a child was all well and good, but why place a Changeling with a Sidhe family? Why not have Alfred or Alistair adopt the boy?

Alfred already has children. A boy around Alexander's age and a baby girl.

But maybe the child is in a good place here. He doesn't have to hide his true nature. Not while he was on the Mannings' property. How did Changelings hide their true faces? Was it an instinct?

The clock chimed the half hour.

"I've kept you long enough," Jacob said. He led Invictus into the hallway. Sean waited by the front door.

"Sean, start the motorcar. Take Mr. Jones wherever he wishes. Here." Jacob handed Invictus a card with his name and two telephone numbers. "The first is the home phone, and the second is my office phone."

Coughing sounded from upstairs. Deep, hacking coughs. Each one sounded more painful than the last. A thin, reedy voice called for help. Footsteps ran overhead. A few moments later, the coughing subsided.

"Your uncle?" Invictus hazarded.

Jacob nodded gravely. "We need a new doctor, but he only trusted Whateley." He sighed heavily.

"What about Alistair Whateley? He's a doctor."

"He is still considering our offer. Alistair is a busy man. The extra hours will only take more of a toll on him." Jacob pointed at the card. "Please, Mr. Jones, the moment you have the murderer's name, call me."

"Why? He will be in police custody."

"Call me regardless. I want to see this monster for myself."

"And then what?" Invictus's blood ran cold.

"Don't worry over the details. Just rest assured that the Face of Justice will shine on him."

Jacob escorted Invictus out the door and watched as he climbed into the motorcar's passenger seat. Sean, white-knuckling the steering wheel, stared straight ahead.

"Goodbye, Mr. Jones, and good luck!" Jacob waved as the motorcar rolled out of the driveway, the wheels crunching on gravel, and onto the quiet street. More mansions with high walls lined the street, and a massive building, four stories tall and twice as wide as the Mannings' mansion, stood on the corner two blocks away. Climbing ivy coated most of the white stone, leaving only the windows visible. The Fae Embassy. They were in the Fae Quarter.

"Where to?" Sean asked, a slight tremor in his voice.

"Clarke Street," Invictus said, the invisible string tugging again. He prayed it would lead him in the right direction.

Chapter 29

Myths

Every nerve in Wulf's body screamed at him to run. He was standing in the middle of a brickyard, surrounded by bricks. Men in dark green armed with guns and nightsticks and handcuffs. And the captain of the bricks stood side by side with him. So close that Wulf could touch him.

You have a gun, Wulf reminded himself. His gloved hand brushed against the smooth handle. A 38 Bricker. Six shots. Ma made him promise not to use a gun again. It created too much risk, made him too much of a target. But Wulf wasn't gonna shoot anyone. Not here. He could just wave the gun around, make a bunch of threats, and maybe fire a hole in the ceiling. And then, he would run like hell.

But he just stood there, frozen.

Captain Reyes whistled sharply, causing Wulf to jump. He cursed under his breath. The last time he was inside a brickyard, he'd help take out a small army of thugs. Now he was acting like a scared little kid. He bit his tongue, the trick Ruthless had taught him to focus his wandering mind. Standing around and actin' scared wasn't gonna help Bookie.

Lawson, Bishop, and all the other bricks gathered around the captain. Three had guns. Wulf spied the impression of brass knuckles in one brick's pocket.

I need to steal me those. Jorge Bishop had a pair of brass knuckles. Real nice and shiny and hurt like hell. Wulf's jaw ached, thinking about the beating Jorge had given him. A beating order by Lewin Manning.

"Was it the Mannings?" Wulf blurted out. His heart threatened to leap out of his chest.

Reyes turned his dark brown eyes on him. The other bricks stared. Some looked surprised, as though Wulf had appeared out of thin air, and not in a good way. One brick, an Eadryn Halfling with green and brown eyes and a small build, looked like he wanted to give Wulf a broken nose or a busted lip. Another brick, a full-blood Shinnok with pale skin and flaming red hair, turning even paler, acted like he had seen a ghost.

"Our job is not to jump to conclusions," Reyes said.

Wulf almost made a smart remark but held his tongue. Bricks always jumped to conclusions in Mull. You were seen near a store when it got robbed? Must be guilty. Looking sideways at a brick? Gotta be hiding something. Wulf bit his tongue.

Reyes addressed the group. "Invictus Jones was grabbed on the street corner. Did anyone happen to look out a window and see this?"

The bricks shifted their feet, murmuring.

"What do you mean he was grabbed?" Lawson asked, the only one to show an ounce of sense.

Reyes turned to Wulf. "Describe what you saw."

Wulf eyed the bricks, keeping one hand on the gun. He could draw and make his escape. But Ma made him promise. He made so many promises to her, promising that he wasn't going to steal no more, that he would stay in school, that he would get a real job one day. He broke every single one. He refused to break this one.

"Two guys grabbed Bookie from behind and put him in a motorcar. Drove that way." He pointed westward.

"What did they look like?" Bishop asked. He studied Wulf warily, as though he were an actual wolf.

So much for believing me. But he wasn't surprised. "One guy was tall, but not wide. Looked Malkinese. The other was shorter, about my height, and he had pale skin."

"Scannie?" asked the Halfling brick with green and brown eyes.

"Don't call folks that!" Wulf snapped. The Halfling took a step back and reached for his nightstick. "And no, not as pale."

"Describe the motorcar," Reyes said.

"It was black and boxy. I don't know. All them motor things look the same." Wulf was fifteen when he saw his first motorcar. Ruthless took him and Dav on a rare trip outside of Mull, teaching them the streets and alleys of the Business District.

At first, Wulf thought a thunderstorm was approaching, but he turned around and his mind broke. A big, black boxy thing on wheels lumbered down the road. But there were no horses. No visible way to see how the damn thing moved, and a faint, flowery scent filled the air. A man sat inside the box, his hands on a little wheel.

"You're looking at the future, boys," Ruthless said as they watched the motorcar roll down the street.

"It's so damn noisy," Wulf said, placing his hands over his ears. Dav watched the motorcar in awe.

"Good. Then you'll always know when one is approaching."

"Did you see the registration plate?" Reyes asked, snapping Wulf back to the present.

"Registration plate?"

"A series of numbers and letters on the rear bumper. Did you see it?"

Wulf closed his eyes, trying to think. The motorcar was pure black, but wasn't there some white symbols on the back? One might have been a number, or letters. But they were all jumbled up. Bloody hell, did he really want a bunch of bricks to know that he could barely read?

"No, didn't see nothing. Was too busy worrying about my friend," he snapped, locking eyes with Reyes.

The captain nodded. "Luckily, I did. Montgomery," he addressed the Eadryn Halfling. "Look up this registration." He rattled off a string of letters and numbers. "Pembroke and Stant, collect a carriage from the First Precinct. Lawson and Bishop, assist Mr. Smith in any way you can."

Wulf's heart skipped a beat. "What?"

"You are a witness in two cases, now," Reyes told him. "Your assistance is needed."

Wulf wanted to refuse. More, he wanted to run the hell out of here and find that motorcar himself. But motorcars moved faster than horses. It could be halfway across town by now. He had no hope of finding Bookie without help.

"Okay." Wulf studied the bricks as Stant and Montgomery obeyed, grumbling. Bloody hell, if Ruthless were in charge here, he would cuff them on the back of the head. Not hard enough to hurt, just to remind them to do their jobs quickly and quietly. "How?"

Turned out, helping bricks meant sitting around and waiting. Wulf watched as Lawson and Bishop wrote down notes and read through records.

His muscles ached. How long had he been sitting here? An hour? Felt like an hour. Was Bookie alright? A lot could happen to a person in an hour. Did those men just wanna question him? Or did they beat him up? Lock him in a warehouse? Throw him into the river?

Wulf flinched, remembering cool water, searching as his eyes stung and his lungs burned.

A telephone rang.

Wulf leapt to his feet, the gun in his hand, ready to fire.

Lawson answered it.

"Jones!"

Wulf ran towards her. "Bookie? Is he okay?"

Lawson held up a finger to silence him. Wulf holstered the gun and shifted on the balls of his feet, his muscles begging to move, to act, to do anything except sit around in a bloody brickyard. Mercy sakes alive, this was worse than being in a holding cell!

"Okay. Got it." Lawson hung up the phone.

"What happened? Is he alright?" Wulf asked. If something bad happened to Bookie, he... He'd... Bloody hell, he didn't know, but he couldn't lose another friend. He had so few friends...

Lawson went over to Bishop and said, "Jones is at his boardinghouse. He wants us to meet him there."

Bishop looked at her sideways. "How the hell—"

"He will explain everything once we get there," Lawson interrupted, sounding like Ma after Wulf had asked her the same question several times, expecting a different answer.

"Okay. I'll tell Reyes, and we'll go," Bishop said.

"What about me?" Wulf asked.

"Don't worry," Lawson replied. "Jones wants you there, too."

***

They rode to Bookie's boardinghouse in one of the brick carriages, powered by a horse. Wulf wished the trains were running. Riding in a carriage was nice and all, but trains moved much faster than horses, and you had more space. Wulf felt cramped sitting between Lawson and Bishop with Montgomery and Pembroke sitting across from them. But all the trains were closed until further notice for safety inspections.

The carriage jolted, and Wulf's knee bumped into Montgomery's. The Eadryn Halfling glared at Wulf as though he'd done it on purpose. And Pembroke looked like he was about to lose his breakfast.

The moment they turned onto Clarke Street, Wulf climbed over Bishop, shoved the door open, and raced down the street.

"Don't shoot him, you idiot!" Bishop yelled.

Wulf turned and saw Stant, the brick driving the carriage, aiming a gun directly at his chest.

"He's running! You saw him run!"

"Yeah, running to the same place we're going!" Bishop yelled.

Is he really gonna shoot me?

Bishop stopped him. Would he have done so a week ago?

Stant stared at Wulf, the gun leveled at his chest.

"47 Clarke Street," Wulf said. "That's where Bookie lives and where I'm going."

The old brick finally holstered his gun. He flicked the reins, and the horse trotted down the street.

Wulf sprinted down Clarke Street. Uprooted trees, broken branches, and leaves littered the street, and puddles pooled along sidewalks. The boardinghouse came into view. The windows were still boarded. He ran up the front steps and banged on the door.

"Bookie! Bookie, it's me!"

A sickening feeling crept into him. What if Bookie wasn't here? Did the people who grabbed Bookie force him to call, saying he was alright?

A Malkinese man, shorter and thinner than the one who grabbed Bookie, answered the door. He eyed Wulf nervously. He then saw the brick carriage and the bricks.

"Um, what...?"

"Official police business, sir," Lawson stated, showing the man her badge. Bishop and Montgomery did the same. Pembroke and Stant stayed with the carriage.

The man relaxed a bit. "I see. How can I help you, officers?"

"Where's Bookie?" Wulf tried to peer inside, but the man blocked him.

"Who?"

"Invictus Jones," Bishop clarified.

The man's eyes widened. "Yes. He's in the sitting room." The man led them inside.

The sitting room was on the first floor, across the hall from the dining room. Bookie sat in one of the plush chairs along with a Malkinese woman and that chemist they talked to at the University. The one who got all cagey when they asked about Dr. Whateley. A little girl sat in the woman's lap, looking at everyone with big, brown eyes.

"Bookie!"

Wulf ran into the sitting room and hugged him.

Bookie tensed up, but he quickly relaxed and gave Wulf a hug before pushing him away.

"Glad to see you, too."

"Oh, you've brought guests," the scientist said, his voice all jittery like he drank too much coffee.

Bookie stood and greeted the bricks. The tenants headed upstairs, the little girl shouting 'goodbye' to everyone. Bishop, Lawson, and Bookie then sat down. Montgomery walked around, studying the sitting room. Wulf stood next to Bookie and looked at him up and down. No cuts or bruises. No tears in his clothes. For a man who just got kidnapped, he seemed surprisingly okay.

"Care to explain what the hell happened?" Bishop asked.

Bookie explained that the two thugs drove him to Taran Manning's house.

"What?!" Wulf snarled, reaching for the borrowed gun. "Those sons of bitches! I'll—"

"Wulf, calm down," Bookie said.

Wulf tried to, but how the hell could he be calm when... His eyes met Montgomery's. The brick Halfling also had a hand on his gun.

He ain't gonna shoot me, is he? Stant had been ready to shoot him. Likely would have if Bishop hadn't intervened. Wulf forced himself to calm down.

Bookie continued, explaining his conversation with Jacob Manning and Dr. Whateley's involvement with the family.

"So, the Sidhe Family ain't guilty?" Wulf asked.

"Not of murder." Bookie's face fell. "Jacob has an adopted son. A Changeling."

"Come again?" Bishop asked.

"Changelings?" Montgomery rolled his eyes. "Those are a myth."

"The hell they are," Wulf said.

Montgomery glared at Wulf and then looked at Lawson and Bishop for confirmation.

"We haven't seen them as Changelings," Lawson said. "But I trust Jones's word."

"And what about him?" he pointed at Wulf.

Wulf had half a mind to break the bastard's finger. "Why would I lie?"

"You're a damn thief!" The Halfling's eyes swirled, the colors mixing.

"Montgomery, do you want Reyes to know you're cursing on the job again?" Bishop asked.

The Halfling fumed but said nothing. Wulf smirked. The Halfling's face turned red, and his eyes swirled faster, turning dark green. Almost the same color as his uniform.

"Back on topic," Lawson said. She leaned on the edge of the chair and locked eyes with Bookie. "You're sure the child was a Changeling?"

"Yes. He had the same red eyes and white skin as the Whateleys." Bookie paused. "He looked about seven years old."

"The same age as Alfred's son," Bishop noted. He drummed his fingers on his knee. "Do you think they're related?"

"Well, I have a theory, but I would like Lawson to explain her theory again."

She did so, theorizing that Dr. Whateley was abusive towards his family and likely caused Arlan's injuries. Once all the facts were straight, Bookie explained Dr. Whateley's dealings with the Manning Family and how Whateley became the Old Man's personal doctor.

"The Five Families?" Montgomery asked incredulously. "You idiots have been reading too many goddamn books."

"I agree," Wulf said, "about the books. But the Families is as real as birds and sprites. Remember Lewin Manning?"

"Of course I remember that f.... That guy," Montgomery quickly corrected himself. "He was a crazy Sidhe who liked to blackmail people. Doesn't mean he's part of an underworld criminal organization."

Wulf smirked. A part of him wanted to introduce this guy to Ruthless and watch as his brain turned to putty.

"That's not entirely true," Bishop said. "Reyes keeps files on the Five Families. Most of it is rumors and hearsay, but Lewin Manning and Emilio Grady's arrests help connect a lot of dots. I wouldn't be surprised if the rest of Lewin's family was involved as well."

"How long has Jacob Manning been on the City Council?" Lawson asked.

"About ten years," Bishop replied. "Before that, he worked at his uncle's investment firm. Has a lot of eggs in a lot of baskets."

"So, y'all gonna arrest them?" Wulf asked.

"Arrest who?" Bishop asked.

"Jacob Manning. He had Bookie kidnapped!"

"He does have a point," Lawson said to Bishop.

"That depends. Do you want to press charges?"

Bookie was quiet for a moment. "No, Manning did not hurt me, and we have more important matters to deal with. I think we should talk to the Whateleys again."

"What, are you insane?" Wulf asked, but he already knew the answer. Of course Bookie wanted to talk to the Changelings again. Granted, this time he would have the bricks by his side.

"Agreed," Lawson said. She and Bishop stood up. "How do you want to go about this?"

"I think you, Wulf, and I should speak with them. Asa, you and Montgomery will be outside as back up. If the Whateleys are somehow involved with the murder, they might try to run."

"That's... a good idea, actually," Bishop said. Montgomery rolled his multi-colored eyes.

"Should we inform Reyes?" Lawson asked.

Bookie thought it over. "No. We should speak with them first. If the Mannings are also involved, they might have people watching the house. Better for them to think it's just routine police work."

The bricks nodded.

"What about Ruthless?" Wulf whispered.

"Do you want his help?" Bookie had the good sense to whisper back.

Wulf shrugged. He went after Lewin without Ruthless's help, and it ended with him beaten to hell and with Dav in a coffin. Could he risk making another foolish mistake?

"We have a phone if you want to call him."

"Who are you talking about?" Bishop asked.

"A friend," Wulf blurted out. He couldn't let the bricks find out about Ruthless. "Uh, never mind, Bookie. Are we going now, or what?"

Bookie looked at the bricks. They nodded in agreement.

Against his better judgment, Wulf climbed into a carriage full of bricks for the second time that day.

Chapter 30

Confrontation

The ringing in Invictus's ear worsened as the carriage neared the Whateley house. He took deep, even breaths, forcing himself to appear outwardly calm.

People milled about the neighboring houses, picking up broken tree limbs, sweeping leaves out of driveways, and removing boards from windows. Invictus couldn't help wondering. Were they all neighbors? Or did the Mannings have people close by? A key person acting as an innocent homeowner?

He shoved the idea out of his mind. If he kept thinking along these lines, fear would take over, preventing him from seeing this case through to the end. Besides, he had a protection from the Seelie Court. It would protect him.

Maybe.

The carriage stopped two houses away. Invictus, Celeste, and Wulf climbed out while Asa and Montgomery remained behind. They would circle around and approach the house from the back road, ensuring nobody tried to sneak away. They had dropped Pembroke off at the Precinct to get reinforcements, and Stant agreed to stay with the horse, parking the carriage next to the corner store.

"Whistle if you need us," Asa said. He and Montgomery walked down the neighboring house's garden path. A man raking leaves gave them a cursory glance but did not question them.

Invictus looked at Celeste and Wulf. Celeste seemed nervous yet confident, but Wulf was shaking. His purple eyes darted this way and that, and he jumped whenever a neighbor made a sudden move. He placed a hand on the empty holster. Wulf had given the gun to Asa on the ride here.

"Made a promise," he said, offering no further explanation.

The Whateley house loomed at the end of the driveway. All the windows were dark with the curtains drawn. Silent.

"Are they still here?" Celeste wondered.

"Yeah. I can hear them," Wulf said, his voice little more than a whisper.

Invictus and Celeste shared a look, nodded, and walked towards the house. Wulf followed on their heels.

Celeste knocked on the door. Nobody answered. She knocked two more times, each more loudly than the last. A maid, the timid young woman who had served Invictus tea a few days ago, answered.

"This is a bad time for visitors," she said, her voice shaking. Dark circles lined her brown eyes. She glanced nervously over her shoulder.

Celeste showed the maid her badge. "Official police business, ma'am."

The maid stared at the badge. Tears welled in her eyes.

Molly. Her name is Molly, Invictus remembered.

"They aren't bad people," Molly said, tears escaping. "Truly. They're just..." She trembled, the tears choking her. "They're just Fae. Like him." She pointed at Wulf. "Please, don't..."

"We only want to help them," Celeste said. Her voice was gentle and calm. Invictus wished he felt half as calm.

The maid wiped away her tears with her sleeve, but new ones quickly replaced them. She resigned to let them fell and led Invictus, Celeste, and Wulf inside.

Save for a gaslamp burning in the hallway, the house was dark. Faint light struggled to pierce the thick curtains, casting pale shadows.

The Whateley family was gathered in the parlor. Alfred and Gina sat on the couch along with their children. Arlan, who was around seven years old, sat on the floor and played with a painted, tin boat and soldiers. Gina held a new baby in her arms, wrapped in a purple blanket embroidered with wildflowers. Alistair, his hair unkept and his face lined with stubble, stood by the empty fireplace, resting his arm on the mantle.

"Dr. Whateley," Molly addressed Alistair in a timid voice, "the police are here."

Alistair turned and glared at them with blood red eyes. His deathly pale face was marred by dark circles surrounding his eyes. Dark fluid leaked out of his eyes, creating new streaks in the pale flesh. He sneered.

"Get the hell out of my house." His voice was hoarse, almost raspy. Like two rocks being scrapped together. Invictus imagined Alexander Manning's voice sounding the same in twenty years.

"Dr. Whateley," Celeste said in a bold voice, "we have some questions—"

"No! Get out!" His eerie eyes turned a darker shade of red as they fell on Invictus and Wulf. He jabbed a finger at them. "They're the ones you should arrest! They broke into our house yesterday!"

"That ain't true!" Wulf snapped. "The door was unlocked."

"But you didn't have permission." Alistair stalked towards them. His red eyes glowed faintly in the low light. Every muscle in Invictus's body screamed at him to run, but he stood his ground. "We did not want you here. You two just barged in. You saw..." Alistair seethed.

"They can see us now," Gina said. The baby started crying, and she held her closer to her chest. Gina's eyes, also blood red and seeping black fluid, watched the three of them warily, like unexpected visitors in the dead of night.

Alistair squeezed his eyes shut, causing more fluid to leak out.

"What the hell is that stuff?" Wulf asked.

"Why do you care?"

Wulf shrugged.

Invictus would have liked an explanation as well, but it was a question for another day.

"Would you care to sit, Dr. Whateley?" Celeste asked.

"No."

"Alistair, we know your father was Taran Manning's personal doctor," Invictus said.

The parlor grew eerily still. Alfred and Gina shared a concerned look, unsure how to respond. Molly wrung her hands, fighting a losing battle against her tears. Alistair stared at Invictus, his face like granite.

"So?"

"We know Taran Manning has several underworld connections." Invictus forced himself to speak, knowing that if he paused for a second, he would never find the courage to begin again. "I'm sure he was controlling your father. Limiting—"

"You know nothing!" Alistair yelled. Invictus flinched. Last time Alistair yelled at him, he had grabbed Invictus, threatening him and Wulf. That had been at the hospital. In public. What would he do in the privacy of his own home? Yes, Celeste was a police officer, but the Whateleys and their household staff outnumbered them. And with their connection to the Sidhe Family...

"Al, that's enough."

Every eye turned to Alfred. He sat quietly, his hands resting on his knees and his eyes fixed on the carpet.

"How did you learn this?" he asked Invictus. His voice sounded tired, so very tired.

"An anonymous tip. And Jacob Manning spoke with me," he added reluctantly.

"Really?" Alfred did not sound surprised. Invictus wondered if Alfred had experienced similar meetings. "Where?"

"At his house."

Alfred's gaze shifted to his son. Arlan clutched the toys to his chest and stared at the adults. His blue eyes were wide, fearful.

Blue eyes. Not red.

"Why doesn't Arlan have red eyes?" Celeste asked a second before Invictus could.

The Whateleys were silent. Alistair glared at his brother. Gina held the baby closer to her chest, as though she believed they would take her away. Alfred looked at his son. He smiled at the boy and held out his arms. Arlan, protectively holding his toys, climbed into Alfred's lap. Alfred hugged him tightly.

"His eyes are blue," Alfred said.

"Freddy." Gina placed a hand on Alfred's shoulder. Tears mixed with the black fluid. "Please."

"Alfred, shut up!" Alistair hissed.

"NO!"

The temperature in the room seemed to drop ten degrees. Wulf placed a hand on the empty holster and cursed under his breath. Celeste did not so much as flinch and kept her eyes on the Whateleys.

"They will find out anyway," Alfred said quietly. "Better for them to hear it from us."

Alistair threw up his hands in disgust and retreated to one of the windows. He pulled the curtain back an inch and gazed into the street. The black fluid seeping out of his eyes seemed more like tears.

Alfred looked at Arlan and smiled, smoothing back the child's blond hair. "Arlan isn't a Changeling. He is human."

Invictus's blood turned cold. "Exchanges. Nor—" He pretended to clear his throat. "No one does exchanges anymore. Right?"

"It's illegal," Gina said. The baby cried. She cooed to her, rocking her gently.

"Technically illegal," Alfred amended.

"Were the Mannings involved?" Invictus asked. The invisible string tugged again.

Alfred stared at Invictus for a long, quiet moment. His red eyes shifted to Wulf. "I'm sorry we got you involved in this mess. We didn't know what else to do. I..." He swallowed. "I'm sorry."

"Holy hell, you did kill him," Wulf said. He looked like Alfred had punched him in the gut. "You killed your father."

"Alfred, is this true?" Celeste asked.

Alfred looked at his brother. Alistair refused to meet his eyes. Alfred then looked at his wife. Gina nodded.

"I never wanted..." Alfred struggled to speak. "It was his idea."

"Your father arranged for the exchange?" Invictus's mind immediately went to Alexander Manning. A Changeling child, about seven years old. The same age as Arlan Whateley, a human.

Jacob Manning claimed that the boy was an orphan, and that Dr. Whateley helped arrange the adoption. But what if it wasn't an adoption? What if it was an exchange?

The invisible string tugged again, stronger this time. Invictus's heart sank with each tug.

"Please sit down," Alfred said. "I'll tell you everything. I will confess to my father's murder."

Chapter 31

No Other Choice

Every word struck Alfred like an arrow to the heart. Each syllable threatened to bleed him dry.

"Are you listening?" Armand Whateley snapped. Alfred had not viewed the hateful creature as a father in years.

Alfred nodded. What other choice did he have? The first time was horrible, a nightmare come to life, but Armand assured him that this was natural. Changelings had done exchanges with human children for centuries. Long before the founding of the Commonwealth. Perhaps even before the Royal Family had risen to power and united the Islands. No one truly knew. Alfred doubted if anyone wanted to know.

Giving up their newborn son was the worst day of his and Gina's lives. They were so happy. For years, they tried to have a child, to start a family of their own. And their dream had finally come true.

Then Armand intervened.

Armand had singlehandedly arranged the exchange. Alfred never learned what became of his son. He only had three months with the child. Three wonderful months. Then Arlan, the real Arlan, was taken. Alfred never had a chance to say goodbye. The exchanged child arrived a few days later, in the dead of night. A human boy of Scanlannish heritage. Alfred had no idea where the child came from. He honestly did not want to know.

Last month, he and Gina welcomed a baby girl. A healthy little Changeling with alabaster skin and rose red eyes. He assumed that she was theirs to keep. They had already exchanged one child. There was no need to exchange a second. But fear crept into the back of his mind. Would Armand allow him to keep this child?

"Ava Ingrid," he whispered into his newborn's ears. Her name. Only he and Gina knew the middle name, her soul name.

This morning, Armand summoned Alfred into his study and confirmed that his fears were true. He would have to say goodbye to both of his children.

Unless he did the impossible.

Unless he stood up to Armand.

"When will the exchange take place?" he asked, struggling to keep his voice level.

"When the child turns three months old."

The child. Not Ava, or his granddaughter. The child.

For half a second, Alfred wondered what life would have been like if he was exchanged. He would have grown up a freak, never truly understanding his nature. But would his new parents have loved him? Would they force him to practice this barbaric ritual?

"I refuse," he whispered, practicing the words.

"What?" Armand leaned forward, seated in his chair by the study's fireplace. His vermillion eyes turned crimson. "What did you say, boy?"

"I refuse," Alfred said. His heart pounded in his throat. "I will not let you steal my daughter."

Armand sighed heavily and beckoned Alfred to step forward. Alfred, knowing what would happen and knowing the consequence if he refused, obeyed. Armand slapped him across the face. Despite Armand's slight build, he had the strength of a man half his age. One of the benefits gifted to Changelings.

"You can't refuse, boy. The exchange has already been arranged. We completed everything the day after the girl was born."

'We'. Always this nebulous 'we'. But who was 'we'? Alfred had his suspicions but giving them voice could put everyone he loved in jeopardy.

"The exchange," Armand continued, "will take place in two months. If you're so attached, I suggest making your goodbyes now." Armand selected one of the medical journals from the small stack on the end table and began reading. The conversation, and any chance Alfred had of protecting the little life gifted to him by God, was over.

Alfred saw himself out of the study, the door closing with a soft click. His face smarted, but in his Changeling state, the redness was barely noticeable.

A black tear fell onto the carpet, followed by a torrent. Alfred pressed his hands against his eyes and managed to stumble into a sitting room, collapsing into a chair. Tears overwhelmed him.

I'm sorry. I'm so sorry, Ava Ingrid.

"Sir?"

Alfred froze. Black tears continued to run down his face, staining the skin. Most of the household staff knew that the Whateleys were Changelings and were paid handsomely for their silence. And in a city full of Fae, the staff honestly did not care. One subspecies was the same as another.

But he did not recognize this voice.

Concentrating, Alfred altered his features by picturing a human face. The faces he saw as a child in Scanlan. Pale white skin turned a fleshy pink. Red eyes to pale blue. Black tears to clear. Only his hair retained its blond color.

The newcomer gasped as he watched the transformation. Bloody hell. How much was this going to cost?

Alfred wiped away the remaining tears and glanced up.

A young man stood in the doorway. His purple eyes, dark red hair, and pointed ears gave him away as a Shinnok or a Halfling. He wore grass-stained khaki pants and a blue shirt, and he held a floppy sunhat in his hands. The Shinnok could not be older than twenty. Just a kid.

"Can I help you?" Alfred asked, his voice hoarse.

"I, um... I work..." He pointed down the hall.

"Wait. Aren't you with the landscaping crew?" Alfred had rolled his eyes when Alistair suggested hiring landscapers. They were perfectly capable of maintaining their own yards, but no. They needed to be modern. Needed to blend in.

The Shinnok nodded. "I, um... I wanted to ask about next week, sir."

"Same day and time will be fine. Do we owe you anything?"

"No, sir. Your brother already paid for the month. We... I..." He wrung the hat. "I heard you arguing." He pointed down the hallway towards the study. "Out there."

Alfred's heart sank. Merciful God, how would Armand react if he discovered that an outsider had learned about the exchange? Would he brush it off, or would 'we' decide to intervene?

He's just a kid.

"How much did you hear?"

The Shinnok cowered and looked like he was going to bolt.

"No, wait!" Alfred stood and gestured for the young Fae to step into the room. He did so. "I mean, what exactly did you hear?"

The boy trembled, wringing the hat. "The old man wants to get rid of your child. I think... I think that's wrong, sir." He paused, studying Alfred with big, purple eyes. "I want to help you."

"How?"

"I know people." He nervously moved the hat in his hands. "They can make things look like accidents."

Alfred's blood turned cold. "What kinds of things?"

The boy focused on his hat. "Will this exchange happen if the old man is dead?"

“I don’t know.” Alfred never thought of that. Never dared. “Other people are involved, but my father is in charge. He arranged it. I don’t know, but maybe.”

The Shinnok nodded. “Good. That’s good. Do you want help?”

Did he want help? Alfred thought of his father. For the first part of his life, his father was gone for long stretches of time, earning a medical degree in Malkin City. A dot on the map. A thousand miles away. Those long stretches were the only times when Alfred had known peace.

After the family immigrated, he thought things would get better. Father would stop shouting and throwing things at them.

“No more hitting,” Alistair, then twelve years old, had promised. He smiled despite the purple bruise on his jaw.

And for a while, there was peace.

A short while.

Alfred contemplated leaving his family. Starting fresh in a new town or province. But a new obstacle always arose. First, he needed to graduate high school. Dropping out was never an option. And then there was University. Armand had a fit when Alfred expressed the slightest doubt in continuing his education. And after graduation, thanks to Armand’s numerous connections, Alfred got a job at an art dealership. An excellent job. His dream job, in fact. How could he walk away from his dream? Then he met Gina. A small piece of perfection in a chaotic world.

Alfred stopped thinking about leaving. What was the point?

A few years later, Arlan was taken. And now, Armand threatened to steal away Ava.

I won’t let you have her!

“What is your name?” Alfred asked, hesitant but strangely hopeful.

“Carlos. Carlos Vallejo,” the young Shinnok replied.

“Who are these people?”

“Professionals. They’ll make it look like an accident or a robbery. Your choice.”

"Why my choice?" Doubt crept into his mind, but he shoved it away.

"Because it's your house, sir."

Of course. These people were likely Fae. They had to obey the Seelie Court.

Alfred considered it.

It didn't take long.

"How much will this cost?"

"Your silence. Don't tell no one the truth. Not even the bricks."

Alfred agreed. Carlos stopped by next week. While the landscapers were busily cutting the grass and trimming hedges, Carlos presented Alfred with a detailed plan. Carlos and two other men would break into the house at night, after everyone was asleep. They would take a few valuables to make it look legitimate and then kill the old man in his sleep.

"It's a good plan. Simple." Alfred spent all week thinking about this, thinking about Gina and Arlan and Ava Ingrid, and thinking about the consequences for them if the plan failed. "But I want to pull the trigger. I want my father to watch as I kill him."

Carlos paled, but he nodded. "Yeah. You decide on a time and date. We'll be there."

"Wait." Doubt threatened to invade his mind again, but it was too late to back out now. Ava Ingrid was almost two months old. A little more than a month shy of being lost forever. "The police will be all over this house. They will want to find the murderer." Even more so, Taran Manning would want to find the murderer. Alfred shivered just thinking about the Old Man and his wrath. Armand was as harmless as a kitten compared to him. "What will we do?"

"Well, see." Carlos nervously shifted on the balls of his feet. "I only work with one of the guys. I'm going to recruit someone who deserves to go to jail. Someone the police will look for the whole time, not you."

"Who?"

"Beowulf Smith."

Alfred recognized the name. Smith was a thief who had helped the police with... something. He hadn't paid much attention to the papers lately. "But why him?"

Carlos shrugged. "Smith does a lot of bad things. He deserves to get punished, don't you think, sir?"

"Yeah." Alfred nodded. "Better him than us, I guess. Will the other guy keep his mouth shut?"

"Course. He will think we're robbing a different place. Do you know if any houses will be empty in the next few weeks?"

The answer came to Alfred immediately. "The Townsend house. Number 368. They will be gone all September." Arlan came home from school the other day with a note explaining his teacher's extended absence. Alfred breathed a silent prayer of thanks.

Arlan accidentally broke a ceramic vase last week. A simple accident. The thing wasn't worth the paint it was decorated with, but seeing the broken pieces drove Armand into a rage. He grabbed Arlan and twisted the boy's arm behind his back, snapping the bones.

"Are you going to break anything else?" Armand demanded, his eyes flashing crimson.

"No!" Arlan wailed. He looked up at Alfred, pleading for him to help. But Alfred could not intervene, could not say a word. Once Armand released the boy and stormed away, Alfred gathered Arlan into his arms and hugged him. The boy cried all the way to the hospital.

The attack left a number of bruises, too.

When the doctors asked, Alfred concocted a believable lie. Arlan fell out of a swing set. The doctors, used to seeing similar childhood accidents, nodded, placed splints to re-set the bones, and put a plaster cast on Arlan's arm.

Mrs. Townsend, however, was not convinced. This was not the first time Arlan had come to school with bruises, and the fact that she lived on their street made matters worse. She always engaged Alfred or Gina in conversation whenever she 'happened to be walking by', asking increasingly personal questions. She even offered to walk Arlan to school a few times, no doubt to learn the truth. Alfred happily agreed, so long as he walked with them.

Her extended vacation gave Alfred one less thing to fear.

And now her absence gave him a new advantage.

"Good. Very good." Carlos nodded. "Will the twelfth work?" The twelfth was two weeks away.

Alfred nodded, and they shook hands.

"I'll hide the gun in the backyard garden the Friday before," Carlos said. "Make sure you don't get any fingerprints on it."

"Understood." The instructions went without saying. Guns were made of steel. Since it was an alloy, it wasn't as toxic as iron, but it would still hurt if Alfred touched it with his bare hands. A pair of leather gloves would solve both problems.

Carlos then left.

All Alfred could do now was wait and pray.

***

Alfred checked the time again. A quarter to eleven. Alistair was working the late shift tonight. His usual weekend schedule. Alfred wanted to include his brother in the plan, but Carlos advised against it.

"The less people who know, the better," the Shinnok said. His voice still held a faint tremble, but he seemed more confident than he was at their first meeting. "This way, when the police question everyone, they'll tell the truth. They don't know anything."

Alfred understood the logic, but a part of him wanted his big brother by his side. To watch over and protect him.

He peered into his bedroom one last time. Gina was fast asleep, and baby Ava slept peacefully in her crib. Her tiny hands were curled into fists, and wisps of blonde hair framed her little, doll-like face.

I'm doing this for you, he wanted to say. *And I'm doing this for you, Arlan.* For both Arlans. For the child he was forced to give away, and for the child who now suffered from Armand's abuse.

Alfred went into the hall closet, donned a pair of thick leather gloves, and retrieved an old hat box from the top shelf. The gun rested inside. Carlos hid it in the garden while he clipped the hedges. A six-shooter pistol. But Alfred only needed one bullet.

Steeling himself, he walked down the stairs to his father's study. If everything was going as planned, Beowulf Smith should be in place.

But what if he isn't? Sure, he's a thief, but he is also a Shinnok Halfling. The subspecies tended to be too smart by half. What if Smith decided not to show? Decided the robbery was too risky? Alfred supposed he could lie and say that he saw Smith running away from the house, but he already felt terrible. Choosing between condemning an innocent man and his own daughter's safety? What kind of choice was that?

One Armand forced you into.

Choosing between Smith and Ava, he chose his daughter.

Alfred stood in front of the study's door, frozen. How many times had he been summoned to this room? How many times had he been yelled at, cursed out, and beaten in this room? Alfred had never once walked in here voluntarily.

The door swung open on well-oiled hinges. Armand sat in his armchair, facing a small fire and reading one of his medical journals. This journal discussed new surgical techniques from the Ruhalleen Empire. Alfred's skin crawled. How many patients had Armand treated with the same hands he used to beat his own family?

Armand glanced up and scowled. "What the hell do you want, boy?"

Alfred's hands began to sweat inside the gloves. He held the gun behind his back, gripping the handle so tightly that his knuckles hurt.

"I asked you a question, boy." Fire reflected in Armand's blood red eyes.

"I..." He cleared his throat. "I want to talk to you about, Ava," he said in Scanlannish.

Armand rolled his eyes. "Not this again," he replied in the same language. "The exchange details are set. I suggest you say your goodbyes." He returned his attention to the journal.

"No!" Alfred's anger boiled. "You won't take her from me!"

"You think I have a choice?" The old man raised an eyebrow.

"What do you mean?"

Armand waved him away.

"No, tell me what you mean." Alfred's hand shook. Merciful heavens, what was he doing? Was he really going to shoot someone? Even someone who deserved it? And where was Smith?

"Leave it alone, boy."

"Stop calling me boy! What do you mean you don't have a choice? I thought this was your idea."

"It's none of your business," he said calmly.

"My business?! Ava is my daughter!"

"And my granddaughter." He sat up straighter. "I have just as much say in—"

Alfred drew the gun, aiming the barrel directly at Armand's heart.

The old man studied him curiously. "Where did you get that gun?"

"You won't take Ava from me. I won't let you."

"Put down the gun, Alfred."

Alfred glared at the old man. His hand trembled, but he kept the gun aimed at Armand's chest. At his heart.

The old man's eyes widened, worried. "Alfred, don't you—"

He pulled the trigger.

Armand slumped over. Blood oozed from a small hole in his chest. Alfred's ears rang as the gunshot's echo faded. His heart pounded in his chest.

He...

He'd done it.

The hallway floorboard creaked.

Smith!

Bloody hell, what would Smith do if he saw Alfred with the gun? Would he call the police? Leave an anonymous tip?

Panic seizing him, Alfred tossed the gun into the hallway. The gun hit the wall and landed on the carpet with a dull thud.

Footsteps turned and raced down the hall, running away.

Alfred dashed out of the study and ran in the opposite direction. He ducked into a storage closet and stuffed the sweat soaked gloves behind a box filled with random odds and ends.

Then, he heard Mrs. Palacio scream.

"Oh my God!" the maid screamed. "He killed him! Smith killed him!"

Alfred broke out in a cold sweat. Arms and legs shaking, he doubled back, acting like he had come down the stairs. He felt strange, a weird mixture of sickness and relief. The plan had worked. Armand Whateley was dead, and soon everyone would believe that Beowulf Smith had murdered him.

You're safe, Ava Ingrid. You're safe.

Chapter 32
Judgment

The sitting room fell silent. Alfred's testimony left Invictus numb and unsure how to respond. He looked to Celeste and Wulf. Both stared at Alfred, shocked and a bit confused.

"Why?" Wulf asked.

The Whateleys looked at one another. Gina was frightened, her eyes wide and lips trembling, but Alistair's face was blank with empty eyes, as though he was still deciding which emotion to express.

"I wanted to protect my family," Alfred said, his voice strained. Alistair turned away and shuddered.

"But why not leave?" Wulf asked. "I mean, you got a good job. Lots of money. You could have moved away."

"He would have found us," Gina said. She gazed down at the baby. Ava had fallen asleep during the confession. "He would have taken Ava away."

"What did Armand mean by not having another choice?" Celeste asked.

"I don't know." A tear ran down Alfred's face. An ink black tear that seeped into his pale skin. "He didn't... He died before..."

"Was it the Manning family?" Invictus asked.

"The Mannings?" Alfred tensed, his eyes turning a lighter shade of red. He hugged Arlan tighter. "What would they have to do with any of this?"

"Because..." Invictus held his tongue. How much did Alfred know about the Mannings? Armand had worked for the family for years, but had Alfred ever met them? Did he ever visit their house? Did he know that Jacob had an adopted Changeling son? A boy the same age as Arlan?

Alexander Manning and the original Arlan Whateley could be one and the same, but what if Invictus's hunch was wrong? It could have been a legitimate adoption.

But what if it wasn't?

How would Alfred and Gina react if they learned about their child's fate? Would they demand that the Mannings give him back? Or would the Mannings make another one of their problems disappear?

Invictus recalled Jacob requesting him to tell him the murderer's identity the moment he discovered it.

The Face of Justice will shine on him.

Invictus shivered. If Jacob discovered Alfred's involvement...

"What are you going to do to me?" Alfred asked. His voice sounded hollow, almost resigned.

Celeste and Invictus shared a glance. Her hazel eyes shimmered with tears. The invisible string tugged at Invictus's mind, pulling him in the right direction. For once, he knew exactly what to do. Celeste sighed and placed a hand on her cuffs.

"Alfred Whateley, you—"

"You are lying," Invictus interrupted.

The Whateleys stared at Invictus, shocked and confused. Wulf shared their expression, but when Invictus locked eyes with Celeste, she nodded.

"You did not shoot and kill your father," Invictus said. The invisible string tugged again, and he knew in his heart that this was the right path. "You are covering for Carlos Vallejo."

"What are you...?" Alfred began. Alistair signaled for him to be quiet.

"Carlos Vallejo is the real murderer, right?"

Alfred struggled to speak. "He created the plan, but..."

"Why create the plan?" Invictus asked. "Did he do it solely out of pity, or was there a deeper reason?"

Alfred shrugged. He looked at his wife and brother. Neither had an explanation. He then looked at Celeste. The policewoman nodded, her hands clasped behind her back.

"I believe you're on to something, Mr. Jones," she replied. "We analyzed your father's financial records and discovered a number of discrepancies. Isn't that right, Jones?"

"Yes." Invictus had not found a single discrepancy in the ledgers. Not a penny out of place. But the hurricane caused extensive damage to the Precinct, and Reyes had yet to see the ledgers. Who was to say they were not heavily water damaged? The precise number and letters reduced to illegible smudges?

"Your father has been paying Carlos Vallejo for years," Celeste continued.

"What?" Alistair stared at her in disbelief.

"That's not true!" Alfred said. "I just met him a few weeks ago."

"Yes, that was when *you* met him," Invictus clarified. He prayed for the right words. "But when did your father meet him?"

"Never. Armand never spoke with the hired staff. Alistair..."

"I hired the landscapers," Alistair said.

"But why this company?" Celeste asked.

Alistair shrugged. "I saw their ad in the paper."

Celeste nodded sagely. "I see."

Alistair looked very confused.

"Bookie, what the hell is going on?" Wulf whispered. Invictus signaled for him to hush.

"The case is very clear now," Celeste continued. "Wouldn't you agree, Mr. Jones?"

"Yes, Officer Lawson." Invictus addressed Alfred. "Mr. Whateley, when I analyzed your father's ledgers, I noted monthly payments to an unknown person. Not a lot, not a first, but it added up to a handsome sum.

"We now believe that Carlos Vallejo was blackmailing your father. We haven't found Vallejo, so his reason is still unknown. However, the amount grew over the years. Vallejo demanded more and more money, but your father finally refused. Perhaps Dr. Whateley threatened to tell the police or have Taran Manning's people deal with Carlos. Either way, he was done.

"So, Vallejo arranged a robbery. While Smith and his colleague stole valuables from the first floor, Vallejo was on the second floor. He confronted your father, demanding the money. Dr. Whateley refused, and Vallejo shot him.

"By this time, Smith grew concerned by Vallejo's absence and went searching for him."

"That ain't true," Wulf said. Invictus stomped on his foot. "Ouch!"

"Smith heard arguing in the study," Invictus continued. "Before he could intervene, Vallejo shot and killed Dr. Whateley. Smith ran away, and the second thief, having heard the gunshot, made his escape through a back door. In the confusion, Vallejo got away, leaving Smith to take the blame. Isn't that right, Mr. Whateley?"

Alfred trembled, hugging Arlan close to his chest. Both the man and the boy looked to their family members, scared, confused.

"I, uh..." Alfred swallowed.

"Bookie, Carlos never—"

"You heard arguing, right?" Invictus questioned Wulf. The Halfling looked startled, almost scared. Invictus felt bad about that, but he needed fast answers.

"Yeah, but..."

"What language was it?"

Wulf shrugged. "Scanlannish?"

"Could it have been Faerie? Dr. Whateley was a Changeling, and Carlos is a Shinnok. It makes sense that both men knew the language."

"My father was fluent in Faerie," Alistair said. He watched Invictus and Celeste warily, as though he could not trust his own senses.

"Well, I…" Wulf grounded his teeth. "Hell, Bookie, I don't know!" He pointed at Alfred. "But he confessed. Y'all heard him confess!"

"He gave a confession," Celeste said. "But is it the truth?"

Wulf stared at her as though she switched from Malkinese to High Speech midsentence and expected him to respond in the same language.

"Mr. Whateley," Celeste continued, "as a member of the Malkin City Police, it is my conclusion, given the evidence, that Carlos Vallejo was blackmailing your father. Dr. Armand Whateley had enough and refused to continue payments. As a result, Vallejo killed him and fled. In order to protect your family from further harm," she emphasized, "you confessed."

The front door opened.

"Lawson?" Asa called out.

"In the parlor."

Asa and Montgomery walked into the room.

"The perimeter is clear," Asa said. "Are y'all okay in here?" He saw the Whateleys and jolted.

"Holy hell!" Montgomery shouted, pointing at the Whateleys in their Changeling form. Alfred and Gina held their children closer. Alistair balled his hands into fists and stepped in front of his family.

"It's rude to point, Officer Montgomery," Celeste admonished him.

Montgomery's face turned crimson. He lowered his arm.

"It appears Alfred Whateley has been withholding evidence," Celeste said to Asa. She explained Carlos's blackmailing scheme and the resulting murder. "Alfred feared that Carlos Vallejo would return and harm his family if he told us the truth. Isn't that right, sir?"

Tears, both clear and black, streamed down Alfred's face. He tried to speak, but the tears choked him. He nodded. Gina hugged him, and Alistair placed a hand on his shoulder.

"Where is Vallejo now?" Asa asked.

"He mostly likely fled the city," Invictus said. "We suspect that he fled shortly before the hurricane made landfall. With everyone preoccupied with preparations, he easily slipped away."

Asa grimaced. "Damn. I was afraid of that." He studied the Whateleys, taking in their expressions, body language, and eerie appearances. "You know this means another round of questioning, right? I want every detail about this Vallejo person. Understood?"

"Yes, officer," Alistair replied. "But I never had any contact with him. Alfred only saw him here a handful of times."

"I thought he worked for the landscaping crew," Alfred managed, his throat thick with tears.

"Okay." Asa massaged the bridge of his nose. He looked at Celeste and Montgomery. "What do we tell Reyes?"

"Place a search for Carlos Vallejo and include a reward," Celeste said. "I think it's unlikely he'll be in the city or province. It's possible he fled to Barra or the Ruhalleen Empire."

Montgomery cursed. "You know how bloody hard it will be to conduct an investigation in the Empire?"

Celeste looked off to the side, thinking. "We can send a letter to the Ruish Embassy, explaining Dr. Whateley's relation to Taran Manning. He's a prominent businessman and former member of Parliament, and his nephew is on the City Council. Hopefully their connections will hold some sway."

"Bloody doubt it," Montgomery muttered.

"I don't get it," Wulf said, scratching his head. "What did the old guy mean by—"

Invictus stomped on his foot again.

"Bloody hell! Can't I ask a question?"

"Shut up, thief," Montgomery snapped. "We got more questions for you, too. Where did you meet Carlos Vallejo?"

"I done told y'all!"

Asa raised his hand. "We will settle this later." He then addressed the Whateleys. "Well, I'm sorry the investigation ended this way. We always try to bring the guilty to justice, but sometimes they slip through our fingers. Rest assured, every officer in the Province will have Vallejo's description within the week. We won't stop looking for him. And if you think you see him, contact us immediately." Asa handed them a business card.

"Thank you, officer." Alfred smiled through his tears. He looked at Invictus and Celeste. "Thank you."

"We're just doing our job, sir." Celeste gave him a curt nod.

Alfred wrapped an arm around Gina's shoulders. With his other arm, he hugged Arlan tightly. He and Gina looked down at baby Ava and smiled. Wonderful, relieved smiles. Alistair gave Celeste and Invictus a solemn nod.

"Thanks," Invictus whispered to Celeste as they left the house. The sky was a brilliant shade of blue, and the sun shone brightly in the cloudless expanse. And the breeze actually felt cool. A promise that autumn was right around the corner.

"Just following a hunch," she replied with a wink. She glanced over her shoulder at Wulf. The Halfling frowned and muttered under his breath. "Are you okay, Beowulf?"

"I don't know." He spared a quick glance at the house. "I honestly don't know. Why did...?" He shook his head. "Bloody bricks. Make no bloody sense."

"What's he muttering about?" Asa asked. He opened the carriage door for them. Montgomery climbed onto the driver's seat with Stant, his arms folded across his chest.

Invictus smiled. "I think he's a bit confused. Usually, he's running away from the police instead of following them."

"Hey, I ain't following nobody!"

"Sure you aren't."

"Bookie," Wulf whispered into his ear. "You and me gotta talk? Hear me?"

"Loud and clear."

He then climbed into the carriage.

Chapter 33

Storm's End

Questions crowded Wulf's brain. Alfred Whateley's confession made perfect sense. Carlos, a Shinnok with excellent hearing, overheard the plot to exchange Alfred's daughter with a human child. He saw Alfred in distress and offered to help. Going to the police would have made more sense, but what if the old man denied it? Made Alfred out to be paranoid? Besides, Changelings technically did not exist.

So, they planned to kill the old man and pin the blame on Wulf. Which also made sense. Wulf was not just a thief anymore. He was a famous thief. Half the folks in Malkin read about him in the papers. And the bricks hated him, so of course they would hunt him down.

Hell, if Wulf and Bookie weren't friends, he'd have no one to turn to. No one to make the bricks see reason. They would have arrested him and shipped him off to Greer or sent him to swing from a noose. It was almost the perfect plan.

But then the world got turned on its head. Bookie making crap up was one thing. The man's brain was infected by books about fake bricks. But Lawson had backed him up. She even lied to the other bricks, saying that it was Carlos the whole time.

In a way, it was true. Carlos planned the murder, planting the idea in Alfred's brain. He also supplied the gun and the fall guy. All Alfred had to do was aim true.

When they arrived at the Precinct, the bricks surrounded Wulf. He feared they would lock him up and ship him to Greer just for the hell of it, but instead, they placed him in an office. Not an interrogation room. The office had a door with a simple turn lock, and the window was cracked open. Perfect for escaping. But they didn't give him a chance. The bricks asked him question after question.

When did he meet Carlos Vallejo?

Who was the second thief?

Where the hell was he?

What did Wulf see, hear, and smell while inside the Whateley house?

Hours of questions.

Wulf answered all of them, and he had some of his own.

Why would a landscaper care enough to help a man murder his abusive, psychopathic father?

Did Carlos given Macsen food poisoning on purpose, or was it just bad timing?

Where did Carlos vanish to?

And most importantly, why did Bookie lie to the bricks?

Wulf asked him once they were alone. Or rather, as alone as they could get. They sat in the middle of the desk area surrounded by green clad bricks. But the bricks were too busy to eavesdrop. They talked to witnesses, cleaned up debris, and argued over the best way to get the tree out of the building. The oak rested in the center of the room, obliterating the work area. They sat at Bishop's desk, one of the few that survived.

"Because it was wrong," Bookie whispered. He had what was left of the doctor's ledgers on the desk. The ledger looked like it got dropped in a bucket. The warped pages were stuck together, and the ink ran, creating black and gray smudges that even Bookie could not read. Only a few pages survived. Lines of numbers with notations off to the side. Bookie told the bricks that the payments to Carlos were recorded on the ruined pages. They had no reason not to believe him.

Wulf was honestly impressed by how well Bookie lied. He had the makings of an okay thief.

"Armand stole his own grandchild," Bookie continued, still whispering.

"Yeah, that's all kinds of messed up. You gonna tell the Whateleys about Manning's Changeling son?"

"Not yet. I told Asa. He promised to look into it." He flipped through another ledger. A not ruined one. It listed expenses and incomes for all three Whateleys. The numbers made Wulf's eyes hurt.

He glanced around. Several bricks looked his way, but none made a move to arrest him. He itched to run, but he was not in danger. Hadn't done anything wrong. Reyes had already absolved him of his involvement with the robbery because of his help.

Bloody hell, does this make me an informant? He groaned. How would he be able to face his gang after this?

Well, Ruthless would understand. Wulf never wanted to be an informant, and he hadn't accepted any money. Informants always accepted money, and most were stupid enough to brag about it. Their rewards were a beating in an alley or a dip in the river.

"What do you think the old guy meant by it not being his choice?" Wulf asked.

Bookie sighed and looked tired, like he hadn't slept in days. "I think Taran Manning forced Dr. Whateley to make the first exchange. Remember, Norri said that the doctor changed after he started medical school. He became more paranoid. I think the Mannings wanted a Changeling child then, but Armand refused to give up his sons. But when his grandson was born, Taran found a new opportunity."

Wulf cursed under his breath. "That's messed up."

Bookie nodded. He closed the ledger and pushed it to the side.

"What about your other idea?" Wulf asked. "The one about Carlos being Whateley's kid?"

"It didn't pan out. There's no evidence."

"Still, makes you wonder why a landscaper would get involved with a murder. He had to have some reason to hate the old guy."

"Whatever reason that is, Carlos took it with him." Bookie sighed again. "I wish we could have found him. Did Ruthless have any luck?"

"None." A bad feeling settled in Wulf's gut. Ruthless had eyes and ears all over the city. Either Carlos Vallejo was real good at hiding and got out before the storm hit, or he had help. A light dawned in his mind. "You think someone hired Carlos to plan the murder? Like how Lewin hired us to rob Ciceron Station?"

Bookie's eyes widened as his face turned ashen. "I think there is a very good chance."

"Then how do we find them?"

"We?" Asa Bishop asked as he and Celeste Lawson strolled up to the desk. "You thinking of joining the force, Smith?"

Wulf bared his teeth. "I'd rather eat broken glass."

Celeste smirked, her hazel eyes shining. "We overheard your conversation. Your theory of someone hiring Vallejo is interesting."

"Wait, really?"

She nodded. "We couldn't find any records for a Shinnok Halfling named Carlos Vallejo in Malkin City. Or in Malkin Province," she added. "We think he used a pseudonym."

"Yeah, and a fake name."

Bookie smirked. "Did you question the Whateleys again?"

"Reyes doesn't think it's necessary right now," Asa replied. "He assigned three officers to watch the house at all times. If Vallejo tries to retaliate, we will catch him."

Wulf doubted it. Carlos was long gone. The bricks had a better chance of catching the common cold.

"So, anybody gettin' arrested?" Wulf asked, a bit afraid to ask.

"Not any time soon," Asa replied. The brick looked disappointed.

"And me? Reyes says I'm in the clear, but..." But he was still a thief.

Asa shrugged. "Depends. Will you be stupid enough to pull another job like this?"

"Hell no."

"Good. I'd hate to have to arrest you after all the help you've given us," Asa said a bit sarcastically.

Officer Pembroke walked up to them. He was a full-blooded Shinnok with bright red hair, purple eyes, and a thin, angular face. His face was paler than normal, like he had seen a ghost.

"Yes, Pembroke?" Asa asked.

"I, um..." Pembroke wrung his hands. "I wanted to say sorry, Mr. Jones."

"Sorry?" Bookie frowned, confused.

The Shinnok nodded.

"What are you sorry for?"

"I followed you," he stammered. "Captain Reyes asked me to."

"Followed us? What do you mean?" Bookie asked.

"Since, um, Monday. Captain Reyes asked me to. I..." He looked like he was on the verge of tears. "I'm sorry, sir."

"That's... amazing," Bookie said. His eyes brightened.

The hairs on the back of Wulf's neck stood on end. This guy was following them for a whole week? But Wulf never saw him. Never smelled or sensed his presence. How the hell...?

He's a full-blooded Shinnok. He can sneak around better than you in his sleep.

Wulf's guts twisted in knots. If Pembroke could follow Wulf without his knowledge, could Carlos have followed him, too?

Pembroke nodded. "Captain Reyes told me to follow you everywhere you went, sir."

"This whole time?" Bookie asked.

"Yes, sir. I went to Mull and Gray Hook and Old City. Everywhere."

"That's how Celeste found us at the library," Bookie said, amazed.

Celeste smiled. "I had excellent help." She placed her arm around Pembroke's narrow shoulders. The Shinnok averted his gaze.

"You was watching us in Gray Hook?" Wulf asked. "You saw where we went and who we spoke to?"

"Yes, but I…" Pembroke looked like he was going to cry or faint. Probably both. Bloody hell, how did this kid wind up as a brick?

"Pembroke reported seeing Alistair Whateley at a fighting ring," Asa said. "He admitted to moonlighting as a ring doc for the last five years."

"But that isn't illegal," Bookie pointed out.

"No, but it's interesting. Reyes thinks one of the ring's wealthier clientele learned about the Whateleys' true nature and used Carlos as a go-between for the blackmail money. Lawson and I will investigate it during our off time."

"Why not immediately?" Bookie asked.

Wulf didn't care. Pembroke saw them talking to Alistair Whateley. Did he also see them talking to Ruthless? He glared at Pembroke. The brick refused to meet his eyes.

You did see us! Wulf needed to report this to Ruthless. The Blydd might take pity on the Shinnok, give him a warning. Or he might create an informant of his own.

"The Whateley case is officially closed," Celeste replied.

Bookie relaxed. "Good." He reached into his pocket, but his hand came out empty. He sighed.

"Still can't find your watch?" Wulf asked.

Bookie shook his head.

Good. Now I don't have to worry about that damn thing burning me again. But Bookie looked so sad. Maybe Wulf could steal him a new watch. A nice harmless one with a glass face and a leather band.

"Hey, we're going out for dinner," Celeste said. "Care to join us?"

"Who else is going?" Bookie asked.

"Me, Asa, Montgomery, and Pembroke. What do you think?"

Bookie thought it over. “Only if Wulf can join.”

Wulf’s heart skipped a beat. “Wait, Bookie, I don’t...” Bloody hell, was he serious?

“Sure.” Celeste smiled. An honest smile. For some reason, Wulf wanted to trust that smile.

“Wulf, what do you think?” Bookie asked.

Wulf thought it was a terrible idea, but he trusted Bookie, and he wanted to trust Celeste. And he might get a chance to corner Pembroke and make a deal with him. The bricks had failed to arrest Ruthless time and again, but Pembroke knew where the Blydd lived. People with that information either joined Ruthless’s gang, or they found a good reason to leave town.

“Okay. I...” Wulf bit his tongue. Should he ask? *If anyone can find the answer, it’s the bricks.* “Do y’all think you can do me a favor?”

“What kind of favor?” Asa asked warily.

“Can you look for death records for a Shinnok named Camden Pritchard? He died around twenty-three or twenty-two years ago.”

“We can try. Who was he?” Celeste asked.

“My dad.”

Celeste and Asa shared a look and then nodded. Wulf didn’t know what to feel. Relief? Guilt, maybe? He wanted the truth, and Ma told him a lot, but in his heart, he knew she was holding back. There was more to Camden Pritchard o’r Shinnok’s story, and Wulf wanted every word.

“Where did you have in mind?” Bookie asked as he and Wulf stood up.

“Philip Jose’s. It’s a Barrish restaurant a block down the street.”

“Sound’s great. I...” Bookie’s eyes grew wide. “My watch! I remember where I left it.”

“Great. Get it tomorrow,” Wulf said.

“No, I will meet you guys there.” Bookie headed for the door.

"Bookie!" Wulf called out, his heart leaping into his throat. Bookie wasn't going to leave him alone with all these bricks, was he?

"I'll only be an hour or so. The trains are working again, right?" he asked Asa and Celeste.

"Most of them," Asa replied.

"Alright. See you there." Bookie vanished through the door.

Wulf looked at the bricks. Three men and one woman all dressed in dark green. The color he was taught to fear. But he didn't feel afraid. Not really. Celeste had treated him kindly and had the decency to listen. Asa and Montgomery were kinda assholes, but they listened to Celeste.

And then there was Pembroke. Another Shinnok.

"Turn every situation to your advantage," Ruthless had taught him.

Well, he was a thief with four bricks for company.

He could definitely turn this situation into an advantage. An advantage for himself and every thief in Mull.

"So," Wulf said with a smirk, "does this place serve crawfish?"

Chapter 34

In the Name of the Seelie Court

Only half of the trains were running again, and Invictus needed to switch tracks twice due to damage and debris blocking the rails. But despite the delays, he managed to arrive at Twenty-first Street in just under an hour.

Pedestrians crowded the street, cleaning up downed tree branches, sweeping up leaves, and removing boards from windows to assess possible damage. A few shady people eyed Invictus, but no one made a move to mug him.

The benefits of being in a gang leader's good graces, he guessed.

He wanted to kick himself. This entire time, he thought he lost his watch while running away from the Whateleys, but he gave it to Vic. The Blydd teen had asked to see the watch, despite the better judgment of every adult in the room. In all the excitement, Invictus had forgotten.

He knocked on the front door. It cracked open.

"Oh, it's you." Mrs. Garcia opened the door wider and allowed Invictus to enter. "Where's the other one?"

"Not here." Would the landlady believe that Wulf was with a group of police officers? No, not unless he was under arrest.

Mrs. Garcia huffed. "You're better than him. I can see it in the way you walk and hear it in your voice. You're too good to be roughing it with that thief. He will only drag you into the gutter."

"I doubt it."

The landlady sadly shook her head and retreated into her own apartment.

Invictus walked up to the third floor, mindful of the creaking stairs. Other than a few broken windows, the building weathered the storm alright, but the hallways were eerily quiet. Where was everybody?

A light shone through the cracked door at the end of the hallway. Voices drifted his way. Maria and Ruthless.

Excellent. He could ask Ruthless for the watch and be on his way.

The invisible string tugged at Invictus, leading him back to the stairs. Weird. Why would the string lead him away from the people he wanted to see? And he did not intend to stay long. The trip here took longer than expected. By the time he got back to the Precinct, dinner would be over. He would retrieve the watch and leave. Two minutes tops.

He continued forward. The invisible string tugged and tugged, begging him to go back. To leave this building.

Why?

What was so important that it couldn't wait two minutes?

"Are you certain it was Talos?" Maria asked, her voice strained.

Talos? Is she talking about the prince? Invictus took a silent step closer.

"My people saw him arrive at the docks this morning," Ruthless replied. "I can help arrange a meeting..."

"No. I..." Maria paused. "I saw him a few months ago. It was too close."

"Did Beowulf see him?"

"No. He and Esmeralda were dancing." She paused again. "Invictus might have seen him, but he was too far away to recognize. Do you know why he is back in the city?"

"Not yet." Ruthless almost sounded worried. "I did some more research on Vallejo. I think he might belong to an offshoot of the Royal Family."

Invictus crept closer, curiosity getting the better of him. The invisible string continued to tug backwards. He ignored it.

"Why would the Royals be involved?" Maria asked.

"Waylinda wasn't pleased with Lewin bringing down her heir. She could have removed the doctor as retaliation, or as a means to place her own doctor in the Manning house."

Maria sighed. "So Waylinda has turned Talos into her new errand boy."

"We don't know that for sure."

"Don't we, Rufus? Being my son's father does not make him a good person. And he has changed so much. I barely..."

"Father?"

Maria and Ruthless jolted and faced the doorway. Both sets of eyes locked onto Invictus. Maria's face turned ashen, her eyes wide and sorrowful.

"Oh, Invictus..."

Ruthless snarled. He grabbed a knife off the kitchen table and lunged at Invictus, the knife aimed at his heart.

The Blydd took two steps and screamed. He dropped the knife and fell to his knees, clutching his head.

"Rufus, what's wrong?" Maria knelt beside him. "Rufus?"

Ruthless glared at Invictus. His silver eyes, now completely bloodshot, flashed twice.

Invictus stood in the doorway, his heart pounding and muscles frozen. Ruthless...

Ruthless Wells, the man he had learned to trust, tried to kill him.

Cradling his head in both hands, Ruthless stood on shaking legs and walked over to the couch. He gingerly lowered himself down.

"You... You tried..." Invictus struggled to find the words. *You tried to kill me.* Why? What did Invictus do to deserve this?

Maria placed a soft hand on his arm. He flinched. Maria had made no move to stop him. She would have watched as Ruthless drove the knife into his chest.

"Please, Invictus, don't hold it against him."

"He wanted to stab me! Why did...?" The invisible string tugged again. Towards the knife on the floor. "What stopped you?"

"The worse headache in my life," Ruthless replied, his voice weak and hoarse. He sounded sick. "God above, it felt like my skull was splitting open. How did you manage that, Jones?"

"Why did you try to kill me?" Invictus felt cold and shaky.

Ruthless studied him for a silent moment. "Because I made a promise."

"What kind of promise?" He rounded on Maria. "Why didn't you try to stop him?"

"I can explain." Her voice was hardly more than a whisper. "Please, sit down."

Invictus sat at the kitchen table, a healthy distance away from Ruthless. The apartment held an empty, hollow feeling. Not a single one of Ruthless's relatives was present, and all of the supply crates were gone.

"Where is everybody?"

"Sent them west," Ruthless replied. "Whole family."

"Why?"

Ruthless sneered, displaying his sharp teeth.

Invictus shrank back. What did he do that was so wrong?

Maria sat at the table with him. "Invictus, how much of our conversation did you overhear?"

A part of him was afraid to answer, but the invisible string tugged again. "I heard that Prince Talos is back in Malkin City, and that he is Wulf's father."

Maria grimaced and looked away.

"Please, speak up, Jones, I don't think they heard you in the Amistad Plains." Ruthless massaged his temples. "That's better. Where did you learn how to create protections?"

Of course, the protection. Thank God it worked.

"From a friend." Invictus's mind swam, struggling to keep afloat. A prince. Wulf's father was a Fae prince. How on earth did that happen?

"You have very good friends," Ruthless said, the strength returning to his voice. "How did you create it? What words did you use?"

Invictus paused. Five minutes ago, Ruthless tried to kill him. He would have succeeded if Norri hadn't taught Invictus about the Seelie Court and its protections. How far could he really trust the Blydd? "I said that any Fae who tried to harm me would have terrible headaches."

"Terrible is an understatement. How did you seal it?"

"Seal?"

"The words you used when creating it. The exact words."

Invictus struggled to remember. He was so terrified, so certain that he was going to die, he said the first words that came to mind. "I said it in the name of the Seelie Court."

Ruthless cursed softly. "Of course. In the name of the Seelie Court. Nothing short of your own death can break that protection."

"Yeah. Kinda the point."

"Sorry for how I reacted, Jones. But I made a promise. I refuse to break it." His voice was calm, almost sad. Yes, he would have killed Invictus to protect Wulf, but he would have done so coldly, mechanically. Like a doctor amputating a mangled limb.

Invictus looked at Maria. Tears welled in her eyes, and she looked away.

"You promise not to reveal the truth?" Invictus guessed.

"And to protect Maria's son. That includes not telling the boy about his father. No matter how often he asked," Ruthless added quietly.

"We couldn't risk the Royals finding him," Maria said. "They would have killed Wulf. And he's so curious, I was afraid he would search for his father on his own. That he would see a picture in the newspaper, see a man who looked like him, or read a name, and then wonder..." The tears fell freely.

"Read." Invictus's blood turned cold. "Is this why you never taught Wulf how to read?"

Maria nodded. "That and him being dyslexic. Talos is the same way. Has trouble reading without help." She smiled weakly and met Invictus's eyes. "I appreciate you helping Wulf learn, but he was getting curious again. I told him as much of the truth as I could, hoping it would be enough."

"Camden Pritchard." Saying the name aloud, he realized how odd it sounded. Pritchard was an Amistadian last name, and Camden sounded Tarrbonnish, possible Kallendonic.

Maria sighed heavily. "Not the best name, I admit. But if he went searching..." She shrugged. Fresh tears made tracks on her face.

"Jones." Ruthless stood and loomed over him. "Beowulf cannot know. The Royals almost killed Talos for having a simple affair with a human. If they learned that he fathered a Halfling, they won't hesitate to kill Beowulf and Maria. Hell, they will probably kill you, too."

"But why?"

"The Royals have strange inheritance laws. The crown always goes to the monarch's favorite. And favorite could mean child or grandchild or niece or nephew. Waylinda's original heir was her favorite grandson, Prince Hastyr. Now, she has chosen her second favorite, Talos. He could easily name Wulf as his heir once he secures the throne."

Invictus's heart skipped a beat. "He could make Wulf a king?"

"A future king, yes."

"That's absurd! Wulf would never accept that."

"They can force him," Maria said. "Talos never wanted the throne, but it's very rare for an heir to refuse. And Waylinda is not someone you say no to."

"Does Talos know about Wulf?" His mind wandered back to that sunny day in July, walking in Valor Park with Wulf and Maria. A man stood off to the side. Hiding in the shade of an oak tree...

Maria nodded. "I made him promise to keep our son a secret, but a promise made between a human and a Fae can be fickle. When I made him swear, Talos swore to protect our child. Wulf isn't a child anymore."

"Merciful heavens." The room began to spin. Invictus's ear rang painfully. "Then, what do we do?"

"You will keep your mouth shut," Ruthless ordered. "And Maria and I will pretend that this conversation never happened."

"But will the Royals try to hurt me?"

Ruthless scoffed. "With that protection over you? I'd like to see them try."

"Why are you here, Invictus?" Maria asked. "Is Wulf alright?"

"Yeah, he's fine. The Whateley case is officially closed, and Wulf is no longer a suspect."

Maria whispered a prayer of thanks.

"I, um, remembered that I left my pocket watch here. Unless Vic took it with him." Where had the family gone? Ruthless said west, but west covered thousands of miles. They could be anywhere between the Attakapas River and the Scalaad Caelum Mountains.

Why did the entire family leave the city? Invictus decided to save the question for later. Too much had happened in the last twenty-four hours. In the last half hour.

Ruthless smiled. "The boy tried, but Verona and his stepfather stopped him. It's on the windowsill."

Invictus retrieved it. The watch was in perfect condition save for the crack in the glass face, the result of the train station robbery. The day he and Wulf met. The inscription read, *Enjoy the journey.*

He doubted his father ever imagined the journey leading Invictus to befriend a Halfling thief who was a prince in disguise.

Wulf would never believe me.

"Invictus, what is your middle name?" Ruthless asked.

"Why?"

"Just tell me. You know I can't hurt you."

Invictus looked at Maria. She nodded.

"Honoratus." It was his father's name.

Ruthless placed his right hand firmly on Invictus's shoulder and locked eyes with him. "Invictus Honoratus Jones, the Esteemed Unconquerable One, I ask that you protect Beowulf Cannell Smith, my foster son, from all who wish him harm. You will not tell him the identity of his father nor allow his father or any member of the Royal Family to have any contact with him. I, Rufus Brychan Wells, ask you this in the name of the Seelie Court. Do you accept?"

Invictus stared into Ruthless's silvery eyes and saw sincerity but also fear. This man, one of the most powerful Fae in Malkin City's underworld, was afraid.

"Yes," Invictus said. "I accept this promise in the name of the Seelie Court."

He shivered violently, as though an icy, winter wind had swept through the apartment. The wind vanished, replaced by the warm, late summer sunlight streaming in through the window.

"Thank you, Invictus," Maria said, placing her hand on his other shoulder. She smiled despite the tears running down her face. A bright, warm smile. "Thank you for protecting my son."

Epilogue: Along the Beach

THE SEA GRASS SWAYED as a warm breeze swept along the shore. The waves broke gently on the beach, signaling the incoming tide. Here and there, bits of debris littered the beach. Pieces of driftwood or rope. A plank with half a boat's name, painted in bright red and blue that was now chipped and faded.

The hurricane had torn through Malkin City like a cannonball, but like cannonballs, the resulting damage was not as terrible as the sound suggested.

Talos Mhin ap Rhydian o'r Shinnok walked along the sandy beach. The breeze tugged at his jacket. A simple black jacket that came down to his waist. He wore his traditional tunic and cloak on the voyage here and while disembarking. The newspaper photographers ate it up, snapping away until they ran out of powder. Talos grinned and bared it. He hated this crap, but being Grandmother's new heir drew attention like moths to a flame.

Thanks to his aides, he slipped out of the Embassy and walked down to the beach. Only a handful of people were out and about, and in these clothes, he was just another Fae in a city of thousands.

In his mind's eye, he saw himself as a child, running back and forth in tandem with the waves behind their family's beach house on the Islands. Niamh had laughed and smiled, her purple eyes like the purest amethysts. Hastyr, the eldest, had stood off to the side with his hands clasped behind his back in perfect imitation of their father, deep in thought.

Plans within plans. That was how his brother's mind worked. Even trapped on the humans' prison island, Hastyr's influence had not diminished. It merely transferred.

A strong gust almost stole Talos's hat. He held onto it tightly. Nobody was nearby, but his red hair stood out like a lighthouse beacon at midnight. Best not to take any chances.

A lone figure emerged from behind a dune. The figure glanced left and right and then hurried over to Talos, leaving tracks in the soft sand. He also had red hair, but the color was darker, almost the color of rust. The young man's purple eyes were the same shade as Niamh's.

Talos's heart ached. Of all the members of the Royal Family, of all the cousins and aunts and uncles and sycophants, why did Niamh have to be taken? Why couldn't she still be here? Talos needed her guidance.

Instead, he just had himself.

"Did I do well?" the young Shinnok Halfling asked. His eyes darted up and down the beach.

"Yes, Miles, you did excellently." Talos placed a hand on Miles Benson's shoulders. The boy was one of Hastyr's bastards, fathered during one of his many diplomatic visits to the Continent. A pathetic Halfling. The Crown had no use for such creatures, but there was no crown on Talos's head.

Not yet.

"What did you think of the Whateleys?" Talos asked Miles as they walked down the beach. Overhead, seagulls cawed.

Where did they shelter during the storm? Talos wondered. Niamh would have encouraged such questions. Hastyr would tell him to shut up and pay attention.

Miles shuddered. "They're terrifying, but Alfred is a good man." He hesitated, tugging at his shirtsleeve. "Are the police going to arrest him?"

"They won't." With help from his most trusted aide, Talos read the papers. Dr. Armand Whateley was the unfortunate victim of blackmail.

The blackmailer killed him after the doctor refused to increase the payments. The reason for the blackmail was unknown, but the theories ranged from medical malpractice to an illegitimate child. Talos doubted they would ever learn the truth.

Talos had discovered the doctor's role accidentally. Armand spent the last thirty years as Taran "The Old Man" Manning's personal physician, heeding his every beck and call. The payments were handsome, but they came at a heavy cost. Taran was fascinated by Changelings. The Royal Family did not recognize the subspecies, and very few studies were conducted.

Taran presented Whateley with a choice: have the world discover his secret or exchange his newborn grandson with a human infant. The Changeling boy would live with Taran as part of a social and medical study. No harm would befall him so long as Whateley stayed in line. And the human child... Well, no one knew where Taran had found him. An orphan most likely.

After Hastyr's arrest, Waylinda named Talos as the Royal liaison to the Sidhe Family, ensuring their fifth of the crime network acted in the Royal Family's best interests. He also gained control of Hastyr's spy network. Through them, he learned that Taran planned the same fate for Whateley's granddaughter, this time selling her to the Barrish Family for their godforsaken experiments.

Talos sensed an opportunity. He chose Alfred as his pressure point. The man had the most to lose and the years spent under his father's tyranny made him desperate. All Talos needed to do was recruit Miles.

He had known about Miles Benson for years. His mother tried blackmailing the Royals, threatening to tell every major newspaper in the Commonwealth that her Halfling son was Prince Hastyr's child. But people who make such threats have very short life expectancies. Talos secreted the boy away while Waylinda's assassins went to work. Hastyr never learned about his son, and Talos gained a valuable pawn.

Guilt panged him. He wished that terrible affair could have ended differently. But Alivia Benson was a threat. Threats to the Royals need to be removed. The same fate almost befell Maria. If she hadn't hidden in that closet, if she hadn't been completely silent, she and their child would have died.

His heart ached. He did not want to involve Beowulf, but the little thief had made a name for himself. The bastard even managed to get his photograph in the papers. The Royals, the ones with keen eyes, were growing suspicious. Asking questions. Was this another threat that needed to be removed?

Talos was left with only one option. Pin the blame on Beowulf. Once the public learned about Dr. Whateley's murder, they would demand his arrest. Thieves, after all, never changed their ways.

After the arrest and trial, Talos planned to secret Beowulf away. Faking a death was not hard. Just bribe the right guards to look the other way and sign the necessary paperwork. Then, they would sail from Greer to the Islands. The Commonwealth's laws would be unable to touch him.

But Talos had been out planned. Beowulf's human friend, the bookish accountant who Lewin Manning and Emilio Grady recruited for their scheme, the one they were certain would be too frightened to work against them, proved the Halfling's innocence.

Now, the police were searching for Carlos Vallejo. A fabrication.

"What about me?" Miles asked. The young man shook like a leaf in a storm. Always so nervous. *Guess I can't blame the poor kid.*

"I will secure passage to the Fae Islands. In the meantime, stay in Ossa City, Barra."

"Barra?"

"Yes, it's just across the river. I will send for you in a week."

Miles tried to smile, but he frowned.

"Is something wrong?"

"Did we do the right thing? I know the doctor was an evil man, but..." He shrugged. "I don't know. This doesn't feel right."

Talos sighed heavily. "Sometimes, people have to do the wrong thing for the right reason. Like you said, Dr. Whateley was evil. Abusive."

"I understand that, but I made Macsen Wells sick. He could have died. And Beowulf Smith almost went to prison." Talos had instructed Miles to recruit both Beowulf and Macsen Wells in order to make Beowulf feel more confident about the job. Then, Miles poisoned Macsen's food so Beowulf would be alone. He would have no witnesses to back up his side of the story.

"Both were necessary." Talos smiled brightly at Miles. "You were a good soldier."

Miles managed a small smile, but it did not reach his eyes. Did his mother know that the name Miles meant 'Soldier' in the High Speech?

"Will I have to do this again?"

"No. This job is done. I think you deserve a rest. Don't you?"

Miles nodded as relief swept over his face.

Talos studied that face. Rusty hair with purple eyes and a skin tone midway between fair and tan. His own son had the same features, but his hair was pitch black.

Just like Maria's.

Talos could still recall the feel of her silky, black hair, and eyes of the deepest brown.

I love you, Maria.

If only his plan had gone perfectly. Instead of walking along the Malkin beachfront, he would be sailing to Greer Island to facilitate Beowulf's release. Then, they would sail home. Beowulf, naturally, would need time to adjust, but Talos would help him every step of the way like a father should.

On his next continental visit, he would have sneaked into Mull District, found Maria, and united their family on the Islands.

Yes, there was his wife and son to deal with, but Nimue knew that their marriage was one of political convenience. No love would be lost. And Lugh would continue to live with them, of course. No need to punish the boy for his parents' failings.

But fate had other plans.

The sun sunk lower in the cloudless sky, dying the ocean shades of orange and red. He closed his eyes, allowing his mind to wander back to that day.

After discovering his affair, Waylinda ordered Talos to stay on the Islands for five years. He could not even leave the palace grounds without her explicit, spoken permission. She controlled every aspect of his life, including arranging a marriage between him and the daughter of a Shinnok noble family.

Somehow, he convinced Waylinda to allow him to accompany Hastyr on a visit to Malkin City, claiming the trip would improve his political acumen. Waylinda relented.

Talos snuck away at the first opportunity and searched every public record for Maria Smith. A far more difficult task than he had expected. Maria had hidden herself well. After three days of searching and evading his brother, he found her.

And a four-year-old Halfling with his mother's beautiful black hair and Talos's purple eyes.

That day, he vowed to make the Royals pay.

Taran Manning was a fond pet of Queen Waylinda's. He saw to her interests and kept the other Families in line, but he was sickly. He required constant medical care, and he only trusted one doctor.

Without Armand Whateley's help, the stubborn bastard was not long for this world.

And without Taran Manning, Waylinda would lose a valuable pawn.

Talos smiled, arranging his pieces on the board.

The End of Book 2

My Travels to the Fae Islands

A Scholarly Report by Varius Sanders

2 JULY 467 F.C.

I noticed the most bizarre sight this afternoon. The day was warm and humid, and my host suggested going to the local marketplace. The sea breezes were a welcome relief from the tropical heat, far more intense than temperatures on the Malkin Continent. (What we would call a warm, summer day, they would call mild spring!)

Vendors in tent booths lined the sandy walkways, calling out their wares, and each one greeted my host and myself cordially. One of the benefits of residing with a noble house, albeit a small one. My host wandered over to a vendor selling hand-woven hats. He is always prone to wandering around and knew his mother would want proof of this trip.

While taking in the sights, my eyes fell on a strange creature. The creature, which I assumed was a Fae subspecies, sat crisscross next to a wagon and wore a ragged tunic and trousers, torn at one knee and frayed at the hems. He had chalky white skin with lanky, black hair, and blood red eyes that seemed to glow in the light. The creature blinked, and an ink-like substance leaked out of the tear duct. His skin quickly absorbed the liquid and turned black.

I walked over to the Fae and introduced myself, explaining that I was a researcher from Malkin City University's Department of Anthropology and wished to catalogue all of the Fae subspecies.

The creature made no reply and merely stared up at me with red, unblinking eyes. I noted that he wore a corded leather necklace, undecorated by gems or beads.

Berating myself for a fool, I introduced myself again in Faerie. My mastery of the language is nowhere near fluency, though my host and his family always compliment that I am a fast learner. However, I attribute this to Fae hospitality and no true skill.

Again, the creature did not respond. I studied him more closely, and revulsion filled me. That necklace was in fact a collar, and a leather leash tied him securely to the wagon's wheel.

I called out to my host, demanding an explanation. His eyes fell on the creature, and he halted several paces short.

"Varius, walk towards me very slowly."

"Whatever for?" I questioned. "Why is this young man tied up?"

Before my host could reply, a Blydd Fae, one who towered head and shoulders taller than my host, charged towards the wagon and placed himself between me and the red-eyed creature. The furious Blydd spoke rapidly in Faerie, far too rapidly for me to understand. My host interceded and was able to placate the Blydd. He then bowed and escorted me away.

"What on earth was that about?" I asked.

My host turned a sharp corner and led me in a circle so we could observe the creature from a distance. But it could not possibly be the same creature. The young man wore the same clothes, sat in the same position, and had the same collar and leash, but he was undeniably Blydd. His once chalky skin now possessed a healthy tan, his black hair was silvery white, and his eyes were a clear, shiny silver.

"That is a Changeling," my host explained.

"I've never heard of that subspecies. Are they dangerous?"

"They're no more dangerous than a human, but they are crafty, and they have a habit of exchanging their children with the children of other subspecies."

"Exchanging?"

My host explained that the Blydd Fae had raised the Changeling for fifteen years, thinking he was his orphaned nephew, but last week, the Changeling grew careless and exposed his true nature. The Blydd did not know when the exchange took place, whether it was before his brother and sister-in-law's illness or shortly after their passing. Either way, he was taking the Changeling to Mabinogia to present him to the Crown for questioning.

"What will become of him after that?" I asked. "He was just a child, after all. Will the Crown declare him innocent?"

"Depends on how young he was, I guess." A pensive frown marred my host's face as he studied the creature.

I felt sorry for the young Fae, wondering what kind of life he led and how difficult it must have been to conceal his true nature. I asked my host how common these Changelings were, but he only stated that they were rare, almost extinct, and refused to answer any more of my questions.

Shortly after supper, I ventured into the marketplace on my own, hoping to speak with the Blydd Fae, but the man and the Changeling were long gone. Those who saw the creature refused to talk about him, as though he were nothing more than a bad dream.

About the author

Beck Todd is an independent science fiction and fantasy author. She was born and raised in Charleston, South Carolina, and started writing while studying biology and psychology at the College of Charleston. She has one tortoiseshell cat and a never-ending TBR list.

For updates, you can follow her at becktoddauthor.com and on Instagram @becktodd_author95.

www.ingramcontent.com/pod-product-compliance
Lightning Source LLC
LaVergne TN
LVHW090550110826
845146LV00001B/86

9798986200781